D A R K N E S S

Darkness

TWO DECADES OF MODERN HORROR

EDITED BY **ELLEN DATLOW**

TACHYON

Interior design by John Coulthart
Cover design by Ann Monn

Tachyon Publications
1459 18th Street #139
San Francisco, CA 94107
(415) 285-5615
www.tachyonpublications.com
tachyon@tachyonpublications.com

Series Editor: Jacob Weisman

ISBN 13: 978-1-892391-95-7
ISBN 10: 1-892391-95-3

Printed in the United States of America
by Worzalla

First Edition: 2010
9 8 7 6 5 4 3 2 1

ACKNOWLEDGMENTS

I'd like to thank Jeff VanderMeer, John
Kessel, Jill Roberts and Jacob Weisman
(the latter two for their patience), and
especially Stefan Dziemianowicz, not
only for his foreword but for providing
photocopies of some of the stories.

DARKNESS: TWO DECADES OF MODERN HORROR

Ellen Datlow has been an editor of short science fiction, fantasy, and horror for almost thirty years.

She was co-editor of *The Year's Best Fantasy and Horror* for twenty-one years and currently edits *The Best Horror of the Year*. Her most recent anthologies are *Inferno*, *The Del Rey Book of Science Fiction and Fantasy*, *Poe: 19 New Tales of Suspense, Dark Fantasy, and Horror Inspired by Edgar Allan Poe*, *Lovecraft Unbound*, and *The Coyote Road: Trickster Tales* and *Troll's Eye View* (the latter two with Terri Windling). Forthcoming are *Naked City: New Tales of Urban Fantasy*, *The Beastly Bride and Other Tales of the Animal People* (with Terri Windling), and *Haunted Legends* (with Nick Mamatas).

Datlow is the winner of multiple awards for her editing, including the World Fantasy, Locus, Hugo, International Horror Guild, Shirley Jackson, and Bram Stoker awards. She was named recipient of the 2007 Karl Edward Wagner Award, given at the British Fantasy Convention for "outstanding contribution to the genre."

She co-hosts the popular Fantastic Fiction reading series at KGB Bar in New York City, where she lives in close proximity to too many books and some very frightening (although not to her) doll heads.

Introduction
Ellen Datlow

I'M NOT A horror critic or expert. I *am* an enthusiast of short horror fiction, and have been for as long as I remember. I've also been reading most of the short horror fiction being published since 1986 when I was a judge for the World Fantasy Awards and then in 1987 I became the editor of the horror half of the ongoing anthology series *The Year's Best Fantasy and Horror*. So I *am* aware of what's out there.

My publisher and I decided to begin with 1985 — which is the year Clive Barker's *Books of Blood* volumes 1–3 won the World Fantasy Award. Although the books were published as mass market paperbacks in the United Kingdom in 1984 and Barker was heralded as "the new voice of horror," their influence didn't really take hold until 1985 — which is also when his second three volumes were published.

This is not to say that short horror fiction was languishing prior to Barker's emergence on the scene. What with the publication of Kirby McCauley's landmark anthology *Dark Forces* in 1980, the general reading public could see writers from all over the spectrum producing excellent horror fiction. Some of the twenty-three contributors were Joyce Carol Oates, Isaac Bashevis Singer, Gene Wolfe, Clifford Simak, Davis Grubb, T.E.D. Klein, Karl Edward Wagner, Stephen King, Joe Haldeman, Gahan Wilson, Edward Gorey, and Ramsey Campbell.

Less monumental but just as important were the horror series anthologies *Shadows*, edited by Charles L. Grant between 1978 and 1991; *Whispers* magazine and then anthology, edited by Stuart Schiff between 1973 and 1987 (with a *Best of Whispers*, including original stories, in 1997); and *Fantasy Tales*, edited by Stephen Jones and David Sutton in the UK from 1977 to 1991. The fiction published in these magazines and anthologies, although actually publishing a variety of types of stories, was perceived by some horror readers as lacking something.

Barker was heralded as introducing a new, more visceral form of horror fiction, something that was dubbed splatterpunk, although Barker's work seemed less influenced by "splatter" films than some of the later members of that loosely connected group of writers. Although the early "splatterpunks" produced some excellent work, the movement unfortunately devolved into shock fiction more concerned with viscera, torture, and grisliness than in creating lasting fear or unease. What it *did* do is start a conversation between those who felt horror needed a punch in the guts and those who felt quiet horror more effective. The only three alumni included in this volume are Clive Barker, David J. Schow (who made up the term "splatterpunk" as a joke), and Poppy Z. Brite; all three of their stories were published between 1990 and 1995, long after the heyday of the movement.

What this volume is not:

It is by no means a definitive collection of the best stories published between 1984 and 2005. Are these stories the best? How does one judge such a thing? Some are award nominees or winners, and most were reprinted by me in my annual *Year's Best Fantasy and Horror*. Are they the stories I love the best of all those published in that period? This week they are. Maybe next week, I'd pick others. With only a little over 180,000 words, this volume can merely be a taste of great fiction. I could easily fill a book twice this size with other stories (plus the brilliant and powerful novellas) that are my favorites. In fact, when pressed to say who/what I left out, although I won't name names, I did an informal count and came up with at least fifty other writers whose stories I'd have liked to include.

What this volume is:

A volume of stories that I'm particularly fond of, some of which I originally published in *OMNI*, *Event Horizon*, or *SCIFICTION*, the three magazines/webzines I've edited since 1981. Some I published in original anthologies. Some were reprinted by me in volumes of *The Year's Best Fantasy and Horror*. What they have in common is that they are the horror stories that have stayed with me. That still thrill me and chill me when I read them. I remember the characters (which indicates *something* for one who reads hundreds of stories a year). I also believe that they are a good representation of the excellent horror that has been published between 1984 and 2005.

So consider this just a sampling of great terror tales, supernatural fiction, and psychological horror.

The stories have been organized by year of publication. It seemed the most natural way. Unlike most anthologies which try to start with a very strong story and end with possibly the strongest story, a book such of this, which is essentially a survey of twenty years worth of strong horror could not work that way. Not every year is represented.

Right around when we were finishing up editing the twentieth volume of *The Year's Best Fantasy and Horror*, James Frenkel, packager of all twenty-one volumes, suggested to me and my fantasy co-editors that we compile a "best of the best" from the first twenty years of the series' existence. That project never came to be. But since much of *Darkness: Two Decades of Modern Horror* covers the same period, and most of the stories have over the years appeared in various volumes of *The Year's Best Fantasy and Horror*, readers might find it useful to think of this volume as an attempt to fulfill that ambition, at least on the horror side. Readers might also consider this as a complementary volume to what I hope will be an annual series: *The Best Horror of the Year*, first published in 2009, taking over where *The Year's Best Fantasy and Horror* left off.

Stefan Dziemianowicz has compiled more than forty anthologies of horror, mystery, and science fiction, and collections of macabre fiction by Louisa May Alcott, Robert Bloch, Joseph Payne Brennan, August Derleth, Henry Kuttner, Jane Rice, Bram Stoker, Henry S. Whitehead, and others. A former editor of *Necrofile: The Review of Horror Fiction* and the Necronomicon Press short fiction series, he co-edited *Supernatural Literature of the World: An Encyclopedia*. He is the author of *Bloody Mary and Other Tales for a Dark Night* and *The Annotated Guide to Unknown and Unknown Worlds*. His reviews have appeared in *Publishers Weekly*, *Locus*, and the *Washington Post Book World*.

Foreword
Stefan Dziemianowicz

LET A THOUSAND voices shriek!

That might well have been the mantra of horror publishing at the start of the 1980s. The trickle of trade horror fiction that began with the publication of Ira Levin's *Rosemary's Baby* in 1967 became a tide with the release of William Peter Blatty's *The Exorcist* and Thomas Tryon's *The Other* in 1971, and of course Stephen King's *Carrie* three years after that. With King's phenomenal success, horror became a best-selling category of popular fiction and the tide turned torrent. Professional writers who for decades had been sublimating their horror impulses into suspense or science fiction suddenly found publishers willing to accommodate them when they channeled their inner Poes. Writers who had honed their skills in the burgeoning horror specialty press were snapped up by an expanding market of trade horror imprints, while a younger generation of writers that had grown up reading King and his colleagues reached their majority and began blitzing publishing houses with manuscripts. The floodgates were open, and while there was much dross silting the stream of fiction that flowed forth, the sheer profusion of talent devoted to horror craft ensured that the horror field and its fiction would enjoy imaginative growth and evolution. Over the next twenty years, through the themes it popularized, the concerns it grappled with, and the arguments it ignited, horror boomed and bloomed, and the generation that cultivated it helped to shape the horror tale of the twenty-first century.

Among the earliest controversies horror's post-Stephen King writers grappled with was how much graphic content horror fiction should tolerate. It was by no means a new issue. Gothic novels of the late-eighteenth and early-nineteenth centuries had scandalized their eras' arbiters of literary taste with (then) shocking scenes of gore, taboo sexuality, and sordid behavior, and their spirit had persisted through a subspecies of exploitative horror fiction that was an ineradicable part of the genre for two centuries. King had pushed the envelope of the physically squeamish in his own writing and established a balance between outrageous and acceptable content. With King's model setting the upward limit for how explicit horror fiction should be Charles L. Grant, through his own writing and the series of *Shadows* anthologies that he inaugurated in 1978, legitimized a subtle approach to horror that was eventually dubbed "dark fantasy" to distinguish it from the seamier fare of "horror." Dark fantasy, as Grant defined it, emphasized people, their problems, and their emotional responses to the dark side of everyday life over the weird phenomena and Gothic grue that had defined much horror fiction of the pulp era and mid-twentieth century. Though not without its mayhem and monsters, dark fantasy most often presented horrors that incarnated or gave shape to the fears and anxieties of ordinary people caught up in extraordinary circumstances. Most of horror's better-selling works between 1967 and 1984 — certainly those that had escaped genre ghettoization — comfortably fit the dark fantasy template and were seen as helping to usher the hitherto stigmatized tale of horror into a new era of literary respectability.

Then came Barker. With the release of Clive Barker's six-volume *Books of Blood* short fiction collections between 1984 and 1985, explicitness thrust itself back onto horror's main stage. Graphic sex and gore were essential inflections in Barker's articulate horror vocabulary, and they helped to refurbish some of the classic horror tropes he put to work in his fiction. What's more, a wide popular audience — including not only non-veteran horror readers, but cinema fans and enthusiasts of other extraliterary artistic media — embraced Barker's fiction and canonized him as the genre's new visionary.

Which kicked open the door for splatterpunk. Even as Barker was basking in the limelight for his type of graphic horror tale, a coterie of younger writers disgruntled with the subtleties that they saw as straitjacketing trade horror fiction and depriving the horror story of its unique and unsettling character, roared onto the scene. Dubbing themselves the splatterpunks — a reference to both contemporary graphic horror (i.e., splatter) films that were a seminal influence not only on their writing, but increasingly on the work of many neophyte writers coming up in the new culture of horror engendered by King's popularity; and cyberpunk, the edgy technophilic subgenre of modern science fiction — David J. Schow, John Skipp, Craig Spector, and a small but vocal band of renegades began promoting their work on the strength of its adrenalized prose, kinetic scenes of physical horror, and inventively outrageous renderings of sex, blood, and (yes, occasionally) rock 'n' roll. The gauntlet was thrown down.

The conflict between splatterpunk and dark fantasy sparked great debates at conventions and in the pages of horror publications: Had the enforcement of a set of core values made the modern horror story stale and predictable? (Perhaps.) Did horror stories that studiously avoided the visceral in favor of the subtle tend sometimes toward the obscure? (Possibly.) Were the shock tactics of splatterpunk an antidote to complacency in horror fiction or merely an excuse for gratuitous exhibitionism? (All depends on the writer and the story.) But the perceived controversy between these two approaches was greatly exaggerated. At their most contentious, they represented opposite extremes of the horror-fiction continuum. Each approach yielded its share of good and bad horror fiction. Most authors worked in the territory between the two poles, but enough produced stories that might have tended toward either extreme that it was pointless to see the issue as somehow dividing horror into warring camps. Regardless, the splatterpunk upsurge was important for calling attention to the aesthetic principles of horror fiction and making writers conscious of their objectives as serious practitioners.

One of the major inspirations for splatterpunk was the zombie movie trilogy that independent film director George Romero had launched with *Night of the Living Dead* in 1968. The transformation of the zombie from a grisly but otherwise non-threatening monster resurrected by black magic into a virally re-animated voracious eating machine that hungers for human flesh is just one example of the many ways in which horror's classic themes and monsters changed in the decades between 1983 and 2003 in response to readers' needs for monsters that spoke directly to fears salient for the times. Following the publication of John Skipp and Craig Spector's anthologies *Book of the Dead* (1989) and *Still Dead: Book of the Dead II* — both stocked with Romeroesque zombie stories by most of modern horror's best and brightest writers — the traditional zombie was all but consigned to the lime pit of horror tropes that had outlived their fearsomeness. Interpreted anew as a symbol for everything from conspicuous consumption run amuck in American society to the mindless obedience and extreme aggression associated with terrorist movements, the zombie enjoyed an unusually imaginative makeover that moved it from the periphery of horror's classic iconography at the start of the Stephen King era to the frontline of horror's most malleable metaphors by the new millennium.

The zombie was joined by the serial killer, who since the 1960s had increasingly supplanted the werewolf as a representation of the monster within struggling to express itself. In the decade following the success of Thomas Harris's *Red Dragon* (1981) and its sequel *The Silence of the Lambs* (1988) — both of which established the character of sociopath Hannibal Lecter as a horror icon openly embraced by the popular culture — serial killer fiction enjoyed a surge of popularity that reflected the interpenetration of crime and horror in the popular fiction market and the increasingly ambiguous boundary separating suspense and thriller fiction from the horror tale. In the minds of many readers, the dispassionate personality of the serial killer and his frequently gruesome methods were little different from the inhuman monsters of supernatural horror and the mayhem they wrought.

The monster most conspicuously transformed within and without horror fiction at the end of the twentieth century, however, was surely the vampire. The two decades between 1985 and 2005 saw more vampire stories written than had been published for the two centuries that preceded them — so many, in fact, that the vampire tale became a genre unto itself, with its own subgenres and sub-subgenres. Traditional depictions of the vampire as a blood despoiling scourge resonated with readers in the age of AIDS and the vampire story's traditional predator-prey relationship seemed vitally relevant to a culture whose members increasingly saw themselves as victimized by a variety of social, political, and domestic threats beyond their control. More important, much vampire fiction during this era refurbished the image of the vampire: depictions of the soulless monster that Bram Stoker and his followers had promulgated for nearly a century gave way to those of a superior but alienated individual who is out of step with society and exiled to its margins. Anne Rice's novel *Interview with the Vampire* (1976), and especially its sequel *The Vampire Lestat* (1985), fine-tuned this image into that of the social outcast whose unique perspective — developed and shaped independent of the common mass — gives it an unusual vantage point from which to view and assess human behavior. Through her fiction, Rice depicted the vampire as attractive and enviable, if not always sympathetic. Her Lestat spawned countless imitators and doppelgängers who could be interpreted as renderings of gay society, modern primitives, and other contemporary subcultures whose behavior might be perceived as rebellious, renegade, and otherwise nonconformist. The enormous popularity of the articulate and sophisticated vampire whose supernatural character seems less an affliction than an alternate lifestyle choice found favor with the modern Goth movement, and writers such as Poppy Z. Brite and Caitlín R. Kiernan, whose tales of disaffected outsiders and their often surreal supernatural experiences resonated with its transgressive mindset.

The popularity of the vampire helped to ignite another trend that significantly impacted the trajectory of horror fiction at the end of the twentieth century. As an immortal creature capable of outliving adventures in any one story, the vampire proved perfectly poised to become a recurring character in chronicles with a vast historical sweep and a scope too broad to be contained by a single book. Imaginative multi-volume vampire sagas by Rice, Chelsea Quinn Yarbro, and Les Daniels legitimized the series horror story and encouraged other writers of both vampire fiction and non-vampire fiction to create their own episodic horror epics. By the beginning of the twenty-first century, one-third to one-half of all trade sales in horror were for series titles. By benefit of their recurring characters and repetitious formulae, these books introduced a new type of horror story, one driven less by mood, atmosphere, and phenomena than by character and complexity of plot.

With each infusion, incursion, and re-invention, horror became a more complex and less clearly defined branch of popular fiction. Perhaps that's as it should be, since the horror story (and in particular the tale of supernatural horror) is, by its nature, concerned with the irrational, the unthinkable, the impalpable, and the unwieldy. In the last quarter century the horror tale has played to appreciative audiences at both loud and soft decibel levels. It has spliced itself with virtually every other genre, ranging from fantasy and science fiction to suspense and romance. It has franchised its most iconic monsters to successful roles in stories that are far from horrifying. It has achieved best-sellerdom with a huge audience of non-horror readers even as it sells in abundance to a core audience of devoted fans who cherish its subversiveness. Above all it has become a ubiquitous presence in the landscape of contemporary fiction, openly embraced by Joyce Carol Oates, Michael Chabon, Dan Chaon, and countless other writers who flirt regularly with the dark side of the fanciful across the rickety fence that separates literary from genre fiction, and in artifacts and emblems regularly referenced in the work of writers who hope to reflect horror's omnipresence in the contemporary culture. Horror is where you find it, and after the past quarter century of growth and development, you find it everywhere. It has come a long way since the 1970s when the paranoia and distrust of authority sown during the Vietnam War era prepared a generation of readers and writers for a type of fiction that explored the dark side of daily life and peeled back the façade of the ordinary to expose unpleasantness squirming beneath. Its enduring popularity and continuing growth and evolution suggest that horror is a story type that will continue to be told as long as there are readers who enjoy its thrills, and who perhaps find it all the more easy to exorcise their fears and anxieties by reading fiction that gives them identifiable shapes and substance.

Darkness: Two Decades of Modern Horror is not only a celebration of horror fiction published in the years 1985 to 2005, but of distinguished short horror stories that appeared in that interval. To that end, it acknowledges the recent resurgence of the short horror story as the showpiece of modern horror. Although the horror tale as we know it today has its origins in the Gothic novels of the late-eighteenth and early-nineteenth centuries, the horror story was refined as an art form at shorter lengths. Through his enormously influential body of work, Edgar Allan Poe helped to establish unities and aesthetic principles for the short horror tale not unlike those for poetic composition that still inform horror fiction today.

Horror thrived in short form throughout the nineteenth century and in the pulp magazines of the early twentieth century, which were tailored almost exclusively for short, sharp, and shocking tales. Story types as different as the antiquarian ghost story perfected by M. R. James, and the tale of cosmic horror promulgated by H. P. Lovecraft, reinforced the perception that the unique character of the horror story best expressed itself at short, compact lengths. With the collapse of the pulp magazines and the decline of horror's popularity in the years immediately following World War II, however, the short horror story found itself with few major venues or proving grounds for its continued evolution and development. The decline of markets for short horror fiction mirrored the diminishing popularity of short fiction in general, and the corresponding increase of interest in the novel as a serious artistic (and commercial) form. By the time Stephen King helped to put horror on the map of modern fiction, the popular wisdom was that the only way to reach beyond the genre market to a general readership and literary success was to produce novel-length works. Even writers who had heretofore specialized in short horror fiction — Ramsey Campbell, Dennis Etchison, Ted Klein, King himself — turned their attention to novel-writing.

Of course short horror fiction was still being published in the 1970s and '80s, but absent the dedicated and diversified markets that supported science fiction and mystery fiction — *Rod Serling's Twilight Zone Magazine* and its short-lived sister publication *Night Cry* were the only two professional magazines for most of the 1980s to specialize in or feature predominantly horror fiction — it appeared primarily in mixed genre magazines such as *The Magazine of Fantasy & Science Fiction*, or outlets known primarily to hardcore genre fans: horror anthologies such as Charles Grant's *Shadows* series and its different offshoots, and especially the specialty press. Small press magazines such as *Whispers, Fantasy Tales, The Horror Show, Weirdbook, Grue,* and *Cemetery Dance* provided established authors with markets for shorter works that they could not place in mainstream publications and nurtured new writers and movements within horror whose raw and sometimes unrefined offerings would not have found favor outside of a genre known for its edginess and provocation.

Inevitably, specialty book publishers helped to take up the slack with anthologies whose contents were the equal of those produced by trade publishers. These were the years that saw the launch of the *Masques, Borderlands, Night Visions,* and *Darklands* series. Not only did these compilations help to erode the distinction between the small and trade press — along with distinguished trade anthology series such as *New Terrors* and *Dark Terrors*, among others — these books helped the all-original anthology to supplant the magazine as the top market for new horror fiction. It wasn't necessarily the best transition — by the time of the collapse of the overexpanded market for horror fiction in the early 1990s, the horror anthology market was glutted with compilations of uninspired stories written to order on narrow themes, rather than culled as a representation of the best possible work on the subject or by the author. Regardless, the proliferation and persistence of markets for the horror short story were proof that the short horror tale would always play a vital role in horror's development, and that it would both lead the genre as well as reflect its dominant trends and interests.

For the brief span of a few years, three annual anthology series featured the best horror stories produced in any calendar year: Karl Edward Wagner's *The Year's Best Horror Stories*, Ellen Datlow and Terri Windling's *The Years Best Fantasy and Horror*, and Steve Jones's (and, for its first six volumes, Ramsey Campbell's) *Best New Horror*. Though all three reflected the personal preferences of their editors, the relative lack of overlap in contents and the professionalism and high caliber of stories selected proved the strength and vitality of the short horror tale. For the contents of *Darkness*, Ellen Datlow draws extensively from the picks she has compiled for more than twenty years as editor of the horror half of *The Year's Best Fantasy and Horror*. Few people if any have read as extensively in the short horror market as Datlow has for the past two decades, so it is inevitable that some readers may look upon this volume as a "best of the best" culling. Yet *Darkness* is a testament to something grander and more significant about contemporary horror fiction. Through the sheer quantity of the quality stories it gathers, it pays tribute to the persistence of the short horror story, and the importance of horror as an outlet of expression for some our most talented writers of short fiction. And in its celebration of creativity and the wide range of talents among horror's best and brightest, it may well be looked to by future generations of horror readers as the anthology that established the benchmark for horror, and the short horror story in particular, at the start of the twenty-first century.

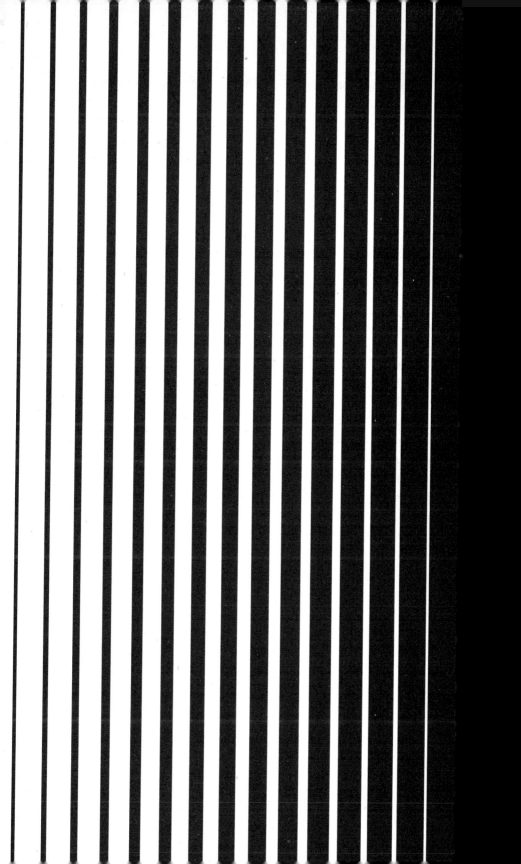

Clive Barker burst onto the horror scene in 1984 with the British publication of his mass market, three-book collection *Books of Blood 1–3* from Sphere. Their publication was momentous in two ways. In addition to it being extremely unusual for an all-original collection to be published in book form (let alone three books) — that is, without any of the stories first being published in magazines — even more important, a new voice in horror was introduced to the world. And the world took note. The *Books of Blood* (1–3) won the World Fantasy Award in 1985. I published one of the stories in *OMNI* Magazine, giving Barker his first u.s. publication in magazine form. The stories were visceral, sexual, graphic, and intense, and for better or worse they heralded what came to be dubbed splatterpunk. "Jacqueline Ess: Her Will and Testament" has certainly retained its power since it was first published over twenty-five years ago.

Barker rarely produces short fiction these days, currently writing prose for adults and children, writing for the screen and stage, and continuing his work as an accomplished artist. His most recent novels are *Coldheart Canyon: A Hollywood Ghost Story, Abarat, Abarat: Days of Magic, Nights of War, Mister B. Gone,* and *Absolute Midnight* (the third book in the projected Abarat Quintet).

Jacqueline Ess: Her Will and Testament
Clive Barker

MY GOD, SHE thought, this can't be living. Day in, day out: the boredom, the drudgery, the frustration.

My Christ, she prayed, let me out, set me free, crucify me if you must, but put me out of my misery.

In lieu of his euthanasian benediction, she took a blade from Ben's razor, one dull day in late March, locked herself in the bathroom, and slit her wrists.

Through the throbbing in her ears, she faintly heard Ben outside the bathroom door.

"Are you in there, darling?"

"Go away," she thought she said.

"I'm back early, sweetheart. The traffic was light."

"Please go away."

The effort of trying to speak slid her off the toilet seat and on to the white-tiled floor, where pools of her blood were already cooling.

"Darling?"

"Go."

"Darling."

"Away."

"Are you all right?"

Now he was rattling at the door, the rat. Didn't he realize she couldn't open it, wouldn't open it?

"Answer me, Jackie."

She groaned. She couldn't stop herself. The pain wasn't as terrible as she'd expected, but there was an ugly feeling, as though she'd been kicked in the head. Still, he couldn't catch her in time, not now. Not even if he broke the door down.

He broke the door down.

She looked up at him through an air grown so thick with death you could have sliced it.

"Too late," she thought she said.

But it wasn't.

My God, she thought, this can't be suicide. I haven't died.

The doctor Ben had hired for her was too perfectly benign. Only the best, he'd promised, only the very best for my Jackie.

"It's nothing," the doctor reassured her, "that we can't put right with a little tinkering."

Why doesn't he just come out with it? she thought. He doesn't give a damn. He doesn't know what it's like.

"I deal with a lot of these women's problems," he confided, fairly oozing a practiced compassion. "It's got to epidemic proportions among a certain age-bracket."

She was barely thirty. What was he telling her? That she was prematurely menopausal?

"Depression, partial or total withdrawal, neuroses of every shape and size. You're not alone, believe me."

Oh yes I am, she thought. I'm here in my head, on my own, and you can't know what it's like.

"We'll have you right in two shakes of a lamb's tail."

I'm a lamb, am I? Does he think I'm a lamb?

Musing, he glanced up at his framed qualifications, then at his manicured nails, then at the pens on his desk and notepad. But he didn't look at Jacqueline. Anywhere but at Jacqueline.

"I know," he was saying now, "what you've been through, and it's been traumatic. Women have certain needs. If they go unanswered —"

What would he know about women's needs?

You're not a woman, she thought she thought.

"What?" he said.

Had she spoken? She shook her head: denying speech. He went on; finding his rhythm once more: "I'm not going to put you through interminable therapy-sessions. You don't want that, do you? You want a little reassurance, and you want something to help you sleep at nights."

He was irritating her badly now. His condescension was so profound it had no bottom. All-knowing, all-seeing Father; that was his performance. As if he were blessed with some miraculous insight into the nature of a woman's soul.

"Of course, I've tried therapy courses with patients in the past. But between you and me —"

He lightly patted her hand. Father's palm on the back of her hand. She was supposed to be flattered, reassured, maybe even seduced.

"— between you and me it's so much talk. Endless talk. Frankly, what good does it do? We've all got problems. You can't talk them away, can you?"

You're not a woman. You don't look like a woman, you don't feel like a woman —

"Did you say something?"

She shook her head.

"I thought you said something. Please feel free to be honest with me."

She didn't reply, and he seemed to tire of pretending intimacy. He stood up and went to the window.

"I think the best thing for you —"

He stood against the light: darkening the room, obscuring the view of the cherry trees on the lawn through the window. She stared at his wide shoulders, at his narrow hips. A fine figure of a man, as Ben would have called him. No child-bearer he. Made to remake the world, a body like that. If not the world, remaking minds would have to do.

"I think the best thing for you —"

What did he know, with his hips, with his shoulders? He was too much a man to understand anything of her.

"I think the best thing for you would be a course of sedatives —"

Now her eyes were on his waist.

"— and a holiday."

Her mind had focussed now on the body beneath the veneer of his clothes. The muscle, bone and blood beneath the elastic skin. She pictured it from all sides, sizing it up, judging its powers of resistance, then closing on it. She thought:

Be a woman.

Simply, as she thought that preposterous idea, it began to take shape. Not a fairy-tale transformation, unfortunately, his flesh resisted such magic. She willed his manly chest into making breasts of itself and it began to swell most fetchingly, until the skin burst and his sternum flew apart. His pelvis, teased to breaking point, fractured at its center; unbalanced, he toppled over on to his desk and from there stared up at her, his face yellow with shock. He licked his lips, over and over again, to find some wetness to talk with. His mouth was dry: his words were still-born. It was from between his legs that all the noise was coming; the splashing of his blood; the thud of his bowel on the carpet.

She screamed at the absurd monstrosity she had made, and withdrew to the far corner of the room, where she was sick in the pot of the rubber plant.

My God, she thought, this can't be murder. I didn't so much as touch him.

What Jacqueline had done that afternoon, she kept to herself. No sense in giving people sleepless nights, thinking about such peculiar talent.

The police were very kind. They produced any number of explanations for the sudden departure of Dr. Blandish, though none quite described how his chest had erupted in that extraordinary fashion, making two handsome (if hairy) domes of his pectorals.

It was assumed that some unknown psychotic, strong in his insanity, had broken in, done the deed with hands, hammers and saws, and exited, locking the innocent Jacqueline Ess in an appalled silence no interrogation could hope to penetrate.

Person or persons unknown had clearly dispatched the doctor to where neither sedatives nor therapy could help him.

She almost forgot for a while. But as the months passed it came back to her by degrees, like a memory of a secret adultery. It teased her with its forbidden delights. She forgot the nausea, and remembered the power. She forgot sordidity, and remembered strength. She forgot the guilt that had seized her afterwards and longed, longed to do it again.

Only better.

"Jacqueline."

Is this my husband, she thought, actually calling me by my name? Usually it was Jackie, or Jack, or nothing at all.

"Jacqueline."

He was looking at her with those big baby blues of his, like the college-boy she'd loved at first sight. But his mouth was harder now, and his kisses tasted like stale bread.

"Jacqueline."

"Yes."

"I've got something I want to speak to you about."

A conversation? she thought; it must be a public holiday.

"I don't know how to tell you this."

"Try me," she suggested.

She knew that she could think his tongue into speaking if it pleased her. Make him tell her what she wanted to hear. Words of love, maybe, if she could remember what they sounded like. But what was the use of that? Better the truth.

"Darling, I've gone off the rails a bit."

"What do you mean?" she said.

Have you, you bastard, she thought.

"It was while you weren't quite yourself. You know, when things had more or less stopped between us. Separate rooms...you wanted separate rooms...and I just went bananas with frustration. I didn't want to upset you, so I didn't say anything. But it's no use me trying to live two lives."

"You can have an affair if you want to, Ben."

"It's not an affair, Jackie. I love her —"

He was preparing one of his speeches, she could see it gathering momentum behind his teeth. The justifications that became accusations, those excuses that always turned into assaults on her character. Once he got into full flow there'd be no stopping him. She didn't want to hear.

"— she's not like you at all, Jackie. She's frivolous in her way. I suppose you'd call her shallow."

It might be worth interrupting here, she thought, before he ties himself in his usual knots.

"She's not moody like you. You know, she's just a normal woman. I don't mean to say you're not normal: you can't help having depressions. But she's not so sensitive."

"There's no need, Ben —"

"No, damn it, I want it all off my chest."

On to me, she thought.

"You've never let me explain," he was saying. "You've always given me one of those damn looks of yours, as if you wished I'd —"

Die.

"— wished I'd shut up."

Shut up.

"You don't care how I feel!" He was shouting now. "Always in your own little world."

Shut up, she thought.

His mouth was open. She seemed to wish it closed, and with the thought his jaws snapped together, severing the very tip of his pink tongue. It fell from between his lips and lodged in a fold of his shirt.

Shut up, she thought again.

The two perfect regiments of his teeth ground down into each other, cracking and splitting, nerve, calcium and spit making a pinkish foam on his chin as his mouth collapsed inwards.

Shut up, she was still thinking as his startled baby blues sank back into his skull and his nose wormed its way into his brain.

He was not Ben any longer, he was a man with a red lizard's head, flattening, battening down upon itself, and, thank God, he was past speech-making once and for all.

Now she had the knack of it, she began to take pleasure in the changes she was willing upon him.

She flipped him head over heels on to the floor and began to compress his arms and legs, telescoping flesh and resistant bone into a smaller and yet smaller space. His clothes were folded inwards, and the tissue of his stomach was plucked from his neatly packaged entrails and stretched around his body to wrap him up. His fingers were poking from his shoulder-blades now, and his feet, still thrashing with fury, were tipped up in his gut. She turned him over one final time to pressure his spine into a foot-long column of muck, and that was about the end of it.

As she came out of her ecstasy she saw Ben sitting on the floor, shut up into a space about the size of one of his fine leather suitcases, while blood, bile and lymphatic fluid pulsed weakly from his hushed body.

My God, she thought, this can't be my husband. He's never been as tidy as that.

This time she didn't wait for help. This time she knew what she'd done (guessed, even, how she'd done it) and she accepted her crime for the too-rough justice it was. She packed her bags and left the home.

I'm alive, she thought. For the first time in my whole, wretched life, I'm alive.

Vassi's Testimony (part one)

"To you who dream of sweet, strong women I leave this story. It is a promise, as surely as it is a confession, as surely as it's the last words of a lost man who wanted nothing but to love and be loved. I sit here trembling, waiting for the night, waiting for that whining pimp Koos to come to my door again, and take everything I own from me in exchange for the key to her room.

I am not a courageous man, and I never have been: so I'm afraid of what may happen to me tonight. But I cannot go through life dreaming all the time, existing through the darkness on only a glimpse of heaven. Sooner or later, one has to gird one's loins (that's appropriate) and get up and find it. Even if it means giving away the world in exchange.

I probably make no sense. You're thinking, you who chanced on this testimony, you're thinking, who was he, this imbecile?

My name was Oliver Vassi. I am now thirty-eight years old. I was lawyer, until a year or more ago, when I began the search that ends tonight with that pimp and that key and that holy of holies.

But the story begins more than a year ago. It is many years since Jacqueline Ess first came to me.

She arrived out of the blue at my offices, claiming to be the widow of a friend of mine from Law School, one Benjamin Ess, and when I thought back, I remembered the face. A mutual friend who'd been at the wedding had shown me a photograph of Ben and his blushing bride. And here she was, every bit as elusive a beauty as her photograph promised.

I remember being acutely embarrassed at that first interview. She'd arrived at a busy time, and I was up to my neck in work. But I was so enthralled by her, I let all the day's interviews fall by the wayside, and when my secretary came in she gave me one of her steely glances as if to throw a bucket of cold water over me. I suppose I was enamored from the start, and she sensed the electric atmosphere in my office. Me, I pretended I was merely being polite to the widow of an old friend. I didn't like to think about passion: it wasn't a part of my nature, or so I thought. How little we know — I mean *really* know — about our capabilities.

Jacqueline told me lies at that first meeting. About how Ben had died of cancer, of how often he had spoken of me, and how fondly. I suppose she could have told me the truth then and there, and I would have lapped it up — I believe I was utterly devoted from the beginning.

But it's difficult to remember quite how and when interest in another human being flares into something more committed, more passionate. It may be that I am inventing the impact she had on me at that first meeting, simply re-inventing history to justify my later excesses. I'm not sure. Anyway, wherever and whenever it happened, however quickly or slowly, I succumbed to her, and the affair began.

I'm not a particularly inquisitive man where my friends, or my bed-partners, are concerned. As a lawyer one spends one's time going through the dirt of other people's lives, and frankly, eight hours a day of that is quite enough for me. When I'm out of the office my pleasure is in letting people be. I don't pry. I don't dig, I just take them on face value.

Jacqueline was no exception to this rule. She was a woman I was glad to have in my life whatever the truth of her past. She possessed a marvellous *sang-froid,* she was witty, bawdy, oblique. I had never met a more enchanting woman. It was none of my business how she'd lived with Ben, what the marriage had been like etc., etc. That was her history. I was happy to live in the present, and let the past die its own death. I think I even flattered myself that whatever pain she had experienced, I could help her forget it.

Certainly her stories had holes in them. As a lawyer, I was trained to be eagle-eyed where fabrications were concerned, and however much I tried to put my perceptions aside I sensed that she wasn't quite coming clean with me. But everyone has secrets: I knew that. Let her have hers, I thought.

Only once did I challenge her on a detail of her pretended life-story. In talking about Ben's death, she let slip that he had got what he deserved. I asked her what she meant. She smiled, that Gioconda smile of hers, and told me that she felt there was a balance to be redressed between men and women. I let the observation pass. After all, I was obsessed by that time, past all hope of salvation; whatever argument she was putting, I was happy to concede it.

She was so beautiful, you see. Not in any two-dimensional sense: she wasn't young, she wasn't innocent, she didn't have that pristine symmetry so favored by ad-men and photographers. Her face was plainly that of a woman in her early forties: it had been used to laugh and cry, and usage leaves its marks. But she had a power to transform herself, in the subtlest way, making that face as various as the sky. Early on, I thought it was a make-up trick. But as we slept together more and more, and I watched her in the mornings, sleep in her eyes, and in the evenings, heavy with fatigue, I soon realized she wore nothing on her skull but flesh and blood. What transformed her was internal: it was a trick of the will.

And, you know, that made me love her all the more.

Then one night I woke with her sleeping beside me. We slept often on the floor, which she preferred to the bed. Beds, she said, reminded her of marriage. Anyway, that night she was lying under a quilt on the carpet of my room, and I, simply out of adoration, was watching her face in sleep.

If one has given oneself utterly, watching the beloved sleep can be a vile experience. Perhaps some of you have known that paralysis, staring down at features closed to your enquiry, locked away from you where you can never, ever go, into the other's mind. As I say, for us who have given ourselves, that is a horror. One knows, in those moments, that one does not exist, except in relation to that face, that personality. Therefore, when that face is closed down, that personality is lost in its own unknowable world, one feels completely without purpose. A planet without a sun, revolving in darkness.

That's how I felt that night, looking down at her extraordinary features, and as I chewed on my soullessness, her face began to alter. She was clearly dreaming; but what dreams must she have been having. Her very fabric was on the move, her muscle, her hair, the down on her cheek moving to the dictates of some internal tide. Her lips bloomed from her bone, boiling up into a slavering tower of skin; her hair swirled around her head as though she were lying in water; the substance of her cheeks formed furrows and ridges like the ritual scars on a warrior; inflamed and throbbing patterns of tissue, swelling up and changing again even as a pattern formed. This fluxion was a terror to me, and I must have made some noise. She didn't wake, but came a little closer to the surface of sleep, leaving the deeper waters where these powers were sourced. The patterns sank away in an instant, and her face was again that of a gently sleeping woman.

That was, you can understand, a pivotal experience, even though I spent the next few days trying to convince myself that I hadn't seen it.

The effort was useless. I knew there was something wrong with her; and at that time I was certain she knew nothing about it. I was convinced that something in her system was awry, and that I was best to investigate her history before I told her what I had seen.

On reflection, of course, that seems laughably naïve. To think she wouldn't have known that she contained such a power. But it was easier for me to picture her as prey to such skill, than mistress of it. That's a man speaking of a woman; not just me, Oliver Vassi, of her, Jacqueline Ess. We cannot believe, we men, that power will ever reside happily in the body of a woman, unless that power is a male child. Not true power. The power must be in male hands, God-given. That's what our fathers tell us, idiots that they are.

Anyway, I investigated Jacqueline, as surreptitiously as I could. I had a contact in York where the couple had lived, and it wasn't difficult to get some enquiries moving. It took a week for my contact to get back to me, because he'd had to cut through a good deal of shit from the police to get a hint of the truth, but the news came, and it was bad.

Ben was dead, that much was true. But there was no way he had died of cancer. My contact had only got the vaguest clues as to the condition of Ben's corpse, but he gathered it had been spectacularly mutilated. And the prime suspect? My beloved Jacqueline Ess. The same innocent woman who was occupying my flat, sleeping by my side every night.

So I put it to her that she was hiding something from me. I don't know what I was expecting in return. What I got was a demonstration of her power. She gave it freely, without malice, but I would have been a fool not to have read a warning into it. She told me first how she had discovered her unique control over the sum and substance of human beings. In her despair, she said, when she was on the verge of killing herself, she had found, in the very deep-water trenches of her nature, faculties she had never known existed. Powers which came up out of those regions as she recovered, like fish to the light.

Then she showed me the smallest measure of these powers, plucking hairs from my head, one by one. Only a dozen; just to demonstrate her formidable skills. I felt them going. She just said: one from behind your ear, and I'd feel my skin creep and then jump as fingers of her volition snatched a hair out. Then another, and another. It was an incredible display; she had this power down to a fine art, locating and withdrawing single hairs from my scalp with the precision of tweezers.

Frankly, I was sitting there rigid with fear, knowing that she was just toying with me. Sooner or later, I was certain the time would be right for her to silence me permanently.

But she had doubts about herself. She told me how the skill, though she had honed it, scared her. She needed, she said, someone to teach her how to use it best. And I was not that somebody. I was just a man who loved her, who had loved her before this revelation, and would love her still, in spite of it.

In fact, after that display I quickly came to accommodate a new vision of Jacqueline. Instead of fearing her, I became more devoted to this woman who tolerated my possession of her body.

My work became an irritation, a distraction that came between me and thinking of my beloved. What reputation I had began to deteriorate; I lost briefs, I lost credibility. In the space of two or three months my professional life dwindled away to almost nothing. Friends despaired of me, colleagues avoided me.

It wasn't that she was feeding on me. I want to be clear about that. She was no lamia, no succubus. What happened to me, my fall from grace with ordinary life if you like, was of my own making. She didn't bewitch me; that's a romantic lie to excuse rape. She was a sea: and I had to swim in her. Does that make any sense? I'd lived my life on the shore, in the solid world of law, and I was tired of it. She was liquid; a boundless sea in a single body, a deluge in a small room, and I will gladly drown in her, if she grants me the chance. But that was my decision. Understand that. This has always been my decision. I have decided to go to the room tonight, and be with her one final time. That is of my own free will.

And what man would not? She was (is) sublime.

For a month after that demonstration of power I lived in a permanent ecstasy of her. When I was with her she showed me ways to love beyond the limits of any other creature on God's earth. I say beyond the limits: with her there were no limits. And when I was away from her the reverie continued: because she seemed to have changed my world.

Then she left me.

I knew why: she'd gone to find someone to teach her how to use strength. But understanding her reasons made it no easier.

I broke down: lost my job, lost my identity, lost the few friends I had left in the world. I scarcely noticed. They were minor losses, beside the loss of Jacqueline..."

"Jacqueline."

My God, she thought, can this really be the most influential man in the country? He looked so unprepossessing, so very unspectacular. His chin wasn't even strong.

But Titus Pettifer was power.

He ran more monopolies than he could count; his word in the financial world could break companies like sticks, destroying the ambitions of hundreds, the careers of thousands. Fortunes were made overnight in his shadow, entire corporations fell when he blew on them, casualties of his whim. This man knew power if any man knew it. He had to be learned from.

"You wouldn't mind if I called you J., would you?"

"No."

"Have you been waiting long?"

"Long enough."

"I don't normally leave beautiful women waiting."

"Yes you do."

She knew him already: two minutes in his presence was enough to find his measure. He would come quickest to her if she was quietly insolent.

"Do you always call women you've never met before by their initials?"

"It's convenient for filing; do you mind?"

"It depends."

"On what?"

"What I get in return for giving you the privilege."

"It's a privilege, is it, to know your name?"

"Yes."

"Well...I'm flattered. Unless of course you grant that privilege widely?"

She shook her head. No, he could see she wasn't profligate with her affections.

"Why have you waited so long to see me?" he said. "Why have I had reports of your wearing my secretaries down with your constant demands to meet with me? Do you want money? Because if you do you'll go away empty-handed. I became rich by being mean, and the richer I get, the meaner I become."

The remark was truth; he spoke it plainly.

"I don't want money," she said, equally plainly.

"That's refreshing."

"There's richer than you."

He raised his eyebrows in surprise. She could bite, this beauty.

"True," he said. There were at least half a dozen richer men in the hemisphere.

"I'm not an adoring little nobody. I haven't come here to screw a name. I've come here because we can be together. We have a great deal to offer each other."

"Such as?" he said.

"I have my body."

He smiled. It was the straightest offer he'd heard in years.

"And what do I offer you in return for such largesse?"

"I want to learn —"

"Learn?"

"— how to use power."

She was stranger and stranger, this one.

"What do you mean?" he replied, playing for time. He hadn't got the measure of her; she vexed him, confounded him.

"Shall I recite it for you again, in bourgeois?" she said, playing insolence with such a smile he almost felt attractive again.

"No need. You want to learn to use power. I suppose I could teach you —"

"I know you can."

"You realize I'm a married man. Virginia and I have been together eighteen years."

"You have three sons, four houses, a maid-servant called Mirabelle. You loathe New York, and you love Bangkok; your shirt collar is 16 ½, your favorite color green."

"Turquoise."

"You're getting subtler in your old age."

"I'm not old."

"Eighteen years a married man. It ages you prematurely."

"Not me."

"Prove it."

"How?"

"Take me."

"What?"

"Take me."

"Here?"

"Draw the blinds, lock the door, turn off the computer terminus, and take me. I dare you."

"Dare?"

How long was it since anyone had *dared* him to do anything?

"Dare?"

He was excited. He hadn't been so excited in a dozen years. He drew the blinds, locked the door, turned off the video display of his fortunes.

My God, she thought, I've got him.

It wasn't an easy passion, not like that with Vassi. For one thing, Pettifer was a clumsy, uncultured lover. For another, he was too nervous of his wife to be a wholly successful adulterer. He thought he saw Virginia everywhere: in the lobbies of the hotels they took a room in for the afternoon, in cabs cruising the street outside their rendezvous, once even (he swore the likeness was exact) dressed as a waitress, and swabbing down a table in a restaurant. All fictional fears, but they dampened the spontaneity of the romance somewhat.

Still, she was learning from him. He was as brilliant a potentate as he was inept a lover. She learned how to be powerful without exercising power, how to keep one's self uncontaminated by the foulness all charisma stirs up in the uncharismatic; how to make the plain decisions plainly; how to be merciless. Not that she needed much education in that particular quarter. Perhaps it was more truthful to say he taught her never to regret her absence of instinctive compassion, but to judge with her intellect alone who deserved extinction and who might be numbered amongst the righteous.

Not once did she show herself to him, though she used her skills in the most secret of ways to tease pleasure out of his stale nerves.

In the fourth week of their affair they were lying side by side in a lilac room, while the mid-afternoon traffic growled in the street below. It had been a bad bout of sex; he was nervous, and no tricks would coax him out of himself. It was over quickly, almost without heat.

He was going to tell her something. She knew it: it was waiting, this revelation, somewhere at the back of his throat. Turning to him she massaged his temples with her mind, and soothed him into speech.

He was about to spoil the day.

He was about to spoil his career.

He was about, God help him, to spoil his life.

"I have to stop seeing you," he said.

He wouldn't dare, she thought.

"I'm not sure what I know about you, or rather, what I *think* I know about you, but it makes me...cautious of you, J. Do you understand?"

"No."

"I'm afraid I suspect you of...crimes,"

"Crimes?"

"You have a history."

"Who's been rooting?" she asked. "Surely not Virginia?"

"No, not Virginia, she's beyond curiosity."

"Who then?"

"It's not your business."

"Who?"

She pressed lightly on his temples. It hurt him and he winced.

"What's wrong?" she asked.

"My head's aching."

"Tension, that's all, just tension. I can take it away, Titus." She touched her finger to his forehead, relaxing her hold on him. He sighed as relief came.

"Is that better?"

"Yes."

"Who's been snooping, Titus?"

"I have a personal secretary. Lyndon. You've heard me speak of him. He knew about our relationship from the beginning. Indeed, he books the hotels, arranges my cover stories for Virginia."

There was a sort of boyishness in this speech that was rather touching. As though he was embarrassed to leave her, rather than heartbroken. "Lyndon's quite a miracle worker. He's maneuvered a lot of things to make it easier between us. So he's got nothing against you. It's just that he happened to see one of the photographs I took of you. I gave them to him to shred."

"Why?"

"I shouldn't have taken them; it was a mistake. Virginia might have..." He paused, began again. "Anyhow, he recognized you, although he couldn't remember where he'd seen you before."

"But he remembered eventually."

"He used to work for one of my newspapers, as a gossip columnist. That's how he came to be my personal assistant. He remembered you from your previous incarnation, as it were. Jacqueline Ess, the wife of Benjamin Ess, deceased."

"Deceased."

"He brought me some other photographs, not as pretty as the ones of you."

"Photographs of what?"

"Your home. And the body of your husband. They said it was a body, though in God's name there was precious little human being left in it."

"There was precious little to start with," she said simply, thinking of Ben's cold eyes, and colder hands. Fit only to be shut up, and forgotten.

"What happened?"

"To Ben? He was killed."

"How?" Did his voice waver a little?

"Very easily." She had risen from the bed, and was standing by the window. Strong summer light carved its way through the slats of the blind, ridges of shadow and sunlight charting the contours of her face.

"You did it."

"Yes." He had taught her to be plain. "Yes, I did it."

He had taught her an economy of threat too. "Leave me, and I'll do the same again."

He shook his head. "Never. You wouldn't dare."

He was standing in front of her now.

"We must understand each other, J. I am powerful and I am pure. Do you see? My public face isn't even touched by a glimmer of scandal. I could afford a mistress, a dozen mistresses, to be revealed. But a murderess? No, that would spoil my life."

"Is he blackmailing you? This Lyndon?"

He stared at the day through the blinds, with a crippled look on his face. There was a twitch in the nerves of his cheek, under his left eye.

"Yes, if you must know," he said in a dead voice. "The bastard has me for all I'm worth."

"I see."

"And if he can guess, so can others. You understand?"

"I'm strong: you're strong. We can twist them around our little fingers."

"No."

"Yes! I have skills, Titus."

"I don't want to know."

"You *will* know," she said.

She looked at him, taking hold of his hands without touching him. He watched, all astonished eyes, as his unwilling hands were raised to touch her face, to stroke her hair with the fondest of gestures. She made him run his trembling fingers across her breasts, taking them with more ardor than he could summon on his own initiative.

"You are always too tentative, Titus," she said, making him paw her almost to the point of bruising. "This is how I like it." Now his hands were lower, fetching out a different look from her face. Tides were moving over it, she was all alive —

"Deeper —"

His finger intruded, his thumb stroked.

"I like that, Titus. Why can't you do that to me without me demanding?"

He blushed. He didn't like to talk about what they did together. She coaxed him deeper, whispering.

"I won't break, you know. Virginia may be Dresden china, I'm not. I want feeling; I want something that I can remember you by when I'm not with you. Nothing is everlasting, is it? But I want something to keep me warm through the night."

He was sinking to his knees, his hands kept, by her design, on her and in her, still roving like two lustful crabs. His body was awash with sweat. It was, she thought, the first time she'd ever seen him sweat.

"Don't kill me," he whimpered.

"I could wipe you out." Wipe, she thought, then put the image out of her mind before she did him some harm.

"I know. I know," he said. "You can kill me easily."

He was crying. My God, she thought, the great man is at my feet, sobbing like a baby. What can I learn of power from this puerile performance? She plucked the tears off his cheeks, using rather more strength than the task required. His skin reddened under her gaze.

"Let me be, J. I can't help you. I'm useless to you."

It was true. He was absolutely useless. Contemptuously, she let his hands go. They fell limply by his sides.

"Don't ever try and find me, Titus. You understand? Don't ever send your minions after me to preserve your reputation, because I will be more merciless than you've ever been."

He said nothing; just knelt there, facing the window, while she washed her face, drank the coffee they'd ordered, and left.

Lyndon was surprised to find the door of his office ajar. It was only 7:36. None of the secretaries would be in for another hour. Clearly one of the cleaners had been remiss, leaving the door unlocked. He'd find out who: sack her.

He pushed the door open.

Jacqueline was sitting with her back to the door. He recognized the back of her head, that fall of auburn hair. A sluttish display; too teased, too wild. His office, an annex to Mr. Pettifer's, was kept meticulously ordered. He glanced over it: everything seemed to be in place.

"What are you doing here?"

She took a little breath, preparing herself.

This was the first time she had planned to do it. Before it had been a spur-of-the-moment decision.

He was approaching the desk, and putting down his briefcase and his neatly folded copy of the *Financial Times*.

"You have no right to come in here without my permission," he said.

She turned on the lazy swivel of his chair; the way he did when he had people in to discipline.

"Lyndon," she said.

"Nothing you can say or do will change the facts, Mrs. Ess," he said, saving her the trouble of introducing the subject, "you are a cold-blooded killer. It was my bounden duty to inform Mr. Pettifer of the situation."

"You did it for the good of Titus?"

"Of course."

"And the blackmail, that was also for the good of Titus, was it?"

"Get out of my office —"

"Was it, Lyndon?"

"You're a whore! Whores know nothing: they are ignorant, diseased animals," he spat. "Oh, you're cunning, I grant you that — but then so's any slut with a living to make."

She stood up. He expected a riposte. He got none; at least not verbally. But he felt a tautness across his face: as though someone was pressing on it.

"What…are…you…doing?" he asked.

"Doing?"

His eyes were being forced into slits like a child imitating a monstrous Oriental, his mouth was hauled wide and tight, his smile brilliant. The words were difficult to say —

"Stop…it…"

She shook her head.

"Whore…" he said again, still defying her.

She just stared at him. His face was beginning to jerk and twitch under the pressure, the muscles going into spasm.

"The police..." he tried to say, "if you lay a finger on me..."

I won't," she said, and pressed home her advantage.

Beneath his clothes he felt the same tension all over his body, pulling his skin, drawing him tighter and tighter. Something was going to give; he knew it. Some part of him would be weak, and tear under this relentless assault. And if he once began to break open, nothing would prevent her ripping him apart. He worked all this out quite coolly, while his body twitched and he swore at her through his enforced grin.

"Cunt," he said. "Syphilitic cunt."

He didn't seem to be afraid, she thought.

In extremis he just unleashed so much hatred of her, the fear was entirely eclipsed. Now he was calling her a whore again; though his face was distorted almost beyond recognition.

And then he began to split.

The tear began at the bridge of his nose and ran up, across his brow, and down, bisecting his lips and his chin, then his neck and chest. In a matter of seconds his shirt was dyed red, his dark suit darkening further, his cuffs and trouser-legs pouring blood. The skin flew off his hands like gloves off a surgeon, and two rings of scarlet tissue lolled down to either side of his flayed face like the ears of an elephant.

His name-calling had stopped.

He had been dead of shock now for ten seconds, though she was still working him over vengefully, tugging his skin off his body and flinging the scraps around the room, until at last he stood, steaming, in his red suit, and his red shirt, and his shiny red shoes, and looked, to her eyes, a little more like a sensitive man. Content with the effect, she released him. He lay down quietly in a blood puddle and slept.

My God, she thought, as she calmly took the stairs out the back way, that was murder in the first degree.

She saw no reports of the death in any of the papers, and nothing on the news bulletins. Lyndon had apparently died as he had lived, hidden from public view.

But she knew wheels, so big their hubs could not be seen by insignificant individuals like herself, would be moving. What they would do, how they would change her life, she could only guess at. But the murder of Lyndon had not simply been spite, though that had been a part of it. No, she'd also wanted to stir them up, her enemies in the world, and bring them after her. Let them show their hands: let them show their contempt, their terror. She'd gone through her life, it seemed, looking for a sign of herself, only able to define her nature by the look in others' eyes. Now she wanted an end to that. It was time to deal with her pursuers.

Surely now everyone who had seen her, Pettifer first, then Vassi, would come after her, and she would close their eyes permanently: make them forgetful of her. Only then, the witnesses destroyed, would she be free.

Pettifer didn't come, of course, not in person. It was easy for him to find agents, men without scruple or compassion, but with a nose for pursuit that would shame a bloodhound.

A trap was being laid for her, though she couldn't yet see its jaws. There were signs of it everywhere. An eruption of birds from behind a wall, a peculiar light from a distant window, footsteps, whistles, dark-suited men reading the news at the limit of her vision. As the weeks passed they didn't come any closer to her, but then neither did they go away. They waited, like cats in a tree, their tails twitching, their eyes lazy.

But the pursuit had Pettifer's mark. She'd learned enough from him to recognize his circumspection and his guile. They would come for her eventually, not in her time, but in theirs. Perhaps not even in theirs: in his. And though she never saw his face, it was as though Titus was on her heels personally.

My God, she thought, I'm in danger of my life and I don't care.

It was useless, this power over flesh, if it had no direction behind it. She had used it for her own petty reasons, for the gratification of nervous pleasure and sheer anger. But these displays hadn't brought her any closer to other people: they just made her a freak in their eyes.

Sometimes she thought of Vassi, and wondered where he was, what he was doing. He hadn't been a strong man, but he'd had a little passion in his soul. More than Ben, more than Pettifer, certainly more than Lyndon. And, she remembered, fondly, he was the only man she'd ever known who called her Jacqueline. All the rest had manufactured unendearing corruptions of her name: Jackie, or J., or, in Ben's more irritating moods, Ju-ju. Only Vassi had called her Jacqueline, plain and simple, accepting, in his formal way, the completeness of her, the totality of her. And when she thought of him, tried to picture how he might return to her, she feared for him.

Vassi's Testimony (part two)

Of course I searched for her. It's only when you've lost someone, you realize the nonsense of that phrase "it's a small world." It isn't. It's a vast, devouring world, especially if you're alone.

When I was a lawyer, locked in that incestuous coterie, I used to see the same faces day after day. Some I'd exchange words with, some smiles, some nods. We belonged, even if we were enemies at the Bar, to the same complacent circle. We ate at the same tables, we drank elbow to elbow. We even shared mistresses, though we didn't always know it at the time. In such circumstances, it's easy to believe the world means you no harm. Certainly you grow older, but then so does everyone else. You even believe, in your self-satisfied way, that the passage of years makes you a little wiser. Life is bearable; even the 3 A.M. sweats come more infrequently as the bank-balance swells.

But to think that the world is harmless is to lie to yourself, to believe in so-called certainties that are, in fact, simply shared delusions.

When she left, all the delusions fell away, and all the lies I had assiduously lived by became strikingly apparent.

It's not a small world, when there's only one face in it you can bear to look upon, and that face is lost somewhere in a maelstrom. It's not a small world when the few, vital memories of your object of affection are in danger of being trampled out by the thousands of moments that assail you every day, like children tugging at you, demanding your sole attention.

I was a broken man.

I would find myself (there's an apt phrase) sleeping in tiny bedrooms in forlorn hotels, drinking more often than eating, and writing her name, like a classic obsessive, over and over again. On the walls, on the pillow, on the palm of my hand. I broke the skin of my palm with my pen, and the ink infected it. The mark's still there, I'm looking at it now. Jacqueline it says. Jacqueline.

Then one day, entirely by chance, I saw her. It sounds melodramatic, but I thought I was going to die at that moment. I'd imagined her for so long, keyed myself up for seeing her again, that when it happened I felt my limbs weaken, and I was sick in the middle of the street. Not a classic reunion. The lover, on seeing his beloved, throws up down his shirt. But then, nothing that happened between Jacqueline and myself was ever quite normal. Or natural.

I followed her, which was difficult. There were crowds, and she was walking fast. I didn't know whether to call out her name or not. I decided not. What would she have done anyway, seeing this unshaven lunatic shambling towards her, calling her name? She would have run probably. Or worse, she would have reached into my chest, seizing my heart in her will, and put me out of my misery before I could reveal her to the world.

So I was silent, and simply followed her, doggedly, to what I assumed was her apartment. And I stayed there, or in the vicinity, for the next two and a half days, not quite knowing what to do. It was a ridiculous dilemma. After all this time of watching for her, now that she was within speaking distance, touching distance, I didn't dare approach.

Maybe I feared death. But then, here I am, in this stinking room in Amsterdam, setting my testimony down and waiting for Koos to bring me her key, and I don't fear death now. Probably it was my vanity that prevented me from approaching her. I didn't want her so see me cracked and desolate; I wanted to come to her clean, her dream-lover.

While I waited, they came for her.

I don't know who they were. Two men, plainly dressed. I don't think policemen: too smooth. Cultured even. And she didn't resist. She went smilingly, as if to the opera.

At the first opportunity I returned to the building a little better dressed, located her apartment from the porter, and broke in. She had been living plainly. In one corner of the room she had set up a table, and had been writing her memoirs. I sat down and read, and eventually took the pages away with me. She had got no further than the first seven years of her life. I wondered, again in my vanity, if I would have been chronicled in the book. Probably not.

I took some of her clothes too; only items she had worn when I had known her. And nothing intimate: I'm not a fetishist. I wasn't going to go home and bury my face in the smell of her underwear. But I wanted something to remember her by; to picture her in. Though on reflection I never met a human being more fitted to dress purely in her skin.

So I lost her a second time, more the fault of my own cowardice than circumstance.

Pettifer didn't come near the house they were keeping Mrs. Ess in for four weeks. She was given more or less everything she asked for, except her freedom, and she only asked for that in the most abstracted fashion. She wasn't interested in escape: though it would have been easy to achieve. Once or twice she wondered if Titus had told the two men and the woman who were keeping her a prisoner in the house exactly what she was capable of: she guessed not. They treated her as though she were simply a woman Titus had set eyes on and desired. They had procured her for his bed, simple as that.

With a room to herself, and an endless supply of paper, she began to write her memoirs again, from the beginning.

It was late summer, and the nights were getting chilly. Sometimes, to warm herself, she would lie on the floor (she'd asked them to remove the bed) and will her body to ripple like the surface of a lake. Her body, without sex, became a mystery to her again; and she realized for the first time that physical love had been an exploration of that most intimate, and yet most unknown region of her being: her flesh. She had understood herself best embracing someone else: seen her own substance clearly only when another's lips were laid on it, adoring and gentle. She thought of Vassi again; and the lake, at the thought of him, was roused as if by a tempest. Her breasts shook into curling mountains, her belly ran with extraordinary tides, currents crossed and recrossed her flickering face, lapping at her mouth and leaving their mark like waves on sand. As she was fluid in his memory, so as she remembered him, she liquified.

She thought of the few times she had been at peace in her life; and physical love, discharging ambition and vanity, had always preceded those fragile moments. There were other ways presumably; but her experience had been limited. Her mother had always said that women, being more at peace with themselves than men, needed fewer distractions from their hurts. But she'd not found it like that at all. She'd found her life full of hurts, but almost empty of ways to salve them.

She left off writing her memoirs when she reached her ninth year. She despaired of telling her story from that point on, with the first realization of on-coming puberty. She burnt the papers on a bonfire she lit in the middle of her room the day that Pettifer arrived.

My God, she thought, this can't be power.

Pettifer looked sick; as physically changed as a friend she'd lost to cancer. One month seemingly healthy, the next sucked up from the inside, self-devoured. He looked like a husk of a man: his skin grey and mottled. Only his eyes glittered, and those like the eyes of a mad dog.

He was dressed immaculately, as though for a wedding.

"J."

"Titus."

He looked her up and down.

"Are you well?"

"Thank you, yes."

"They give you everything you ask for?"

"Perfect hosts."

"You haven't resisted."

"Resisted?"

"Being here. Locked up. I was prepared, after Lyndon, for another slaughter of the innocents."

"Lyndon was not innocent, Titus. These people are. You didn't tell them."

"I didn't deem it necessary. May I close the door?"

He was her captor: but he came like an emissary to the camp of a greater power. She liked the way he was with her, cowed but elated. He closed the door, and locked it.

"I love you, J. And I fear you. In fact, I think I love you because I fear you. Is that a sickness?"

"I would have thought so."

"Yes, so would I."

"Why did you take such a time to come?"

"I had to put my affairs in order. Otherwise there would have been chaos. When I was gone."

"You're leaving?"

He looked into her, the muscles of his face ruffled by anticipation.

"I hope so."

"Where to?"

Still she didn't guess what had brought him to the house, his affairs neatened, his wife unknowingly asked forgiveness of as she slept, all channels of escape closed, all contradictions laid to rest.

Still she didn't guess he'd come to die.

"I'm reduced by you, J. Reduced to nothing. And there is nowhere for me to go. Do you follow?"

"No."

"I cannot live without you," he said. The cliché was unpardonable. Could he not have found a better way to say it? She almost laughed, it was so trite.

But he hadn't finished.

"— and I certainly can't live *with* you." Abruptly, the tone changed. "Because you revolt me, woman, your whole being disgusts me."

"So?" she asked, softly.

"So..." He was tender again and she began to understand. "...kill me."

It was grotesque. The glittering eyes were steady on her.

"It's what I want," he said. "Believe me, it's all I want in the world. Kill me, however you please. I'll go without resistance, without complaint."

She remembered the old joke. Masochist to Sadist: Hurt me! For God's sake, hurt me! Sadist to Masochist: No.

"And if I refuse?" she said.

"You can't refuse. I'm loathsome."

"But I don't hate you, Titus."

"You should. I'm weak. I'm useless to you. I taught you nothing."

"You taught me a great deal. I can control myself now."

"Lyndon's death was controlled, was it?"

"Certainly."

"It looked a little excessive to me."

"He got everything he deserved."

"Give me what I deserve, then, in my turn. I've locked you up. I've rejected you when you needed me. Punish me for it."

"I survived."

"J.!"

Even in this extremity he couldn't call her by her full name.

"Please to God. Please to God. I need only this one thing from you. Do it out of whatever motive you have in you. Compassion, or contempt, or love. But do it, please do it."

"No," she said.

He crossed the room suddenly, and slapped her, very hard.

"Lyndon said you were a whore. He was right; you are. Gutterslut, nothing better."

He walked away, turned, walked back, hit her again, faster, harder, and again, six or seven times, backwards and forwards.

Then he stopped, panting.

"You want money?" Bargains now. Blows, then bargains.

She was seeing him twisted through tears of shock, which she was unable to prevent.

"Do you want money?" he said again.

"What do you think?"

He didn't hear her sarcasm, and began to scatter notes around her feet, dozens and dozens of them, like offerings around the Statue of the Virgin.

"Anything you want," he said, *"Jacqueline."*

In her belly she felt something close to pain as the urge to kill him found birth, but she resisted it. It was playing into his hands, becoming the instrument of his will: powerless. Usage again; that's all she ever got. She had been bred like a cow, to give a certain supply. Of care to husbands, of milk to babies, of death to old men. And, like a cow, she was expected to be compliant with every demand made of her, whenever the call came. Well, not this time.

She went to the door.

"Where are you going?"

She reached for the key.

"Your death is your own business, not mine," she said.

He ran at her before she could unlock the door, and the blow — in its force, in its malice — was totally unexpected.

"Bitch!" he shrieked, a hail of blows coming fast upon the first.

In her stomach, the thing that wanted to kill grew a little larger.

He had his fingers tangled in her hair, and pulled her back into the room, shouting obscenities at her, an endless stream of them, as though he'd opened a dam full of sewer-water on her. This was just another way for him to get what he wanted she told herself, if you succumb to this you've lost: he's just manipulating you. Still the words came: the same dirty words that had been thrown at generations of unsubmissive women. Whore; heretic; cunt; bitch; monster.

Yes, she was that.

Yes, she thought: monster I am.

The thought made it easy. She turned. He knew what she intended even before she looked at him. He dropped his hands from her head. Her anger was already in her throat coming out of her — crossing the air between them.

Monster he calls me: monster I am.

I do this for myself, not for him. Never for him. For myself!

He gasped as her will touched him, and the glittering eyes stopped glittering for a moment, the will to die became the will to survive, all too late of course, and he roared. She heard answering shouts, steps, threats on the stairs. They would be in the room in a matter of moments.

Darkness: Two Decades of Modern Horror

"You are an animal," she said.

"No," he said, certain even now that his place was in command.

"You don't exist," she said, advancing on him. "They'll never find the part that was Titus. Titus is gone. The rest is just —"

The pain was terrible. It stopped even a voice coming out from him. Or was that her again, changing his throat, his palate, his very head? She was unlocking the plates of his skull, and reorganizing him.

No, he wanted to say, this isn't the subtle ritual I had planned. I wanted to die folded into you, I wanted to go with my mouth clamped to yours, cooling in you as I died. This is not the way I want it.

No. No. No.

They were at the door, the men who'd kept her here, beating on it. She had no fear of them, of course, except that they might spoil her handiwork before the final touches were added to it.

Someone was hurling themselves at the door now. Wood splintered: the door was flung open. The two men were both armed. They pointed their weapons at her, steady-handed.

"Mr. Pettifer?" said the younger man. In the corner of the room, under the table, Pettifer's eyes shone.

"Mr. Pettifer?" he said again, forgetting the woman.

Pettifer shook his snouted head. Don't come any closer, please, he thought.

The man crouched down and stared under the table at the disgusting beast that was squatting there; bloody from its transformation, but alive. She had killed his nerves: he felt no pain. He just survived, his hands knotted into paws, his legs scooped up around his back, knees broken so he had the look of a four-legged crab, his brain exposed, his eyes lidless, lower jaw broken and swept up over his top jaw like a bulldog, ears torn off, spine snapped, humanity bewitched into another state.

"You are an animal," she'd said. It wasn't a bad facsimile of beasthood.

The man with the gun gagged as he recognized fragments of his master. He stood up, greasy-chinned, and glanced around at the woman.

Jacqueline shrugged.

"You did this?" Awe mingled with the revulsion.

She nodded.

"Come Titus," she said, clicking her fingers.

The beast shook its head, sobbing.

"Come Titus," she said more forcefully, and Titus Pettifer waddled out of his hiding place, leaving a trail like a punctured meat-sack.

The man fired at Pettifer's remains out of sheer instinct. Anything, anything at all to prevent this disgusting creature from approaching him.

Titus stumbled two steps back on his bloody paws, shook himself as if to dislodge the death in him, and failing, died.

"Content?" she asked.

The gunman looked up from the execution. Was the power talking to him? No; Jacqueline was staring at Pettifer's corpse, asking the question of him.

Content?

The gunman dropped his weapon. The other man did the same.

"How did this happen?" asked the man at the door. A simple question: a child's question.

"He asked," said Jacqueline. "It was all I could give him."

The gunman nodded, and fell to his knees.

Vassi's Testimony (final part)

Chance has played a worryingly large part in my romance with Jacqueline Ess. Sometimes it's seemed I've been subject to every tide that passes through the world, spun around by the merest flick of accident's wrist. Other times I've had the suspicion that she was masterminding my life, as she was the lives of a hundred others, a thousand others, arranging every fluke meeting, choreographing my victories and my defeats, escorting me, blindly, towards this last encounter.

I found her without knowing I'd found her, that was the irony of it. I'd traced her first to a house in Surrey, a house that had a year previous seen the murder of one Titus Pettifer, a billionaire shot by one of his own bodyguards. In the upstairs room, where the murder had taken place, all was serenity. If she had been there, they had removed any sign. But the house, now in virtual ruin, was prey to all manner of graffiti; and on the stained plaster wall of that room someone had scrawled a woman. She was obscenely over-endowed, her gaping sex blazing with what looked like lightning. And at her feet there was a creature of indeterminate species. Perhaps a crab, perhaps a dog, perhaps even a man. Whatever it was it had no power over itself. It sat in the light of her agonizing presence and counted itself amongst the fortunate. Looking at that wizened creature, with its eyes turned up to gaze on the burning Madonna, I knew the picture was a portrait of Jacqueline.

I don't know how long I stood looking at the graffiti, but I was interrupted by a man who looked to be in a worse condition than me. A beard that had never been trimmed or washed, a frame so wasted I wondered how he managed to stand upright, and a smell that would not have shamed a skunk.

I never knew his name: but he was, he told me, the maker of the picture on the wall. It was easy to believe that. His desperation, his hunger, his confusion were all marks of a man who had seen Jacqueline.

If I was rough in my interrogation of him I'm sure he forgave me. It was an unburdening for him, to tell everything he'd seen the day that Pettifer had been killed, and know that I believed it all. He told me his fellow bodyguard, the man who had fired the shots that had killed Pettifer, had committed suicide in prison.

His life, he said, was meaningless. She had destroyed it. I gave him what reassurances I could; that she meant no harm, and that he needn't fear that she would come for him. When I told him that, he cried, more, I think, out of loss than relief.

Finally I asked him if he knew where Jacqueline was now. I'd left that question to the end, though it had been the most pressing enquiry, because I suppose I didn't dare hope he'd know. But my God, he did. She had not left the house immediately after the shooting of Pettifer. She had sat down with this man, and talked to him quietly about his children, his tailor, his car. She'd asked him what his mother had been like, and he'd told her his mother had been a prostitute. Had she been happy? Jacqueline had asked. He'd said he didn't know. Did she ever cry? she'd asked. He'd said he never saw her laugh or cry in his life. And she'd nodded, and thanked him.

Later, before his suicide, the other gunman had told him Jacqueline had gone to Amsterdam. This he knew for a fact, from a man called Koos. And so the circle begins to close, yes?

I was in Amsterdam seven weeks, without finding a single clue to her whereabouts, until yesterday evening. Seven weeks of celibacy, which is unusual for me. Listless with frustration I went down to the red-light district, to find a woman. They sit there you know, in the windows, like mannequins, beside pink-fringed lamps. Some have miniature dogs on their laps; some read. Most just stare out at the street, as if mesmerized.

There were no faces there that interested me. They all seemed joyless, light-less, too much unlike her. Yet I couldn't leave. I was like a fat boy in a sweet shop, too nauseous to buy, too gluttonous to go.

Towards the middle of the night, I was spoken to out of the crowd by a young man who, on closer inspection, was not young at all, but heavily made up. He had no eyebrows, just pencil marks drawn on to his shiny skin. A cluster of gold earrings in his left ear, a half-eaten peach in his white-gloved hand, open sandals, lacquered toenails. He took hold of my sleeve, proprietorially.

I must have sneered at his sickening appearance, but he didn't seem at all upset by my contempt. You look like a man of discernment, he said. I looked nothing of the kind: you must be mistaken, I said. No, he replied, I am not mistaken. You are Oliver Vassi.

My first thought, absurdly, was that he intended to kill me. I tried to pull away; his grip on my cuff was relentless.

You want a woman, he said. Did I hesitate enough for him to know I meant yes, though I said no? I have a woman like no other, he went on, she's a miracle. I know you'll want to meet her in the flesh.

What made me know it was Jacqueline he was talking about? Perhaps the fact that he had known me from out of the crowd, as though she was up at a window somewhere, ordering her admirers to be brought to her like a diner ordering lobster from a tank. Perhaps too the way his eyes shone at me, meeting mine without fear because fear, like rapture, he felt only in the presence of one creature on God's cruel earth. Could I not also see myself reflected in his perilous look? He knew Jacqueline, I had no doubt of it.

He knew I was hooked, because once I hesitated he turned away from me with a mincing shrug, as if to say: you missed your chance. Where is she? I said, seizing his twig-thin arm. He cocked his head down the street and I followed him, suddenly as witless as an idiot, out of the throng. The road emptied as we walked; the red lights gave way to gloom, and then to darkness. If I asked him where we were going once I asked him a dozen times; he chose not to answer, until we reached a narrow door in a narrow house down some razor-thin street. We're here, he announced, as though the hovel were the Palace of Versailles.

Up two flights in the otherwise empty house there was a room with a black door. He pressed me to it. It was locked.

"See," he invited, "she's inside."

"It's locked," I replied. My heart was fit to burst: she was near, for certain, I knew she was near.

"See," he said again, and pointed to a tiny hole in the panel of the door. I devoured the light through it, pushing my eye towards her through the tiny hole.

The squalid interior was empty, except for a mattress and Jacqueline. She lay spreadeagled, her wrists and ankles bound to rough posts set in the bare floor at the four corners of the mattress.

"Who did this?" I demanded, not taking my eye from her nakedness.

"She asks," he replied. "It is her desire. She asks."

She had heard my voice; she cranked up her head with some difficulty and stared directly at the door. When she looked at me all the hairs rose on my head, I swear it, in welcome, and swayed at her command.

"Oliver," she said.

"Jacqueline." I pressed the word to the wood with a kiss.

Her body was seething, her shaved sex opening and closing like some exquisite plant, purple and lilac and rose.

"Let me in," I said to Koos.

"You will not survive one night with her."

"Let me in."

"She is expensive," he warned.

"How much do you want?"

"Everything you have. The shirt off your back, your money, your jewelry; then she is yours."

I wanted to beat the door down, or break his nicotine-stained fingers one by one until he gave me the key. He knew what I was thinking.

"The key is hidden," he said, "and the door is strong. You must pay, Mr. Vassi. You want to pay."

It was true. I wanted to pay.

"You want to give me all you have ever owned, all you have ever been. You want to go to her with nothing to claim you back. I know this. It's how they all go to her."

"All? Are there many?"

"She is insatiable," he said, without relish. It wasn't a pimp's boast: it was his pain, I saw that clearly. "I am always finding more for her, and burying them."

Burying them.

That, I suppose, is Koos' function; he disposes of the dead. And he will get his lacquered hands on me after tonight; he will fetch me off her when I am dry and useless to her, and find some pit, some canal, some furnace to lose me in. The thought isn't particularly attractive.

Yet here I am with all the money I could raise from selling my few remaining possessions on the table in front of me, my dignity gone, my life hanging on a thread, waiting for a pimp and a key.

It's well dark now, and he's late. But I think he is obliged to come. Not for the money, he probably has few requirements beyond his heroin and his mascara. He will come to do business with me because she demands it and he is in thrall to her, every bit as much as I am. Oh, he will come. Of course he will come.

Well, I think that is sufficient.

This is my testimony. I have no time to re-read it now. His footsteps are on the stairs (he limps) and I must go with him. This I leave to whoever finds it, to use as they think fit. By morning I shall be dead, and happy. Believe it.

My God, she thought, Koos has cheated me.

Vassi had been outside the door, she'd felt his flesh with her mind and she'd embraced it. But Koos hadn't let him in, despite her explicit orders. Of all men, Vassi was to be allowed free access, Koos knew that. But he'd cheated her, the way they'd all cheated her except Vassi. With him (perhaps) it had been love.

She lay on the bed through the night, never sleeping. She seldom slept now for more than a few minutes: and only then with Koos watching her. She'd done herself harm in her sleep, mutilating herself without knowing it, waking up bleeding and screaming with every limb sprouting needles she'd made out of her own skin and muscle, like a flesh cactus.

It was dark again, she guessed, but it was difficult to be sure. In this heavily curtained, bare-bulb lit room, it was a perpetual day to the senses, perpetual night to the soul. She would lie, bed-sores on her back, on her buttocks, listening to the far sounds of the street, sometimes dozing for a while, sometimes eating from Koos' hand, being washed, being toileted, being used.

A key turned in the lock. She strained from the mattress to see who it was. The door was opening...opening...opened.

Vassi. Oh God, it was Vassi at last, she could see him crossing the room towards her.

Let this not be another memory, she prayed, please let it be him this time: true and real.

"Jacqueline."

He said the name of her flesh, the whole name.

"Jacqueline." It *was* him.

Behind him, Koos stared between her legs, fascinated by the dance of her labia.

"Koo…" she said, trying to smile.

"I brought him," he grinned at her, not looking away from her sex.

"A day," she whispered. "I waited a day, Koos. You made me wait —"

"What's a day to you?" he said, still grinning.

She didn't need the pimp any longer, not that he knew that. In his innocence he thought Vassi was just another man she'd seduced along the way; to be drained and discarded like the others. Koos believed he would be needed tomorrow; that's why he played this fatal game so artlessly.

"Lock the door," she suggested to him. "Stay if you like."

"Stay?" he said, leering. "You mean, and watch?"

He watched anyway. She knew he watched through that hole he had bored in the door; she could hear him pant sometimes. But this time, let him stay forever.

Carefully, he took the key from the outside of the door, closed it, slipped the key into the inside and locked it. Even as the lock clicked she killed him, before he could even turn round and look at her again. Nothing spectacular in the execution; she just reached into his pigeon chest and crushed his lungs. He slumped against the door and slid down, smearing his face across the wood.

Vassi didn't even turn round to see him die; she was all he ever wanted to look at again.

He approached the mattress, crouched, and began to untie her ankles. The skin was chafed, the rope scabby with old blood. He worked at the knots systematically, finding a calm he thought he'd lost, a simple contentment in being here at the end, unable to go back, and knowing that the path ahead was deep in her.

When her ankles were free, he began on her wrists, interrupting her view of the ceiling as he bent over her. His voice was soft.

"Why did you let him do this to you?"

"I was afraid."

"Of what?"

"To move; even to live. Every day, agony."

"Yes."

He understood so well that total incapacity to exist.

She felt him at her side, undressing, then laying a kiss on the sallow skin of the stomach of the body she occupied. It was marked with her workings; the skin had been stretched beyond its tolerance and was permanently criss-crossed.

He lay down beside her, and the feel of his body against hers was not unpleasant.

She touched his head. Her joints were stiff, the movements painful, but she wanted to draw his face up to hers. He came, smiling, into her sight, and they exchanged kisses.

My God, she thought, we are together.

And thinking they were together, her will was made flesh. Under his lips her features dissolved, becoming the red sea he'd dreamt of, and washing up over his face, that was itself dissolving: common waters made of thought and bone.

Her keen breasts pricked him like arrows; his erection, sharpened by her thought, killed her in return with his only thrust. Tangled in a wash of love they thought themselves extinguished, and were.

Outside, the hard world mourned on, the chatter of buyers and sellers continuing through the night. Eventually indifference and fatigue claimed even the eagerest merchant. Inside and out there was a healing silence: an end to losses and to gains.

Edward Bryant began writing professionally in 1968 and has had more than a dozen books published, including *Among the Dead, Cinnabar, Phoenix Without Ashes* (with Harlan Ellison), *Wyoming Sun, Particle Theory, Fetish* (a novella chapbook), and *The Baku: Tales of the Nuclear Age.* In the beginning, he was known as a science fiction writer and although he still occasionally dabbles in sf with great success (he won the Nebula Award for short story in both 1978 and 1979, and in 1994 published "The Fire That Scours," an excellent story about love and evolution), he gradually strayed into horror and mostly has remained there, writing a series of sharply etched stories about Angie Black, a contemporary witch, the brilliant zombie story "A Sad Last Love at the Diner of the Damned," and other marvelous tales.

"Dancing Chickens," originally slated to be published in *New Dimension 13* edited by Marta Randall, along with some other edgy stories (including "All My Darling Daughters" by Connie Willis), was orphaned when the book was cancelled by the publisher while in galleys. I felt compelled to turn it down for *OMNI* but passed it on to Michael Bishop, who was soliciting original fiction for the one-off original anthology *Light Years and Dark.* Initially, he turned it down but on reconsidering, acquired it for his anthology.

To me, it's the perfect story demonstrating Bryant's movement from sf to horror because it's both. And it still shocks.

Dancing Chickens
Edward Bryant

WHAT DO ALIENS want?

Their burnished black ships, humming with the ominous power of a clenched fist, ghost across our cities. At first we turned our faces to the skies in the chill of every moving shadow. Now we seem to feel the disinterest bred of familiarity. It's not a sense of ease, though. The collective apprehension is still there — even if diminished. For many of us, I believe, the feeling is much like awaiting a dentist's drill.

Do aliens have expectations?

If human beings know, no one's telling. Our leaders dissemble, the news media speculate, but facts and truths alike submerge in murky communications. Extraterrestrial secrets, if they do have answers, remain quietly and tastefully enigmatic. Most of us have read about the government's beamed messages, all apparently ignored.

Do humans care?

I'm not really sure anymore. The ships have been up there for months — a year or more. People do become blasé, even about those mysterious craft and their unseen pilots. When the waiting became unendurable, most humans simply seemed to tune out the ships and thought about other things again: mortgages, spiraling inflation, Mideast turmoil, and getting laid. Yet the underlying tension remained.

Some of us in the civilian sector have retained our curiosity. Right here in the neighborhood, David told us he sat in the aloneness of the early morning hours and pumped out Morse to the silhouettes as they cruised out of the dark above the mountains and slid into the dim east. If there were replies, David couldn't interpret them. "You'd think at least they'd want to go out for a drink," David had said.

Riley used the mirror in his compact to send up heliograph signals. In great excitement he claimed to have detected a reply, messages in kind. We suggested he saw, if anything, reflections from the undersides of the dark hulls. None of that diminished his ecstasy. He believed he was noticed. I felt for him.

Hawk — both job description and name — didn't hold much with guesses. "In good time," he said, "they'll tell us what they want; tell us, then buy it, take it, use it. They'll give us the word." Hawk had plucked me, runaway and desperate young man, literally out of the gutter along the Boulevard. Since before the time of the ships, he had cared for me. He had taken me home, cleaned, fed, and warmed me. He used me, sometimes well. Sometimes he only used me.

Whether Hawk loved me was debatable.

Watching the ships gave me no answer.

I attempted to communicate every day. It was a little like what my case worker told me about what dentists did to kids' mouths before anyone had invented braces. When he was a boy with protruding teeth, my case worker was instructed to push fingers gently against those front teeth every time he thought of his mouth and how people were making fun. "Hey, Trigger! Where's Roy?" Years of gentle, insistent touches did what braces do now.

I tried to do something like that with the alien ships. Every time I fantasized smooth, alien features when I shivered in the chilly wake of an alien shadow, I gathered my mental energies, concentrated, shot an inquiring thought after the diminishing leviathan.

Ship, come to me... I wanted it to carry me away, to take charge, to save me from any sense of responsibility about my own actions in my own life. I knew better, but that didn't stop the temptation.

Once, only once, I thought I felt a reply, the slightest tickling just at the border of my mind. At the time it was neither pleasant nor unpleasant, more a textural thing: slick surfaces, cool, moist, one whole enclosing another. (A fist fills the glove. One hand, damp, warm: the wrist — twists.)

I tried to describe the sensation to some of the people on the street. I'm not sure who disbelieved me. I know Hawk believed. He stared at me with his dark raptor eyes and touched my arm. I danced skittishly away.

"You fit, Ricky," he said. "You really do."

"Not like that," I answer. The conversation has taken place in many variations, in many bedrooms and on many streets, and still does. "No longer. No more."

Hawk nods, almost sadly, I think. "Still going to leave?"

"I'll dance again," I say. "I'm young." Dancing was the only thing the therapists ever gave me that I loved.

"You're that," he agrees. "But you're out of shape." His voice is sad again. "At least for dancing."

"I can get back," I say helplessly, spreading my hands. "Soon." I try to ignore the fact that, as young as I am, I've abandoned my best years.

"I wish you could do it." The tone is as gentle as Hawk's voice ever gets. "It's the sticks, kiddo," he says. "You're a runaway on the skids, just off the street, in the sticks."

I don't like being reminded. He makes me remember every foster home, every set of possible parents who threw me back in the pool.

Hawk nods toward the stairs. "Come up."

I look at the darkness beyond the landing. I look at the faceted rings on the knuckles of Hawk's right hand. I stare at the floor. "No." I feel the circle tighten.

"Rick..." His voice shines dark and faceted.

"No." But I follow Hawk up the steps and into freezing alien shadows.

I'm planning my escape. I keep telling myself that. But that's all I do. Plan. If I left, I'd have to go someplace. There's nowhere I've ever realistically wanted to go.

Come, ships...

At one time I thought about hitching to Montana. I'd seen *Comes a Horseman* on late-night TV. Then I made the mistake of turning to Hawk and mentioning my plan. He raised his head from the pillow and said, "Ricky, you want to be a dancer again *and* go to Montana? You're maybe going to dance for the Great Falls Repertory Ballet?" I pretended to ignore the mockery. Someday I *would* leave. Just as soon as I made up my mind.

I gave up the Montana idea. But I still plan my escape. I've saved a few hundred dollars in tips waiting on tables at Richard's Coffee Shop. I have a dog-eared copy of *Ecotopia* and a Texaco road map of Oregon. I think Portland's probably a whole lot larger and more cosmopolitan than Great Falls. Certainly more cultural. Oregon seems familiar to me. I read a tattered paperback of *One Flew over the Cuckoo's Nest* in that fragmented past when I bounced from home to home, always waiting for them to tell my case worker I wasn't quite what they wanted.

If I really wanted to go, I'd leave. Right? Hawk jokes about it because he simply doesn't believe me. He doesn't know me. He never did find the passage to my mind.

Tonight I'm at a party at David and Lee's apartment. There are plenty of times when I wish I had the kind of relationship with someone, loving and supportive, that the two of them share.

David and Lee's apartment is on the fourteenth floor of a high-rise, rearing improbably out of a restored Victorian neighborhood. The balcony faces east and I can see all the way across the city, almost to the plains. There are maybe thirty people in the apartment, smoking, talking, drinking. Lee had laid out some lines he got at work on the big heart-shaped mirror on the coffee table, but those vanished early on. While some of the party guests watch, David is at his ham set, flashing out *dah-dit, dah-dit, dah-dah-dit* messages to the aliens.

Riley, resplendent in ermine and pearls, rushes up to my elbow. "Oh, Ricky, you've *got* to see!" I turn, look past him. People are thronging around the bar. The laughter rises and crashes uproariously. "Ricky, come *on*." He takes my arm and propels me into the apartment.

I crane my neck to see what's going on. For once unladylike, Riley climbs onto a chair. Somebody I don't know, shiny in full leathers, is standing behind the mahogany bar. For a second I think he's wearing a white glove, but *only* for a second.

It's a chicken. The man has stuffed his fist into a plucked, pale chicken right out of a cello-wrapped package from a Safeway meat department. He wears it like a naked hand puppet. I find it hard to believe.

The man holds the chicken close to his face and talks to it like a ventriloquist crooning to his dummy. "That's a good boy, you like the party? Want to entertain the nice folks with a little dance?" I realize the headless chicken has a small black bolo tie with a dime-sized silver concho tied around its neck. Tasteful, basic black. The drumsticks are wearing doll shoes. The sheen of chicken juice on the rubbery, stippled skin starts to make me queasy.

It ought to be funny — but it's not.

The man addresses us, the audience. "And now," he says, "the award-winning performance by a featherless biped." He nods toward David, who has come away from his radio set to watch. "Maestro, if you please." The expensive stereo crackles and we hear a tinkling piano version of "Tea for Two." The man with the chicken half crouches behind the bar top so that most of his arm is hidden.

The chicken stands onstage. And starts to dance.

Evidently the joints have been cracked, because the dancer's limbs swing loose. The little shoes clatter on the Formica bar. The wings flap up and down wildly. Fluid drips to the bar.

"An *obscene* featherless biped," someone says accurately. But we all keep watching. The pimpled skin catches the light wetly. I don't think this is what the Greek philosopher who defined human beings as featherless bipeds had in mind.

The tune changes, the tempo alters — faster — "If You Knew Susie" — and the dancer is in trouble. It seems to be sliding off the manipulator's hand. The man behind the bar impatiently reaches with his free hand and screws the chicken down firmly on his fist. It makes a squelching sound like adjusting a rubber glove. Now I can smell the raw flesh. I turn suddenly and head for the balcony and the clean air that should steady my stomach.

I walk by Hawk. He lightly touches my wrist as I pass, but his eyes don't deviate from the scene on the bar. He doesn't have to look at me.

On the balcony I lean over the railing and retch. It's dark now and I have no idea who or what is fourteen stories below. Crazily I hope it will all evaporate before it hits the ground, like those immensely long and beautiful South American waterfall veils that dissolve into mist and then vanish before ever hitting the jungle floor.

Travelogs again. I want to escape.

My mind skips erratically. I also have to find a new doctor. My appointment this morning arrived at the point I've come to dread. There always comes a time when my current doctor looks at me quizzically and says, "Son, those aren't ordinary hemorrhoids." I stammer and leave.

Leave.

Good-bye, Hawk.

I'm leaving.

"But what do they want?" someone is saying as I walk across the floor. Oregon is, more or less, on the other side of that door. What do they want? Alien ships are still sliding silently between us and the stars. The watchers are out on the balcony, no longer discreet now that I've finished my purgation.

Ship, come to me...

Inside the apartment, the dancing chicken episode is triggering debate. I am amazed to see a confrontation between David and Lee. That they would fight is enough to make me pause.

"Sick," says Lee. "Tasteless. How could you let him spoil the party? You *helped* him."

"He's *your* friend," David says.

"*Colleague*. He stacks boxes. That's all." Lee's expression is furious. "The two of you! What sort of people think it's amusing to stick their hand inside a dead chicken?"

David says defensively, "Everyone was watching."

"And that makes it real!" Lee's amazement and anger are palpable. "Jesus! We're part of the most technologically sophisticated civilization on Earth, and yet we do this."

Riley has come up to us, looking cool and demure. "All societies are just individuals," he says reasonably. "You have to allow for a wide variation in" — he smiles sweetly — "individual tastes."

"Don't give me platitudes!" says Lee angrily. He stalks off toward the kitchen.

"Sulky, sulky," says Riley, and shrugs.

The three of us hear a chorus of *ooh*'s and *aah*'s from behind. We turn as one toward the balcony.

"I've never seen one so close," says a voice suffused with wonder. I imagine it's like sitting helplessly in a rowboat being passed by a whale. It seems as though the shining metallic skin of the alien ship is gliding past only yards from the balcony. The ship is so huge I can't accurately gauge the distance. The *whooosh* of displaced air flows through the windows. Chilly currents cocoon us.

The cold breaks the spell.

"I'm leaving," I say to the people around me. Lee and Riley seem fixed in place by the passing ship. They don't hear me. But then I don't think they ever did. "Good-bye," I say. "I'm leaving." Nobody hears.

So, finally, I carry out my plans, my threat, my promise to myself.

I leave, and it feels better than I'd expected.

Someone does notice my departure, and he catches up with me at the elevator.

I try to ignore Hawk. He lounges beside the door until it slides open. Then he follows me into the car. I slap the ground-floor button with my fist.

"Stay," Hawk says.

I look at the sharpness of his eyes. "Why?"

He smiles slightly. "I haven't finished using you."

"At least that's honest."

"I've got no need to lie," he says. "I know you well enough, I can say that."

The sureness in his voice and the agreement I feel combine internally to make me feel again the sickness I felt upstairs watching the chicken dance. But now I have nothing left to purge.

The elevator brakes and I feel it all through my gut — it's the burn you get gulping ice water. The door hisses open. Hawk follows me into the apartment lobby. "Just let me go," I say without turning.

His words catch me as I reach for the outer door. "You know, Ricky, in my own way, I do love you."

I wonder if he knows the cruelty of that. I stare at him, startled. He's the first I remember saying that to me. Tears I haven't felt since childhood slide down my cheeks. I turn away.

"Stick around, kiddo," Hawk calls after me. "Please?"

"No." This time I mean it. I've made my decision. I don't look back at him. I stiff-arm the door open and lunge past a pair of aging queens; I am running as I hit the sidewalk. I barely see through the tears as a shadow deeper than the surrounding night envelops me. Rubbing eyes with wet knuckles, I look up to see an alien ship cross my vision and recede into the east. There are other ships in the sky now. Huge as they are, they still seem to dance and dart like enormous moths. What I see must be true, because others around me on the street are also gawking at the sky. Perhaps we all simply share the delusion.

"Rick!" Hawk's voice sinuously seeks me from behind.

I lower my head and bull forward.

"Ricky, look out!"

I register what my eyes must have seen all the time. The bus. The driver, wide-eyed and staring upward. The rushing chrome bumpers —

I feel no pain at first. Just the brutal physical force, the crushing motion, the slamming against the pavement. I feel — broken. Parts of me are no longer whole, that I know. When I try to move, some things don't, and those that do, don't move in the right places.

I am lying on my back. I think one leg is twisted beneath me.

Come to me, ship...

One of the swooping, agitated, alien ships has parked poised, stationary above the block, above the street, above me. It masks both the city glow and the few stars penetrating that radiance. The angles are peculiar. Hawk's face enters my field of vision. I expect him to look stricken, or at least concerned. He only looks — I don't know — *possessive,* a boy whose doll has broken. Other faces now, all staring on with confusion, some with a sort of interest. I saw those faces at the party, those expressions.

As I stare past Hawk at the immobile alien ship, I know that I am dying here in the street. *And I was on the way to Oregon....* Why is the alien ship above me? They'll start somewhere, Hawk had said. Sometime. With someone.

Then I feel the ice. At least I can feel something. I feel that knotted — *something,* an agency from outside me coming within, a chilly intrusion into my core.

The ship seems closer, dwarfing everything else, monopolizing my vision. They'll give us the word, Hawk had said. I had wanted the word. Now I feel very tight and unwilling.

From deep inside, spreading, flexing, tearing, ice impales me. The cold burns with a flame. I try to shrink away from it — and cannot. And then something moves. My foot. It spasms once, twice. My ankle jerks. My knee separates, cartilage wrenching apart, sliding back together, but wrong. My whole body quivers, each limb rebelling. Joints grind.

But I start to move. Slowly, horribly, without my orders, I rear up. *Stop it,* I will myself. I can't stop it.

I wonder if the aliens define featherless bipeds too?

The faces around me mirror pain as my body struggles to its knees. No one watches the ship anymore. All eyes fix on my performance.

I am called... At last I am wanted.

Why aren't I dead? I'm moving and I cannot help it. My body lurches to its feet, limbs pivoting at wrong, odd angles. The fist inside me tentatively twists. I struggle to fall, to rest, but I am not allowed the luxury of ending this. Death doesn't save me. I waited too long and forfeit escape. At least I finally tried. It isn't fair, but then it never was.

The fist in me flexes, testing again.

My eyes flicker. Hawk has come to me. He watches with impassive eyes of shining black metal.

What do aliens want?

Chickens, dancing.

Thomas Ligotti's first collection of stories, *Songs of a Dead Dreamer* (now collectible), was published in 1986, with an expanded version issued three years later. Other collections include *Grimscribe, Noctuary, My Work Is Not Yet Done,* and *Teatro Grottesco.*

Ligotti is the recipient of multiple Bram Stoker Awards given by the Horror Writers Association, and also the British Fantasy and the International Horror Guild Awards. In 2007, a short film based on "The Frolic" was released. In addition, two graphic novel adaptations from Ligotti's 1996 collection *The Nightmare Factory* were published in 2007 and 2008.

Ligotti has been cited as the most curious and remarkable figure in horror literature since H. P. Lovecraft. His work is imaginatively grotesque and richly evocative.

The Greater Festival of Masks
Thomas Ligotti

THERE ARE ONLY a few houses in the district where Noss begins his excursions. Nonetheless, they are spaced in such a way that suggests some provision has been made to accommodate a greater number of them, like a garden from which certain growths have been removed or have yet to appear. It even seems to Noss that these hypothetical houses, the ones now absent, may at some point change places with those which can be seen, in order to enrich the lapses in the landscape and give the visible a rest within nullity. And of these houses now stretching high or spreading low there will remain nothing to be said, for they will have entered the empty spaces, which are merely blank faces waiting to gain features. Such are the declining days of the festival, when the old and the new, the real and the imaginary, truth and deception, all join in the masquerade.

But even at this stage of the festival some have yet to take a large enough interest in tradition to visit one of the shops of costumes and masks. Until recently Noss was among this group, for reasons neither he nor anyone else could clearly explain. Now, however, he is on his way to a shop whose every shelf is crammed and flowing over, even at this late stage of the festival, with costumes and masks. In the course of his little journey, Noss keeps watching as buildings become more numerous, enough to make a street, many narrow streets, a town. He also observes numerous indications of the festival season. These signs are sometimes subtle, sometimes blatant in nature. For instance, not a few doors have been kept ajar, even throughout the night, and dim lights are left burning in empty rooms. On the other hand, someone has ostentatiously scattered a bunch of filthy rags in a certain street, shredded rags that are easily disturbed by the wind and twist gaily about. But there are many other gestures of festive abandonment: a hat, all style mangled out of it, has been jammed into the space where a board is missing in a high fence; a poster stuck to a crumbling wall has been diagonally torn in half, leaving a scrap of face fluttering at its edges; and into strange pathways of caprice revelers will go, but to have *shorn* themselves in doorways, to have littered the shadows with such wiry clippings and tumbling fluff. Reliquiae of the hatless, the faceless, the tediously groomed. And Noss passes it all by with no more, if no less, than a glance.

His attention appears more sharply awakened as he approaches the center of the town, where the houses, the shops, the fences, the walls are more, much more…close. There seems barely enough space for a few stars to squeeze their bristling light between the roofs and towers above, and the outsized moon — not a familiar face in this neighborhood — must suffer to be seen only as a fuzzy anonymous glow mirrored in silvery windows. The streets are more tightly strung here, and a single one may have several names compressed into it from end to end. Some of the names may be credited less to deliberate planning, or even the quirks of local history, than to an apparent need for the superfluous, as if a street sloughed off its name every so often like an old skin, the extra ones insuring that it would not go completely nameless. Perhaps a similar need could explain why the buildings in this district exhibit so many pointless embellishments: doors which are elaborately decorated yet will not budge in their frames; massive shutters covering blank walls behind them; enticing balconies, well-railed and promising in their views, but without any means of entrance; stairways that enter dark niches…and a dead end. These structural adornments are mysterious indulgences in an area so pressed for room that even shadows must be shared. And so must other things. Backyards, for example, where a few fires still burn, the last of the festival pyres. For in this part of town the season is still at its peak, or at least the signs of its termination have yet to appear. Perhaps revelers hereabouts are still nudging each other in corners, hinting at preposterous things, coughing in the middle of jokes. Here the festival is not dead. For the delirium of this rare celebration does not radiate out from the center of things, but seeps inward from remote margins. Thus, the festival may have begun in an isolated hovel at the edge of town, if not in some lonely residence in the woods beyond. In any case, its agitations have now reached the heart of this dim region, and Noss has finally resolved to visit one of the many shops of costumes and masks.

A steep stairway leads him to a shrunken platform of a porch, and a little slot of a door puts him inside the shop. And indeed its shelves *are* crammed and flowing over with costumes and masks. The shelves are also very dark and mouth-like, stuffed into silence by the wardrobes and faces of dreams. Noss pulls at a mask that is over-hanging the edge of one shelf — a dozen fall down upon him. Backing away from the avalanche of false faces, he looks at the sardonically grinning one in his hand.

"Excellent choice," says the shopkeeper, who steps out from behind a long counter in the rearguard of shadows. "Put it on and let's see. Yes, my gracious, this is excellent. You see how your entire face is well-covered, from the hairline to just beneath the chin and no farther. And at the sides it clings snugly. It doesn't pinch, am I right?" The mask nods in agreement. "Good, that's how it should be. Your ears are unobstructed — you have very nice ones, by the way — while the mask holds on to the sides of the head. It is comfortable, yet secure enough to stay put and not fall off in the heat of activity. You'll see, after a while you won't even know you're wearing it! The holes for the eyes, nostrils, and mouth are perfectly placed for your features; no natural function is inhibited, that is a must. And it looks so good on you, especially up close, though I'm sure also at a distance. Go stand over there in the moonlight. Yes, it was made for you, what do you say? I'm sorry, what?"

Noss walks back toward the shopkeeper and removes the mask.

"I said alright, I suppose I'll take this one."

"Fine, there's no question about it. Now let me show you some of the other ones, just a few steps this way."

The shopkeeper pulls something down from a high shelf and places it in his customer's hands. What Noss now holds is another mask, but one that somehow seems to be...impractical. While the other mask possessed every virtue of conformity with its wearer's face, this mask is neglectful of such advantages. Its surface forms a strange mass of bulges and depressions which appear unaccommodating at best, possibly pain-inflicting. And it is so much heavier than the first one.

"No," says Noss, handing back the mask, "I believe the other will do."

The shopkeeper looks as if he is at a loss for words. He stares at Noss for many moments before saying: "May I ask a personal question? Have you lived, how shall I say this, *here* all your life?"

The shopkeeper is now gesturing beyond the thick glass of the shop's windows.

Noss shakes his head in reply.

"Well, then there's no rush. Don't make any hasty decisions. Stay around the shop and think it over, there's still time. In fact, it would be a favor to me.

I have to go out for a while, you see, and if you could keep an eye on things I would greatly appreciate it. You'll do it, then? Good. And don't worry," he says, taking a large hat from a peg that poked out of the wall, "I'll be back in no time, no time at all. If someone pays us a visit, just do what you can for them," he shouts before closing the front door behind him.

Now alone, Noss takes a closer look at those outlandish masks the shopkeeper had just shown him. While differing in design, as any good assortment of masks must, they all share the same impracticalities of weight and shape, as well as having some very oddly placed apertures for ventilation, and too many of them. Outlandish indeed! Noss gives these new masks back to the shelves from which they came, and he holds on tightly to the one that the shopkeeper had said was so perfect for him, so practical in every way. After a vaguely exploratory shuffle about the shop, Noss finds a stool behind the long counter and there falls asleep.

It seems only a few moments later that he is awakened by some sound or other. Collecting his wits, he gazes around the dark shop, as if searching for the source of hidden voices which are calling to him. Then the sound returns, a soft thudding sound behind him and far off into the shadowy rooms at the rear of the shop. Hopping down from the stool, Noss passes through a narrow doorway, descends a brief flight of stairs, passes through another doorway, ascends another brief flight of stairs, walks down a short and very low hallway, and at last arrives at the back door. It rumbles again once or twice.

"Just do what you can for them," Noss remembers. But he looks uneasy. On the other side of that door there is only a tiny plot of ground surrounded by a high fence.

"Why don't you come around the front?" he shouts through the door. But there is no reply, only a request.

"Please bring five of those masks to the other side of the fence. That's where we are now. There's a fire, you'll see us. Well, can you do this or not?"

Noss leans his head into the shadows by the wall: one side of his face is now in darkness while the other is indistinct, blurred by a strange glare which is only an impostor of true light. "Give me a moment, I'll meet you there," he finally replies. "Did you hear me?"

There is no response from the other side. Noss turns the door handle, which is unexpectedly warm, and through a thread-like crack peers out into the backyard. There is nothing to be seen except a square of blackness surrounded by the tall wooden slabs of the fence, and a few thin branches twisting against a pale sky. But whatever signs of pranksterism Noss perceives or is able to fabricate to himself, there is no defying the traditions of the festival, even if one can claim to have merely adopted this town and its seasonal practices, however *rare* they may be. For innocence and excuses are not harmonious with the spirit of this fabulously infrequent occasion. Therefore, Noss retrieves the masks and brings them to the rear door of the shop. Cautiously, he steps out.

When he reaches the far end of the yard — a much greater distance from the shop than it had seemed — he sees a faint glow of fire through the cracks in the fence. There is a small door with clumsy black hinges and only a hole for a handle. Setting the five masks aside for a moment, Noss squats down and peers through the hole. On the other side of the fence is a dark yard exactly like the one on his side, save for the fire burning upon the ground. Gathered around the blaze are several figures — five, perhaps four — with hunched shoulders and spines curving toward the light of the flames. They are all wearing masks which at first seem securely fitted to their faces. But, one by one, these masks appear to loosen and slip down, as if each is losing hold upon its wearer. Finally, one of the figures pulls his off completely and tosses it into the fire, where it curls and shrinks into a wad of bubbling blackness. The others follow this action when their time comes. Relieved of their masks, the figures resume their shrugging stance. But the light of the fire now shines on four, yes four, smooth and faceless faces.

"These are the wrong ones, you little idiot," says someone who is standing in the shadows by the fence. And Noss can only stare dumbly as a hand snatches up the masks and draws them into the darkness. "We have no more use for *these!*" the voice shouts.

Noss runs in retreat toward the shop, the five masks striking his narrow back and falling face-up on the ground. For he has gained a glimpse of the speaker in the shadows and now understands why *those* masks are no good to them now.

Once inside the shop, Noss leans upon the long counter to catch his breath. Then he looks up and sees that the shopkeeper has returned.

"There were some masks I brought out to the fence. They were the wrong ones," he says to the shopkeeper.

"No trouble at all," the other replies. "I'll see that the right ones are delivered. Don't worry, there's still time. And how about you, then?"

"Me?"

"And the masks, I mean."

"Oh, I'm sorry to have bothered you in the first place. It's not at all what I thought… That is, maybe I should just —"

"Nonsense! You can't leave now, you see. Let me take care of everything. Listen to me, I want you to go to a place where they know how to handle cases like this, at times like this. You're not the only one who is a little frightened tonight. It's right around the corner, this — no, *that* way, and across the street. It's a tall gray building, but it hasn't been there very long so watch you don't miss it. And you have to go down some stairs around the side. Now will you please follow my advice?"

Noss nods obediently.

"Good, you won't be sorry. Now go straight there. Don't stop for anyone or anything. And here, don't forget these," the shopkeeper reminds Noss, handing him an unmatching pair of masks. "Good luck!"

Though there doesn't seem to be anyone or anything to stop for, Noss does stop once or twice and dead in his tracks, as if someone behind him has just called his name. Then he thoughtfully caresses his chin and his smooth cheeks; he also touches other parts of his face, frantically, before proceeding toward the tall gray building. By the time he reaches the stairway at the side of the building, he cannot keep his hands off himself. Finally Noss puts on one of the masks — the sardonically grinning one. But somehow it no longer fits him the way it once did. It keeps slipping, little by little, as he descends the stairs, which look worn down by countless footsteps, bowed in the middle by the invisible tonnage of time. Yet Noss remembers the shopkeeper saying that this place hadn't been here very long.

The room at the bottom, which Noss now enters, also looks very old and is very…quiet. At this late stage of the festival the room is crowded with occupants who do nothing but sit silently in the shadows, with a face here and there reflecting the dull light. These faces are horribly simple; they have no expression at all, or very slight expressions and ones that are strange. But they are finding their way back, little by little, to a familiar land of faces. And the process, if the ear listens closely, is not an entirely silent one. Perhaps this is how a garden would sound if it could be heard growing in the dead of night. It is that soft creaking of new faces breaking through old flesh. And they are growing very nicely. At length, with a torpid solemnity, Noss removes the old mask and tosses it away. It falls to the floor and lies there grinning in the dim glow of that room, fixed in an expression that, in days to come, many will find strange and wonder at.

For the old festival of masks has ended, so that a greater festival may begin. And of the old time nothing will be said, because nothing will be known. But the old masks, false souls, will find something to remember, and perhaps they will speak of those days when they are alone behind doors that do not open, or in the darkness at the summit of stairways leading nowhere.

George R. R. Martin is best known today for his epic fantasy series A Song of Ice and Fire, which began with *A Game of Thrones* in 1996. Before that, he was already a multi award-winning science fiction and horror writer, having won the Hugo award for his novella "A Song for Lya," and then Hugo and Nebula awards for his novelette "Sandkings" (subsequently made into a *Twilight Zone* episode) and the Hugo Award the same year for his short story "The Way of Cross and Dragon." He's also won multiple Locus Awards, as well as the Bram Stoker, and the World Fantasy Award. His earlier novels ranged from science fiction, with *Dying of the Light,* and science fantasy *Windhaven* (with Lisa Tuttle), to the historical vampire novel *Fevre Dream,* and the rock 'n' roll apocalyptic novel *The Armageddon Rag,* all written between 1977 and 1983.

Martin became story editor for *The New Twilight Zone in 1986* and later was Executive Story Consultant for the television series *Beauty and the Beast,* on which he worked for several years. He also helped create and edit the Wild Cards shared world series of anthologies in 1987 and they continue to be published today.

"The Pear-Shaped Man" was originally published in *OMNI* Magazine and went on to win the first Bram Stoker Award in 1988. It's a fine example of Martin's horror with its clear and lucid style. And it might just put you off Cheez Doodles for life.

The Pear-Shaped Man
George R. R. Martin

THE PEAR-SHAPED MAN lives beneath the stairs. His shoulders are narrow and stooped, but his buttocks are impressively large. Or perhaps it is only the clothing he wears; no one has ever admitted to seeing him nude, and no one has ever admitted to wanting to. His trousers are brown polyester double knits, with wide cuffs and a shiny seat; they are always baggy, and they have big, deep, droopy pockets so stuffed with oddments and bric-a-brac that they bulge against his sides. He wears his pants very high, hiked up above the swell of his stomach, and cinches them in place around his chest with a narrow brown leather belt. He wears them so high that his drooping socks show clearly, and often an inch or two of pasty white skin as well.

His shirts are always short-sleeved, most often white or pale blue, and his breast pocket is always full of Bic pens, the cheap throwaway kind that write with blue ink. He has lost the caps or tossed them out, because his shirts are all stained and splotched around the breast pockets. His head is a second pear set atop the first; he has a double chin and wide, full, fleshy cheeks, and the top of his head seems to come almost to a point. His nose is broad and flat, with large, greasy pores; his eyes are small and pale, set close together. His hair is thin, dark, limp, flaky with dandruff; it never looks washed, and there are those who say that he cuts it himself with a bowl and a dull knife. He has a smell, too, the Pear-shaped Man; it is a sweet smell, a sour smell, a rich smell, compounded of old butter and rancid meat and vegetables rotting in the garbage bin. His voice, when he speaks, is high and thin and squeaky; it would be a funny little voice, coming from such a large, ugly man, but there is something unnerving about it, and something even more chilling about his tight, small smile. He never shows any teeth when he smiles, but his lips are broad and wet.

Of course you know him. Everyone knows a Pear-shaped Man.

Jessie met hers on her first day in the neighborhood, while she and Angela were moving into the vacant apartment on the first floor. Angela and her boyfriend, Donald the student shrink, had lugged the couch inside and accidentally knocked away the brick that had been holding open the door to the building. Meanwhile Jessie had gotten the recliner out of the U-Haul all by herself and thumped it up the steps, only to find the door locked when she backed into it, the recliner in her arms. She was hot and sore and irritable and ready to scream with frustration.

And then the Pear-shaped Man emerged from his basement apartment under the steps, climbed onto the sidewalk at the foot of the stoop, and looked up at her with those small, pale, watery eyes of his. He made no move to help her with her chair. He did not say hello or offer to let her into the building. He only blinked and smiled a tight, wet smile that showed none of his teeth and said in a voice as squeaky and grating as nails on a blackboard, "Ahhhh. *There* she is." Then he turned and walked away. When he walked he swayed slightly from side to side.

Jessie let go of the recliner; it bumped down two steps and turned over. She suddenly felt cold, despite the sweltering July heat. She watched the Pear-shaped Man depart. That was her first sight of him. She went inside and told Donald and Angela about him, but they were not much impressed. "Into every girl's life a Pear-shaped Man must fall," Angela said, with the cynicism of the veteran city girl. "I bet I met him on a blind date once."

Donald, who didn't live with them but spent so many nights with Angela that sometimes it seemed as though he did, had a more immediate concern. "Where do you want this recliner?" he wanted to know.

Later they had a few beers, and Rick and Molly and the Heathersons came over to help them warm the apartment, and Rick offered to pose for her (wink wink, nudge nudge) when Molly wasn't there to hear, and Donald drank too much and went to sleep on the sofa, and the Heathersons had a fight that ended with Geoff storming out and Lureen crying; it was a night like any other night, in other words, and Jessie forgot all about the Pear-shaped Man. But not for long.

The next morning Angela roused Donald, and the two of them went off, Angie to the big downtown firm where she was a legal secretary, Don to study shrinking. Jessie was a freelance commercial illustrator. She did her work at home, which as far as Angela and Donald and her mother and the rest of Western civilization were concerned meant that she didn't work at all. "Would you mind doing the shopping?" Angie asked her just before she left. They had pretty well devastated their refrigerator in the two weeks before the move, so as not to have a lot of food to lug across town. "Seeing as how you'll be home all day? I mean, we really need some food."

So Jessie was pushing a full cart of groceries down a crowded aisle in Santino's Market, on the corner, when she saw the Pear-shaped Man the second time. He was at the register, counting out change into Santino's hand. Jessie felt like making a U-turn and busying herself until he'd gone. But that would be silly. She'd gotten everything she needed, and she was a grown woman, after all, and he was standing at the only open register. Resolute, she got in line behind him.

Santino dumped the Pear-shaped Man's coins into the old register and bagged up his purchase: a big plastic bottle of Coke and a one-pound bag of Cheez Doodles. As he took the bag, the Pear-shaped Man saw her and smiled that little wet smile of his. "Cheez Doodles are the best," he said. "Would you like some?"

"No, thank you," Jessie said politely. The Pear-shaped Man put the brown paper sack inside a shapeless leather bag of the sort that schoolboys use to carry their books, gathered it up, and waddled out of the store. Santino, a big grizzled man with thinning salt-and-pepper hair, began to ring up Jessie's groceries. "He's something, ain't he?" he asked her.

"Who is he?" she asked.

Santino shrugged. "Hell, I dunno. Everybody just calls him the Pear-shaped Man. He's been around here forever. Comes in every morning, buys a bottle of Coke and a big bag of Cheez Doodles. Once we run out of Cheez Doodles, so I tell him he oughta try them Cheetos or maybe even potato chips, y'know, for a change? He wasn't having none of it, though."

Jessie was bemused. "He must buy something besides Coke and Cheez Doodles."

"Wanna bet, lady?"

"Then he must shop somewhere else."

"Besides me, the nearest supermarket is nine blocks away. Charlie down at the candy store tells me the Pear-shaped Man comes in every afternoon at 4:30 and has himself a chocolate ice-cream soda, but far as we can tell, that's all he eats." He rang for a total. "That's seventy-nine eighty-two, lady. You new around here?"

"I live just above the Pear-shaped Man," Jessie confessed.

"Congratulations," Santino said.

Later that morning, after she lined the shelves and put away the groceries, set up her studio in the spare bedroom, made a few desultory dabs on the cover she was supposed to be painting for Pirouette Publishing, ate lunch and washed the dishes, hooked up the stereo and listened to some Carly Simon, and rearranged half of the living room furniture, Jessie finally admitted a certain restlessness and decided this would be a good time to go around the building and introduce herself to her new neighbors. Not many people bothered with that in the city, she knew, but she was still a small-town kid at heart, and it made her feel safer to know the people around her. She decided to start with the Pear-shaped Man down in the basement and got as far as descending the stairs to his door. Then a funny feeling came over her. There was no name on the doorbell, she noticed. Suddenly she regretted her impulse. She retreated back upstairs to meet the rest of the building.

The other tenants all knew him; most of them had spoken to him, at least once or twice, trying to be friendly. Old Sadie Winbright, who had lived across the hall in the other first-floor apartment for twelve years, said he was very quiet. Billy Peabody, who shared the big second-floor apartment with his crippled mother, thought the Pear-shaped Man was creepy, especially that little smile of his. Pete Pumetti worked the late shift, and told her how those basement lights were always on, no matter what hour of the night Pete came swaggering home, even though it was hard to tell on account of the way the Pear-shaped Man had boarded up his windows. Jess and Ginny Harris didn't like their twins playing around the stairs that led down to his apartment and had forbidden them to talk to him. Jeffries the barber, whose small two-chair shop was down the block from Santino's, knew him and had no great desire for his patronage. All of them, every one, called him the Pear-shaped Man. That was who he was. "But who is he?" Jessie asked. None of them knew. "What does he do for a living?" she asked.

"I think he's on welfare," Old Sadie Winbright said. "The poor dear, he must be feebleminded."

"Damned if I know," said Pete Pumetti. "He sure as hell don't work. I bet he's a queer."

"Sometimes I think he might be a drug pusher," said Jeffries the barber, whose familiarity with drugs was limited to witch hazel.

"I betcha he writes them pornographic books down there," Billy Peabody surmised.

"He doesn't do anything for a living," said Ginny Harris. "Jess and I have talked about it. He's a shopping-bag man, he has to be."

That night, over dinner, Jessie told Angela about the Pear-shaped Man and the other tenants and their comments. "He's probably an attorney," Angie said. "Why do you care so much, anyway?"

Jessie couldn't answer that. "I don't know. He gives me goose bumps. I don't like the idea of some maniac living right underneath us."

Angela shrugged. "That's the way it goes in the big, glamorous city. Did the guy from the phone company come?"

"Maybe next week," said Jessie. "That's the way it goes in the big, glamorous city."

Jessie soon learned that there was no avoiding the Pear-shaped Man. When she visited the laundromat around the block, there he was, washing a big load of striped boxer shorts and ink-stained short-sleeved shirts, snacking on Coke and Cheez Doodles from the vending machines. She tried to ignore him, but whenever she turned around, there he was, smiling wetly, his eyes fixed on her, or perhaps on the underthings she was loading into the dryer.

When she went down to the corner candy store one afternoon to buy a paper, there he was, slurping his ice cream soda, his buttocks overflowing the stool on which he was perched. "It's homemade," he squeaked at her. She frowned, paid for her newspaper, and left.

One evening when Angela was seeing Donald, Jessie picked up an old paperback and went out on the stoop to read and maybe socialize and enjoy the cool breeze that was blowing up the street. She got lost in the story, until she caught a whiff of something unpleasant, and when she looked up from the page, there he was, standing not three feet away, staring at her. "What do you want?" she snapped, closing the book.

"Would you like to come down and see my house?" the Pear-shaped Man asked in that high, whiny voice.

"No," she said, retreating to her own apartment. But when she looked out a half hour later, he was still standing in the same exact spot, clutching his brown bag and staring at her windows while dusk fell around him. He made her feel very uneasy. She wished that Angela would come home, but she knew that wouldn't happen for hours. In fact, Angie might very well decide to spend the night at Don's place.

Jessie shut the windows despite the heat, checked the locks on her door, and then went back to her studio to work. Painting would take her mind off the Pear-shaped Man. Besides, the cover was due at Pirouette by the end of the week.

She spent the rest of the evening finishing off the background and doing some of the fine detail on the heroine's gown. The hero didn't look quite right to her when she was done, so she worked on him, too. He was the usual dark-haired, virile, strong-jawed type, but Jessie decided to individualize him a bit, an effort that kept her pleasantly occupied until she heard Angie's key in the lock.

She put away her paints and washed up and decided to have some tea before calling it a night. Angela was standing in the living room, with her hands behind her back, looking more than a little tipsy, giggling. "What's so funny?" Jessie asked.

Angela giggled again. "You've been holding out on me," she said. "You got yourself a new beau and you didn't tell."

"What are you talking about?"

"'He was standing on the stoop when I got home," Angie said, grinning. She came across the room. "He said to give you these." Her hand emerged from behind her back. It was full of fat, orange worms, little flaking twists of corn and cheese that curled between her fingers and left powdery stains on the palm of her hand. "For you," Angie repeated, laughing. "For you."

That night Jessie had a long, terrible dream, but when the daylight came she could remember only a small part of it. She was standing at the door to the Pear-shaped Man's apartment under the stairs; she was standing there in darkness, waiting, waiting for something to happen, something awful, the worst thing she could imagine. Slowly, oh so slowly, the door began to open. Light fell upon her face, and Jessie woke, trembling.

He might be dangerous, Jessie decided the next morning over Rice Krispies and tea. Maybe he had a criminal record. Maybe he was some kind of mental patient. She ought to check up on him. But she needed to know his name first. She couldn't just call up the police and say, "Do you have anything on the Pear-shaped Man?"

After Angela had gone to work, Jessie pulled a chair over by the front window and sat down to wait and watch. The mail usually arrived about eleven. She saw the postman ascend the stairs, heard him putting the mail in the big hall mailbox. But the Pear-shaped Man got his mail separately, she knew. He had his own box, right under his doorbell, and if she remembered right it wasn't the kind that locked, either. As soon as the postman had departed, she was on her feet, moving quickly down the stairs. There was no sign of the Pear-shaped Man. The door to his apartment was down under the stoop, and farther back she could see overflowing garbage cans, smell their rich, sickly sweet odor. The upper half of the door was a window, boarded up. It was dark under the stoop. Jessie barked her knuckles on the brick as she fumbled for his mailbox. Her hand brushed the loose metal lid. She got it open, pulled out two thin envelopes. She had to squint and move toward the sunlight to read the name. They were both addressed to Occupant.

She was stuffing them back into the box when the door opened. The Pear-shaped Man was framed by bright light from within his apartment. He smiled at her, so close she could count the pores on his nose, see the sheen of the saliva on his lower lip. He said nothing.

"I," she said, startled, "I, I... I got some of your mail by mistake. Must be a new man on the route. I, I was just bringing it back."

The Pear-shaped Man reached up and into his mailbox. For a second his hand brushed Jessie's. His skin was soft and damp and seemed much colder than it ought to be, and the touch gave her goose bumps all up and down her arm. He took the two letters from her and looked at them briefly and then stuffed them into his pants pocket. "It's just garbage," squeaked the Pear-shaped Man. "They shouldn't be allowed to send you garbage. They ought to be stopped. Would you like to see my things? I have things inside to look at."

"I," said Jessie, "uh, no. No, I can't. Excuse me." She turned quickly, moved out from under the stairs, back into the sunlight, and hurried back inside the building. All the way, she could feel his eyes on her.

She spent the rest of that day working, and the next as well, never glancing outside, for fear that he would be standing there. By Thursday the painting was finished. She decided to take it in to Pirouette herself and have dinner downtown, maybe do a little shopping. A day away from the apartment and the Pear-shaped Man would do her good, soothe her nerves. She was being overimaginative. He hadn't actually done anything, after all. It was just that he was so damned *creepy.*

Adrian, the art director at Pirouette, was glad to see her, as always. "That's my Jessie," he said after he'd given her a hug. "I wish all my artists were like you. Never miss a deadline, never turn in anything but the best work, a real pro. Come on back to my office, we'll look at this one and talk about some new assignments and gossip a bit." He told his secretary to hold his calls and escorted her back through the maze of tiny little cubicles where the editors lived. Adrian himself had a huge corner office with two big windows, a sign of his status in Pirouette Publishing. He gestured Jessie to a chair, poured her a cup of herb tea, then took her portfolio and removed the cover painting and held it up at arm's length.

The silence went on far too long.

Adrian dragged out a chair, propped up the painting, and retreated several feet to consider it from a distance. He stroked his beard and cocked his head this way and that. Watching him, Jessie felt a thin prickle of alarm. Normally, Adrian was given to exuberant outbursts of approval. She didn't like this quiet. "What's wrong?" she said, setting down her teacup. "Don't you like it?"

"Oh," Adrian said. He put out a hand, palm open and level, waggled it this way and that. "It's well executed, no doubt. Your technique is very professional. Fine detail."

"I researched all the clothing," she said in exasperation. "It's all authentic for the period; you know it is."

"Yes, no doubt. And the heroine is gorgeous, as always. I wouldn't mind ripping her bodice myself. You do amazing things with mammaries, Jessie."

She stood up. "Then what is it?" she said. "I've been doing covers for you for three years now, Adrian. There's never been any problem."

"Well," he said. He shook his head, smiled. "Nothing, really. Maybe you've been doing too many of these. I know how it can go. They're so much alike, it gets boring, painting all those hot embraces one after another; so pretty soon you feel an urge to experiment, to try something a little bit different." He shook a finger at her. "It won't do, though. Our readers just want the same old shit with the same old covers. I understand, but it won't do."

"There's nothing experimental about this painting." Jessie said, exasperated. "It's the same thing I've done for you a hundred times before. *What* won't do?"

Adrian looked honestly surprised. "Why, the man, of course," he said. "I thought you'd done it deliberately." He gestured. "I mean, look at him. He's almost *unattractive*."

"What?" Jessie moved over to the painting. "He's the same virile jerk I've painted over and over again."

Adrian frowned. "Really now," he said. "Look." He started pointing things out. "There, around his collar, is that or is that not just the faintest hint of a double chin? And look at that lower lip! Beautifully executed, yes, but it looks, well, gross. Like it was wet or something. Pirouette heroes rape, they plunder, they seduce, they threaten, but they do not drool, darling. And perhaps it's just a trick of perspective, but I could swear" — he paused, leaned close, shook his head — "no, it's not perspective, the top of his head is definitely narrower than the bottom. A pinhead! We can't have pinheads on Pirouette books, Jessie. Too much fullness in the cheeks, too. He looks as though he might be storing nuts for the winter." Adrian shook his head. "It won't do, love. Look, no big problem. The rest of the painting is fine. Just take it home and fix him up. How about it?"

Jessie was staring at her painting in horror, as if she were seeing it for the first time. Everything Adrian had said, everything he had pointed out, was true. It was all very subtle, to be sure; at first glance the man looked almost like your normal Pirouette hero, but there was something just the tiniest bit off about him, and when you looked closer, it was blatant and unmistakable. Somehow the Pear-shaped Man had crept into her painting. "I," she began, "I, yes, you're right, I'll do it over. I don't know what happened. There's this man who lives in my building, a creepy-looking guy, everybody calls him the Pear-shaped Man. He's been getting on my nerves. I swear, it wasn't intentional. I guess I've been thinking about him so much it just crept into my work subconsciously."

"I understand," Adrian said. "Well, no problem, just set it right. We do have deadline problems, though."

"I'll fix it this weekend, have it back to you by Monday," Jessie promised.

"Wonderful," said Adrian. "Let's talk about those other assignments then." He poured her more Red Zinger, and they sat down to talk. By the time Jessie left his office, she was feeling much better.

Afterward she enjoyed a drink in her favorite bar, met a few friends, and had a nice dinner at an excellent new Japanese restaurant. It was dark by the time she got home. There was no sign of the Pear-shaped Man. She kept her portfolio under her arm as she fished for her keys and unlocked the door to the building.

When she stepped inside, Jessie heard a faint noise and felt something crunch underfoot. A nest of orange worms clustered against the faded blue of the hallway carpet, crushed and broken by her foot.

She dreamed of him again. It was the same shapeless, terrible dream. She was down in the dark beneath the stoop, near the trash bins crawling with all kinds of things, waiting at his door. She was frightened, too frightened to knock or open the door yet helpless to leave. Finally the door crept open of its own accord. There he stood, smiling, smiling. "Would you like to stay?" he said, and the last words echoed, *to stay to stay to stay to stay,* and he reached out for her, and his fingers were as soft and pulpy as earthworms when he touched her on the cheek.

The next morning Jessie arrived at the offices of Citywide Realty just as they opened their doors. The receptionist told her that Edward Selby was out showing some condos; she couldn't say when he'd be in. "That's all right," Jessie said. "I'll wait." She settled down to leaf through some magazines, studying pictures of houses she couldn't afford.

Selby arrived just before eleven. He looked momentarily surprised to see her, before his professional smile switched on automatically. "Jessie," he said, "how nice. Something I can do for you?"

"Let's talk," she said, tossing down the magazines.

They went to Selby's desk. He was still only an associate with the rental firm, so he shared the office with another agent, but she was out, and they had the room to themselves. Selby settled himself into his chair and leaned back. He was a pleasant-looking man, with curly brown hair and white teeth, his eyes careful behind silver aviator frames. "Is there a problem?" he asked.

Jessie leaned forward. "The Pear-shaped Man," she said.

Selby arched one eyebrow. "I see. A harmless eccentric."

"Are you sure of that?"

He shrugged. "He hasn't murdered anybody yet, at least that I know of."

"How much do you know about him? For starters, what's his name?"

"Good question," Selby said, smiling. "Here at Citywide Realty we just think of him as the Pear-shaped Man. I don't think I've ever gotten a name out of him."

"What the hell do you mean?" Jessie demanded. "Are you telling me his checks have THE PEAR-SHAPED MAN printed on them?"

Selby cleared his throat. "Well, no. Actually, he doesn't use checks. I come by on the first of every month to collect, and knock on his door, and he pays me in cash. One-dollar bills, in fact. I stand there, and he counts out the money into my hand, dollar by dollar. I'll confess, Jessie, that I've never been inside the apartment, and I don't especially care to. Kind of a funny smell, you know? But he's a good tenant, as far as we're concerned. Always has his rent paid on time. Never bitches about rent hikes. And he certainly doesn't bounce checks on us." He showed a lot of teeth, a broad smile to let her know he was joking.

Jessie was not amused. "He must have given a name when he first rented the apartment."

"I wouldn't know about that," Selby said. "I've only handled that building for six years. He's been down in the basement a lot longer than that."

"Why don't you check his lease?"

Selby frowned. "Well, I could dig it up, I suppose. But really, is his name any of your business? What's the problem here, anyway? Exactly what has the Pear-shaped Man *done?*"

Jessie sat back and crossed her arms. "He looks at me."

"Well," Selby said, carefully, "I, uh, well, you're an attractive woman, Jessie. I seem to recall asking you out myself."

"That's different," she said. "You're normal. It's the way he looks at me."

"Undressing you with his eyes?" Selby suggested.

Jessie was nonplussed. "No," she said. "That isn't it. It's not sexual, not in the normal way, anyhow. I don't know how to explain it. He keeps asking me down to his apartment. He's always hanging around."

"Well, that's where he lives."

"He bothers me. He's crept into my paintings."

This time both of Selby's eyebrows went up. "Into your paintings?" he said. There was a funny hitch in his voice.

Jessie was getting more and more discomfited; this wasn't coming out right at all. "Okay, it doesn't sound like much, but he's *creepy*, I tell you. His lips are always wet. The way he smiles. His eyes. His squeaky little voice. And that smell. Jesus Christ, you collect his rent, you ought to know."

The realtor spread his hands helplessly. "It's not against the law to have body odor. It's not even a violation of his lease."

"Last night he snuck into the building and left a pile of Cheez Doodles right where I'd step in them."

"Cheez Doodles?" Selby said. His voice took on a sarcastic edge. "God, not *Cheez Doodles*! How fucking heinous! Have you informed the police?"

"It's not funny. What was he doing inside the building anyway?"

"He lives there."

"He lives in the basement. He has his own door, he doesn't need to come into our hallway. Nobody but the six regular tenants ought to have keys to that door."

"Nobody does, as far as I know," Selby said. He pulled out a notepad. "Well, that's something, anyway. I'll tell you what, I'll have the lock changed on the outer door. The Pear-shaped Man won't get a key. Will that make you happy?"

"A little," said Jessie, slightly mollified.

"I can't promise that he won't get in," Selby cautioned. "You know how it is. If I had a nickel for every time some tenant has taped over a lock or propped open a door with a doorstop because it was more convenient, well…"

"Don't worry, I'll see that nothing like that happens. What about his name? Will you check the lease for me?"

Selby sighed. "This is really an invasion of privacy. But I'll do it. A personal favor. You owe me one." He got up and went across the room to a black metal filing cabinet, pulled open a drawer, rummaged around, and came out with a legal-sized folder. He was flipping through it as he returned to his desk.

"Well?" Jessie asked, impatiently.

"Hmmmm," Selby said. "Here's your lease. And here's the others." He went back to the beginning and checked the papers one by one. "Winbright, Peabody, Pumetti, Harris, Jeffries." He closed the file, looked up at her, and shrugged. "No lease. Well, it's a crummy little apartment, and he's been there forever. Either we've misfiled his lease or he never had one. It's not unknown. A month-to-month basis…"

"Oh, great," Jessie said. "Are you going to do anything about it?"

"I'll change that lock," Selby said. "Beyond that, I don't know what you expect of me. I'm not going to evict the man for offering you Cheez Doodles."

The Pear-shaped Man was standing on the stoop when Jessie got home, his battered bag tucked up under one arm. He smiled when he saw her approach. *Let him touch me,* she thought; *just let him touch me when I walk by, and I'll have him booked for assault so fast it'll make his little pointy head swim.* But the Pear-shaped Man made no effort to grab her. "I have things to show you downstairs," he said as Jessie ascended the stairs. She had to pass within a foot of him; the smell was overwhelming today, a rich odor like yeast and decaying vegetables. "Would you like to look at my things?" he called after her. Jessie unlocked the door and slammed it behind her.

I'm not going to think about him, she told herself inside, over a cup of tea. She had work to do. She'd promised Adrian the cover by Monday, after all. She went into her studio, drew back the curtains, and set to work, determined to eradicate every hint of the Pear-shaped Man from the cover. She painted away the double chin, firmed up the jaw, redid those tight wet lips, darkened the hair, made it blacker and bushier and more wind tossed so the head didn't seem to come to such a point. She gave him sharp, high, pronounced cheekbones — cheekbones like the blade of a knife — made the face almost gaunt. She even changed the color of his eyes. Why had she given him those weak, pale eyes? She made the eyes green, a crisp, clean, commanding green, full of vitality.

It was almost midnight by the time she was done, and Jessie was exhausted, but when she stepped back to survey her handiwork, she was delighted. The man was a real Pirouette hero now: a rakehell, a rogue, a hell-raiser whose robust exterior concealed a brooding, melancholy, poetic soul. There was nothing the least bit pear-shaped about him. Adrian would have puppies.

It was a good kind of tiredness. Jessie went to sleep feeling altogether satisfied. Maybe Selby was right; she was too imaginative, she'd really let the Pear-shaped Man get to her. But work, good hard old-fashioned work, was the perfect antidote for these shapeless fears of hers. Tonight, she was sure, her sleep would be deep and dreamless.

She was wrong. There was no safety in her sleep. She stood trembling on his doorstep once again. It was so dark down there, so filthy. The rich, ripe smell of the garbage cans was overwhelming, and she thought she could hear things moving in the shadows. The door began to open. The Pear-shaped Man smiled at her and touched her with cold, soft fingers like a nest of grubs. He took hold of her by the arm and drew her inside, inside, inside, inside....

Angela knocked on her door the next morning at ten. "Sunday brunch," she called out. "Don is making waffles. With chocolate chips and fresh strawberries. And bacon. And coffee. And O.J. Want some?"

Jessie sat up in bed. "Don? Is he here?"

"He stayed over," Angela said.

Jessie climbed out of bed and pulled on a paint-splattered pair of jeans. "You know I'd never turn down one of Don's brunches. I didn't even hear you guys come in."

"I snuck my head into your studio, but you were painting away, and you didn't even notice. You had that intent look you get sometimes, you know, with the tip of your tongue peeking out of one corner of your mouth. I figured it was better not to disturb the artist at work." She giggled. "How you avoided hearing the bed-springs, though, I'll never know."

Breakfast was a triumph. There were times when Jessie couldn't understand just what Angela saw in Donald the student shrink, but mealtimes were not among them. He was a splendid cook. Angela and Donald were still lingering over coffee, and Jessie over tea, at eleven, when they heard noises from the hall. Angela went to check. "Some guy's out there changing the lock," she said when she returned. "I wonder what that's all about."

"I'll be damned," Jessie said. "And on the weekend, too. That's time and a half. I never expected Selby to move so fast."

Angela looked at her curiously. "What do you know about this?"

So Jessie told them all about her meeting with the realtor and her encounters with the Pear-shaped Man. Angela giggled once or twice, and Donald slipped into his wise shrink face. "Tell me, Jessie," he said when she had finished, "don't you think you're overreacting a bit here?"

"No," Jessie said curtly.

"You're stonewalling," Donald said. "Really now, try and look at your actions objectively. What has this man done to you?"

"Nothing, and I intend to keep it that way," Jessie snapped. "I didn't ask for your opinion."

"You don't have to ask," Donald said. "We're friends, aren't we? I hate to see you getting upset over nothing. It sounds to me as though you're developing some kind of phobia about a harmless neighborhood character."

Angela giggled. "He's just got a crush on you, that's all. You're such a heartbreaker."

Jessie was getting annoyed. "You wouldn't think it was funny if he was leaving Cheez Doodles for you," she said angrily. "There's something...well, something *wrong* there. I can feel it."

Donald spread his hands. "Something wrong? Most definitely. The man is obviously very poorly socialized. He's unattractive, sloppy, he doesn't conform to normal standards of dress or personal hygiene, he has unusual eating habits and a great deal of difficulty relating to others. He's probably a very lonely person and no doubt deeply neurotic as well. But none of this makes him a killer or a rapist, does it? Why are you becoming so obsessed with him?"

"I am not becoming obsessed with him."

"Obviously you are," Donald said.

"She's in love," Angela teased.

Jessie stood up. "I am not becoming obsessed with him!" she shouted, "and this discussion has just ended."

That night, in her dream, Jessie saw inside for the first time. He drew her in, and she found she was too weak to resist. The lights were very bright inside, and it was warm and oh so humid, and the air seemed to move as if she had entered the mouth of some great beast, and the walls were orange and flaky and had a strange, sweet smell, and there were empty plastic Coke bottles everywhere and bowls of half-eaten Cheez Doodles, too, and the Pear-shaped Man said, "You can see my things, you can have my things," and he began to undress, unbuttoning his short-sleeved shirt, pulling it off, revealing dead, white, hairless flesh and two floppy breasts, and the right breast was stained with blue ink from his leaking pens, and he was smiling, smiling, and he undid his thin belt, and then pulled down the fly on his brown polyester pants, and Jessie woke screaming.

On Monday morning, Jessie packed up her cover painting, phoned a messenger service, and had them take it down to Pirouette for her. She wasn't up to another trip downtown. Adrian would want to chat, and Jessie wasn't in a very sociable mood. Angela kept needling her about the Pear-shaped Man, and it had left her in a foul temper. Nobody seemed to understand. There was something wrong with the Pear-shaped Man, something serious, something horrible. He was no joke. He was frightening. Somehow she had to prove it. She had to learn his name, had to find out what he was hiding.

She could hire a detective, except detectives were expensive. There had to be something she could do on her own. She could try his mailbox again. She'd be better off if she waited until the day the gas and electric bills came, though. He had lights in his apartment, so the electric company would know his name. The only problem was that the electric bill wasn't due for another couple of weeks.

The living room windows were wide open, Jessie noticed suddenly. Even the drapes had been drawn all the way back. Angela must have done it that morning before taking off for work. Jessie hesitated and then went to the window. She closed it, locked it, moved to the next, closed it, locked it. It made her feel safer. She told herself she wouldn't look out. It would be better if she didn't look out.

How could she not look out? She looked out. He was there, standing on the sidewalk below her, looking up. "You could see my things," he said in his high, thin voice. "I knew when I saw you that you'd want my things. You'd like them. We could have food." He reached into a bulgy pocket, brought out a single Cheez Doodle, held it up to her. His mouth moved silently.

"Get away from here, or I'll call the police!" Jessie shouted.

"I have something for you. Come to my house and you can have it. It's in my pocket. I'll give it to you."

"No you won't. Get away, I warn you. Leave me alone." She stepped back, closed the drapes. It was gloomy in here with the drapes pulled, but that was better than knowing that the Pear-shaped Man was looking in. Jessie turned on a light, picked up a paperback, and tried to read. She found herself turning pages rapidly and realized she didn't have the vaguest idea of what the words meant. She slammed down the book, marched into the kitchen, made a tuna salad sandwich on whole wheat toast. She wanted something with it, but she wasn't sure what. She took out a dill pickle and sliced it into quarters, arranged it neatly on her plate, searched through her cupboard for some potato chips. Then she poured a big fresh glass of milk and sat down to lunch.

She took one bite of the sandwich, made a face, and shoved it away. It tasted funny. Like the mayonnaise had gone bad or something. The pickle was too sour, and the chips seemed soggy and limp and much too salty. She didn't want chips anyway. She wanted something else. Some of those little orange cheese curls. She could picture them in her head, almost taste them. Her mouth watered.

Then she realized what she was thinking and almost gagged. She got up and scraped her lunch into the garbage. She had to get out of here, she thought wildly. She'd go see a movie or something, forget all about the Pear-shaped Man for a few hours. Maybe she could go to a singles' bar somewhere, pick someone up, get laid. At his place. Away from here. Away from the Pear-shaped Man. That was the ticket. A night away from the apartment would do her good.

She went to the window, pulled aside the drapes, peered out.

The Pear-shaped Man smiled, shifted from side to side. He had his misshapen briefcase under his arm. His pockets bulged. Jessie felt her skin crawl. He was *revolting,* she thought. But she wasn't going to let him keep her prisoner.

She gathered her things together, slipped a little steak knife into her purse just in case, and marched outside. "Would you like to see what I have in my case?" the Pear-shaped Man asked her when she emerged. Jessie had decided to ignore him. If she did not reply at all, just pretended he wasn't there, maybe he'd grow bored and leave her alone. She descended the steps briskly and set off down the street. The Pear-shaped Man followed close behind her. "They're all around us," he whispered. She could smell him hurrying a step or two behind her, puffing as he walked. "They are. They laugh at me. They don't understand, but they want my things. I can show you proof. I have it down in my house. I know you want to come see."

Jessie continued to ignore him. He followed her all the way to the bus stop.

The movie was a dud. Having skipped lunch, Jessie was hungry. She got a Coke and a tub of buttered popcorn from the candy counter. The Coke was three-quarters crushed ice, but it still tasted good. She couldn't eat the popcorn. The fake butter they used had a vaguely rancid smell that reminded her of the Pear-shaped Man. She tried two kernels and felt sick.

Afterward, though, she did a little better. His name was Jack, he said. He was a sound man on a local TV news show, and he had an interesting face: an easy smile, Clark Gable ears, nice gray eyes with friendly little crinkles in the corners. He bought her a drink and touched her hand; but the way he did it was a little clumsy, like he was a bit shy about this whole scene, and Jessie liked that. They had a few drinks together, and then he suggested dinner back at his place. Nothing fancy, he said. He had some cold cuts in the fridge; he could whip up some jumbo sandwiches and show her his stereo system, which was some kind of special super setup he'd rigged himself. That all sounded fine to her.

His apartment was on the twenty-third floor of a midtown high rise, and from his windows you could see sailboats tacking off on the horizon. Jack put the new Linda Ronstadt album on the stereo while he went to make the sandwiches. Jessie watched the sailboats. She was finally beginning to relax. "I have beer or ice tea," Jack called from the kitchen. "What'll it be?"

"Coke," she said absently.

"No Coke," he called back. "Beer or ice tea."

"Oh," she said, somehow annoyed. "Ice tea, then."

"You got it. Rye or wheat?"

"I don't care," she said. The boats were very graceful. She'd like to paint them someday. She could paint Jack, too. He looked like he had a nice body.

"Here we go," he said, emerging from the kitchen carrying a tray. "I hope you're hungry."

"Famished," Jessie said, turning away from the window. She went over to where he was setting the table and froze.

"What's wrong?" Jack said. He was holding out a white stoneware plate. On top of it was a truly gargantuan ham-and-Swiss sandwich on fresh deli rye, lavishly slathered with mustard, and next to it, filling up the rest of the plate, was a pile of puffy orange cheese curls. They seemed to writhe and move, to edge toward the sandwich, toward her. "Jessie?" Jack said.

She gave a choked, inarticulate cry and pushed the plate away wildly. Jack lost his grip; ham, Swiss cheese, bread, and Cheez Doodles scattered in all directions. A Cheez Doodle brushed against Jessie's leg. She whirled and ran from the apartment.

Jessie spent the night alone at a hotel and slept poorly. Even here, miles from the apartment, she could not escape the dream. It was the same as before, the same, but each night it seemed to grow longer, each night it went a little further. She was on the stoop, waiting, afraid. The door opened, and he drew her inside, the orange warm, the air like fetid breath, the Pear-shaped Man smiling. "You can see my things," he said, "you can have my things," and then he was undressing, his shirt first, his skin so white, dead flesh, heavy breasts with a blue ink stain, his belt, his pants falling, polyester puddling around his ankles, all the trash in his pockets scattering on the floor, and he really was pear-shaped, it wasn't just the way he dressed, and then the boxer shorts last of all, and Jessie looked down despite herself and there was no hair and it was small and wormy and kind of yellow, like a cheese curl, and it moved slightly and the Pear-shaped Man was saying, "I want your things now, give them to me, let me see your things," and why couldn't she run, her feet wouldn't move, but her hands did, her hands, and she began to undress.

The hotel detective woke her, pounding on her door, demanding to know what the problem was and why she was screaming.

She timed her return home so that the Pear-shaped Man would be away on his morning run to Santino's Market when she arrived. The house was empty. Angela had already gone to work, leaving the living room windows open again. Jessie closed them, locked them, and pulled the drapes. With luck, the Pear-shaped Man would never know that she'd come home.

Already the day outside was swelteringly hot. It was going to be a real scorcher. Jessie felt sweaty and soiled. She stripped, dumped her clothing into the wicker hamper in her bedroom, and immersed herself in a long, cold shower. The icy water hurt, but it was a good clean kind of hurting, and it left her feeling invigorated. She dried her hair and wrapped herself in a huge, fluffy blue towel, then padded back to her bedroom, leaving wet footprints on the bare wood floors.

A halter top and a pair of cutoffs would be all she'd need in this heat, Jessie decided. She had a plan for the day firmly in mind. She'd get dressed, do a little work in her studio, and after that she could read or watch some soaps or something. She wouldn't go outside; she wouldn't even look out the window. If the Pear-shaped Man was at his vigil, it would be a long, hot, boring afternoon for him.

Jessie laid out her cutoffs and a white halter top on the bed, draped the wet towel over a bedpost, and went to her dresser for a fresh pair of panties. She ought to do laundry soon, she thought absently as she snatched up a pair of pink bikini briefs.

A Cheez Doodle fell out.

Jessie recoiled, shuddering. It had been *inside,* she thought wildly, it had been inside the briefs. The powdery cheese had left a yellow stain on the fabric. The Cheez Doodle lay where it had fallen, in the open drawer on top of her underwear. Something like terror took hold of her. She balled the bikini briefs up in her fist and tossed them away with revulsion. She grabbed another pair of panties, shook them, and another Cheez Doodle leapt out. And then another. Another. She began to make a thin, hysterical sound, but she kept on. Five pairs, six, nine, that was all, but that was enough. Someone had opened her drawer and taken out every pair of panties and carefully wrapped a Cheez Doodle in each and put them all back.

It was a ghastly joke, she thought. Angela, it had to be Angela who'd done it, maybe she and Donald together. They thought this whole thing about the Pear-shaped Man was a big laugh, so they decided to see if they could really freak her out.

Except it hadn't been Angela. She knew it hadn't been Angela.

Jessie began to sob uncontrollably. She threw her balled-up panties to the floor and ran from the room, crushing Cheez Doodles into the carpet.

Out in the living room, she didn't know where to turn. She couldn't go back to her bedroom, *couldn't,* not just now, not until Angela got back, and she didn't want to go to the windows, even with the drapes closed. He was out there, Jessie could feel it, could feel him staring up at the windows. She grew suddenly aware of her nakedness and covered herself with her hands. She backed away from the windows, step by uncertain step, and retreated to her studio.

Inside she found a big square package leaning up against the door, with a note from Angela taped to it. "Jess, this came for you last evening," signed with Angie's big winged A. Jessie stared at the package, uncomprehending. It was from Pirouette. It was her painting, the cover she'd rushed to redo for them. Adrian had sent it back. Why?

She didn't want to know. She had to know.

Wildly, Jessie ripped at the brown paper wrappings, tore them away in long, ragged strips, baring the cover she'd painted. Adrian had written on the mat; she recognized his hand. "Not funny, kid," he'd scrawled. "Forget it."

"No," Jessie whimpered, backing off.

There it was, her painting, the familiar background, the trite embrace, the period costumes researched so carefully, but no, she hadn't done that, someone had changed it, it wasn't her work, the woman was her, her, her, slender and strong with sandy blond hair and green eyes full of rapture, and he was crushing her to him, to *him,* the wet lips and white skin, and he had a blue ink stain on his ruffled lace shirtfront and dandruff on his velvet jacket and his head was pointed and his hair was greasy and the fingers wrapped in her locks were stained yellow, and he was smiling thinly and pulling her to him and her mouth was open and her eyes half closed and it was him and it was her, and there was her own signature, there, down at the bottom.

"No," she said again. She backed away, tripped over an easel, and fell. She curled up into a little ball on the floor and lay there sobbing, and that was how

Angela found her, hours later.

Angela laid her out on the couch and made a cold compress and pressed it to her forehead. Donald stood in the doorway between the living room and the studio, frowning, glancing first at Jessie and then in at the painting and then at Jessie again. Angela said soothing things and held Jessie's hand and got her a cup of tea; little by little her hysteria began to ebb. Donald crossed his arms and scowled. Finally, when Jessie had dried the last of her tears, he said, "This obsession of yours has gone too far."

"Don, don't," Angela said. "She's terrified."

"I can see that," Donald said. "That's why something has to be done. She's doing it to herself, honey."

Jessie had a hot cup of Morning Thunder halfway to her mouth. She stopped dead still. "I'm doing it to myself?" she repeated incredulously.

"Certainly," Donald said.

The complacency in his tone made Jessie suddenly, blazingly angry. "You stupid ignorant callous son of a bitch," she roared. "I'm doing it to myself, *I'm* doing it, *I'm* doing it, how *dare* you say that *I'm* doing it." She flung the teacup across the room, aiming for his fat head. Donald ducked; the cup shattered and the tea sent three long brown fingers running down the off-white wall. "Go on, let out your anger," he said. "I know you're upset. When you calm down, we can discuss this rationally, maybe get to the root of your problem."

Angela took her arm, but Jessie shook off the grip and stood, her hands balled into fists. "Go into my bedroom, you jerk, go in there right now and look around and come back and tell me what you see."

"If you'd like," Donald said. He walked over to the bedroom door, vanished, reemerged several moments later. "All right," he said patiently.

"Well?" Jessie demanded.

Donald shrugged. "It's a mess," he said. "Underpants all over the floor, lots of crushed cheese curls. Tell me what you think it means."

"He broke in here!" Jessie said.

"The Pear-shaped Man?" Donald queried pleasantly.

"*Of course* it was the Pear-shaped Man," Jessie screamed. "He snuck in here while we were all gone and he went into my bedroom and pawed through all my things and put Cheez Doodles in my underwear. He was *here!* He was touching my stuff."

Donald wore an expression of patient, compassionate wisdom. "Jessie, dear, I want you to think about what you just told us."

"There's nothing to think about!"

"Of course there is," he said. "Let's think it through together. The Pear-shaped Man was here, you think?"

"Yes."

"Why?"

"To do...to do what he did. It's disgusting. He's disgusting."

"Hmmm," Don said. "How, then? The locks were changed, remember? He can't even get in the building. He's never had a key to this apartment. There was no sign of forced entry. How did he get in with his bag of cheese curls?"

Jessie had him there. "Angela left the living room windows open," she said.

Angela looked stricken. "I did," she admitted. "Oh, Jessie, honey, I'm so sorry. It was hot. I just wanted to get a breeze, I didn't mean..."

"The windows are too high to reach from the sidewalk," Donald pointed out. "He'd have needed a ladder or something to stand on. He'd have needed to do it in broad daylight, from a busy street, with people coming and going all the time. He'd have had to have left the same way. There's the problem of the screens. He doesn't look like a very athletic sort, either."

"He did it," Jessie insisted. "He was here, wasn't he?"

"I know you think so, and I'm not trying to deny your feelings, just explore them. Has this Pear-shaped Man ever been invited into the apartment?"

"Of course not!" Jessie said. "What are you suggesting?"

"Nothing, Jess. Just consider. He climbs in through the windows with these cheese curls he intends to secrete in your drawers. Fine. How does he know which room is yours?"

Jessie frowned. "He... I don't know...he searched around, I guess."

"And found what clue? You've got three bedrooms here, one a studio, two full of women's clothing. How'd he pick the right one?"

"Maybe he did it in both."

"Angela, would you go check your bedroom, please?" Donald asked.

Angela rose hesitantly. "Well," she said, "okay." Jessie and Donald stared at each other until she returned a minute or so later. "All clean," she said.

"I don't know how he figured out which damned room was mine," Jessie said. "All I know is that he did. He had to. How else can you explain what happened, huh? Do you think I did it *myself?*"

Donald shrugged. "I don't know," he said calmly. He glanced over his shoulder into the studio. "Funny, though. That painting in there, him and you, he must have done that some other time, after you finished it but before you sent it to Pirouette. It's good work, too. Almost as good as yours."

Jessie had been trying very hard not to think about the painting. She opened her mouth to throw something back at him, but nothing flew out. She closed her mouth. Tears began to gather in the corners of her eyes. She suddenly felt weary, confused, and very alone. Angela had walked over to stand beside Donald. They were both looking at her. Jessie looked down at her hands helplessly and said, "What am I going to do? God. What am I going to *do?*"

God did not answer; Donald did. "Only one thing *to* do," he said briskly. "Face up to your fears. Exorcise them. Go down there and talk to the man, get to know him. By the time you come back up, you may pity him or have contempt for him or dislike him, but you won't fear him any longer; you'll see that he's only a human being and a rather sad one."

"Are you sure, Don?" Angela asked him.

"Completely. Confront this obsession of yours, Jessie. That's the only way you'll ever be free of it. Go down to the basement and visit with the Pear-shaped Man."

"There's nothing to be afraid of," Angela told her again.

"That's easy for you to say."

"Look, Jess, the minute you're inside, Don and I will come out and sit on the stoop. We'll be just an earshot away. All you'll have to do is let out the teeniest little yell and we'll come rushing right down. So you won't be alone, not really. And you've still got that knife in your purse, right?"

Jessie nodded.

"Come on, then, remember the time that purse snatcher tried to grab your shoulder bag? You decked him good. If this Pear-shaped Man tries anything, you're quick enough. Stab him. Run away. Yell for us. You'll be perfectly safe."

"I suppose you're right," Jessie said with a small sigh. They *were* right. She knew it. It didn't make any sense. He was a dirty, foul-smelling, unattractive man, maybe a little retarded, but nothing she couldn't handle, nothing she had to be afraid of, she didn't want to be crazy, she was letting this ridiculous obsession eat her alive and it had to end now, Donald was perfectly correct, she'd been doing it to herself all along and now she was going to take hold of it and stop it, certainly, it all made perfect sense and there was nothing to worry about, nothing to be afraid of, what could the Pear-shaped Man do to her, after all, what could he possibly do to her that was so terrifying? Nothing. Nothing.

Angela patted her on the back. Jessie took a deep breath, took the doorknob firmly in hand, and stepped out of the building into the hot, damp evening air. Everything was under control.

So why was she so scared?

Night was falling, but down under the stairs it had fallen already. Down under the stairs it was always night. The stoop cut off the morning sun, and the building itself blocked the afternoon light. It was dark, so dark. She stumbled over a crack in the cement, and her foot rang off the side of a metal garbage can. Jessie shuddered, imagining flies and maggots and other, worse things moving and breeding back there where the sun never shone. *No, mustn't think about that, it was only garbage, rotting and festering in the warm, humid dark, mustn't dwell on it.* She was at the door.

She raised her hand to knock, and then the fear took hold of her again. She could not move. *Nothing to be frightened of,* she told herself, *nothing at all.* What could he possibly *do* to her? Yet still she could not bring herself to knock. She stood before his door with her hand raised, her breath raw in her throat. It was so hot, so suffocatingly hot. She had to breathe. She had to get out from under the stoop, get back to where she could breathe.

A thin vertical crack of yellow light split the darkness. *No,* Jessie thought, *oh, please no.*

The door was opening.

Why did it have to open so slowly? Slowly, like in her dreams. Why did it have to open at all?

The light was so bright in there. As the door opened, Jessie found herself squinting.

The Pear-shaped Man stood smiling at her.

"I," Jessie began, "I, uh, I…"

"There she is," the Pear-shaped Man said in his tinny little squeak.

"What do you want from me?" Jessie blurted.

"I knew she'd come," he said, as though she wasn't there. "I knew she'd come for my things."

"No," Jessie said. She wanted to run away, but her feet would not move.

"You can come in," he said. He raised his hand, moved it toward her face. He touched her. Five fat white maggots crawled across her cheek and wriggled through her hair. His fingers smelled like cheese curls. His pinkie touched her ear and tried to burrow inside. She hadn't seen his other hand move until she felt it grip her upper arm, pulling, pulling. His flesh felt damp and cold. Jessie whimpered.

"Come in and see my things," he said. "You have to. You know you have to." And somehow she was inside then, and the door was closing behind her, and she was there, inside, alone with the Pear-shaped Man.

Jessie tried to get a grip on herself. *Nothing to be afraid of,* she repeated to herself, a litany, a charm, a chant, *nothing to be afraid of, what could he do to you, what could he do?* The room was L-shaped, low ceilinged, filthy. The sickly sweet smell was overwhelming. Four naked light bulbs burned in the fixture above, and along one wall was a row of old lamps without shades, bare bulbs blazing away. A three-legged card table stood against the opposite wall, its fourth corner propped up by a broken TV set with wires dangling through the shattered glass of its picture tube. On top of the card table was a big bowl of Cheez Doodles. Jessie looked away, feeling sick. She tried to step backward, and her foot hit an empty plastic Coke bottle. She almost fell. But the Pear-shaped Man caught her in his soft, damp grip and held her upright.

Jessie yanked herself free of him and backed away. Her hand went into her purse and closed around the knife. It made her feel better, stronger. She moved close to the boarded-up window. Outside she could make out Donald and Angela talking. The sound of their voices, so close at hand — that helped, too. She tried to summon up all of her strength. "How do you live like this?" she asked him. "Do you need help cleaning up the place? Are you sick?" It was so hard to force out the words.

"Sick," the Pear-shaped Man repeated. "Did they tell you I was sick? They lie about me. They lie about me all the time. Somebody should make them stop." If only he would stop smiling. His lips were so wet. But he never stopped smiling. "I knew you would come. Here. This is for you." He pulled it from a pocket, held it out.

"No," said Jessie. "I'm not hungry. Really." But she was hungry, she realized. She was famished. She found herself staring at the thick orange twist between his fingers, and suddenly she wanted it desperately. "No," she said again, but her voice was weaker now, barely more than a whisper, and the cheese curl was very close.

Her mouth sagged open. She felt it on her tongue, the roughness of the powdery cheese, the sweetness of it. It crunched softly between her teeth. She swallowed and licked the last orange flakes from her lower lip. She wanted more.

"I knew it was you," said the Pear-shaped Man. "Now your things are mine." Jessie stared at him. It was like in her nightmare. The Pear-shaped Man reached up and began to undo the little white plastic buttons on his shirt. She struggled to find her voice. He shrugged out of the shirt. His undershirt was yellow, with huge damp circles under his arms. He peeled it off, dropped it. He moved closer, and heavy white breasts flopped against his chest. The right one was covered by a wide blue smear. A dark little tongue slid between his lips. Fat white fingers worked at his belt like a team of dancing slugs. "These are for you," he said.

Jessie's knuckles were white around the hilt of the knife. "Stop," she said in a hoarse whisper.

His pants settled to the floor.

She couldn't take it. No more, no more. She pulled the knife free of her bag, raised it over her head. *"Stop!"*

"Ahh," said the Pear-shaped Man, "there it is."

She stabbed him.

The blade went in right to the hilt, plunged deep into his soft, white skin. She wrenched it down and out. The skin parted, a huge, meaty gash. The Pear-shaped Man was smiling his little smile. There was no blood, no blood at all. His flesh was soft and thick, all pale dead meat.

He moved closer, and Jessie stabbed him again. This time he reached up and knocked her hand away. The knife was embedded in his neck. The hilt wobbled back and forth as he padded toward her. His dead, white arms reached out and she pushed against him and her hand sank into his body like he was made of wet, rotten bread. "Oh," he said, "oh, oh, oh." Jessie opened her mouth to scream, and the Pear-shaped Man pressed those heavy wet lips to her own and swallowed at her sound. His pale eyes sucked at her. She felt his tongue darting forward, and it was round and black and oily, and then it was snaking down inside her, touching, tasting, feeling all her things. She was drowning in a sea of soft, damp flesh.

She woke to the sound of the door closing. It was only a small click, a latch sliding into place, but it was enough. Her eyes opened, and she pulled herself up. It was so hard to move. She felt heavy, tired. Outside they were laughing. They were laughing at her. It was dim and far-off, that laughter, but she knew it was meant for her.

Her hand was resting on her thigh. She stared at it and blinked. She wiggled her fingers, and they moved like five fat maggots. She had something soft and yellow under her nails and deep dirty yellow stains up near her fingertips.

She closed her eyes, ran her hand over her body, the soft heavy curves, the thicknesses, the strange hills and valleys. She pushed, and the flesh gave and gave and gave. She stood up weakly. There were her clothes, scattered on the floor. Piece by piece she pulled them on, and then she moved across the room. Her briefcase was down beside the door; she gathered it up, tucked it under her arm, she might need something, yes, it was good to have the briefcase. She pushed open the door and emerged into the warm night. She heard the voices above her: "...were right all along," a woman was saying, "I couldn't believe I'd been so silly. There's nothing sinister about him, really, he's just pathetic. Donald, I don't know how to thank you."

She came out from under the stoop and stood there. Her feet hurt so. She shifted her weight from one to the other and back again. They had stopped talking, and they were staring at her, Angela and Donald and a slender, pretty woman in blue jeans and work shirt. "Come back," she said, and her voice was thin and high. "Give them back. You took them, you took my things. You have to give them back."

The woman's laugh was like ice cubes tinkling in a glass of Coke.

"I think you've bothered Jessie quite enough," Donald said.

"She has my things," she said. "Please."

"I saw her come out, and she didn't have anything of yours," Donald said.

"She took all my things," she said.

Donald frowned. The woman with the sandy hair and the green eyes laughed again and put a hand on his arm. "Don't look so serious, Don. He's not all there."

They were all against her, she knew, looking at their faces. She clutched her briefcase to his chest. They'd taken her things, he couldn't remember exactly what, but they wouldn't get her case, he had stuff in there and they wouldn't get it. She turned away from them. He was hungry, she realized. She wanted something to eat. He had half a bag of Cheez Doodles left, she remembered. Downstairs. Down under the stoop.

As she descended, the Pear-shaped Man heard them talking about her. He opened the door and went inside to stay. The room smelled like home. He sat down, laid his case across his knees, and began to eat. He stuffed the cheese curls into his mouth in big handfuls and washed them down with sips from a glass of warm Coke straight from the bottle he'd opened that morning, or maybe yesterday. It was good. Nobody knew how good it was. They laughed at him, but they didn't know, they didn't know about all the nice things he had. No one knew. No one. Only someday he'd see somebody different, somebody to give his things to, somebody who would give him all their things. Yes. He'd like that. He'd know her when he saw her.

He'd know just what to say.

Peter Straub is the author of seventeen novels, including *Ghost Story, Koko, Mr. X,* two collaborations with Stephen King, *The Talisman* and *Black House,* and his most recent, *In the Night Room.* He has also written two volumes of poetry and two collections of short fiction. He edited *Conjunctions 39: The New Wave Fabulists,* the Library of America's *H. P. Lovecraft: Tales, Poe's Children,* and the Library of America two volume set, *American Fantastic Tales:Terror and the Uncanny from Poe to the Pulps* and *American Fantastic Tales:Terror and the Uncanny from the 1940's Until Now.* He has won the British Fantasy Award, four Bram Stoker Awards, two International Horror Guild Awards, and two World Fantasy Awards. In 1998, he was named Grand Master at the World Horror Convention.

Straub is best known for his novels, but his short fiction writing is infused by a poetry of language and jazz as he joyously explores and experiments and creates marvelous riffs.

"The Juniper Tree"— subtle, disturbing, and very powerful — features Straub's recurring character, Vietnam war veteran turned horror writer, Tim Underhill.

The Juniper Tree
Peter Straub

It is a school yard in my Midwest of empty lots, waving green and brilliant with tiger lilies, of ugly new "ranch" houses set down in rows in glistening clay, of treeless avenues cooking in the sun. Our school yard is black asphalt — on June days, patches of the asphalt loosen and stick like gum to the soles of our high-top basketball shoes.

Most of the playground is black empty space from which heat radiates up like the wavery images on the screen of a faulty television set. Tall wire mesh surrounds it. A new boy named Paul is standing beside me.

Though it is now nearly the final month of the semester, Paul came to us, carroty-haired, pale-eyed, too shy to ask even the whereabouts of the lavatory, only six weeks ago. The lessons baffle him, and his Southern accent is a fatal error of style. The popular students broadcast in hushed, giggling whispers the terrible news that Paul "talks like a nigger." Their voices are *almost* awed — they are conscious of the enormity of what they are saying, of the enormity of its consequences.

Paul is wearing a brilliant red shirt too heavy, too enveloping, for the weather. He and I stand in the shade at the rear of the school, before the cream-colored brick wall in which is placed at eye level a newly broken window of pebbly green glass reinforced with strands of copper wire. At our feet is a little scatter of green, edible-looking pebbles. The pebbles dig into the soles of our shoes, too hard to shatter against the softer asphalt. Paul is singing to me in his slow, lilting voice that he will never have friends in this school. I put my foot down on one of the green candy pebbles and feel it push up, hard as a bullet, against my foot. "Children are so cruel," Paul casually sings. I think of sliding the pebble of broken glass across my throat, slicing myself wide open to let death in.

Paul did not return to school in the fall. His father, who had beaten a man to death down in Mississippi, had been arrested while leaving a movie theater near my house named the Orpheum-Oriental. Paul's father had taken his family to see an Esther Williams movie costarring Fernando Lamas, and when they came out, their mouths raw from salty popcorn, the baby's hands sticky with spilled Coca-Cola, the police were waiting for them. They were Mississippi people, and I think of Paul now, seated at a desk on a floor of an office building in Jackson filled with men like him at desks: his tie perfectly knotted, a good shine on his cordovan shoes, a necessary but unconscious restraint in the set of his mouth.

In those days I used to spend whole days in the Orpheum-Oriental.

I was seven. I held within me the idea of a disappearance like Paul's, of never having to be seen again. Of being an absence, a shadow, a place where something no longer visible used to be.

Before I met that young-old man whose name was "Frank" or "Stan" or "Jimmy," when I sat in the rapture of education before the movies at the Orpheum-Oriental, I watched Alan Ladd and Richard Widmark and Glenn Ford and Dane Clark. *Chicago Deadline.* Martin and Lewis, tangled up in the same parachute in *At War with the Army.* William Boyd and Roy Rogers. Openmouthed, I drank down movies about spies and criminals, wanting the passionate and shadowy ones to fulfill themselves, to gorge themselves on what they needed.

The feverish gaze of Richard Widmark, the anger of Alan Ladd, Berry Kroeger's sneaky eyes, girlish and watchful — vivid, total elegance.

When I was seven, my father walked into the bathroom and saw me looking at my face in the mirror. He slapped me, not with his whole strength, but hard, raging instantly. "What do you think you're looking at?" His hand cocked and ready. "What do you think you see?"

"Nothing," I said.

"Nothing is right."

A carpenter, he worked furiously, already defeated, and never had enough money — as if, permanently beyond reach, some quantity of money existed that would have satisfied him. In the mornings he went to the job site hardened like cement into anger he barely knew he had. Sometimes he brought men from the taverns home with him at night. They carried transparent bottles of

Darkness: Two Decades of Modern Horror

Miller High Life in paper bags and set them down on the table with a bang that said: Men are here! My mother, who had returned from her secretary's job a few hours earlier, fed my brothers and me, washed the dishes, and put the three of us to bed while the men shouted and laughed in the kitchen.

He was considered an excellent carpenter. He worked slowly, patiently; and I see now that he spent whatever love he had in the rented garage that was his workshop. In his spare time he listened to baseball games on the radio. He had professional, but not personal, vanity, and he thought that a face like mine should not be examined.

Because I saw "Jimmy" in the mirror, I thought my father, too, had seen him.

One Saturday my mother took the twins and me on the ferry across Lake Michigan to Saginaw — the point of the journey was the journey, and at Saginaw the boat docked for twenty minutes before wallowing back out into the lake and returning. With us were women like my mother, her friends, freed by the weekend from their jobs, some of them accompanied by men like my father, with their felt hats and baggy weekend trousers flaring over their weekend shoes. The women wore blood-bright lipstick that printed itself onto their cigarettes and smeared across their front teeth. They laughed a great deal and repeated the words that had made them laugh. "Hot dog," "slippin' 'n' slidin'," "opera singer." Thirty minutes after departure, the men disappeared into the enclosed deck bar; the women, my mother among them, arranged deck chairs into a long oval tied together by laughter, attention, gossip. They waved their cigarettes in the air. My brothers raced around the deck, their shirts flapping, their hair glued to their skulls with sweat — when they squabbled, my mother ordered them into empty deck chairs. I sat on the deck, leaning against the railings, quiet. If someone had asked me: What do you want to do this afternoon, what do you want to do for the rest of your life? I would have said, I want to stay right here, I want to stay here forever.

After a while I stood up and left the women. I went across the deck and stepped through a hatch into the bar. Dark, deeply grained imitation wood covered the walls. The odors of beer and cigarettes and the sound of men's voices filled the enclosed space. About twenty men stood at the bar, talking and gesturing with half-filled glasses. Then one man broke away from the others with a flash of dirty-blond hair. I saw his shoulders move, and my scalp tingled and my stomach froze and I thought: Jimmy. "Jimmy." But he turned all the way around, dipping his shoulders in some ecstasy of beer and male company, and I saw that he was a stranger, not "Jimmy," after all.

I was thinking: Someday when I am free, when I am out of this body and in some city whose name I do not even know now, I will remember this from beginning to end and then I will be free of it.

The women floated over the empty lake, laughing out clouds of cigarette smoke, the men, too, as boisterous as the children on the sticky asphalt playground with its small green spray of glass like candy.

In those days I knew I was set apart from the rest of my family, an island between my parents and the twins. Those pairs that bracketed me slept in double beds in adjacent rooms at the back of the ground floor of the duplex owned by the blind man who lived above us. My bed, a cot coveted by the twins, stood in their room. An invisible line of great authority divided my territory and possessions from theirs.

This is what happened in the mornings in our half of the duplex. My mother got up first — we heard her showering, heard drawers closing, the sounds of bowls and milk being set out on the table. The smell of bacon frying for my father, who banged on the door and called out my brothers' names. "Don't you make me come in there, now!" The noisy, puppyish turmoil of my brothers getting out of bed. All three of us scramble into the bathroom as soon as my father leaves it. The bathroom was steamy, heavy with the odor of shit and the more piercing, almost palpable smell of shaving — lather and amputated whiskers. We all pee into the toilet at the same time. My mother frets and frets, pulling the twins into their clothes so that she can take them down the street to Mrs. Candee, who is given a five-dollar bill every week for taking care of them. I am supposed to be running back and forth on the playground in Summer Play School, supervised by two teenage girls who live a block away from us. (I went to Play School only twice.) After I dress myself in clean underwear and socks and put on my everyday shirt and pants, I come into the kitchen while my father finishes his breakfast. He is eating strips of bacon and golden-brown pieces of toast shiny with butter. A cigarette smolders in the ashtray before him. Everybody else has already left the house. My father and I can hear the blind man banging on the piano in his living room. I sit down before a bowl of cereal. My father looks at me, looks away.

Angry at the blind man for banging at the piano this early in the morning, he is sweating already. His cheeks and forehead shine like the golden toast. My father glances at me, knowing he can postpone this no longer, and reaches wearily into his pocket and drops two quarters on the table. The high-school girls charge twenty-five cents a day, and the other quarter is for my lunch. "Don't lose that money," he says as I take the coins. My father dumps coffee into his mouth, puts the cup and his plate into the crowded sink, looks at me again, pats his pockets for his keys, and says, "Close the door behind you." I tell him that I will close the door. He picks up his gray toolbox and his black lunch pail, claps his hat on his head, and goes out, banging his toolbox against the door frame. It leaves a broad gray mark like a smear left by the passing of some angry creature's hide.

Then I am alone in the house. I go back to the bedroom, close the door and push a chair beneath the knob, and read *Blackhawk* and *Henry* and *Captain Marvel* comic books until at last it is time to go to the theater.

While I read, everything in the house seems alive and dangerous. I can hear the telephone in the hall rattling on its hook, the radio clicking as it tries to turn itself on and talk to me. The dishes stir and chime in the sink. At these times all objects, even the heavy chairs and sofa, become their true selves, violent as the fire that fills the sky I cannot see, and races through the secret ways and passages beneath the streets. At these times other people vanish like smoke.

When I pull the chair away from the door, the house immediately goes quiet, like a wild animal feigning sleep. Everything inside and out slips cunningly back into place, the fires bank, men and women reappear on the sidewalks. I must open the door and I do. I walk swiftly through the kitchen and the living room to the front door, knowing that if I look too carefully at any one thing, I will wake it up again. My mouth is so dry, my tongue feels fat. "I'm leaving," I say to no one. Everything in the house hears me.

The quarter goes through the slot at the bottom of the window, the ticket leaps from its slot. For a long time, before "Jimmy," I thought that unless you kept your stub unfolded and safe in a shirt pocket, the usher could rush down the aisle in the middle of the movie, seize you, and throw you out. So into the pocket it goes, and I slip through the big doors into the cool, cross the lobby, and pass through a swinging door with a porthole window.

Most of the regular daytime patrons of the Orpheum-Oriental sit in the same seats every day — I am one of those who comes here every day. A small, talkative gathering of bums sits far to the right of the theater, in the rows beneath the sconces fastened like bronze torches to the walls. The bums choose these seats so that they can examine their bits of paper, their "documents," and show them to each other during the movies. Always on their minds is the possibility that they might have lost one of these documents, and they frequently consult the tattered envelopes in which they are kept.

I take the end seat, left side of the central block of seats, just before the broad horizontal middle aisle. There I can stretch out. At other times I sit in the middle of the last row, or the first; sometimes when the balcony is open I go up and sit in its first row. From the first row of the balcony, seeing a movie is like being a bird and flying down into the movie from above. To be alone in the theater is delicious. The curtains hang heavy, red, anticipatory; the mock torches glow on the walls. Swirls of gilt wind through the red paint. On days when I sit near a wall, I reach out toward the red, which seems warm and soft, and find my fingers resting on a chill dampness. The carpet of the Orpheum-Oriental must once have been a bottomlessly rich brown; now it is a dark noncolor, mottled with the pink and gray smears, like melted Band-Aids, of chewing gum. From about a third of the seats dirty gray wool foams from slashes in the worn plush.

On an ideal day I sit through a cartoon, a travelogue, a sequence of previews, a movie, another cartoon, and another movie before anyone else enters the theater. This whole cycle is as satisfying as a meal. On other mornings, old women in odd hats and young women wearing scarves over their rollers, a few teenage couples are scattered throughout the theater when I come in. None of these people ever pays attention to anything but the screen and, in the case of the teenagers, each other.

Once, a man in his early twenties, hair like a haystack, sat up in the wide middle aisle when I took my seat. He groaned. Rusty-looking dried blood was spattered over his chin and his dirty white shirt. He groaned again and then got to his hands and knees. The carpet beneath him was spotted with what looked like a thousand red dots. The young man stumbled to his feet and began reeling up the aisle. A bright, depthless pane of sunlight surrounded him before he vanished into it.

At the beginning of July, I told my mother that the high-school girls had increased the hours of the Play School because I wanted to be sure of seeing both features twice before I had to go home. After that I could learn the rhythms of the theater itself, which did not impress themselves upon me all at once but revealed themselves gradually, so that by the middle of the first week, I knew when the bums would begin to move toward the seats beneath the sconces — they usually arrived on Tuesdays and Fridays shortly after eleven o'clock, when the liquor store down the block opened up to provide them with the pints and half-pints that nourished them. By the end of the second week, I knew when the ushers left the interior of the theater to sit on padded benches in the lobby and light up their Luckies and Chesterfields, when the old men and women would begin to appear. By the end of the third week, I felt like the merest part of a great, orderly machine. Before the beginning of the second showing of *Beautiful Hawaii* or *Curiosities Down Under*, I went out to the counter and with my second quarter purchased a box of popcorn or a packet of Good & Plenty candy.

In a movie theater nothing is random except the customers and hitches in the machine. Filmstrips break and lights fail; the projectionist gets drunk or falls asleep; and the screen presents a blank yellow face to the stamping, whistling audience. These inconsistencies are summer squalls, forgotten as soon as they have ended.

The occasion for the lights, the projectionist, the boxes of popcorn and packets of candy, the movies, enlarged when seen over and over. The truth gradually came to me that this deepening and widening out, this enlarging, was why movies were shown over and over all day long. The machine revealed itself most surely in the exact, limpid repetitions of the actors' words and gestures as they moved through the story. When Alan Ladd asked "Blacky Franchot," the dying gangster, "Who did it, Blacky?" his voice widened like a river, grew *sandier* with an almost unconcealed tenderness I had to learn to hear — the voice within the speaking voice.

Chicago Deadline was the exploration by a newspaper reporter named "Ed Adams" (Alan Ladd) of the tragedy of a mysterious young woman, "Rosita Jean D'ur," who had died alone of tuberculosis in a shabby hotel room. The reporter soon learns that she had many names, many identities. She had been in love with an architect, a gangster, a crippled professor, a boxer, a millionaire, and had given a different facet of her being to each of them. Far too predictably, the adult me complains, the obsessed "Ed" falls in love with "Rosita." When I was seven, little was predictable — I had not yet seen *Laura* — and I saw a man driven by the need to understand, which became identical to the need to protect. "Rosita Jean D'ur" was the embodiment of memory, which was mystery.

Through the sequences of her identities, the various selves shown to brother, boxer, millionaire, gangster, all the others, her memory kept her whole. I saw, twice a day, for two weeks, before and during "Jimmy," the machine deep within the machine. Love and memory were the same. Both love and memory accommodated us to death. (I did not understand this, but I saw it.) The reporter, Alan Ladd, with his dirty-blond hair, his perfect jawline, and brilliant, wounded smile, gave her life by making her memory his own.

"I think you're the only one who ever understood her," Arthur Kennedy — "Rosita's" brother — tells Alan Ladd.

Most of the world demands the kick of sensation, most of the world must gather and spend money, hunt for easier and more temporary forms of love, must feed itself, sell newspapers, destroy the enemy's plots with plots of its own....

"I don't know what you want," "Ed Adams" says to the editor of *The Journal*. "You got two murders..."

"...and a mystery woman," I say along with him. His voice is tough and detached, the voice of a wounded man acting. The man beside me laughs. Unlike his normal voice, his laughter is breathless and high-pitched. It is the second showing today of *Chicago Deadline*, early afternoon — after the next showing of *At War with the Army* I will have to walk up the aisle and out of the theater. It will be twenty minutes to five, and the sun will still burn high over the cream-colored buildings across wide, empty Sherman Boulevard.

I met the man, or he met me, at the candy counter. He was at first only a tall presence, blond, dressed in dark clothing. I cared nothing for him, he did not matter. He was vague even when he spoke. "Good popcorn." I looked up at him — narrow blue eyes, bad teeth smiling at me. Stubble on his face. I looked away and the uniformed man behind the counter handed me popcorn. "Good for you, I mean. Good stuff in popcorn — comes right out of the ground. Grows on big plants tall as I am, just like other corn. You know that?"

When I said nothing, he laughed and spoke to the man behind the counter. "*He* didn't know that — the kid thought popcorn grew inside poppers." The counterman turned away. "You come here a lot?" the man asked me.

I put a few kernels of popcorn in my mouth and turned toward him. He was showing me his bad teeth.

"You do," he said. "You come here a lot."

I nodded.

"Every day?"

I nodded again.

"And we tell little fibs at home about what we've been doing all day, don't we?" he asked, and pursed his lips and raised his eyes like a comic butler in a movie. Then his mood shifted and everything about him became serious. He was looking at me, but he did not see me. "You got a favorite actor? I got a favorite actor. Alan Ladd."

And I saw — both saw and understood — that he thought he looked like Alan Ladd. He did, too, at least a little bit. When I saw the resemblance, he seemed like a different person, more glamorous. Glamour surrounded him, as though he were acting, impersonating a shabby young man with stained, irregular teeth.

"The name's Frank," he said, and stuck out his hand. "Shake?"

I took his hand.

"Real good popcorn," he said, and stuck his hand into the box. "Want to hear a secret?"

A secret.

"I was born twice. The first time, I died. It was on an Army base. Everybody *told* me I should have joined the Navy, and everybody was right. So I just had myself get born somewhere else. Hey — the Army's not for everybody, you know?" He grinned down at me. "Now I told you my secret. Let's go in — I'll sit with you. Everybody needs company, and I like you. You look like a good kid."

He followed me back to my seat and sat down beside me. When I quoted the lines along with the actors, he laughed.

Then he said —

Then he leaned toward me and said —

He leaned toward me, breathing sour wine over me, and took —

No.

"I was just kidding out there," he said. "Frank ain't my real name. Well, it was my name. Before. See? Frank *used* to be my name for a while. But now my good friends call me Stan. I like that. Stanley the Steamer. Big Stan. Stan the Man. See? It works real good."

You'll never be a carpenter, he told me. You'll never be anything like that — because you got that look; *I* used to have that look, okay? So I know. I know about you just by looking at you.

He said he had been a clerk at Sears; after that he had worked as the custodian for a couple of apartment buildings owned by a guy who used to be a friend of his but was no longer. Then he had been the janitor at the high school where my grade school sent its graduates. "Good old booze got me fired, story of my life," he said. "Tight-ass bitches caught me drinking down in the basement, in a room I used there, and threw me out without a fare-thee-well. Hey, that was my *room*. My *place*. The best things in the world can do the worst things to you; you'll find that out someday. And when you go to that school, I hope you'll remember what they done to me there."

These days he was resting. He hung around, he went to the movies.

He said: You got something special in you. Guys like me, we're funny, we can tell.

We sat together through the second feature, Dean Martin and Jerry Lewis, comfortable and laughing. "Those guys are bigger bums than us," he said. I thought of Paul backed up against the school in his enveloping red shirt, imprisoned within his inability to be like anyone around him.

You coming back tomorrow? If I get here, I'll check around for you.

Hey. Trust me. I know who you are.

You know that little thing you pee with? Leaning sideways and whispering into my ear. That's the best thing a man's got. Trust me.

The big providential park near our house, two streets past the Orpheum-Oriental, is separated into three different areas. Nearest the wide iron gates on Sherman Boulevard through which we enter was a wading pool divided by a low green hedge, so rubbery it seemed artificial, from a playground with a climbing frame, swings, and a row of seesaws. When I was a child of two and three, I splashed in the warm pool and clung to the chains of the swings, making myself go higher and higher, terror and joy and grim duty so woven together that no one could pull them apart.

Beyond the children's pool and playground was the zoo. My mother walked my brothers and me to the playground and wading pool and sat smoking on a bench while we played; both of my parents took us into the zoo. An elephant extended his trunk to my father's palm and delicately lipped peanuts toward his maw. The giraffe stretched toward the constantly diminishing supply of leaves, ever fewer and higher, above his cage. The lions drowsed on amputated branches and paced behind the bars, staring out not at what was there but at the long, grassy plains imprinted on their memories. I knew the lions had the power not to see us, to look straight through us to Africa. But when they saw you instead of Africa, they looked right into your bones, they saw the blood traveling through your body. The lions were golden-brown, patient, green-eyed. They recognized me and could read thoughts. The lions neither liked nor disliked me, they did not miss me during their long weekdays, but they took me into the circle of known beings.

("You shouldn't have looked at me like that," June Havoc — "Leona" — tells "Ed Adams." She does not mean it, not at all.)

Past the zoo and across a narrow park road down which khaki-clothed park attendants pushed barrows heavy with flowers stood a wide, unexpected lawn bordered with flower beds and tall elms — open space hidden like a secret between the caged animals and the elm trees. Only my father brought me to this section of the park. Here he tried to make a baseball player of me.

"Get the bat off your shoulders," he says. "For God's sake, will you try to hit the ball, anyhow?"

When I fail once again to swing at his slow, perfect pitch, he spins around, raises his arm, and theatrically asks everyone in sight, "Whose kid is this, anyway? Can you answer me that?"

He has never asked me about the Play School I am supposed to be attending, and I have never told him about the Orpheum-Oriental — I will never come any closer to talking to him than now, for "Stan," "Stanley the Steamer," has told me things that cannot be true, that must be inventions and fables, part of the world of children wandering lost in the forest, of talking cats and silver boots filled with blood. In this world, dismembered children buried beneath juniper trees can rise and speak, made whole once again. Fables boil with underground explosions and hidden fires, and for this reason, memory rejects them, thrusts them out of its sight, and they must be repeated over and over. I cannot remember "Stan's" face — cannot even be sure I remember what he said. Dean Martin and Jerry Lewis are bums like us. I am certain of only one thing: tomorrow I am again going to see my newest, scariest, most interesting friend.

"When I was your age," my father says, "I had my heart set on playing pro ball when I grew up. And you're too damned scared or lazy to even take the bat off your shoulder. Kee-rist! I can't stand looking at you anymore."

He turns around and begins to move quickly toward the narrow park road and the zoo, going home, and I run after him. I retrieve the softball when he tosses it into the bushes.

"What the hell do you think you're going to do when you grow up?" my father asks, his eyes still fixed ahead of him. "I wonder what you think life is all *about*. I wouldn't give you a job, I wouldn't trust you around carpenter tools, I wouldn't trust you to blow your nose right — to tell you the truth, I wonder if the hospital mixed up the goddamn babies."

I follow him, dragging the bat with one hand, in the other cradling the softball in the pouch of my mitt.

At dinner my mother asks if Summer Play School is fun, and I say yes. I have already taken from my father's dresser drawer what "Stan" asked me to get for him, and it burns in my pocket as if it were alight. I want to ask: Is it actually true and not a story? Does the worst thing always have to be the true thing? Of course, I cannot ask this. My father does not know about worse things — he sees what he wants to see, or he tries so hard, he thinks he does see it.

"I guess he'll hit a long ball someday. The boy just needs more work on his swing." He tries to smile at me, a boy who will someday learn to hit a long ball. The knife is upended in his fist — he is about to smear a pat of butter on his steak. He does not see me at all. My father is not a lion, he cannot make the switch to seeing what is really there in front of him.

Late at night Alan Ladd knelt beside my bed. He was wearing a neat gray suit, and his breath smelled like cloves. "You okay, son?" I nodded. "I just wanted to tell you that I like seeing you out there every day. That means a lot to me."

"Do you remember what I was telling you about?"

And I knew: it was true. He had said those things, and he would repeat them like a fairy tale, and the world was going to change because it would be seen through changed eyes. I felt sick — trapped in the theater as if in a cage.

"You think about what I told you?"

"Sure," I said.

"That's good. Hey, you know what? I feel like changing seats. You want to change seats too?"

"Where to?"

He tilted his head back, and I knew he wanted to move to the last row. "Come on. I want to show you something."

We changed seats.

For a long time we sat watching the movie from the last row, nearly alone in the theater. Just after eleven, three of the bums filed in and proceeded to their customary seats on the other side of the theater — a rumpled graybeard I had seen many times before; a fat man with a stubby, squashed face, also familiar; and one of the shaggy, wild-looking young men who hung around the bums until they became indistinguishable from them. They began passing a flat brown bottle back and forth. After a second I remembered the young man — I had surprised him awake one morning, passed out and spattered with blood, in the middle aisle.

Then I wondered if "Stan" was not the young man I had surprised that morning; they looked as alike as twins, though I knew they were not.

"Want a sip?" "Stan" said, showing me his own pint bottle. "Do you good."

Bravely, feeling privileged and adult, I took the bottle of Thunderbird and raised it to my mouth. I wanted to like it, to share the pleasure of it with "Stan," but it tasted horrible, like garbage, and the little bit I swallowed burned all the way down my throat.

I made a face, and he said, "This stuff's really not so bad. Only one thing in the world can make you feel better than this stuff."

He placed his hand on my thigh and squeezed. "I'm giving you a head start, you know. Just because I liked you the first time I saw you." He leaned over and stared at me. "You believe me? You believe the things I tell you?"

I said I guessed so.

"I got proof. I'll show you it's true. Want to see my proof?"

When I said nothing, "Stan" leaned closer to me, inundating me with the stench of Thunderbird. "You know that little thing you pee with? Remember how I told you how it gets real big when you're about thirteen? Remember I told you about how incredible that feels? Well, you have to trust Stan now, because Stan's going to trust you." He put his face right beside my ear. "Then I'll tell you another secret."

He lifted his hand from my thigh and closed it around mine and pulled my hand down onto his crotch. "Feel anything?"

I nodded, but I could not have described what I felt any more than the blind men could describe the elephant.

"Stan" smiled tightly and tugged at his zipper in a way even I could tell was nervous. He reached inside his pants, fumbled, and pulled out a thick, pale club that looked like nothing human. I was so frightened I thought I would throw up, and I looked back up at the screen. Invisible chains held me to my seat.

"See? Now you understand me."

Then he noticed that I was not looking at him. "Kid. Look. I said, look. It's not going to hurt you."

I could not look down at him. I saw nothing.

"Come on. Touch it, see what it feels like."

I shook my head.

"Let me tell you something. I like you a lot. I think the two of us are friends. This thing we're doing, it's unusual to you because this is the first time, but people do this all the time. Your mommy and daddy do it all the time, but they just don't tell you about it. We're pals, aren't we?"

I nodded dumbly. On the screen, Berry Kroeger was telling Alan Ladd, "Drop it, forget it, she's poison."

"Well, this is what friends do when they really like each other, like your mommy and daddy. Look at this thing, will you? Come on."

Did my mommy and daddy like each other? He squeezed my shoulder, and I looked.

Now the thing had folded up into itself and was drooping sideways against the fabric of his trousers. Almost as soon as I looked, it twitched and began to push itself out like the slide of a trombone.

"There," he said. "He likes you, you got him going. Tell me you like him too."

Terror would not let me speak. My brains had turned to powder.

"I know what — let's call him Jimmy. We'll say his name is Jimmy. Now that you've been introduced, say hi to Jimmy."

"Hi, Jimmy," I said, and, despite my terror, could not keep myself from giggling.

"Now go on, touch him."

I slowly extended my hand and put the tips of my fingers on "Jimmy."

"Pet him. Jimmy wants you to pet him."

I tapped my fingertips against "Jimmy" two or three times, and he twitched up another few degrees, as rigid as a surfboard.

"Slide your fingers up and down on him."

If I run, I thought, he'll catch me and kill me. If I don't do what he says, he'll kill me.

I rubbed my fingertips back and forth, moving the thin skin over the veins.

"Can't you imagine Jimmy going in a woman? Now you can see what you'll be like when you're a man. Keep on, but hold him with your whole hand. And give me what I asked you for."

I immediately took my hand from "Jimmy" and pulled my father's clean white handkerchief from my back pocket.

He took the handkerchief with his left hand and with his right guided mine back to "Jimmy." "You're doing really great," he whispered.

In my hand "Jimmy" felt warm and slightly gummy. I could not join my fingers around its width. My head was buzzing. "Is Jimmy your secret?" I was able to say.

"My secret comes later."

"Can I stop now?"

"I'll cut you into little pieces if you do," he said, and when I froze, he stroked my hair and whispered, "Hey, can't you tell when a guy's kidding around? I'm really happy with you right now. You're the best kid in the world. You'd want this, too, if you knew how good it felt."

After what seemed an endless time, while Alan Ladd was climbing out of a taxicab, "Stan" abruptly arched his back, grimaced, and whispered, "Look!" His entire body jerked, and too startled to let go, I held "Jimmy" and watched thick, ivory-colored milk spurt and drool almost unendingly onto the handkerchief. An odor utterly foreign but as familiar as the toilet or the Lakeshore rose from the thick milk. "Stan" sighed, folded the handkerchief, and pushed the softening "Jimmy" back into his trousers. He leaned over and kissed the top of my head. I think I nearly fainted. I felt lightly, pointlessly dead. I could still feel him pulsing in my palm and fingers.

When it was time for me to go home, he told me his secret — his own real name was Jimmy, not Stan. He had been saving his real name until he knew he could trust me.

"Tomorrow," he said, touching my cheek with his fingers. "We'll see each other again tomorrow. But you don't have anything to worry about. I trust you enough to give you my real name. You trusted me not to hurt you, and I didn't. We have to trust each other not to say anything about this, or both you and me'll be in a lot of trouble."
"I won't say anything," I said.

I love you.

I love you, yes I do.

Now *we're* a secret, he said, folding the handkerchief into quarters and putting it back in my pocket. A lot of love has to be secret. Especially when a boy and a man are getting to know each other and learning how to make each other happy and be good, loving friends — not many people can understand that, so the friendship has to be protected. When you walk out of here, he said, you have to forget that this happened. Otherwise people will try to hurt us both.

Afterward I remembered only the confusion of *Chicago Deadline,* how the story had abruptly surged forward, skipping over whole characters and entire scenes, how for long stretches the actors had moved their lips without speaking. I could see Alan Ladd stepping out of the taxicab, looking straight through the screen into my eyes, knowing me.

My mother said that I looked pale, and my father said that I didn't get enough exercise. The twins looked up from their plates, then went back to spooning macaroni and cheese into their mouths. "Were you ever in Chicago?" I asked my father, who asked what was it to me. "Did you ever meet a movie actor?" I asked, and he said, "This kid must have a fever." The twins giggled.

Alan Ladd and Donna Reed came into my bedroom together late that night, moving with brisk, cool theatricality, and kneeled down beside my cot. They smiled at me. Their voices were very soothing. I saw you missed a few things today, Alan said. Nothing to worry about. I'll take care of you. I know, I said, I'm your number-one fan.

Then the door cracked open, and my mother put her head inside the room. Alan and Donna smiled and stood up to let her pass between them and the cot. I missed them the second they stepped back. "Still awake?" I nodded. "Are you feeling all right, honey?" I nodded again, afraid that Alan and Donna would leave if she stayed too long. "I have a surprise for you," she said. "The Saturday after this, I'm taking you and the twins all the way across Lake Michigan on the ferry. There's a whole bunch of us. It'll be a lot of fun." Good, that's nice, I'll like that.

"I thought about you all last night and all this morning."
        When I came into the lobby, he was leaning forward on one of the padded benches where the ushers sat and smoked, his elbows on his knees and his chin in his hand, watching the door. The metal tip of a flat bottle protruded from his side pocket. Beside him was a package rolled up in brown paper. He winked at me, jerked his head toward the door into the theater, stood up, and went inside in an elaborate charade of not being with me. I knew he would be just inside the door, sitting in the middle of the last row, waiting for me. I gave my ticket to the bored usher, who tore it in half and handed over the stub. I knew exactly what had happened yesterday, just as if I had never forgotten any of it, and my insides began shaking. All the colors of the lobby, the red and the shabby gilt, seemed much brighter than I remembered them. I could smell the popcorn in the case and the oily butter heating in the machine. My legs moved me over a mile of sizzling brown carpet and past the candy counter.
        Jimmy's hair gleamed in the empty, darkening theater. When I took the seat next to him, he ruffled my hair and grinned down and said he had been thinking about me all night and all morning. The package in brown paper was a sandwich for my lunch — a kid had to eat more than popcorn.
        The lights went all the way down as the series of curtains opened over the screen. Loud music, beginning in the middle of a note, suddenly jumped from the

speakers, and the Tom and Jerry cartoon "Bull Dozing" began. When I leaned back, Jimmy put his arm around me. I felt sweaty and cold at the same time, and my insides were still shaking. I suddenly realized that part of me was glad to be in this place, and I shocked myself with the knowledge that all morning I had been looking forward to this moment as much as I had been dreading it.

"You want your sandwich now? It's liver sausage, because that's my personal favorite." I said no, thanks, I'd wait until the first movie was over. Okay, he said, just as long as you eat it. Then he said, Look at me. His face was right above mine, and he looked like Alan Ladd's twin brother. You have to know something, he said. You're the best kid I ever met. Ever. The man squeezed me up against his chest and into a dizzying funk of sweat and dirt and wine, along with a trace (imagined?) of that other, more animal odor that had come from him yesterday. Then he released me.

You want me to play with your little "Jimmy" today?

No.

Too small, anyhow, he said with a laugh. He was in perfect good humor.

Bet you wish it was the same size as mine.

That wish terrified me, and I shook my head.

Today we're just going to watch the movies together, he said. I'm not greedy.

Except for when one of the ushers came up the aisle, we sat like that all day, his arm around my shoulders, the back of my neck resting in the hollow of his elbow. When the credits for *At War with the Army* rolled up the screen, I felt as though I had fallen asleep and missed everything. I couldn't believe that it was time to go home. Jimmy tightened his arm around me and in a voice full of amusement said, *Touch me.* I looked up into his face. Go on, he said, I want you to do that little thing for me. I prodded his fly with my index finger. "Jimmy" wobbled under the pressure of my fingers, seeming as long as my arm, and for a second of absolute wretchedness I saw the other children running up and down the school playground behind the girls from the next block.

"Go on," he said.

Trust me, he said, investing "Jimmy" with an identity more concentrated, more focused, than his own. "Jimmy" wanted "to talk," "to speak his piece," "was hungry," "was dying for a kiss." All these words meant the same thing. *Trust me:* I trust you, so you must trust me. Have I ever hurt you? No. Didn't I give you a sandwich? Yes. Don't I love you? You know I won't tell your parents what you do — as long as you keep coming here, I won't tell your parents anything because I won't *have* to, see? And you love me too, don't you?

There. You see how much I love you?

I dreamed that I lived underground in a wooden room. I dreamed that my parents roamed the upper world, calling out my name and weeping because the animals had captured and eaten me. I dreamed that I was buried beneath a juniper tree, and the cut-off pieces of my body called out to each other and wept because they were separate. I dreamed that I ran down a dark forest path toward my parents, and when I finally reached the small clearing where they sat before a bright fire, my mother was Donna and Alan was my father. I dreamed that I could remember everything that was happening to me, every second of it, and that when the teacher called on me in class, when my mother came into my room at night, when the policeman went past me as I walked down Sherman Boulevard, I had to spill it out. But when I tried to speak, I could not remember what it was that I remembered, *only that there was something to remember,* and so I walked again and again toward my beautiful parents in the clearing, repeating myself like a fable, like the jokes of the women on the ferry.

Don't I love you? Don't I show you, can't you tell, that I love you? *Yes.* Don't you, can't you, love me too?

He stares at me as I stare at the movie. He could see me, the way I could see him, with his eyes closed. He has me memorized. He has stroked my hair, my face, my body into his memory, stroke after stroke, stealing me from myself. Eventually he took me in his mouth and his mouth memorized me too, and I knew he wanted me to place my hands on that dirty-blond head resting so hugely in my lap, but I could not touch his head.

I thought: I have already forgotten this, I want to die, I am dead already, only death can make this not have happened.

When you grow up, I bet you'll be in the movies and I'll be your number-one fan.

By the weekend, those days at the Orpheum-Oriental seemed to have been spent underwater; or underground. The spiny anteater, the lyrebird, the kangaroo, the Tasmanian devil, the nun bat, and the frilled lizard were creatures found only in Australia. Australia was the world's smallest continent, its largest island. It was cut off from the earth's great landmasses. Beautiful girls with blond hair strutted across Australian beaches, and Australian Christmases were hot and sunbaked — everybody went outside and waved at the camera, exchanging presents from lawn chairs. The middle of Australia, its heart and gut, was a desert. Australian boys excelled at sports. Tom Cat loved Jerry Mouse, though he plotted again and again to murder him, and Jerry Mouse loved Tom Cat, though to save his life he had to run so fast, he burned a track through the carpet. Jimmy loved me and he would be gone someday, and then I would miss him a lot. Wouldn't I? *Say you'll miss me.*

I'll —

I'll miss —

I think I'd go crazy without you.

When you're all grown-up, will you remember me?

Each time I walked back out past the usher, who stood tearing in half the tickets of the people just entering, handing them the stubs, every time I pushed open the door and walked out onto the heat-filled sidewalk of Sherman Boulevard and saw the sun on the buildings across the street, I lost my hold on what had happened inside the darkness of the theater. I didn't know what I wanted. I had two murders and a… My right hand felt as though I had been holding a smaller child's sticky hand very tightly between my palm and fingers. If I lived in Australia, I would have blond hair like Alan Ladd and run forever across tan beaches on Christmas Day.

I walked through high school in my sleep, reading novels, daydreaming in classes I did not like but earning spuriously good grades; in the middle of my senior year Brown University gave me a full scholarship. Two years later I amazed and disappointed all my old teachers and my parents and my parents' friends by dropping out of school shortly before I would have failed all my courses but English and history, in which I was getting A's. I was certain that no one could teach anyone else how to write. I knew exactly what I was going to do, and all I would miss of college was the social life.

For five years I lived inexpensively in Providence, supporting myself by stacking books in the school library and by petty thievery. I wrote when I was not working or listening to the local bands; then I destroyed what I had written and wrote it again. In this way I saw myself to the end of a novel, like walking through a park one way and then walking backward and forward through the same park, over and over, until every nick on every swing, every tawny hair on every lion's hide, had been witnessed and made to gleam or allowed to sink back into the importunate field of details from which it had been lifted. When this novel was rejected by the publisher to whom I sent it, I moved to New York City and began another novel while I rewrote the first all over again at night. During this period an almost impersonal happiness, like the happiness of a stranger, lay beneath everything I did. I wrapped parcels of books at the Strand Book Store. For a short time, no more than a few months, I lived on shredded wheat and peanut butter. When my first book was accepted, I moved from a single room on the Lower East Side into another, larger single room, a "studio apartment," on Ninth Avenue in Chelsea, where I continue to live. My apartment is just large enough for my wooden desk, a convertible couch, two large crowded bookshelves, a shelf of stereo equipment, and dozens of cardboard boxes of records. In this apartment everything has its place and is in it.

My parents have never been to this enclosed, tidy space, though I speak to my father on the phone every two or three months. In the past ten years I have returned to the city where I grew up only once, to visit my mother in the hospital after her stroke. During the four days I stayed in my father's house I slept in my old room; my father slept upstairs. After the blind man's death my father bought the duplex — on my first night home he told me that we were both successes. Now when we speak on the telephone he tells me of the fortunes of the local baseball and basketball teams and respectfully inquires about my progress on "the new book." I think: This is not my father, he is not the same man.

My old cot disappeared long ago, and late at night I lay on the twins' double bed. Like the house as a whole, like everything in my old neighborhood, the bedroom was larger than I remembered it. I brushed the wallpaper with my fingers, then looked up to the ceiling. The image of two men tangled up in the ropes of the same parachute, comically berating each other as they fell, came to me, and I wondered if the image had a place in the novel I was writing, or if it was a gift from the as yet unseen novel that would follow it. I could hear the floor creak as my father paced upstairs in the blind man's former territory. My inner weather changed, and I began brooding about Mei-Mei Levitt, whom fifteen years earlier at Brown I had known as Mei-Mei Cheung.

Divorced, an editor at a paperback firm, she had called to congratulate me after my second novel was favorably reviewed in the *Times,* and on this slim but well-intentioned foundation we began to construct a long and troubled love affair. Back in the surroundings of my childhood, I felt profoundly uneasy, having spent the day beside my mother's hospital bed without knowing if she understood or even recognized me, and I thought of Mei-Mei with sudden longing. I wanted her in my arms, and I yearned for my purposeful, orderly, dreaming, adult life in New York. I wanted to call Mei-Mei, but it was past midnight in the Midwest, an hour later in New York, and Mei-Mei, no owl, would have gone to bed hours earlier. Then I remembered my mother lying stricken in the narrow hospital bed, and suffered a spasm of guilt for thinking about my lover. For a deluded moment I imagined that it was my duty to move back into the house and see if I could bring my mother back to life while I did what I could for my retired father. At that moment I remembered, as I often did, an orange-haired boy enveloped in a red wool shirt. Sweat poured from my forehead, my chest.

Then a terrifying thing happened to me. I tried to get out of bed to go to the bathroom and found that I could not move. My arms and legs were cast in cement; they were lifeless and *would not move.* I thought that I was having a stroke, like my mother. I could not even cry out — my throat, too, was paralyzed. I strained to push myself up off the double bed and smelled that someone very near, someone just out of sight or around the corner, was making popcorn and heating butter. Another wave of sweat gouted out of my inert body, turning the sheet and the pillowcase slick and cold.

I saw — as if I were writing it — my seven-year-old self hesitating before the entrance of a theater a few blocks from this house. Hot, flat, yellow sunlight fell over everything, cooking the life from the wide boulevard. I saw myself turn away, felt my stomach churn with the smoke of underground fires, saw myself begin to run. Vomit backed up in my throat. My arms and legs convulsed, and I fell out of bed and managed to crawl out of the room and down the hall to throw up in the toilet behind the closed door of the bathroom.

My age, as I write these words, is forty-three. I have written five novels over a period of nearly twenty years, "only" five, each of them more difficult, harder to write than the one before. To maintain this hobbled pace of a novel every four years, I must sit at my desk at least six hours every day; I must consume hundreds of boxes of typing paper, scores of yellow legal pads, forests of pencils, miles of black ribbon. It is a fierce, voracious activity. Every sentence must be tested three or four ways, made to clear fences like a horse. The purpose of every sentence is to be an arrow into the secret center of the book. To find my way into the secret center I must hold the entire book, every detail and rhythm, in my memory. This comprehensive act of memory is the most crucial task of my life.

My books get flattering reviews, which usually seem to describe other, more linear novels, and they win occasional awards — I am one of those writers whose advances are funded by the torrents of money spun off by best-sellers. Lately I have had the impression that the general perception of me, to the extent that such a thing exists, is that of a hermetic painter inscribing hundreds of tiny, grotesque, fantastical details over every inch of a large canvas. (My books are unfashionably long.) I teach writing at various colleges, give occasional lectures, am modestly enriched by grants. This is enough, more than enough. Now and then I am both dismayed and amused to discover that a young writer I have met at a PEN reception or a workshop regards my life with envy. Envy misses the point completely.

"If you were going to give me one piece of advice," a young woman at a conference asked me, "I mean, *real* advice, not just the obvious stuff about keeping on writing, what would it be? What would you tell me to do?"

I won't tell you, but I'll write it out, I said, and picked up one of the conference flyers and printed a few words on its back. Don't read this until you are out of the room, I said, and watched while she folded the flyer into her bag.

What I had printed on the back of the flyer was: Go to a lot of movies.

On the Sunday after the ferry trip I could not hit a single ball in the park. My eyes kept closing, and as soon as my eyelids came down, visions started up like movies — quick, automatic dreams. My arms seemed too heavy to lift. After I had trudged home behind my dispirited father, I collapsed on the sofa and slept straight through to dinner. In a dream a spacious box confined me, and I drew colored pictures of elm trees, the sun, wide fields, mountains, and rivers on its walls. At dinner loud noises, never scarce around the twins, made me jump. That kid's not right, I swear to you, my father said. When my mother asked if I wanted to go to Play School on Monday, my stomach closed up like a fist. I have to, I said, I'm really fine, I have to go. Sentences rolled from my mouth, meaning nothing, or meaning the wrong thing. For a moment of confusion I thought that I really was going to the playground, and saw black asphalt, deep as a field, where a few children, diminished by perspective, clustered at the far end. I went to bed right after dinner. My mother pulled down the shades, turned off the light, and finally left me alone. From above came the sound, like a beast's approximation of music, of random notes struck on a piano. I knew only that I was scared, not why. The next day I had to go to a certain place, but I could not think where until my fingers recalled the velvety plush of the end seat on the middle aisle. Then black-and-white images, full of intentional menace, came to me from the previews I had seen for two weeks — *The Hitch-Hiker,* starring Edmund O'Brien. The spiny anteater and nun bat were animals found only in Australia.

I longed for Alan Ladd, "Ed Adams," to walk into the room with his reporter's notebook and pencil, and knew that I had *something to remember* without knowing what it was.

After a long time the twins cascaded into the bedroom, undressed, put on pajamas, brushed their teeth. The front door slammed — my father had gone out to the taverns. In the kitchen, my mother ironed shirts and talked to herself in a familiar, rancorous voice. The twins went to sleep. I heard my mother put away the ironing board and walk down the hall to the living room.

I saw "Ed Adams" calmly walking up and down on the sidewalk outside our house, as handsome as a god in his neat gray suit. "Ed" went all the way to the end of the block, put a cigarette in his mouth, and leaned into a sudden, round flare of brightness before exhaling smoke and walking away. I knew I had fallen asleep only when the front door slammed for the second time that night and woke me up.

In the morning my father struck his fist against the bedroom door and the twins jumped out of bed and began yelling around the bedroom, instantly filled with energy. As in a cartoon, into the bedroom drifted tendrils of the odor of frying bacon. My brothers jostled toward the bathroom. Water rushed into the sink and the toilet bowl, and my mother hurried in, her face tightened down over her cigarette, and began yanking the twins into their clothes. "You made your decision," she said to me, "now I hope you're going to make it to the playground on time." Doors opened, doors slammed shut. My father shouted from the kitchen, and I got out of bed. Eventually I sat down before the bowl of cereal. My father smoked and did not meet my eyes. The cereal tasted of dead leaves. "You look the way that asshole upstairs plays piano," my father said. He dropped quarters on the table and told me not to lose that money.

After he left, I locked myself in the bedroom. The piano dully resounded overhead like a sound track. I heard the cups and dishes rattle in the sink, the furniture moving by itself, looking for something to hunt down and kill. *Love me, love me,* the radio called from beside a family of brown-and-white porcelain spaniels. I heard some light, whispery thing, a lamp or a magazine, begin to slide around the living room. *I am imagining all this,* I said to myself, and tried to concentrate on a *Blackhawk* comic book. The pictures jigged and melted in their panels. *Love me,* Blackhawk cried out from the cockpit of his fighter as he swooped down to exterminate a nest of yellow, slant-eyed villains. Outside, fire raged beneath the streets, trying to pull the world apart. When I dropped the comic book and closed my eyes, the noises ceased and I could hear the hovering stillness of perfect attention. Even Blackhawk, belted into his airplane within the comic book, was listening to what I was doing.

In thick, hazy sunlight I went down Sherman Boulevard toward the Orpheum-Oriental. Around me the world was motionless, frozen like a frame in a comic strip. After a time I noticed that the cars on the boulevard and the few people on the sidewalk had not actually frozen into place but instead were moving with great slowness. I could see men's legs advancing within their trousers, the knee coming forward to strike the crease, the cuff slowly lifting off the shoe, the shoe drifting up like Tom Cat's paw when he crept toward Jerry Mouse. The warm, patched skin of Sherman Boulevard... I thought of walking along Sherman Boulevard forever, moving past the nearly immobile cars and people, past the theater, past the liquor store, through the gates and past the wading pool and swings, past the elephants and lions reaching out to be fed, past the secret park where my father flailed in a rage of disappointment, past the elms and out the opposite gate, past the big houses on the opposite side of the park, past picture windows and past lawns with bikes and plastic pools, past slanting driveways and basketball hoops, past men getting out of cars, past playgrounds where children raced back and forth on a surface shining black. Then past fields and crowded markets, past high yellow tractors with mud dried like old wool inside the enormous hubs, past eloquent cats and fearful lions on wagons piled high with hay, past deep woods where lost children followed trails of bread crumbs to a gingerbread door, past other cities where nobody would see me because nobody knew my name, past everything, past everybody.

At the Orpheum-Oriental, I stopped still. My mouth was dry and my eyes would not focus. Everything around me, so quiet and still a moment earlier, jumped into life as soon as I stopped walking. Horns blared, cars roared down the boulevard. Beneath these sounds I heard the pounding of great machines, and the fires gobbling up oxygen beneath the street. As if I had eaten them from the air, fire and smoke poured into my stomach. Flame slipped up my throat and sealed the back of my mouth. In my mind I saw myself taking the first quarter from my pocket, exchanging it for a ticket, pushing through the door, and moving into the cool air. I saw myself holding out the ticket to be torn in half, going over an endless brown carpet toward the inner door. From the last row of seats on the other side of the inner door, inside the shadowy but not yet dark theater, a shapeless monster whose wet black mouth said *Love me, love me* stretched yearning arms toward me. Shock froze my shoes to the sidewalk, then shoved me firmly in the small of the back, and I was running down the block, unable to scream because I had to clamp my lips against the smoke and fire trying to explode from my mouth.

The rest of that afternoon remains vague. I wandered through the streets, not in the clean, hollow way I had imagined but almost blindly, hot and uncertain. I remember the taste of fire in my mouth and the loudness of my heart. After a time I found myself before the elephant enclosure in the zoo. A newspaper reporter in a neat gray suit passed through the space before me, and I followed him, knowing that he carried a notebook in his pocket, and that he had been beaten by gangsters, that he could locate the speaking secret that hid beneath the disconnected and dismembered pieces of the world. He would fire his pistol on an empty chamber and trick evil "Solly Wellman," Berry Kroeger, with his girlish, watchful eyes. And when "Solly Wellman" came gloating out of the shadow, the reporter would shoot him dead.

Dead.

Donna Reed smiled down from an upstairs window: Has there ever been a smile like that? Ever? I was in Chicago, and behind a closed door "Blacky Franchot" bled onto a brown carpet. "Solly Wellman," something like "Solly

Wellman," called and called to me from the decorated grave where he lay like a secret. The man in the gray suit finally carried his notebook and his gun through a front door, and I saw that I was only a few blocks from home.

Paul leans against the wire fence surrounding the playground, looking out, looking backward. Alan Ladd brushes off "Leona," for she has no history that matters and exists only in the world of work and pleasure, of cigarettes and cocktail bars. Beneath this world is another, and "Leona's" life is a blind, strenuous denial of that other world.

My mother held her hand to my forehead and declared that I not only had a fever but had been building up to it all week. I was not to go to the playground that next day; I had to spend the day lying down on Mrs. Candee's couch. When she lifted the telephone to call one of the high-school girls, I said not to bother, other kids were gone all the time, and she put down the receiver.

I lay on Mrs. Candee's couch staring up at the ceiling of her darkened living room. The twins squabbled outside, and maternal, slow-witted Mrs. Candee brought me orange juice. The twins ran toward the sandbox, and Mrs. Candee groaned as she let herself fall into a wobbly lawn chair. The morning newspaper folded beneath the lawn chair said that *The Hitch-Hiker* and *Double Cross* had begun playing at the Orpheum-Oriental. *Chicago Deadline* had done its work and traveled on. It had broken the world in half and sealed the monster deep within. Nobody but me knew this. Up and down the block, sprinklers whirred, whipping loops of water onto the dry lawns. Men driving slowly up and down the street hung their elbows out of their windows. For a moment free of regret and nearly without emotion of any kind, I understood that I belonged utterly to myself. Like everything else, I had been torn asunder and glued back together with shock, vomit, and orange juice. The knowledge sifted into me that I was all alone. "Stan," "Jimmy," whatever his name was, would never come back to the theater. He would be afraid that I had told my parents and the police about him. I knew that I had killed him by forgetting him, and then I forgot him again.

The next day I went back to the theater and went through the inner door and saw row after row of empty seats falling toward the curtained screen. I was all alone. The size and grandeur of the theater surprised me. I went down the long, descending aisle and took the last seat, left side, on the broad middle aisle. The next row seemed nearly a playground's distance away. The lights dimmed and the curtains rippled slowly away from the screen. Anticipatory music filled the air, and the first letters appeared on the screen.

What I am, what I do, why I do it. I am simultaneously a man in his early forties, that treacherous time, and a boy of seven before whose bravery I shall forever fall short. I live underground in a wooden room and patiently, in joyful concentration, decorate the walls. Before me, half unseen, hangs a large and appallingly complicated vision I must explore and memorize, must witness again and again in order to locate its hidden center. Around me, everything is in its proper place. My typewriter sits on the sturdy table. Beside the typewriter a cigarette smolders, raising a gray stream of smoke. A record revolves on the turntable, and my small apartment is dense with music. ("Bird of Prey Blues," with Coleman Hawkins, Buck Clayton, and Hank Jones.) Beyond my walls and windows is a world toward which I reach with outstretched arms and an ambitious and divided heart. As if "Bird of Prey Blues" has evoked them, the voices of sentences to be written this afternoon, tomorrow, or next month stir and whisper, beginning to speak, and I lean over the typewriter toward them, getting as close as I can.

Dan Simmons has published twenty-four books since 1985, twenty-one of them novels — including the World Fantasy Award-winning *Song of Kali* and the 2007 *New York Times* bestseller *The Terror*. His most recently published novel is *Drood*, a tale of the last five years of Charles Dickens's life.

I've been following Dan Simmons's career since I bought and published his story "Eyes I Dare Not Meet in Dreams" in *OMNI*. It was his second published story. His first, "The River Styx Runs Upstream," won the *Twilight Zone Magazine* award for first story. I also published "Carrion Comfort," the novelette subsequently expanded into a novel, and continued to publish stories and novellas by Dan in *OMNI* and then in *OMNI* online.

"Two Minutes, Forty-Five Seconds" was commissioned by me for a grouping of horror short shorts published in 1988. It remains one of my favorites of Dan's stories, for its terrifying, believable horror and its economy at creating it.

Two Minutes Forty-Five Seconds
Dan Simmons

ROGER COLVIN CLOSED his eyes, and the steel bar clamped down across his lap, and they began the steep climb. He could hear the rattle of the heavy chain and the creak of steel wheels on steel rails as they clanked up the first hill of the roller coaster. Someone behind him laughed nervously. Terrified of heights, heart pounding painfully against his ribs, Colvin peeked out from between spread fingers.

The metal rails and white wooden frame rose steeply ahead of him. Colvin was in the first car. He lowered both hands and tightly gripped the metal restraining bar. Someone giggled in the car behind him. He turned his head only far enough to peer over the side of the rails.

They were very high and still rising. The midway and parking lots grew smaller, individuals growing too tiny to be seen and the crowds becoming mere carpets of color, fading into a larger mosaic of geometries of streets and lights as the entire city became visible, then the entire county. They clanked higher. The sky darkened to a deeper blue. Colvin could see the curve of the earth in the haze-blued distance. He realized that they were far out over the edge of a lake now as he caught the glimmer of light on wave tops miles below through the wooden ties. Colvin closed his eyes as they briefly passed through the cold breath of a cloud, then snapped them open again as the pitch of chain rumble changed as the steep gradient lessened, as they reached the top.

And went over.

There was nothing beyond. The two rails curved out and down and ended in air.

Colvin gripped the restraining bar as the car pitched forward and over. He opened his mouth to scream. The fall began.

"Hey, the worst part's over." Colvin opened his eyes to see Bill Montgomery handing him a drink. The sound of the Gulfstream's jet engines was a dull rumble under the gentle hissing of air from the overhead ventilator nozzle. Colvin took the drink, turned down the flow of air, and glanced out the window. Logan International was already out of sight behind them, and Colvin could make out Nantasket Beach below, a score of small white triangles of sail in the expanse of bay and ocean beyond. They were still climbing.

"Damn, we're glad you decided to come with us this time, Roger," Montgomery said to Colvin. "It's good having the whole team together again. Like the old days." Montgomery smiled. The three other men in the cabin raised their glasses. Colvin played with the calculator in his lap and sipped his vodka. He took a breath and closed his eyes. Afraid of heights. *Always* afraid. Six years old and in the barn, tumbling from the loft, the fall seemingly endless, time stretching out, the sharp tines of the pitchfork rising toward him. Landing, wind knocked out of him, cheek and right eye against the straw, three inches from the steel points of the pitchfork.

"The company's ready to see better days," said Larry Miller. "Two and a half years of bad press is certainly enough. It will be good to see the launch tomorrow. Get things started again."

"Hear, hear," said Tom Weiscott. It was not yet noon but Tom had already had too much to drink.

Colvin opened his eyes and smiled. Counting himself, there were four corporate vice presidents in the plane. Weiscott was still a project manager. Colvin put his cheek to the window and watched Cape Cod Bay pass below. He guessed their altitude to be eleven or twelve thousand feet and climbing.

Colvin imagined a building nine miles high. From the hall of the top floor he would step into the elevator. The floor of the elevator would be made of glass. The elevator shaft drops away forty-six hundred floors beneath him, each floor marked with halogen lights, the parallel lights drawing closer in the nine miles of black air beneath him until they merged in a blur below.

He would look up in time to see the cable snap, separate. He falls, clutching futilely at the inside walls of the elevator, walls which have grown as slippery as the clear-glass floor. Lights rush by, but already the concrete floor of the shaft is visible miles below — a tiny blue concrete square, growing as the elevator car plummets. He knows that he has almost three minutes to watch that blue square come closer, rise up to smash him. Colvin screams, and the spittle floats in the air in front of him, falling at the same velocity, hanging there. The lights rush past. The blue square grows.

Colvin took a drink, placed the glass in the circle set in the wide arm of his chair, and tapped away at his calculator.

Falling objects in a gravity field follow precise mathematical rules, as precise as the force vectors and burn rates in the shaped charges and solid fuels Colvin had designed for twenty years, but just as oxygen affects combustion rates, so air controls the speed of a falling body. Terminal velocity depends upon atmospheric pressure, mass distribution, and surface area as much as upon gravity.

Colvin lowered his eyelids as if to doze, and saw what he saw every night when he pretended to sleep: the billowing white cloud, expanding outward like a time-lapse film of a slanting, tilting stratocumulus blossoming against a dark blue sky; the reddish-brown interior of nitrogen tetroxide flame; and — just visible below the two emerging, mindless contrails of the SRBs — the tumbling, fuzzy square of the forward fuselage, flight deck included. Even the most amplified images had not shown him the closer details — the intact pressure vessel that was the crew compartment, scorched on the right side where the runaway SRB had played its flame upon it, tumbling, falling free, trailing wires and cables and shreds of fuselage behind it like an umbilical and afterbirth. The earlier images had not shown these details, but Colvin had seen them, touched them, after the fracturing impact with the merciless blue sea. There were layers of tiny barnacles growing on the ruptured skin. Colvin imagined the darkness and cold waiting at the end of that fall, small fish feeding.

"Roger," said Steve Cahill, "where'd you get your fear of flying?"

Colvin shrugged, finished his vodka. "I don't know."

In Vietnam — not "Nam" or "in-country" — a place Colvin still wanted to think of as a place rather than a condition, he had flown. Already an expert on shaped charges and propellants. Colvin was being flown out to Bong Son Valley near the coast to see why a shipment of standard C-4 plastic explosives was not detonating for an ARVN unit when the Jesus nut came off their Huey, and the helicopter fell, rotorless, two hundred eighty feet into the jungle, tore through almost a hundred feet of thick vegetation, and came to a stop, upside down, in vines ten feet above the ground. The pilot had been neatly impaled by a limb that smashed up through the floor of the Huey. The copilot's skull had smashed through the windshield. The gunner was thrown out, breaking his neck and back, and died the next day. Colvin walked away with a sprained ankle.

Colvin looked down as they crossed Nantucket. He estimated their altitude at eighteen thousand feet and climbing steadily. Their cruising altitude, he knew, was to be thirty-two thousand feet. Much lower than forty-six thousand, especially lacking the vertical thrust vector, but so much depended upon surface area.

When Colvin was a boy in the 1950s, he saw a photograph in the "old" *National Enquirer* of a woman who had jumped off the Empire State Building and landed on the roof of a car. Her legs were crossed almost casually at the ankles; there was a hole in the toe of one of her nylon stockings. The roof of the car was flattened, folded inward, almost like a large goose-down mattress, molding itself to the weight of a sleeping person. The woman's head looked as if it were sunk deep in a soft pillow.

Colvin tapped at his calculator. A woman stepping off the Empire State Building would fall for almost fourteen seconds before hitting the street. Someone falling in a metal box from forty-six thousand feet would fall for two minutes and forty-five seconds before hitting the water. What did she think about? What did *they* think about?

Most popular songs and rock videos are about three minutes long, thought Colvin. It is a good length of time: not so long one gets bored, long enough to tell a story.

"We're damned glad you're with us," Bill Montgomery said again.

"God damn it," Bill Montgomery had whispered to Colvin outside the teleconference room twenty-seven months earlier. "Are you with us or against us on this?"

A teleconference was much like a séance. The group sat in semidarkened rooms hundreds or thousands of miles apart and communed with voices which came from nowhere.

"Well, that's the weather situation here," came the voice from KSC. "What's it to be?"

"We've seen your telefaxed stuff," said the voice from Marshall, "but still don't understand why we should consider scrubbing based on an anomaly that small. You assured us that this stuff was so fail-safe that you could kick it around the block if you wanted to."

Phil McGuire, the chief engineer on Colvin's project team, squirmed in his seat and spoke too loudly. The teleconference phones had speakers by each chair and could pick up the softest tones. "You *don't* understand, do you?"

McGuire almost shouted. "It's the *combination* of cold temperatures and the likelihood of electrical activity in that cloud layer that causes the problems. In the past five flights there've been three transient events in the leads that run from SRB linear-shaped charges to the Range Safety command antennas."

"Transient events," said the voice from KSC, "but they are within flight certification parameters?"

"Well...yes," said McGuire. He sounded close to tears. "But it's within parameters because we keep signing waivers and rewriting the goddamn parameters. We just don't *know* why the C-12B shaped range safety charges on the SRBs and ET record a transient current flow when no enable functions have been transmitted. Roger thinks that maybe the LSC enable leads or the C-12 compound itself can accidentally allow the static discharge to simulate a command signal.... Oh, hell, *tell* them, Roger."

"Mr. Colvin?"

Colvin cleared his throat. "We've been watching that for some time. Preliminary data suggests temperatures below twenty-eight degrees Fahrenheit allow the zinc oxide residue in the C-12B stacks to conduct a false signal...if there's enough static discharge...theoretically..."

"But no solid database on this yet?" said the voice from Marshall.

"No," said Colvin.

"And you did sign the Criticality One waiver certifying flight readiness on the last three flights?"

"Yes," said Colvin.

"Well," said the voice from KSC, "we've heard from the engineers at Beunet-HCS. What do you say we have recommendations from management there?"

Bill Montgomery had called a five-minute break, and the management team met in the hall. "God damn it, Roger, are you with us or against us on this one?"

Colvin had looked away.

"I'm serious," snapped Montgomery. "The LCS division has brought this company two hundred and fifteen million dollars in *profit* this year, and your work has been an important part of that success, Roger. Now you seem ready to flush that away on some goddamn transient telemetry readings that don't mean *anything* when compared to the work we've done as a team. There's a vice presidency opening in a few months, Roger. Don't screw your chances by losing your head like that hysteric McGuire."

"Ready?" said the voice from KSC when five minutes had passed.

"Go," said Vice President Montgomery.

"Go," said Vice President Miller.

"Go," said Vice President Cahill.

"Go," said Project Manager Weiscott.

"Go," said Project Manager Colvin.

"Fine," said KSC. "I'll pass along the recommendation. Sorry you gentlemen won't be here to watch the lift-off tomorrow."

Colvin turned his head as Bill Montgomery called from his side of the cabin. "Hey, I think I see Long Island."

"Bill," said Colvin, "approximately how much did the company make this year on the C-12B redesign?"

Montgomery took a drink and stretched his legs in the roomy interior of the Gulfstream. "About four hundred million, I think, Rog. Why?"

"And did the agency ever seriously consider going to someone else after... after?"

"Shit," said Tom Weiscott, "where else could they go? We got them by the short hairs. They thought about it for a few months and then came crawling back. You know you're the best designer of shaped range safety devices and solid hypergolics in the country, Rog."

Colvin nodded, worked with his calculator a minute and closed his eyes. The steel bar clamped down across his lap, and the car he rode in clanked higher and higher. The air grew thin and cold, the screech of wheel on rail dwindling into a thin scream as the roller coaster lumbered above the six-mile mark.

In case of loss of cabin pressure, oxygen masks will descend from the ceiling. Please fasten them securely over your mouth and nose and breathe normally.

Colvin peeked ahead, up the terrible incline of the roller coaster, sensing the summit of the climb ahead and the emptiness beyond that point.

The tiny air-tank-and-mask combinations were called PEAPs — Personal Egress Air Packs. PEAPs from four of the five crew members were recovered from the ocean bottom. All had been activated. Two minutes and forty-five seconds of each five-minute air supply had been used up.

Colvin watched the summit of the roller coaster's first hill arrive.

There was a raw metallic noise and a lurch as the roller coaster went over the top and off the rails. People in the cars behind Colvin screamed and kept on screaming.

Colvin lurched forward and grabbed the restraining bar as the roller coaster plummeted into nine miles of nothingness. He opened his eyes. A single glimpse out the Gulfstream window told him that the thin lines of shaped charge he had placed there had removed all of the port wing cleanly, surgically. The tumble rate suggested that enough of a stub of the starboard wing was left to provide the surface area needed to keep the terminal velocity a little lower than maximum. Two minutes and forty-five seconds, plus or minus four seconds.

Colvin reached for his calculator, but it had flown free in the cabin, colliding with hurtling bottles, glasses, cushions, and bodies that had not been securely strapped in. The screaming was very loud.

Two minutes and forty-five seconds. Time to think of many things. And perhaps, just perhaps, after two and a half years of no sleep without dreams, perhaps it would be time enough for a short nap with no dreams at all. Colvin closed his eyes.

Pat Cadigan has twice won the Arthur C. Clarke Award, for her novels *Synners* and *Fools*, and has been nominated for just about every other science fiction and fantasy award. Although primarily known as a science fiction writer (and as one of the original — and only female — cyberpunks), she also writes fantasy and horror, which can be found in her collections *Patterns*, *Dirty Work*, and *Home by the Sea*. The author of fifteen books, including two nonfiction titles and one young adult novel, she currently has two new novels in progress.

"The Power and the Passion" is one of my favorite Cadigan stories. In it, she manages to merge two major tropes of horror and creates a disturbing yet fascinating point-of-view character.

The Power and the Passion
Pat Cadigan

THE VOICE ON the phone says, "We need to talk to you, Mr. Soames," so I know to pick the place up. Company coming. I don't like for company to come into no pigsty, but one of the reasons the place is such a mess all the time is, it's so small, I got nowhere to keep shit except around, you know. But I shove both the dirty laundry and the dirty dishes in the oven — my mattress is right on the floor so I can't shove stuff under the bed, and what won't fit in the oven I put in the tub and just before I pull the curtain, I think, well, shit, I shoulda just put it all in the tub and filled it and got it all washed at once. Or, well, just the dishes, because I can take the clothes over to the laundromat easier than washing them in the tub.

So, hell, I just pull the shower curtain, stack the newspapers and the magazines — newspapers on top of the magazines, because most people don't take too well to my taste in magazines, and they wouldn't like a lot of the newspapers much either, but I got the Sunday paper to stick on top and hide it all, so it's okay. Company'll damned well know what's under those Sunday funnies because they know *me*, but as long as they don't have to have it staring them in the face, it's like they can pretend it don't exist.

I'm still puttering and fussing around when the knock on the door comes and I'm crossing the room (the only room unless you count the bathroom, which I do when I'm in it) when it comes to me I ain't done dick about myself. I'm still in my undershirt and shorts, for chrissakes.

"Hold on," I call out, "I ain't decent, quite," and I drag a pair of pants outa the closet. But all my shirts are either in the oven or the tub and company'll get fanny-antsy standing in the hall — this is not the watchamacallit, the place where Lennon bought it, the Dakota, yeah. Anyway, I answer the door in my one hundred percent cotton undershirt, but at least I got my fly zipped.

Company's a little different this time. The two guys as usual, but today they got a woman with them. Not a broad, not a bitch, not a bimbo. She's standing between and a little behind them, looking at me the way women always look at me when I happen to cross their path — chin lifted up a little, one hand holding her coat together at the neck in a fist, eyes real cold, like, "Touch me and die horribly, I wish," standing straight fuckin' up, like they're Superman, and the fear coming off them like heat waves from an open furnace.

They all come in and stand around and I wish I'd straightened the sheets out on the mattress so it wouldn't look so messy, but then they'd see the sheets ain't clean, so six of one, you know. And I got nothing for anyone to sit on, except that mattress, so they just keep standing around.

The one guy, Steener, says, "Are you feeling all right, Mr. Soames?" looking around like there's puke and snot all over the floor. Steener don't bother me. He's a pretty man who probably was a pretty boy and a pretty baby before that, and thinks the world oughta be a pretty place. Or he wants to prove pretty guys are really tougher and better and more man than guys like me, because he's afraid it's vice versa, you know. Maybe even both, depending on how he got up this morning.

The other guy, Villanueva, I could almost respect him. He didn't put on no face to look at me, and he didn't have no power fantasies about who he was to me or vice versa. I think Villanueva probably knows me better than anyone in the world. But then, he was the one took my statement when they caught up with me. He was a cop then. If he'd still been a cop, I'd probably respect him.

So I look right at the woman and I say, "So, what's this, you brought me a date?" I know this will get them because they know what I do to dates.

"You speak when spoken to, Mr. Soames," Steener says, kinda barking like a dog that wishes it were bigger.

"You spoke to me," I point out.

Villanueva takes a few steps in the direction of the bathroom — he knows what I got in there and how I don't want company to see it, so this is supposed to distract me, and it does a little. The woman steps back, clutching her light coat tighter around her throat, not sure who to hide behind. Villanueva's the better bet, but she doesn't want to get any further into my stinky little apartment, so she edges toward Steener.

And it comes to me in a two-second flash-movie just how to do it. Steener'd be easy to take out. He's a rusher, don't know dick about fighting. He'd just go for me and I'd just whip my hand up between his arms and crunch goes the windpipe. Villanueva'd be trouble, but I'd probably end up doing him, too.

Villanueva's smart enough to know that. First, though, I'd bop the woman, just bop her to keep her right there — punch in the stomach does it for most people, man or woman — and then I'd do Villanueva, break his neck.

Then the woman. I'd do it all, pound one end, pound the other, switching off before either one of us got too used to one thing or the other. Most people, man or woman, blank out about then. Can't face it, you know, so after that, it's free-for-fuckin'-all. You can do just any old thing you want to a person in shock, they just don't believe it's happening by then. This one I would rip up sloppy, I would send her to hell and then kill her. I can see how it would look, the way her body would be moving, how her flesh would jounce flabby —

But I won't. I can't look at a woman without the flash-movie kicking in, but it's only a movie, you know. This is company, they got something else for me.

"Do you feel like working?" Villanueva asks. He's caught it just now, what I was thinking about, he knows, because I told him how it was when I gave him my statement after I got caught.

"Sure," I say, "what else have I got to do?"

He nods to Steener, who passes me a little slip of paper. The name and address. "It's nothing you haven't done before," he says. "There are two of them. You do as you like, but you *must* follow the procedure as it has been described to you —"

I give a great big nod. "I know how to do it. I've studied on it, got it all right up here." I tap my head. "Second nature to me now."

"I don't want to hear the word 'nature' out of *you,*" Steener sneers. "You've got nothing to do with nature."

"That's right," I agree. I'm mild mannered because it's just come to me what is Steener's problem here. It is that he is like me. He enjoys doing to me what he does the way I enjoy doing what I do, and the fact that he's wearing a white hat and I'm not is just a watchamacallit, a technicality. Deep down at heart, it's the same fuckin' feeling and he's going between loving it and refusing to admit he's like me, boing-boing, boing-boing. And if he ever gets stuck on the loving-it side, well, son of a bitch will there be trouble.

I look over at Villaneuva and point at the woman, raising my eyebrows. I don't know exactly what words to use for a question about her and anything I say is gonna upset everybody.

"This person is with us as an observer," Villanueva says quietly, which means I can just mind my own fuckin' business and don't ask questions unless it's about the job. I look back at the woman and she looks me right in the face. The hand clenched high up on her coat relaxes just a little and I see the purple-black bruises on the side of her neck before she clutches up again real fast. She's still holding herself the same way, but it's like she spoke to me. The lines of communication, like the shrinks say, are open, which is not the safest thing to do with me. She's gotta be a nurse or a teacher or a social worker, I think, because those are the ones that can't help opening up to someone. It's what they're trained to do, reach out. Or hell, maybe she's just somebody's mother. She don't look too motherly, but that don't mean dick these days.

"When?" I say to Steener.

"As soon as you can pack your stuff and get to the airport. There's a cab downstairs and your ticket is waiting at the airline counter, in your name."

"You mean the Soames name," I say, because Soames is not my name for real.

"Just get ready, get going, get it done, and get back here," Steener says. "No side trips, or it's finished. Don't even *attempt* a side trip or it's finished." He starts to turn toward the door and then stops. "And you know that if you're caught in or after the act —"

"Yeah, yeah, I'm on my own and you don't know dick about squat, and nobody ever hearda me, case closed." I keep myself from smiling; he watched too much *Mission Impossible* when he was a kid. Like everyone else in his outfit. I think it's where they got the idea, kind of, some of it anyway.

Villanueva tosses me a fat roll of bills in a rubber band just as he's following Steener and the woman out the door. "Expenses," he says. "You have a rental car on the other end, which you'll have to use cash for. You can only carry cash, so don't get mugged and robbed. You know the drill."

"Drill?" I say, acting perked up, like I'm thinking, *Wow, what a good idea.*

Villanueva refuses to turn green for me, but he shuts the door behind him a little too hard.

I don't waste no time; I go to the closet and pull out my traveling bag. Everything's in it, but I always take a little inventory anyway, just to be on the safe side. Helluva thing to come up empty handed at the wrong moment, you know. Really, though, I just like to handle the stuff: hacksaw, mallet, boning blade, iodized salt, lighter fluid, matches, spray bottle of holy water, four pieces of wood pointed sharp on one end, half a dozen rosaries, all blessed, and two full place settings of silverware, not stainless, mind you, but real silver. And the shirts I don't never put in the tub. What do they make of this at airport security? Not a fuckin' thing. Ain't no gun. Guns don't work for this. Anyway, this bag's always checked.

The flight is fine. It's always fine because they always put me in first class and nobody next to me if possible. On the night flights, it's generally possible and tonight, I have the whole first-class section to myself, hot and cold running stews, who are (I can tell) forcing themselves to be nice to me. I don't know what it is, and I don't mind it, but it makes me wonder all the same: Is it a smell, or just the way my eyes look? Villanueva told me once, it's just something about me gives everyone the creeps. I lean back, watch the flash-movies, don't bother nobody, and everybody's happy to see me go when the plane finally lands.

I get my car, nice midsize job with a phone, and head right into the city. I know this city real good, I been here before for them, but it ain't the only one they send me to when they need to TCB.

Do an easy fifty-five into the city and go to the address on the paper. Midtown, two blocks east of dead center, medium-size Victorian. I can see the area's starting to get a watchamacallit, like a facelift, the rich ones coming in and fixing up the houses because the magazines and the TV told them it's time to love old houses and fix them up.

I think about the other houses all up and down the street of the one I gotta go to, what's in them, what I could do. I sure feel like it, and it would be a lot less trouble, but I made me a deal of my own free will and I will stick to it as long as they do, Steener and Villanueva and the people behind them. But if they bust it up somehow, if they fuck me, that will be real different, and they will be real sorry.

I call the house; nobody home. That's about right. I got to wait, which don't bother me none, because there's the flash-movies to watch. I can think on what I want to do after I get through what I have to do, and those things are not so different from each other. What Steener calls the procedure I just call a new way to play. Only not so new, because I thought of some of those things all on my own when I was watchamacallit, freelance so to say, and done some of them, kind of, which I guess is what made them take me for this stuff, instead of letting me take a quick shot in a quiet room and no funeral after.

So, it gets to be four in the morning and here we come. Somehow, I know as soon as I see the figure coming up the sidewalk across the street that this is the one in the house. I can always tell them, and I don't know what it is, except maybe it takes a human monster to know an inhuman monster. And I don't feel nothing except a little nervous about getting into the house, which is always easier than you'd think it would be, but I get nervous on it anyway.

Figure comes into the light and I see it's a man, and I see it's not alone, and then I get pissed, because that fucking Steener, that fucking Villanueva, they didn't say nothing about no kid. And then I settle some, because I can tell the kid is one, too. Ten, maybe twelve from the way he walks. I take the razor and I give myself a little one just inside my hairline, squeeze the blood out to get it running down my face, and then I get out of the car just as they put their feet on the first step up to the house.

"Please, you gotta help me," I call, not too loud, just so they can hear, "they robbed me, they took everything but my clothes, all my ID, my credit cards, my cash —"

They stop and look at me running across the street at them and the first thing they see is the blood, of course. This would scare anybody but them (or me, naturally). I trip myself on the curb and collapse practically at their feet. "Can I use your phone? Please? I'm scared to stay out here, my car won't start, they might be still around —"

The man leans down and pulls me up under my arm. "Of course. Come in, we'll call the police. I'm a doctor."

I have to bite my lip to keep from laughing at that one. He's an operator maybe but no fucking doctor. Then I taste blood, so I let it run out of my mouth and the two of them, the man and the kid get so hot they can't get me in the house fast enough.

Nice house. All the Victorian shit restored, even the fuzzy stuff on the wallpaper, watchamacallit, flocked wallpaper. I get a glimpse of the living room before the guy's rushing me upstairs, saying he's got his medical bag up there. I just bet he does, and I got mine right in my hand, which they do not bother wondering about what with all this blood and this guy with no ID and out at four in the morning, must be a criminal anyway. I used to ask Villanueva, don't they ever get full, like they can't drink another drop, but Villanueva told me no, they always had room for one more, it was time they were pressed for. Dawn. I'd be through long before then, but even if I wasn't, dawn would take care of the rest of it for me.

They're getting so excited it's getting me even more excited. I look at the kid and man, if I'd been anyone else, I woulda started screaming and trying to get away, because he's all gone. I mean, the kid part is all gone and just this fucking hungry thing from hell. So I stop feeling funny about there being a kid, because like I said, there ain't no kid, just a short one along with the tall one.

And shit if he don't twig, right there on the stairs. I musta looked like I recognized him.

"We're burned! We're burned!" he yells and tries to elbow me in the face. I dip and he goes right the fuck over my head and down, ka-boom, ka-boom. Guess what, they can't fly. It don't do him, but they can feel pain, and if you break their legs, they can't walk for a while until they can get extra blood to heal them up. The kid's fucking neck is broke, you can see it plain as anything.

But I don't get no chance to study on it because the big one growls like a fucking attack dog and grabs me up from behind around the waist. They really are stronger than normal and you better believe it hurt like a motherfucker. He squeezes and there go two ribs and the soft drinks I had on the plane, like a fucking fountain.

"You'll go slow for that," he says, "you'll go for days, and you'll beg to die."

Obviously, he don't know me. I'm hurting all right, but it takes a lot more than a couple of ribs to put me down and I never had to beg for nothing, but these guys get all their dialogue off the late show anyway and they ain't thinking of nothing except sticking it to you and drinking you dry. Fucking undead got a, a watchamacallit, a narrow perspective and they think everyone's scared of them.

That's why they send me, because I don't see no undead and I don't see no human being, I just see something to play with. I gotta narrow perspective, too, I guess.

But then everything is not so good because he tears the bag outa my hand and flings it away up in the hallway. Then he carries me the rest of the way upstairs and down the opposite end and tosses me into a dark room and slams the door and locks it.

I hold still until I can figure out how to move and cause myself the least pain, and I start taking off my shirts. I'm wearing a corduroy shirt with a pure linen lining sewn into the front and two heavy one-hundred-percent cotton T-shirts underneath. I have to tear one of the T-shirts off, biting through the neck, and I bite through the neck of the other one but leave it on (thinking about the guy biting through necks while I do it), and put the corduroy shirt back on, keeping it open. Ready to go.

The guy has gone downstairs. I hear the kid scream and then muffle it, and I hear footsteps coming back up the stairs. There's a pause, and then I see his feet at the bottom of the door in the light, and he unlocks the door and opens it.

"Whoever you think you are," he says, "you're about to find out what you really are."

I give a little whimper, which makes him sure enough to grab me by one leg and start dragging me out into the hallway, where the kid is lying on his back. When we're out in the light, he stops and stands over me, one leg on each side, and looks down at my crotch. I know what he's thinking, because I'm looking up at his and thinking something not too different.

He squats on my thighs, and I rip my shirts open.

It's like an invisible giant hand hit him in the face; he goes backwards with a scream, still bent at the knees, on top of my legs. I heave him off quick. He's so fucked I have time to get to him, roll him over on his back and give him a nice full frontal while I sit on his stomach.

It is a truly def tattoo. This is not like bragging, because I didn't do it, though I did name it: The Power and the Passion. A madwoman with a mean needle in Coney did it, one-handed with her hair standing on end, fingering her rosary beads with the other hand, and when I saw it finished, with the name I had given it on a banner above it, I knew she was the best tattoo artist in the whole world and so I did not do her, I did *not*. It was some very ignorant asshole who musta come in after I did that split her open and nailed her to the wall with a stud gun, but I caught the beef on it, and the tattoo that saved her from me saved me from the quick shot and gave me to Steener's people, courtesy of Villanueva who is, I should mention, also Catholic.

So it's a tattoo that means a lot to me in many ways, you see, but mostly I love it because it is so perfect. It runs from just below where my shirt collars are to my navel, and full across my chest, and if you saw it, you would swear it had been done by someone who had been there to see what happened.

The cross is not just two boards, but a tree trunk and a crossbar, and the spikes are driven into the wrists where the two bones make a natural holder for that kind of thing — you couldn't hang on a cross from spikes driven through your palms like a lot of people think. They'd rip through. The crown of thorns has driven into the flesh to the bone, and the blood drips from the matted beard *distinctly* — the madwoman was careful and skilled so that the different shades of red didn't muddy up. Nothing muddied up; you can see the face clear as you can see where the whips came down, as clear as the wound in his side (which is not some wimpy slit but the best watchamacallit, rendering of a stab wound I have seen outside of real life), as clear as you can see how the arms have pulled out of the sockets, and how the legs are broken.

You just can't find no better picture of slow murder. I know; I seen photos of all kinds, I seen some righteous private art, and I seen the inside of plenty of churches, and ain't nobody done justice to nothing anybody ever done to someone, including the Crucifixion. Especially the Crucifixion, I guess.

Because, you see, you cannot take a vamp out with a cross, that don't mean dick to them, a fucking plus-sign, that's all. It's the Crucifixion that gets them, you gotta have a good crucifix, or some other representation of the Crucifixion, and it has to be sacred in some way, to inflict the agony of the real thing on them: Mine is sacred — that madwoman mumbling her rosary all the way through the work, don't it just figure that she was a runaway nun? I wouldn'ta thought it would matter, but I guess when you take them vows, you can't give them back. Sorta like a tattoo.

Well, that's what that madwoman believed, anyway, and I believe it, too, because I like believing that picture happened, and the vamp I'm sitting on, it don't mean shit if he believes or not, because I got him and he don't understand how I could even get close to him. So while I go get my bag (giving a good flash to the kid, who goes into shock), I explain about pure fibers found in nature like the linen they say they wrapped that man on the cross in (I think that's horseshit myself, but it's all in it being natural and not watchamacallit, synthetic, so that don't matter), and how it keeps the power from getting out till I need it to.

And then it's showtime.

I have a little fun with the silver for a while, just laying it against his skin here and there, and it crosses my mind not for the first time how a doctor could do some interesting research on burns, before I start getting serious. Like a hot knife through butter, you can put it that way and be dead on. Or undead on, ha, ha.

You know what they got for insides? Me neither, but it's as bad for them as anyone. And I wouldn't call *that* a heart, but if you drive a pure wood stake through it, it's lights out.

It lasts forever for him, but not half long enough for me. Come dawn, it's pretty much over. Them watchamacallits, uv rays, they're all over the place.

Skin cancer on fast forward, you can put it that way. I leave myself half an hour for the kid, who is not really a kid because if he was, he'd be the first kid I ever killed, and I ain't no fucking kid killer, because I seen what *they* get in prison and I said, whoa, not *my* ass.

I stake both hearts at the same time, a stake in each hand, sending them to hell together. Call me sentimental. Set their two heads to burning in the cellar and hang in just long enough to make sure we got a good fire going before I'm outa there. House all closed up the way it is, it'll be a while before it's time to call the fire department.

I'm halfway to the airport when I realize my ribs ain't bothered me for a long time. Healed up, just like that.

Hallelujah, gimme that old-time religion.

"As usual," Steener says, snotty as all get-out, "the bulk of the fee has been divided up among your victims' families, with a percentage to the mission downtown. Your share this time is three hundred." Nasty grin. "The check's in the mail."

"Yeah," I say, "you're from the government and you're here to help me. Well, don't worry, Steener, I won't come in your *mouth.*"

He actually cocks a fist and Villanueva steps in front of him. The woman with them gives Steener a really sharp look, like she's gonna come to my defense, which don't make sense. Villanueva starts to rag my ass about pushing Steener's hot button but I'm feeling important enough to wave a hand at him.

"Fuck that," I say, "it's time to tell me who *she* is."

Villanueva looks to the woman like he's asking her permission, but she steps forward and lets go of her coat, and I see the marks on her neck are all gone. "I'm the mother. And the wife. They tried to —" she bites her lips together and makes a stiff little motion at her throat. "I got away. I tried to go to church, but I was…tainted." She takes a breath. "The priest told me about —" she dips her head at Villanueva and Steener, who still wants a piece of me. "You really…put them away?"

The way she says it, it's like she's talking about a couple of rabid dogs. "Yeah," I tell her, smiling. "They're all gone."

"I want to see the picture," she says, and for a moment, I can't figure out what she's talking about. And then I get it.

"Sure," I say, and start to raise my undershirt.

Villanueva starts up. "I don't think you *really* want —"

"Yeah, she does," I say. "It's the only way she can tell she's all right now."

"The marks disappeared," Villanueva snaps. "She's fine. You're fine," he adds to her, almost polite.

She feels the side of her neck. "No, he's right. It *is* the only way I'll know for sure."

I'm shaking my head as I raise the shirt slowly. "You guys didn't think to sprinkle any holy water on her or nothing?"

"I wouldn't take the chance," she says, "it might have —"

But that's as far as she gets, because she's looking at my chest now and her face — oh, man, I start thinking I'm in love, because that's the look, that's the look you oughta have when you see The Power and the Passion. I know, because it's the look on my own face when I stand before the mirror and stare, and stare, and stare. It's so fucking *there.*

Villanueva and Steener are looking off in the opposite direction. I give it a full two-minute count before I lower my shirt. The look on her face goes away and she's just another character for a flash-movie again. Easy come, easy go. But now I know why she was so scared when she was here before. Guess they didn't think to tell her about pure natural fibers.

"You're perfect," she says, and turns to Steener and Villanueva. "He's perfect, isn't he? They can't tempt him into joining them, because he can't. He couldn't if he wanted to."

"Fuckin' A," I tell her.

Villanueva says, "Shut up," to me and looks at her like he's kinda sick. "You don't know what you're talking to. You don't know what's standing in this room with us. I couldn't bring myself to tell you, and I was a cop for sixteen years —"

"You told me what would have to be done with my husband and son," she says, looking him straight in the eye and I start thinking maybe I'm in love after all. "You spelled that out easily enough. The agony of the Crucifixion, the burning and the cutting open of the bodies with silver knives, the stakes through the hearts, the beheadings, the fire. That didn't bother you, telling me what was going to happen to my family —"

"That's because they're the white hats," I say to her, and I can't help smiling, smiling, smiling. "If they had to do it, they'd do it because they're on the side of Good and Right."

Suddenly Steener and Villanueva are falling all over each other to hustle her out and she don't resist, but she don't cooperate, either. The last thing I see before the door closes is her face looking at me, and what I see in that face is not understanding, because she couldn't go that far, but acceptance. Which is one fucking hell of a lot more than I'll ever get from Steener or Villanueva or anybody-the-fuck-else.

And Steener and Villanueva, they don't even get it, I know it just went right by them, what I told her. They'd do it because they're on the side of Good and Right.

I do it because I like to.

And I don't pretend like I ain't no monster, not for Good and Right, and not for Bad and Wrong. I know what I am, and the madwoman who put The Power and the Passion on my chest, she knew, too, and I think now she did it so the vamps would never get me, because God help you all if they had.

Just a coincidence, I guess, that it's my kind of picture.

Joe R. Lansdale has been a freelance writer since 1973, and a full time writer since 1981. He is the author of thirty novels and eighteen short story collections and has received the Edgar Award, seven Bram Stoker Awards, the British Fantasy Award, and Italy's Grinzani Prize for Literature, among others. As obvious from his awards, he writes in several different genres and is proficient in them all.

The novella "Bubba Ho-Tep" was filmed by Don Coscarelli and is now considered a cult classic, and his story "Incident On and Off a Mountain Road" was filmed for Showtime's *Masters of Horror*.

He has written for film, television, comics, and is the author of numerous essays and columns. His most recent work is the collection *Sanctified and Chicken-Fried: The Portable Lansdale*, and *Vanilla Ride*, his latest in the Hap Collins and Leonard Pine mystery series.

Lansdale is best known for his often bloody, ironic, and occasionally humorous horror stories about the denizens of East Texas. "The Phone Woman" is in a different vein entirely.

The Phone Woman
Joe R. Lansdale

Journal Entries

A WEEK TO remember…

After this, my little white page friend, you shall have greater security, kept under not only lock and key, but you will have a hiding place. If I were truly as smart as I sometimes think I am, I wouldn't write this down. I know better. But, I am compelled.

Compulsion. It comes out of nowhere and owns us all. We put a suit and tie and hat on the primitive part of our brain and call it manners and civilization, but ultimately, it's just a suit and tie and a hat. The primitive brain is still primitive, and it compels, pulses to the same dark beat that made our less civilized ancestors and the primordial ooze before them, throb to simple, savage rhythms of sex, death and destruction.

Our nerves call out to us to touch and taste life, and without our suits of civilization, we can do that immediately. Take what we need if we've muscle enough. Will enough. But all dressed up in the trappings of civilization, we're forced to find our thrills vicariously. And eventually, that is not enough. Controlling our impulses that way, is like having someone eat your food for you. No taste. No texture. No nourishment. Pitiful business.

Without catering to the needs of our primitive brains, without feeding impulses, trying instead to get what we need through books and films and the lives of the more adventurous, we cease to live. We wither. We bore ourselves and others. We die. And are glad of it.

Whatcha gonna do, huh?

Saturday Morning, June 10th, through Saturday 17th:

I haven't written in a while, so I'll cover a few days, beginning with a week ago today.

It was one of those mornings when I woke up on the wrong side of the bed, feeling a little out of sorts, mad at the wife over something I've forgotten and she probably hasn't forgotten, and we grumbled down the hall, into the kitchen, and there's our dog, a Siberian Husky — my wife always refers to him as a Suburban Husky because of his pampered life-style, though any resemblance to where we live and suburbia requires a great deal of faith — and he's smiling at us, and then we see why he's smiling. Two reasons: (1) He's happy to see us. (2) He feels a little guilty.

He has reason to feel guilty. Not far behind him, next to the kitchen table, was a pile of shit. I'm not talking your casual little whoopsie-doo, and I'm not talking your inconvenient pile, and I'm not talking six to eight turds the size of large bananas. I'm talking a certified, pure-dee, goddamn prize-winning SHIT. There were enough dog turds there to shovel out in a pickup truck and dump on the lawn and let dry so you could use them to build an adobe hut big enough to keep your tools in and have room to house your cat in the winter.

And right beside this sterling deposit, was a lake of piss wide enough and deep enough to go rowing on.

I had visions of a Siberian Husky hat and slippers, or possibly a nice throw rug for the bedroom, a necklace of dog claws and teeth; maybe cut that smile right out of his face and frame it.

But the dog-lover in me took over, and I put him outside in his pen where he cooled his dew-claws for a while. Then I spent about a half-hour cleaning up dog shit while my wife spent the same amount of time keeping our two-year-old son, Kevin, known to me as Fruit of my Loins, out of the shit.

Yep, Oh Great White Page of a Diary, he was up now. It always works that way. In times of greatest stress, in times of greatest need for contemplation or privacy, like when you're trying to get that morning piece off the Old Lady, the kid shows up, and suddenly it's as if you've been deposited inside an ant farm and the ants are crawling and stinging. By the time I finished cleaning up the mess, it was time for breakfast, and I got to tell you, I didn't want anything that looked like link sausage that morning.

So Janet and I ate, hoping that what we smelled while eating was the aroma of disinfectant and not the stench of shit wearing a coat of disinfectant, and we watched the kid spill his milk eighty-lebben times and throw food and drop stuff on the floor, and me and the wife we're fussing at each other more and more, about whatever it was we were mad about that morning — a little item intensified by our dog's deposits — and by the time we're through eating our meal, and Janet leaves me with Fruit of My Loins and his View Master and goes out to the laundry room to do what the room is named for — probably went out there to beat the laundry clean with rocks or bricks, pretending shirts and pants were my head — I'm beginning to think things couldn't get worse. About that time the earth passes through the tail of a comet or something, some kind of dimensional gate is opened, and the world goes weird.

There's a knock at the door.

At first I thought it was a bird pecking on the glass, it was that soft. Then it came again and I went to the front door and opened it, and there stood a woman about five feet tall wearing a long, wool coat, and untied, flared-at-the-ankles shoes, and a ski cap decorated with a silver pin. The wool ski cap was pulled down so tight over her ears her face was pale. Keep in mind that it was probably eighty degrees that morning, and the temperature was rising steadily, and she was dressed like she was on her way to plant the flag at the summit of Everest. Her age was hard to guess. Had that kind of face. She could have been twenty-two or forty-two.

She said, "Can I use your phone, mister? I got an important call to make."

Well, I didn't see any ready-to-leap companions hiding in the shrubbery, and I figured if she got out of line I could handle her, so I said, "Yeah, sure. Be my guest," and let her in.

The phone was in the kitchen, on the wall, and I pointed it out to her, and me and Fruit of My Loins went back to doing what we were doing, which was looking at the View Master. We switched from Goofy to Winnie the Pooh, the one about Tigger in the tree, and it was my turn to look at it, and I couldn't help but hear that my guest's conversation with her mother was becoming stressful — I knew it was her mother because she addressed her by that title — and suddenly Fruit of My Loins yelled, "Wook, Daddy wook."

I turned and "wooked," and what do I see but what appears to be some rare tribal dance, possibly something having originated in higher altitudes where the lack of oxygen to the brain causes wilder abandon with the dance steps. This gal was all over the place. Fred Astaire with a hot coat hanger up his ass couldn't have been any brisker. I've never seen anything like it. Then, in mid-dossey-do, she did a leap like cheerleaders do, one of those things where they kick their legs out to the side, open up like a nut-cracker and kick the palms of their hands, then she hit the floor on her ass, spun, and wheeled as if on a swivel into the hallway and went out of sight. Then there came a sound from in there like someone on speed beating the bongos. She hadn't dropped the phone either. The wire was stretched tight around the corner and was vibrating like a big fish was on the line.

I dashed over there and saw she was lying crosswise in the hallway, bamming her head against the wall, clutching at the phone with one hand and pulling her dress up over her waist with the other, and she was making horrible sounds and rolling her eyes, and I immediately thought: this is it, she's gonna die. Then I saw she wasn't dying, just thrashing, and I decided it was an epileptic fit.

I got down and took the phone away from her, took hold of her jaw, got her tongue straight without getting bit, stretched her out on the floor away from the wall, picked up the phone and told her mama, who was still fussing about something or another, that things weren't so good, hung up on her in mid-sentence and called the ambulance.

I ran out to the laundry room, told Janet a strange woman was in our hallway puffing her dress over her head and that an ambulance was coming. Janet, bless her heart, has become quite accustomed to weird events following me around, and she went outside to direct the ambulance, like one of those people at the airport with light sticks.

I went back to the woman and watched her thrash awhile, trying to make sure she didn't choke to death, or injure herself, and Fruit of My Loins kept clutching my leg and asking me what was wrong. I didn't know what to tell him.

After what seemed a couple of months and a long holiday, the ambulance showed up with a whoop of siren, and I finally decided the lady was doing as good as she was going to do, so I went outside. On either side of my walk were all these people. It's like Bradbury's story "The Crowd." The one where when there's an accident all these strange people show up out of nowhere and stand around and watch.

I'd never seen but two of these people before in my life, and I've been living in this neighborhood for years.

One lady immediately wanted to go inside and pray for the woman, who she somehow knew, but Janet whispered to me that there wasn't enough room for our guest in there, let alone this other woman and her buddy, God, so I didn't let her in.

All the other folks are just a jabbering, and about all sorts of things. One woman said to another: "Mildred, how you been?"

"I been good. They took my kids away from me this morning, though. I hate that. How you been?"

"Them hogs breeding yet?" one man says to another, and the other goes into not only that they're breeding, but he tells how much fun they're having at it.

Then here comes the ambulance boys with a stretcher. One of the guys knew me somehow, and he stopped and said, "You're that writer, aren't you?"

I admitted it.

"I always wanted to write. I got some ideas that'd make a good book and a movie. I'll tell you about 'em. I got good ideas, I just can't write them down. I could tell them to you and you could write them up and we could split the money."

"Could we talk about this later?" I said. "There's a lady in there thrashing in my hallway."

So they went in with the stretcher, and after a few minutes the guy I talked to came out and said, "We can't get her out of there and turned through the door. We may have to take your back door out."

That made no sense to me at all. They brought the stretcher through and now they were telling me they couldn't carry it out. But I was too addled to argue and told them to do what they had to do.

Well, they managed her out the back door without having to remodel our home after all, and when they came around the edge of the house I heard the guy I'd talked to go, "Ahhh, damn, I'd known it was her I wouldn't have come."

I thought they were going to set her and the stretcher down right there, but they went out to the ambulance and jerked open the door and tossed her and the stretcher inside like they were tossing a dead body over a cliff. You could hear the stretcher strike the back of the ambulance and bounce forward and slide back again.

I had to ask: "You know her?"

"Dark enough in the house there, I couldn't tell at first. But when we got outside, I seen who it was. She does this all the time, but not over on this side of town in a while. She don't take her medicine on purpose so she'll have fits when she gets stressed, or she fakes them, like this time. Way she gets attention. Sometimes she hangs herself, cuts off her air. Likes the way it feels. Sexual or something. She's damn near died half-dozen times. Between you and me, wish she'd go on and do it and save me some trips."

And the ambulance driver and his assistant were out of there. No lights. No siren.

Well, the two people standing in the yard that we knew were still there when I turned around, but the others, like mythical creatures, were gone, turned to smoke, dissolved, become one with the universe, whatever. The two people we knew, elderly neighbors, said they knew the woman, who by this time, I had come to think of as the Phone Woman.

"She goes around doing that," the old man said. "She stays with her mamma who lives on the other side of town, but they get in fights on account of the girl likes to hang herself sometimes for entertainment. Never quite makes it over the ridge, you know, but gets her mother worked up. They say her mother used to do that too, hang herself, when she was a girl. She outgrowed it. I guess the girl there...you know I don't even know her name...must have seen her mamma do that when she was little, and it kind of caught on. She has that 'lepsy stuff too, you know thrashing around and all, biting on her tongue?"

I said I knew and had seen a demonstration of it this morning.

"Anyway," he continued, "they get in fights and she comes over here and tries to stay with some relatives that live up the street there, but they don't cotton much to her hanging herself to things. She broke down their clothesline post last year. Good thing it was old, or she'd been dead. Wasn't nobody home that time. I hear tell they sometimes go off and leave her there and leave rope and wire and stuff laying around, sort of hoping, you know. But except for that time with the clothesline, she usually does her hanging when someone's around. Or she goes in to use the phone at houses and does what she did here."

"She's nutty as a fruitcake," said the old woman. "She goes back on behind here to where that little trailer park is, knocks on doors where the wet backs live, about twenty to a can, and they ain't got no phone, and she knows it. She's gotten raped couple times doing that, and it ain't just them Mex's that have got to her. White folks, niggers. She tries to pick who she thinks will do what she wants. She wants to be raped. It's like the hanging. She gets some kind of attention out of it, some kind of living. Course, I ain't saying she chose you cause you're that kind of person."

I assured her I understood.

The old couple went home then, and another lady came up, and sure enough, I hadn't seen her before either, and she said, "Did that crazy ole girl come over here and ask to use the phone, then fall down on you and flop?"

"Yes, ma'am."

"Does that all the time."

Then this woman went around the corner of the house and was gone, and I never saw her again. In fact, with the exception of the elderly neighbors and the Phone Woman, I never saw any of those people again and never knew where they came from. Next day there was a soft knock on the door. It was the Phone Woman again. She asked to use the phone.

I told her we had taken it out.

She went away and I saw her for several times that day. She'd come up our street about once every half hour, wearing that same coat and hat and those sad shoes, and I guess it must have been a hundred and ten out there. I watched her from the window. In fact I couldn't get any writing done because I was watching for her. Thinking about her lying there on the floor, pulling her dress up, flopping. I thought too of her hanging herself now and then, like she was some kind of suit on a hanger.

Anyway, the day passed and I tried to forget about her, then the other night, Monday probably, I went out on the porch to smoke one of my rare cigars (about four to six a year), and I saw someone coming down the dark street, and from the way that someone walked, I knew it was her, the Phone Woman.

She went on by the house and stopped down the road a piece and looked up and I looked where she was looking, and through the trees I could see what she saw. The moon.

We both looked at it awhile, and she finally walked on, slow, with her head down, and I put my cigar out well before it was finished and went inside and brushed my teeth and took off my clothes, and tried to go to sleep. Instead, I lay there for a long time and thought about her, walking those dark streets, maybe thinking about her mom, or a lost love, or a phone, or sex in the form of rape because it was some kind of human connection, about hanging herself because it was attention and it gave her a sexual high…and then again, maybe I'm full of shit and she wasn't thinking about any of these things.

Then it struck me suddenly, as I lay there in bed beside my wife, in my quiet house, my son sleeping with his teddy bear in the room across the way, that maybe she was the one in touch with the world, with life, and that I was the one gone stale from civilization. Perhaps life had been civilized right out of me.

The times I had truly felt alive, in touch with my nerve centers, were in times of violence or extreme stress.

Where I had grown up, in Mud Creek, violence simmered underneath everyday life like lava cooking beneath a thin crust of earth, ready at any time to explode and spew. I had been in fights, been cut by knives. I once had a job bouncing drunks. I had been a bodyguard in my earlier years, had illegally carried a .38. On one occasion, due to a dispute the day before while protecting my employer, who sometimes dealt with a bad crowd, a man I had insulted and hit with my fists, pulled a gun on me, and I had been forced to pull mine. The both of us ended up with guns in our faces, looking into each other's eyes, knowing full well our lives hung by a thread and the snap of a trigger.

I had killed no one, and had avoided being shot. The Mexican standoff ended with us both backing away and running off, but there had been that moment when I knew it could be all over in a flash. Out of the picture in a blaze of glory. No old folks home for me. No drool running down my chin and some young nurse wiping my ass, thinking how repulsive and old I was, wishing for quitting time so she could roll up with some young stud some place sweet and cozy, open her legs to him with a smile and a sigh, and later a passionate scream, while in the meantime, back at the old folks ranch, I lay in the bed with a dead dick and an oxygen mask strapped to my face.

Something about the Phone Woman had clicked with me. I understood her suddenly. I understood then that the lava that had boiled beneath the civilized fa-cade of my brain was no longer boiling. It might be bubbling way down low, but it wasn't boiling, and the realization of that went all over me and I felt sad, very, very sad. I had dug a grave and crawled into it and was slowly pulling the dirt in after me. I had a home. I had a wife. I had a son. Dirt clods all. Dirt clods filling in my grave while life simmered somewhere down deep and useless within me.

I lay there for a long time with tears on my cheeks before exhaustion took over and I slept in a dark world of dormant passion.

Couple days went by, and one night after Fruit of My Loins and Janet were in bed, I went out on the front porch to sit and look at the stars and think about what I'm working on — a novella that isn't going well — and what do I see but the Phone Woman, coming down the road again, walking past the house, stopping once more to look at the moon.

I didn't go in this time, but sat there waiting, and she went on up the street and turned right and went out of sight. I walked across the yard and went out to the center of the street and watched her back going away from me, mixing into the shadow of the trees and houses along the street, and I followed.

I don't know what I wanted to see, but I wanted to see something, and I found for some reason that I was thinking of her lying there on the floor in my hallway, her dress up, the mound of her sex, as they say in porno novels, pushing up at me. The thought gave me an erection, and I was conscious of how silly this was, how unattractive this woman was to me, how odd she looked, and then another thought came to me: I was a snob. I didn't want to feel sexual towards anyone ugly or smelly in a winter coat in the dead of summer.

But the night was cool and the shadows were thick, and they made me feel all right, romantic maybe, or so I told myself.

I moved through a neighbor's backyard where a dog barked at me a couple of times and shut up. I reached the street across the way and looked for the Phone Woman, but didn't see her.

I took a flyer, and walked on down the street toward the trailer park where those poor illegal aliens were stuffed in like sardines by their unscrupulous employers, and I saw a shadow move among shadows, and then there was a split in the trees that provided the shadows, and I saw her, the Phone Woman. She was standing in a yard under a great oak, and not far from her was a trailer. A pathetic air conditioner hummed in one of its windows.

She stopped and looked up through that split in the trees above, and I knew she was trying to find the moon again, that she had staked out spots that she traveled to at night; spots where she stood and looked at the moon or the stars or the pure and sweet black eternity between them.

Like the time before, I looked up too, took in the moon, and it was beautiful, as gold as if it were a great glob of honey. The wind moved my hair, and it seemed solid and purposeful, like a lover's soft touch, like the beginning of foreplay. I breathed deep and tasted the fragrance of the night, and my lungs felt full and strong and young.

I looked back at the woman and saw she was reaching out her hand to the moon. No, a low limb. She touched it with her fingertips. She raised her other hand, and in it was a short, thick rope. She tossed the rope over the limb and made a loop and pulled it taut to the limb. Then she tied a loop to the other end, quickly expertly, and put that around her neck.

Of course, I knew what she was going to do. But I didn't move. I could have stopped her, I knew, but what was the point? Death was the siren she had called on many a time, and finally, she had heard it sing.

She jumped and pulled her legs under her and the limb took her jump and held her. Her head twisted to the left and she spun about on the rope and the moonlight caught the silver pin on her ski cap and it threw out a cool beacon of silver light, and as she spun, it hit me once, twice, three times.

On the third spin her mouth went wide and her tongue went out and her legs dropped down and hit the ground and she dangled there, unconscious.

I unrooted my feet and walked over there, looking about as I went.

I didn't see anyone. No lights went on in the trailer.

I moved up close to her. Her eyes were open. Her tongue was out. She was swinging a little. Her knees were bent and the toes and tops of her silly shoes dragged the ground. I walked around and around her, an erection pushing at my pants. I observed her closely, tried to see what death looked like.

She coughed. A little choking cough. Her eyes shifted toward me. Her chest heaved. She was beginning to breathe. She made a feeble effort to get her feet under her, to raise her hands to the rope around her neck.

She was back from the dead.

I went to her, I took her hands, gently pulled them from her throat, let them go. I looked into her eyes. I saw the moon there. She shifted so that her legs held her weight better. Her hands went to her dress. She pulled it up to her waist. She wore no panties. Her bush was like a nest built between the boughs of a snow-white elm.

I remembered the day she came into the house. Everything since then, leading up to this moment, seemed like a kind of perverse mating ritual. I put my hand to her throat. I took hold of the rope with my other hand and jerked it so that her knees straightened, then I eased behind her, put my forearm against the rope around her throat, and I began to tighten my hold until she made a soft noise, like a virgin taking a man for the first time. She didn't lift her hands. She continued to tug her dress up. She was trembling from lack of oxygen. I pressed myself against her buttocks, moved my hips rhythmically, my hard-on bound by my underwear and pants. I tightened the pressure on her throat.

And choked her.

And choked her.

She gave up what was left of her life with a shiver and a thrusting of her pelvis, and finally she jammed her buttocks back into me and I felt myself ejaculate, thick and hot and rich as shaving foam.

Her hands fell to her side. I loosened the pressure on her throat but clung to her for a while, getting my breath and my strength back. When I felt strong enough, I let her go. She swung out and around on the rope and her knees bent and her head cocked up to stare blindly at the gap in the trees above, at the honey-golden moon.

I left her there and went back to the house and slipped into the bedroom and took off my clothes. I removed my wet underwear carefully and wiped them out with toilet paper and flushed the paper down the toilet. I put the underwear in the clothes hamper. I put on fresh and climbed into bed and rubbed my hands over my wife's buttocks until she moaned and woke up. I rolled her on her stomach and mounted her and made love to her. Hard, violent love, my forearm around her throat, not squeezing, but thinking about the Phone Woman, the sound she had made when I choked her from behind, the way her buttocks had thrust back into me at the end. I closed my eyes until the sound that Janet made was the sound the Phone Woman made and I could visualize her there in the moonlight, swinging by the rope.

When it was over, I held Janet and she kissed me and joked about my arm around her throat, about how it seemed I had wanted to choke her. We laughed a little. She went to sleep. I let go of her and moved to my side of the bed and looked at the ceiling and thought about the Phone Woman. I tried to feel guilt. I could not. She had wanted it. She had tried for it many times. I had helped her do what she had never been able to manage. And I had felt alive again. Doing something on the edge. Taking a risk.

Well, journal, here's the question: Am I a sociopath?

No. I love my wife. I love my child. I even love my Suburban Husky. I have never hunted and fished, because I thought I didn't like to kill. But there are those who want to die. It is their one moment of life; to totter on the brink between light and darkness, to take the final, dark rush down a corridor of black, hot pain.

So, Oh Great White Pages, should I feel guilt, some inner torment, a fear that I am at heart a cold-blooded murderer?

I think not.

I gave the sweet gift of truly being alive to a woman who wanted someone to participate in her moment of joy. Death ended that, but without the threat of it, her moment would have been nothing. A stage rehearsal for a high school play in street clothes.

Nor do I feel fear. The law will never suspect me. There's no reason to. The Phone Woman had a record of near suicides. It would never occur to anyone to think she had died by anyone's hand other than her own.

I felt content, in touch again with the lava beneath the primal crust. I have allowed it to boil up and burst through and flow, and now it has gone down once more. But it's no longer a distant memory. It throbs and rolls and laps just below, ready to jump and give me life. Are there others out there like me? Or better yet, others for me, like the Phone Woman?

Most certainly.

And now I will recognize them. The Phone Woman has taught me that. She came into my life on a silly morning and brought me adventure, took me away from the grind, and then she brought me more, much, much more. She helped me recognize the fine but perfect line between desire and murder; let me know that there are happy victims and loving executioners.

I will know the happy victims now when I see them, know who needs to be satisfied. I will give them their desire, while they give me mine.

This last part with the Phone Woman happened last night and I am recording it now, while it is fresh, as Janet sleeps. I think of Janet in there and I have a hard time imagining her face. I want her, but I want her to be the Phone Woman, or someone like her.

I can feel the urge rising up in me again. The urge to give someone that tremendous double-edged surge of life and death.

It's like they say about sex. Once you get it, you got to have it on a regular basis. But it isn't sex I want. It's something like it, only sweeter.

I'll wrap this up. I'm tired. Thinking that I'll have to wake Janet and take the edge off my need, imagine that she and I are going to do more than fornicate; that she wants to take that special plunge and that she wants me to shove her.

But she doesn't want that. I'd know. I have to find that in my dreams, when I nestle down into the happy depths of the primitive brain.

At least until I find someone like the Phone Woman, again, that is. Someone with whom I can commit the finest of adultery.

And until that search proves fruitful and I have something special to report, dear diary, I say, goodnight.

In 1991, Kathe Koja's first novel, *The Cipher*, inaugurated the high profile Abyss line of horror and won the Stoker Award for First Novel. In 2008, her novel *Headlong* was featured in the *New Yorker's* "Book Bench" roundtable. In between these milestones, her dozen novels include *Skin*, *The Blue Mirror*, *Talk*, and *Kissing the Bee* (*Under the Poppy* and *Floor Candy* are forthcoming), and a collection of stories, *Extremities*. Her fiction has been honored by the ASPCA, the International Reading Association, the Gustavus Myers Book Award, the Horror Writers Association, and the Parents' Choice Award. *The Cipher* has recently been optioned for film.

Koja's adult novels and short stories stand out for her linguistic experimentation and oblique yet dense storytelling. "Teratisms," a short tale of three siblings, published in 1991, exemplifies this earlier work.

Teratisms
Kathe Koja

"Beaumont." Dreamy, Alex's voice. Sitting in the circle of the heat, curtains drawn in the living room: laddered magenta scenes of birds and dripping trees. "Delcambre. Thibodaux." Slow-drying dribble like rusty water on the bathroom floor. "Abbeville," car door slam, "Chinchuba," screen door slam. Triumphant through its echo, "Baton Rouge!"

Tense hoarse holler almost childish with rage: "Will you shut the fuck *up?*"

From the kitchen, woman's voice, Randle's voice, drawl like cooling blood: "Mitch's home."

"You're damn right Mitch is home." Flat slap of his unread newspaper against the cracked laminate of the kitchen table, the whole set from the Goodwill for thirty dollars. None of the chairs matched. Randle sat in the cane-bottomed one, leg swinging back and forth, shapely metronome, making sure the ragged gape of her tank top gave Mitch a good look. Fanning herself with four slow fingers.

"Bad day, big brother?"

Too tired to sit, propping himself jackknife against the counter. "They're all bad, Francey."

"Mmmm, forgetful. My name's Randle now."

"Doesn't matter what your name is, you're still a bitch."

Soft as dust, from the living room: "De Quincy. Longville." Tenderly, "Bewelcome."

Mitch's sigh. "Numbnuts in there still at it?"

"All day."

Another sigh, he bent to prowl the squat refrigerator, let the door fall shut. Half-angry again, "There's nothing in here to eat, Fran — Randle."

"So what?"

"So what'd you eat?"

More than a laugh, bubbling under. "I don't think you really want to know." Deliberately exposing half a breast, palm lolling beneath like a sideshow, like a street-corner card trick. Presto. "Big brother."

His third sigh, lips closed in decision. "I don't need this," passing close to the wall, warding the barest brush against her, her legs in the chair as deliberate, a sluttish spraddle but all of it understood: an old, unfunny family joke; like calling names; nicknames.

The door slamming, out as in, and in the settling silence of departure: "Is he gone?"

Stiff back, Randle rubbing too hard the itchy tickle of sweat. Pushing at the table to move the chair away. "You heard the car yourself, Alex. You know he's gone."

Pause, then plaintive, "Come sit with me." Sweet; but there are nicknames and nicknames, jokes and jokes; a million ways to say I love you. Through the raddled arch into the living room, Randle's back tighter still, into the smell, and Alex's voice, bright.

"Let's talk," he said.

Mitch, so much later, pausing at the screenless front door, and on the porch Randle's cigarette, drawing lines in the dark like a child with a sparkler.

"Took your time," she said.

Defensively, "It's not that late."

"I know what time it is."

He sat down, not beside her but close enough to speak softly and be heard. "You got another cigarette?"

She took the pack from somewhere, flipped it listless to his lap. "Keep 'em. They're yours anyway."

He lit the cigarette with gold foil matches, JUDY'S DROP-IN. An impulse, shaming, to do as he used to, light a match and hold it to her fingertips to see how long it took to blister. No wonder she hated him. "Do you hate me?"

"Not as much as I hate him." He could feel her motion, half a head-shake. "Do you know what he did?"

"The cities."

"Besides the cities." He did not see her fingers, startled twitch as he felt the pack of cigarettes leave the balance of his thigh. "He was down by the grocery store, the dumpster. Playing. It took me almost an hour just to talk him home."

A black sigh. "He's getting worse."

"You keep saying that."

"It keeps being true, Mitch, whether you want to think so or not. Something really bad's going to happen if we don't get him —"

"Get him what?" Sour. No, bitter. "A doctor? A shrink? How about a one-way ticket back to Shitsburg so he —"

"Fine, that's fine. But when the cops come knocking I'll let you answer the door," and her quick feet bare on the step, into the house. Tense unconscious rise of his shoulders: Don't slam the door. Don't wake him up.

Mitch slept, weak brittle doze in the kitchen, head pillowed on the Yellow Pages. Movement, the practiced calm of desire. Stealth, until denouement, a waking startle to Alex's soft growls and tweaks of laughter, his giggle and spit. All over the floor. All over the floor and his hands, oh God Alex your *hands* —

Showing them off the way a child would, elbows turned, palms up. Showing them in the jittery bug-light of the kitchen in the last half hour before morning, Mitch bent almost at the waist, then sinking back, nausea subsiding but unbanished before the immensity, the drip and stutter, there was some on his mouth too. His chin, Mitch had to look away from what was stuck there.

"Go on," he said. "Go get your sister."

And waited there, eyes closed, hands spread like a medium on the Yellow Pages. While Alex woke his sister. While Randle used the washcloth. Again.

Oxbow lakes. Flat country. Randle sleeping in the back seat, curled and curiously hot, her skin ablush with sweat in the sweet cool air. Big creamy Buick with all the windows open. Mitch was driving, slim black sunglasses like a cop in a movie, while Alex sat playing beside him. Old wrapping paper today, folding in his fingers, disappearing between his palms. Always paper. Newsprint ink under his nails. Glossy foilwrap from some party, caught between the laces of his sneakers. Or tied there. Randle might have done that, it was her style. Grim droll jokery. Despite himself he looked behind, into the back seat, into the stare of her open eyes, so asphalt blank that for one second fear rose like a giant waiting to be born and he thought, Oh no, oh not her too.

Beside him Alex made a playful sound.

Randle's gaze snapped true into her real smile; bared her teeth in burlesque before she rolled over, pleased.

"Fucking bitch," with dry relief. With feeling.

Alex said, "I'm hungry."

Mitch saw he had begun to eat the paper. "We'll find a drive-through somewhere," he said, and for a moment dreamed of flinging the wheel sideways, of fast and greasy death. Let someone else clean up for a change.

There was a McDonald's coming up, garish beside the blacktop; he got into the right lane just a little too fast. "Randle," coldly, "put your shirt on."

Chasing the end of the drive-through line, lunchtime and busy and suddenly Alex was out of the car, leaned smiling through the window to say, "I want to eat inside." And gone, trotting across the parking lot, birthday paper forgotten on the seat beside.

"Oh God," Mitch craning, tracking his progress, "go after him, Randle," and Randle's snarl, the bright slap of her sandals as she ran. Parking, he considered driving off. Alone. Leaving them there. Don't you ever leave them, swear me. You have to swear me, Mitchie. Had she ever really said that? Squeezed out a promise like a dry log of shit? I hope there is a hell, he thought, turning off the car, I hope it's big and hot and eternal and that she's in it.

They were almost to the counter, holding hands. When Randle saw him enter, she looked away; he saw her fingers squeeze Alex's, twice and slow. What was it like for her? Middleman. Alex was staring at the wall menu as if he could read. "I'll get a booth," Mitch said.

A table, instead; there were no empty booths. One by one Alex crumbled the chocolate-chip cookies, licked his fingers to dab up the crumbs. Mitch drank coffee.

"That's making me sick," he said to Randle.

Her quick sideways look at Alex. "What?" through half a mouthful, a tiny glob of tartar sauce rich beside her lower lip.

"That smell," nodding at her sandwich. "Fish."

Mouth abruptly stretched, chewed fish and half-smeared sauce, he really was going to be sick. Goddamned *bitch*. Nudging him under the table with one bare foot. Laughing into her Coke.

"Do you always have to make it worse?"

Through another mouthful, "It can't get any worse." To Alex, "Eat your cookies."

Mitch drank more coffee; it tasted bitter, boiled. Randle stared over his head as she ate: watching the patrons? staring at the wall? Alex coughed on cookie crumbs, soft dry cough. Gagged a little. Coughed harder.

"Alex?" Randle put down her sandwich. "You okay? Slap his back," commandingly to Mitch, and he did, harder as Alex kept coughing, almost a barking sound now and heads turned, a little, at the surrounding tables, the briefest bit of notice that grew more avid as Alex's distress increased, louder whoops and Randle suddenly on her feet, trying to raise him up as Mitch saw the first flecks of blood.

"Oh *shit,*" but it was too late, Alex spitting blood now, spraying it, coughing it out in half-digested clots as Randle, frantic, working to haul him upright as Mitch in some stupid reflex swabbed with napkins at the mess. Tables emptied around them. Kids crying, loud and scared, McDonald's employees surrounding them but not too close, Randle shouting, *"Help* me, you asshole!" and Mitch in dumb paralysis watched as a tiny finger, red but recognizable, flew from Alex's mouth to lie wetly on the seat.

Hammerlock, no time to care if it hurts him, Randle already slamming her back against the door to hold it open and Alex's staining gurgle hot as piss against his shoulder, Randle screaming, "Give me the keys! Give me the keys!" Her hand digging hard into his pocket as he swung Alex, white-faced, into the back seat, lost his balance as the car jerked into gear and fell with the force of motion to his temple, dull and cool, against the lever of the seat release.

And lay there, smelling must and the faint flavor of motor oil, Alex above collapsed into silence, lay a long time before he finally thought to ask, "Where're we going?" He had to ask it twice to cut the blare of the radio.

Randle didn't turn around. "Hope there's nothing in that house you wanted."

Night, and the golden arches again. This time they ate in the car, taking turns to go inside to pee, to wash, the rest rooms small as closets. Gritty green soap from the dispenser. Alex ate nothing. Alex was still asleep.

Randle's lolling glance, too weary to sit up straight anymore. "You drive for a while," she said. "Keep on I-10 till you get —"

"I know," louder than he meant; he was tired too. It was a chore just to keep raising his hand to his mouth. Randle was feeling for something, rooting slowly under the seat, in her purse. When he raised his eyebrows at her she said, "You got any cigarettes?"

"Didn't you just buy a pack?"

Silence, then, "I left them at the house. On the back of the toilet," and without fuller warning began to weep, one hand loose against her mouth. Mitch turned his head, stared at the parking lot around them, the fluttering jerk of headlights like big fat clumsy birds. "I'm sick of leaving stuff places," she said. Her hand muffled her voice, made it sound like she spoke from underwater, some calm green place where voices could never go. "Do you know how long I've been wearing this shirt?" and before he could think if it was right to give any answer, "Five days. That's how long. Five fucking days in this same fucking shirt."

From the back seat Alex said, "Breaux Bridge," in a tone trusting and tender as a child's. Without turning, without bothering to look, Randle pistoned her arm in a backhand punch so hard Mitch flinched watching it.

Flat-voiced, "You just shut up," still without turning, as if the back seat had become impossible for her. "That's all you have to do. Just shut up."

Mitch started the car. Alex began to moan, a pale whimper that undercut the engine noise. Randle said, "I don't care what happens, don't wake me up." She pulled her T-shirt over her head and threw it out the window.

"Randle, for God's sake! At least wait till we get going."

"Let them look." Her breasts were spotted in places, a rashy speckle strange in the greenish dashlight, like some intricate tattoo the details of which became visible only in hard daylight. She lay with her head on his thigh, the flesh beneath her area of touch asleep before she was. He drove for almost an hour before he lightly pushed her off.

And in the back seat the endless sound of Alex, his rustling paper, the marshy odor of his tears. To Mitch it was as if the envelope of night had closed around them not forever but for so long there was no difference to be charted or discerned. Like the good old days. Like Alex staggering around and around, newspaper carpets and the funnies especially, vomiting blood that eclipsed the paler smell of pigeon shit from the old pigeon coop. Pigeonnier. Black dirt, alluvial crumble and sprayed like tarot dust across the blue-tiled kitchen floor. Wasn't it strange that he could still remember that tile, its gaudy Romanesque patterns? Remember it as he recalled his own nervous shiver, hidden like treasure behind the mahogany boards. And Randle's terrified laughter. Momma. Promises, his hands between her dusty palms; they were so small then, his hands. Alex wiping uselessly at the scabby drip of his actions, even then you had to watch him all the time. Broken glasses, one after another. Willow bonfires. The crying cicadas, no, that was happening now, wasn't it? Through the

Buick's open windows. Through the hours and hours of driving until the air went humid with daylight and the reeking shimmer of exhaust, and Randle stirring closed-eyed on the front seat beside him and murmuring, anxious in her sleep, "Alex?"

He lay one hand on her neck, damp skin, clammy. "Shhhh, he's all right. It's still my turn. He's all right."

And kept driving. The rustle of paper in the back seat. Alex's soft sulky hum, like some rare unwanted engine that no lack of fuel could hamper, that no one could finally turn off.

And his hands on the wheel as silent as Randle's calmed breathing, as stealthy as Alex's cities, the litany begun anew: Florien, Samtown, Echo, Lecomte, drifting forward like smoke from a secret fire, always burning, like the fires on the levees, like the fire that took their home. Remember that? Mouth open, catching flies his mother would have said. Blue flame like a gas burner. What color does blood burn?

And his head hanging down as if shamefaced, as if dunned and stropped by the blunt hammer of anger, old anger like the fires that never burned out. And his eyes closing, sleeping, though he woke to think, Pull over, had to, sliding heedless as a drunken man over to the shoulder to let himself fall, forehead striking gentle against the steering wheel as if victim of the mildest of accidents. Randle still asleep on the seat beside. Alex, was he still saying his cities? Alex? Paper to play with? "Alex," but he spoke the word without authority, in dreams against a landscape not welcome but necessary: in which the rustle of Alex's paper mingled with the slower dribble of his desires, the whole an endless pavane danced through the cities of Louisiana, the smaller, the hotter, the better. And he, and Randle too, were somehow children again, kids at the old house where the old mantle of protection fell new upon them, and they unaware and helpless of the burden, ignorant of the loss they had already and irrevocably sustained, loss of life while living it. You have to swear me, Mitchie. And Randle, not Randle then, not Francey but Marie-Claire, that was her name, Marie-Claire promising as he did, little sister with her hands outstretched.

The car baked slow and thorough in the shadeless morning, too far from the trees. Alex, grave as a gargoyle chipped cunningly free, rose, in silence the back door handle and through the open windows his open palms, let the brownish flakes cascade down upon Mitch and Randle both, swirling like the glitter-snow in a paperweight, speckles, freckles, changing to a darker rain, so lightly they never felt it, so quiet they never heard. And gone.

The slap of consciousness, Randle's cry, disgust, her hands grubby with it, scratching at the skin of her forearms so new blood rose beneath the dry. Scabbed with blood, painted with it. Mitch beside her, similarly scabbed, brushing with a detached dismay, not quite fastidious, as if he were used to waking covered with the spoor of his brother's predilections.

"I'm not his mother!" Screaming. She was losing it, maybe already had. Understandable. Less so his own lucidity, back calm against the seat; shock-free? Maybe he was crazier than she was. Crazier than Alex, though that would be pushing it. She was still screaming, waves of it that shook her breasts. He was getting an erection. Wasn't that something.

"I'm sick of him being a monster. I can't —"

"We have to look for him."

"You look! You look! I'm tired of looking!" Snot on her lips. He grabbed her by the breasts, distant relish, and shoved her very hard against the door. She stopped screaming and started crying, a dry drone that did not indicate if she had actually given in or merely cracked. *Huh-huh-huh.* "Put your shirt on," he said, and remembered she didn't have one, she had thrown it away. Stupid bitch. He gave her his shirt, rolled his window all the way down. Should they drive, or go on foot? How far? How long had they slept? He remembered telling her it was his turn to watch Alex. Staring out the window. Willows. Floodplain. Spanish moss. He had always hated Spanish moss. So *hot,* and Randle's sudden screech, he hated that too, hated the way her lips stretched through mucus and old blood and new blood and her pointing finger, pointing at Alex. Walking toward them.

Waving, extravagant, exuberant, carrying something, something it took both hands to hold. Even from this distance Mitch could see that Alex's shirt was soaked. Saturated. Beside him Randle's screech had shrunk to a blubber that he was certain, this time, would not cease. Maybe ever. Nerves, it got on his nerves, mosquito with a dentist's drill digging at your ear. At your brain. At his fingers on the car keys or maybe it was just the itch of blood as he started the car, started out slow, driving straight down the middle of the road to where he, and Randle, and Alex, slick and sticky to the hairline, would intersect. His foot on the gas pedal was gentle, and Alex's gait rocked like a chair on the porch as he waved his arms again, his arms and the thing within.

Randle spoke, dull through a mouthful of snot. "Slow down," and he shook his head without looking at her, he didn't really want to see her at this particular moment.

"I don't think so," he said as his foot dipped, elegant, like the last step in a dance. Behind Alex, the diagonal shadows of willow trees, old ones; sturdy? Surely. There was hardly any gas left in the car, but he had just enough momentum for all of them.

Stephen King needs little introduction. Since the publication of his first novel, *Carrie*, King has been entertaining readers by writing exactly what he wants to write, when he wants to write it. And this includes the occasional short story published in such varied venues as *OMNI, Playboy, The Magazine of Fantasy & Science Fiction, Cemetery Dance,* and *The New Yorker.* He won the O'Henry Award and the World Fantasy Award in 1995 for his story "The Man in the Black Suit."

"Chattery Teeth," in which King takes a simple toy and imbues it with... personality, has been a favorite of mine since its publication in 1992.

Chattery Teeth

Stephen King

LOOKING INTO THE display case was like looking through a dirty pane of glass into the middle third of his boyhood, those years from seven to fourteen when he had been fascinated by stuff like this. Hogan leaned closer, forgetting the rising whine of the wind outside and the gritty *spick-spack* sound of sand hitting the windows. The case was full of fabulous junk, all of it undoubtedly made in Taiwan and Korea, but there was no doubt at all about the pick of the litter. They were the biggest Chattery Teeth he'd ever seen. They were also the only ones he'd ever seen with feet — big orange cartoon shoes with white spats. A real scream.

Hogan looked up at the fat woman behind the counter. She was wearing a T-shirt that said NEVADA IS GOD'S COUNTRY on top (the words swelling and receding across her enormous breasts) and about an acre of jeans on the bottom. She was selling a pack of cigarettes to a skinny young man with a lot of blonde hair tied back in a pony tail. The young man, who had the face of an intelligent rat, was paying in small change, counting it laboriously out of a grimy hand.

"Pardon me, ma'am?" Hogan asked.

She looked at him briefly, and then the back door banged open. A skinny man wearing a bandanna over his mouth and nose came in. The wind swirled gritty desert dust around him in a cyclone and rattled the pin-up cutie on the Valvoline calendar thumbtacked to the wall. The newcomer was pulling a handcart. Three wire-mesh cages were stacked on it. There was a tarantula in the one on top. In the cages below it were a pair of rattlesnakes. They were coiling rapidly back and forth and shaking their rattles in agitation.

"Shut the damn door, Scooter, was you born in a barn?" the woman behind the counter bawled.

He glanced at her briefly, eyes red and irritated from the blowing sand. "Gimme a chance, woman! Can't you see I got my hands full here? Ain't you got *eyes?* Christ!" He reached over the dolly and slammed the door. The dancing sand fell dead to the floor and he pulled the dolly toward the storeroom at the back, still muttering.

"That the last of em?" the woman asked.

"All but Wolf." He pronounced it *Woof.* "I'm gonna stick him in the lean-to back of the gas pumps."

"You ain't not!" the big woman retorted. "Wolf's our star attraction, in case you forgot. You get him in here. Radio says this is gonna get worse before it gets better. A lot worse."

"Just who do you think you're foolin?" The skinny man (her husband, Hogan supposed) stood looking at her with a kind of weary truculence, his hands on his hips. "Damn thing ain't nothin but a Minnesota coydog, as anyone who took more'n half a look could plainly see."

The wind gusted, moaning along the eaves of Scooter's Grocery & Roadside Zoo, throwing sheaves of dry sand against the windows. It *was* getting worse, Hogan realized. He hoped he could drive out of it. He had promised Lita and Jack that he would be home by seven, eight at the latest, and he was a man who liked to keep his promises.

"Just take care of him," the big woman said, and turned irritably back to the rat-faced boy.

"Ma'am?" Hogan said again.

"Just a minute, hold your water," Mrs. Scooter said. She spoke with the air of one who is all but drowning in impatient customers, although Hogan and the rat-faced boy were in fact the only ones present.

"You're a dime short, Sunny Jim," she told the blonde kid after a quick glance at the coins on the counter-top.

The boy regarded her with wide, innocent eyes. "I don't suppose you'd trust me for it?"

"I doubt if the Pope of Rome smokes Merit 100's, but if he did, I wouldn't trust *him* for it."

The look of wide-eyed innocence disappeared. The rat-faced boy looked at her with an expression of sullen dislike for a moment (this expression looked much more at home on the kid's face, Hogan thought), and then slowly began to investigate his pockets again.

Just forget it and get out of here, Hogan thought. *You'll never make it to L.A. by eight if you don't get moving, and this is one of those places that has only two speeds — slow and stop. You got your gas and paid for it, so just get back on the road before the storm gets any worse.*

He almost followed his left brain's good advice...and then he looked at the Chattery Teeth in the display case again, the Chattery Teeth standing there on those big orange cartoon shoes. And white spats! That was the killer. Jack, his right brain told him, would love them. *And tell the truth, Bill, old buddy: if it turns out Jack doesn't want them, you do. You may see another set of Jumbo Chattery Teeth at some point in your life, anything's possible, but ones that also walk on big orange feet? Huh-uh. I really don't think so.*

It was the right brain he listened to that time...and everything else followed.

The kid with the ponytail was still going through his pockets; the sullen expression on his face deepened each time he came up dry. Hogan was no fan of smoking — his father, a two-pack-a-day man, had died of lung cancer — but he had visions of still waiting to be waited on an hour from now. "Hey! Kid!"

The kid looked around and Hogan flipped him a quarter.

"Thanks, dude!"

"Think nothing of it."

The kid concluded his transaction with the beefy Mrs. Scooter. He put the cigarettes in one pocket and the remaining fifteen cents in another. He made no offer of the change to Hogan, who was not very surprised. Boys and girls like this were legion these days — they cluttered the highways from coast to coast, blowing along like tumbleweeds. Perhaps they had always been there, but to Hogan the current breed seemed both unpleasant and a little scary, like the rattlers Scooter was now storing in the back room.

The snakes in pissant little roadside menageries like this one couldn't kill you; their venom was bled twice a week and sold to clinics that made drugs with them. You could count on that just as you could count on the winos to show up at the local Red Cross every Tuesday and Thursday to sell their blood. But the snakes could still give you one hell of a painful bite if you made them mad and then got too close. That, Hogan thought, was what the current breed of road-kids had in common with them.

Mrs. Scooter came drifting down the counter, the words on her T-shirt drifting up and down and side to side as she did. "Whatcha need?" she asked. Her tone was still truculent. The west had a reputation for friendliness, and during the twenty years he had spent selling there Hogan had come to feel the reputation was deserved, but this woman had all the charm of a Brooklyn shopkeeper who has been stuck up three times in the last two weeks. Her kind was also on the rise, Hogan reflected.

"How much are these?" Hogan asked, pointing through the dirty glass. The case was filled with novelty items — Chinese finger-pullers, Pepper Gum, Dr. Wacky's Sneezing Powder, cigarette loads (A Laff Riot! according to the package — Hogan guessed they were more likely a great way to get your teeth knocked out), X-ray glasses, plastic vomit (So Realistic!), joy-buzzers.

"I dunno," Mrs. Scooter said. "Where's the box, I wonder?"

The object of Hogan's interest was the only item in the case that wasn't packaged. A crudely lettered card beside them read JUMBO CHATTERY TEETH! THEY *WALK!* They certainly *were* jumbo, Hogan thought — *super*-jumbo, in fact. They were five times the size of the sets of wind-up teeth which had so amused him as a kid growing up in Maine. Take away the joke feet and they would look like the teeth of some fallen Biblical giant — the cuspids were big white blocks and the canine teeth looked like tentpegs sunk in the improbably red plastic gums. A key jutted from one gum. The teeth were held together in a clench by a thick rubber band.

Mrs. Scooter blew the dust from the Chattery Teeth, then turned them over, looking on the soles of the orange shoes for a price sticker. She didn't find one. "*I* don't know," she said crossly, eyeing Hogan as if he might have taken the sticker off himself. "Only Scooter'd buy a piece of trash like that. Been around a thousand years. I'll have to ask him."

Hogan was suddenly tired of the woman and of Scooter's Grocery & Roadside Zoo. They were great Chattery Teeth, and Jack would undoubtedly love them, but he had promised — eight at the latest.

"Never mind," he said. "I was just an —"

"Them teeth was supposed to go for $5.95," Scooter said from behind them. "They ain't just plastic — those're metal teeth painted white. They could give you a helluva bite if they worked...but *she* dropped em on the floor two-three years ago when she was dustin' the inside of the case and they're busted."

"Oh," Hogan said, disappointed. "That's too bad. I never saw a pair with, you know, feet."

"There are lots of em like that now," Scooter said. "They sell em at the novelty stores in Vegas and Dry Springs. But I never saw a set as big as those. It was funnier'n hell to watch em walk across the floor, snappin' like a crocodile.

Shame the old lady dropped em."

Scooter glanced at her, but his wife was looking out at the blowing sand. There was an expression on her face which Hogan couldn't quite decipher — was it sadness, or disgust, or both?

Scooter looked back at Hogan. "I could let em go for fifty cents, if you wanted em. We're gettin rid of the novelties, anyway. Gonna put rental video-tapes in that counter." He pulled the storeroom door closed. The bandanna was now pulled down, lying on the dusty front of his shirt. His face was haggard and too thin. Hogan saw what might have been the shadow of serious illness lurking just beneath his desert tan.

"You could do no such a thing, Scooter!" the big woman snapped, and turned toward him...almost turned *on* him.

"Shutcha head, Myra," Scooter told her. "You make my fillins ache."

"I told you to get Wolf —"

"If you want him back there in the storeroom, go get him yourself," he said. He began to advance on her, and Hogan was surprised — almost wonder-struck, in fact — when she gave ground. "Ain't nothin' but a Minnesota coydog anyway. Fifty cents for the teeth, friend, and for a buck you can take Myra's Woof, too. If you got five, I'll deed the whole place to you. Ain't worth a dogfart since the turnpike went through, anyway."

The long-haired kid was standing by the door, tearing the top from the pack of cigarettes Hogan had helped buy, and watching this small comic opera with an expression of mean amusement. His small blue eyes gleamed, flicking back and forth between Scooter and his wife.

"Hell with you," Myra said gruffly, and Hogan realized she was close to tears. "If you won't get my sweet baby, I will." She stalked past him, almost striking him with one boulder-sized breast. Hogan thought it would have knocked the little man flat if it had connected.

"Look," Hogan said, "I think I'll just shove along."

"Aw, hell," Scooter said. "Don't mind Myra. I got cancer and she's got the change, and it ain't my problem she's havin the most trouble livin with. Take the teeth. Bet you got a boy might like em. Besides, it's probably just a cog knocked a little off-track. I bet a man who was handy could get em walkin' and chompin' again."

He looked around, his expression helpless and musing. Outside, the wind rose to a brief, thin shriek as the kid opened the door and slipped out. He had decided the show was over, apparently. A cloud of fine grit swirled down the middle aisle, between the canned goods and the dog food.

"I was pretty handy myself, at one time," Scooter confided.

Hogan did not reply for a long moment. He could not think of anything — quite literally not one single thing — to say. He looked down at the Jumbo Chattery Teeth standing on the scratched and cloudy display case, nearly desperate to break the silence (now that Scooter was standing right in front of him, he could see that the man was more than pale — his eyes were huge and dark, glittering with pain and some heavy dope…Darvon, or perhaps morphine), and he spoke the first words that popped into his head: "Gee, they don't *look* broken."

He picked the teeth up. They were metal, all right — too heavy to be anything else — and when he looked through the slightly parted jaws, he was surprised at the size of the mainspring that ran the thing. He supposed it would take one that size to make the teeth not only chatter but walk, as well. What had Scooter said? *They could give you a helluva bite if they worked.* Hogan gave the thick rubber band an experimental tweak, then stripped it off. He was still looking at the teeth so he wouldn't have to look into Scooter's dark, pain-haunted eyes. He grasped the key and at last he risked a look up. He was relieved to see that now the thin man was smiling a little.

"Do you mind?" Hogan asked.

"Not me, pilgrim — let er rip."

Hogan turned the key. At first it was all right; there was a series of small, ratcheting clicks, and he could see the mainspring winding up. Then, on the third turn, there was a *spronk!* noise from inside, and the key simply slid bonelessly around in its hole.

"See?"

"Yes," Hogan said. He set the teeth down on the counter. They simply stood there on their unlikely orange feet and did nothing.

Scooter poked the clenched molars on the lefthand side with the tip of one horny finger. The jaws of the teeth opened. One orange foot rose and took a dreamy half-step forward. Then the teeth stopped moving and the whole rig fell sideways. The Chattery Teeth came to rest on the wind-up key, a slanted, disembodied grin out here in the middle of no-man's land. After a moment or two, the big teeth came together again with a slow (and rather ominous) click. That was all.

Hogan, who had never had a precognitive thought in his life, was suddenly filled with a clear certainty that was both eerie and sickening. *A year from now, this man will have been eight months in his grave, and if someone exhumed his coffin and pried off the lid, they'd see teeth just like these poking out of his dried-out dead face like some sort of animal trap — a set of footless Chattery Teeth that don't work anymore. And why? Because something called cancer came along and knocked all of Scooter's cogs just a little off-track.*

He glanced up into Scooter's eyes, glittering like dark gems in tarnished settings, and suddenly it was no longer a question of *wanting* to get out of here; he *had* to get out of here.

"Well," he said (hoping frantically that Scooter would not stick out his hand to be shaken). "I have to go. Best of luck to you, sir."

Scooter *did* put his hand out, but not to be shaken. Instead, he snapped the rubber band back around the Chattery Teeth (Hogan had no idea why, since they didn't work), set them on their funny cartoon feet, and pushed them across the scratched surface of the counter. "Go on," he said. "Take em. No charge. Give em to your boy. He'll get a kick out of em standin' on the shelf in his room even if they don't work. I know a little about boys. Raised three of em."

"How did you know I had a son?" Hogan asked.

Scooter winked. The gesture was terrifying and pathetic at the same time. "Seen it in your face," he said. "Go on, take em."

The wind gusted again, this time hard enough to make the boards of the building moan. The sand hitting the windows sounded like fine snow. Hogan picked up the teeth by the plastic feet, surprised all over again by how heavy they were.

"Here," Scooter said. He produced a paper bag, almost as wrinkled and crumpled about the edges as his own face, from beneath the counter. "Stick em in here. That's a real nice sport-coat you got there. If you carry them choppers in the pocket, it'll get pulled out of shape."

He put the bag on the counter as if he understood how little Hogan wanted to touch him.

"Thanks," Hogan said. He put the Chattery Teeth in the bag and rolled down the top. "My boy, Jack, thanks you, too."

Scooter smiled, revealing a set of teeth just as false (but nowhere near as large) as the ones in the paper bag. "My pleasure, mister. You drive careful until you get out of the blow. You'll be fine once you get in the foothills."

"I know." Hogan cleared his throat. "Thanks again. I hope you...uh... recover soon."

"That'd be nice," Scooter said evenly, "but I don't think it's in the cards, do you?"

"Uh. Well. Okay." Hogan realized with dismay that he didn't have the slightest idea how to conclude this encounter. "Take care of yourself."

Scooter nodded. "You too."

Hogan retreated toward the door, opened it, and had to hold on tight as the wind tried to rip it out of his hand and bang the wall. Fine sand scoured his face and he slitted his eyes against it.

He stepped out, closed the door behind him, and pulled the lapel of his real nice sport-coat over his mouth and nose as he crossed the porch, descended the steps, and headed toward the Dodge Fiesta camper-van parked just beyond the gas-pumps. The wind pulled his hair and the sand stung his cheeks. He was going around to the driver's side door when someone tugged his arm.

"Mister! Hey, mister!"

He turned. It was the blonde-haired boy. He hunched against the wind and blowing sand, wearing nothing but a T-shirt and a pair of faded 501 jeans. Behind him, Mrs. Scooter was dragging a mangy beast on a choke-chain toward the back door of the store. Wolf the Minnesota Coydog looked like a half-starved German Shepherd pup — and the runt of the litter, at that.

"What?" Hogan shouted, knowing very well what.

"Can I have a ride?" the kid shouted back over the wind.

Hogan did not ordinarily pick up hitchhikers — not since one afternoon five years ago. He had stopped for a young girl on the outskirts of Tonapah. Standing by the side of the road, the girl had resembled one of those sad-eyed waifs in the velvet paintings you could buy in the discount stores, a kid who looked like her mother and her last friend had both died in the same housefire about a month ago. Once she was in the car, however, Hogan had seen the bad skin and mad eyes of the long-time junkie. By then it had been too late. She had stuck a pistol in his face and demanded his wallet. The pistol was old and rusty. Its grip was wrapped in tattered electrician's tape. Hogan had doubted if it was loaded, or if it would fire if it was...but he had a wife and a kid back in L.A., and even if he had been single, was a hundred and forty bucks worth risking your life over? He hadn't thought so even then, when he had just been getting his feet under him in his new line of work. He gave the girl his wallet. By then her boyfriend had been parked beside the van (in those days it had been a Ford Econoline, nowhere near as nice as the Fiesta XRT) in a dirty blue sedan. Hogan asked the girl if she would leave him his driver's license, and the pictures of Lita and Jack. "Fuck you, sugar," she said, and slapped him across the face, hard, with his own wallet before getting out and running to the blue car.

Hitchhikers were trouble.

But the storm was getting worse, and the kid didn't even have a jacket. What was he supposed to tell him? Fuck you, sugar, crawl under a rock until the wind drops?

"Get in," he said.

"Thanks, dude! Thanks a lot!"

The kid ran toward the passenger door, tried it, found it locked, and just stood there, waiting to be let in, hunching his shoulders up around his ears. The wind billowed out the back of his shirt like a sail, revealing glimpses of his thin, pimple-studded back.

Hogan glanced back at Scooter's Grocery & Roadside Zoo as he went around to the driver's door. Scooter was standing at the window, looking out at him. He raised his hand, solemnly, palm out. Hogan raised his own in return, then slipped his key into the lock and turned it. He opened the door, pushed the unlock button next to the power window switch, and motioned for the kid to get in.

He did, then had to use both hands to pull the door shut again. The wind howled around the Fiesta, actually making it rock a little from side to side.

"*Wow!*" the kid gasped, and rubbed his fingers briskly through his hair (it had come loose from the rubber band and now it lay on his shoulders in lank clots). "Some storm, huh?"

"Yeah," Hogan said. There was a console between the two front seats — the kind of seats the brochures liked to call "captain's chairs" — and Hogan placed the paper bag in one of the cup-holders. Then he turned the ignition key. The engine started at once with a good-tempered rumble.

The kid twisted around in his seat and looked appreciatively into the back of the van. There was a bed (now folded back into a couch), a small LP gas stove, several storage compartments where Hogan kept his various sample cases, and a toilet cubicle at the rear.

"Not bad, dude!" the kid said. "All the comforts." He glanced back at Hogan. "Where you headed?"

"Los Angeles."

The kid grinned. "Hey, great! So am I!" He took out his just-purchased pack of Merits and tapped one loose.

Hogan had put on his headlights and dropped the transmission into drive. Now he shoved the gearshift back into park and turned to the kid. "Let's get a couple of things straight," he said.

The kid gave Hogan his wide-eyed innocent look. "Sure, dude — you bet."

"First, I don't pick up hitchhikers as a rule. I had a bad experience with one a few years back. It vaccinated me. I'll take you through the Santa Clara foothills. There's a truckstop on the other side — Sammy's. It's close to the turnpike. That's where we part company. Okay?"

"Okay. Sure, dude. You bet." Still with the wide-eyed look.

"Second, if you really have to smoke, we part company right now. *That* okay?"

For just a moment Hogan saw the kid's other look (and even on short acquaintance, Hogan was almost willing to bet the kid only had the two) — the mean, watchful look, and then he was all wide-eyed, sure-you-bet-right-on-dude innocence again. He tucked the cigarette behind his ear and showed Hogan his empty hands.

"No prob," he said. "Okay?"

"Okay. Bill Hogan." He held out his hand.

"Bryan Adams," the kid said, and shook Hogan's hand briefly.

Hogan dropped the transmission into drive again and began to roll slowly toward Route 46. As he did, his eyes dropped briefly to a cassette box lying on the dashboard. It was *Reckless,* by Bryan Adams.

Sure, he thought. *You're Bryan Adams and I'm really Don Henley. We just stopped by Scooter's Grocery & Roadside Zoo to get a little material for our next albums, right dude?*

As he pulled out onto the highway, already straining to see through the blowing dust, he found himself thinking of the girl again, the one outside of Tonapah who had slapped him across the face with his own wallet before fleeing. He was starting to get a very bad feeling about this.

Then a hard gust of wind tried to push him into the eastbound lane, and he concentrated on his driving.

They rode in silence for a while. When Hogan glanced once to his right he saw the kid was lying back with his eyes closed — maybe asleep, maybe dozing, maybe just pretending because he didn't want to talk. That was okay; Hogan didn't want to talk, either. For one thing, he didn't know what he might have to say to Mr. Bryan Adams from Nowhere, u.s.a. It was a cinch young Mr. Adams wasn't in the market for labels or universal price-code readers, which was what Hogan sold. For another, he needed all his concentration for driving.

As Mrs. Scooter had warned, the storm was intensifying. The road was a dim phantom crossed at irregular intervals by tan ribs of sand. These drifts were like speed-bumps, and they forced Hogan to creep along at no more than twenty-five. He could live with that. At some points, however, the sand had spread more evenly across the road's surface, camouflaging it, and then Hogan had to drop down to fifteen miles an hour, navigating by the dim bounceback of his headlights from the reflector-posts which marched along the side of the road.

Every now and then an approaching car or truck would loom out of the blowing sand like a prehistoric phantom with round blazing eyes. One of these, an old Lincoln Mark IV as big as a cabin cruiser, was driving straight down the center of 46. Hogan hit the horn and squeezed right, feeling the suck of the sand against his tires, feeling his lips peel away from his teeth in a helpless snarl. Just as he became sure the oncomer was going to force him into the ditch, the Lincoln swerved back onto its own side just enough for Hogan to make it by. He thought he heard the metallic click of his bumper kissing off the Mark IV's rear bumper, but given the steady shriek of the wind, that was almost certainly his own imagination. He *did* catch just a glimpse of the driver — an old bald-headed man sitting bolt-upright behind the wheel, peering into the blowing sand with a concentrated glare that was almost maniacal. Hogan shook his fist at him, but the old codger did not so much as glance at him. *Probably didn't even realize I was there,* Hogan thought, *let alone how close he came to hitting me.*

For a few seconds he was very close to going off the road anyway. He could feel the sand sucking harder at the rightside wheels, felt the Fiesta trying to tip. His instinct was to twist the wheel hard to the left. Instead, he fed the van gas and only urged it in that direction, feeling sweat dampen his last good shirt at the armpits. At last the suck on the tires diminished and he began to feel in control of the van again. Hogan blew his breath out in a long sigh.

"Good piece of driving, dude."

His attention had been so focused he had forgotten his passenger, and in his surprise he almost twisted the wheel all the way to the left, which would have put them in trouble again. He looked around and saw the blonde kid watching him. His gray-green eyes were unsettlingly bright; there was no sign of sleepiness in them.

"It was just luck," Hogan said. "If there was a place to pull over, I would... but I know this piece of road. It's Sammy's or bust. Once we're in the foothills, it'll get better."

The thing was, he did not add, it might take them three hours to cover the seventy miles between here and there.

"You're a salesman, right?"

"Right."

"Right."

He wished the kid wouldn't talk. He wanted to concentrate on his driving. Up ahead, fog-lights loomed out of the murk like yellow ghosts. They were followed by an IROC-Z with California plates. The Fiesta and the Z crept past each other like old ladies in a nursing home corridor. In the corner of his eye, Hogan saw the kid take the cigarette from behind his ear and begin to play with it. Bryan Adams indeed. Why had the kid given him a false name? It was like something out of an old Republic movie, the kind of thing you could still see on the late-late show, a black-and-white crime movie where the travelling salesman (probably played by Ray Milland) picks up the tough young con (played by Nick Adams, maybe) who has just broken out of jail in Gabbs or Deeth or some place like that —

"What do you sell, dude?"

"Labels."

"Labels?"

"That's right. The ones with the universal price code on them. It's a little block with a pre-set number of black bars in it."

The kid surprised Hogan by nodding. "Sure — they whip em over an electric-eye gadget in the supermarket and the price shows up on the cash register like magic, right?"

"Yes. Except it's not magic, and it's not an electric eye. It's a laser reader. I sell those, too. Both the big ones and the portables."

"Far out, dude." The tinge of sarcasm in the kid's voice was faint...but it was there.

"Bryan?"

"Yeah?"

"The name's Bill, not dude."

He found himself wishing more and more strongly that he could roll back in time to Scooter's, and just say no when the kid asked him for a ride. The Scooters weren't bad sorts; they would have let the kid stay until the storm blew itself out this evening. Maybe Mrs. Scooter would even have given him five bucks to babysit the tarantula, the rattlers, and Woof, the Amazing Minnesota Coydog. Hogan found himself liking those gray-green eyes less and less. He could feel their weight on his face, like small stones.

"Yeah — Bill. Bill the Label Dude."

Bill didn't reply. The kid laced his fingers together and bent his hands backward, cracking the knuckles.

"Well, it's like my old mamma used to say — it may not be much, but it's a living. Right, Label Dude?"

Hogan grunted something noncommittal and concentrated on his driving. The feeling that he had made a mistake had grown to a certainty. When he'd picked up the girl that time, God had let him get away with it. *Please*, he prayed. *One more time, okay, God? Better yet, let me be wrong about this kid — let it just be paranoia brought on by low barometer, high winds, and the coincidence of a name that can't, after all, be that uncommon.*

Here came a huge Mack truck from the other direction, the silver bulldog atop the grille seeming to peer into the flying grit. Hogan squeezed right until he felt the sand piled up along the edge of the road grabbing greedily at his tires again. The long silver box the Mack was pulling blotted out everything on Hogan's left side. It was six inches away — maybe even less — and it seemed to pass forever.

When it was finally gone, the blonde kid asked: "You look like you're doin' pretty well, Bill — rig like this must have set you back at least thirty big ones. So why —"

"It was a lot less than that." Hogan didn't know if "Bryan Adams" could hear the edgy note in his voice, but *he* sure could. "I did a lot of the work myself."

"All the same, you sure ain't staggerin' around hungry. So why aren't you up above all this shit, flying the friendly skies?"

It was a question Hogan had often asked himself in the long empty miles between Tempe and Tucson or Las Vegas and Los Angeles, the kind of question you *had* to ask yourself when you couldn't find anything on the radio but crappy syntho-pop or threadbare oldies and you'd listened to the last cassette of the current best-seller from Books on Tape, when there was nothing to look at but miles of gullywashes and scrubland, all of it owned by Uncle Sam.

He could say that he got a better feel for his customers and their needs by travelling through the country where his customers lived and sold their goods, and it was true, but it wasn't the reason. He could say that checking his sample cases, which were much too bulky to fit under an airline seat, was a pain in the ass and waiting for them to show up on the conveyor belt at the other end was always an adventure (he'd once had a packing case filled with five thousand soft-drink labels show up in Hilo, Hawaii, instead of Hilsdale, New Mexico). That was *also* true, but it also wasn't the reason.

The reason was that in 1982 he had been on board a Western Pride commuter flight which had crashed in the high country seventeen miles north of Reno. Fifteen of the nineteen passengers on board and both crew-members had been killed. Hogan had suffered a broken back. He had spent four months in bed and another ten in a heavy brace his wife Lita called the Iron Maiden. They (whoever *they* were) said that if you got thrown from a horse, you should get right back on. William I. Hogan said that was bullshit, and with the exception of a white-knuckle, two-Valium flight to attend his brother's wedding in Oakland, he had never been on a plane since.

He came out of these thoughts all at once, realizing two things: he had had the road to himself since the passage of the Mack, and the kid was still looking at him with those unsettling eyes, waiting for him to answer the question.

"I had a bad experience on a commuter flight once," he said. "Since then, I've pretty much stuck to transport where you can coast into the breakdown lane if your engine quits."

"You sure have had a lot of bad experiences, Bill-dude," the kid said. A tone of bogus regret crept into his voice. "And now you're gonna have another one." There was a sharp metallic click. Hogan looked over and was not very surprised to see the kid was holding a switchknife with a glittering eight-inch blade.

Oh shit, Hogan thought. Now that it was here, now that it was right in front of him, he didn't feel very scared. Only tired. *Oh shit, and only four hundred miles from home. Goddam.*

"Pull over, Bill-dude. Nice and slow."

"What do you want?"

"If you really don't know the answer to that one, you're even dumber than you look." A little smile played around the corners of the kid's mouth. "I want your dough, and I want your van. But don't worry — there's this little truck-stop not too far from here. Sammy's. Close to the turnpike. Someone'll give you a ride. The people who don't stop will look at you like you're dogshit they found on their shoe, of course, and you might have to beg a little, but I'm sure you'll get a ride in the end. Now *pull over.*"

Hogan was surprised to find that he felt more than tired — he felt angry, as well. Had he been angry at the girl who had stolen his wallet that other time? He couldn't honestly remember.

"Look," he said, turning to the kid. "I gave you a ride when you needed one, and I didn't make you beg for it. If it wasn't for me, you'd be back at Scooter's, eating sand with your thumb out. So why don't you just put that thing away? We'll —"

The kid suddenly lashed forward with the knife, and Hogan felt a thread of burning pain across his right hand. The van swerved, then shuddered as it passed over another of those sandy speed-bumps.

"Pull *over*, I said. You're either walking, salesman, or you're lying in the nearest gully with your throat cut and one of your own price-reading gadgets jammed up your ass. I get what's in your wallet either way. The van, too. I'm going to chain-smoke all the way to Los Angeles, and you know what? Each time I finish a cigarette I'm going to butt it out on your dashboard."

Hogan glanced down at his hand and saw a diagonal line of blood which stretched from the last knuckle of his pinky to the base of his thumb. And here was the anger again…only now it was something close to rage, and if the tiredness was still there, it was buried somewhere in the middle of that irrational red eye. He tried to summon a mental picture of Lita and Jack to damp that feeling down before it got the better of him and made him do something crazy, but the images were fuzzy and out of focus. There *was* a clear image in his mind, but it was the wrong one — it was the face of the girl outside of Tonapah, the girl with the snarling mouth below the big dime-store waif eyes, the girl who had said *Fuck you, sugar* before slapping him across the face with his own wallet.

He stepped down on the gas-pedal and the Fiesta began to move faster. The red needle moved past thirty.

The kid looked surprised, then puzzled, then angry. "What are you doing? I told you to pull over! Do you want your guts in your lap, or what?"

"I don't know," Hogan said. He kept his foot on the gas. Now the needle was trembling just above forty. The van ran across a series of dunelets and shivered like a dog with a fever. "What do *you* want, kid. How about a broken neck. All it takes is one twist of the wheel. I fastened *my* seatbelt. I notice you forgot yours."

The kid's gray-green eyes were huge now, glittering with a mixture of fear and fury. *You're supposed to pull over,* those eyes said. *That's the way it's supposed to work when I'm holding a knife on you — don't you* know *that?*

"You won't wreck us," the kid said, but Hogan thought he was trying to convince himself.

"Why not?" Hogan turned toward the kid again. "After all, I'm pretty sure I'll walk away, and the van's insured. You call the play, asshole. What about that?"

"You —" the kid began, and then his eyes widened and he lost all interest in Hogan. *"Look out!"* he screamed...

Hogan snapped his eyes forward and saw four huge white headlamps bearing down on him through the flying wrack outside. It was a tanker truck, probably carrying gasoline, propane, or maybe fertilizer. An air-horn beat the air like the cry of a gigantic, enraged goose: *WHONK! WHONK! WHONNNK!*

The Fiesta had drifted while Hogan was trying to deal with the kid; now *he* was the one halfway across the road. He yanked the wheel hard to the right, knowing it would do no good, knowing it was already too late. But the approaching truck was also moving, squeezing over just as Hogan had done to try and accommodate the Mark IV. The two vehicles danced past each other through the flying sand with less than a gasp between them. Hogan felt his rightside wheels bite into the sand again and knew that this time he didn't have a chance in hell of holding the van on the road — not at forty-two miles an hour. As the dim shape of the big steel tank (CARTER'S DAIRY MILK FROM CONTENTED COWS was painted along the side) slid from view, he felt the steering wheel go mushy in his hands, dragging further to the right. And from the corner of his eye, he saw the kid lunge forward with his knife.

What's the matter with you, are you crazy? he wanted to scream, but there was no time left for screaming, and besides, he already knew the answer — of *course* the kid was crazy. That was the message in those gray-green eyes, and it had been there long before the kid pulled the knife. Pure craziness.

He tried his level best to plant the blade in Hogan's neck, but the van had begun to tilt by then, running deeper and deeper into the sand-choked gully. Hogan pulled back from the blade, letting go of the wheel, and thought he had gotten clear until he felt the wet warmth of blood drench the side of his neck.

The knife had unzipped his right cheek from jaw to temple. He flailed with his right hand, trying to get the kid's wrist, and then the Fiesta's left front wheel struck a rock the size of a pay telephone and the van flipped high and hard, like a stunt vehicle in one of those movies this rootless kid undoubtedly loved. It rolled in midair, all four wheels turning, still doing thirty miles an hour according to the speedometer, and Hogan felt his seatbelt lock painfully across his chest and belly. It was like reliving the plane-crash — now, as then, he could not get it through his head that this was really happening.

The kid was thrown upward and forward, still holding onto the knife. His head bounced off the roof as the van's top and bottom swapped places. Hogan saw his left hand waving wildly, and realized with amazement that the kid was *still* trying to stab him. The kid was a rattler, all right, he'd been right about that, but no one had milked his poison sacs.

Then the van struck the desert hardpan, peeling off the luggage racks, and the kid's head connected with the roof again, much harder this time. The knife was jolted from his hand. The cabinets at the rear of the van sprang open, spraying sample-books and laser label-readers everywhere. Hogan was dimly aware of an inhuman screaming sound — the long, drawn-out squall of the Fiesta's roof sliding across the gravelly desert surface on the far side of the gully — and thought: *So this is what it would be like to be inside a tin can when someone was using the opener.*

The windshield shattered, blowing inward in a sagging shield clouded by a million zigzagging cracks. Hogan shut his eyes and threw his hands up to shield his face as the van continued to roll, thumping down on Hogan's side long enough to shatter the driver's side window and admit a rattle of rocks and dusty earth before staggering upright again. It rocked as if meaning to go over on the kid's side...and then came to rest.

Hogan sat where he was without moving for perhaps five seconds, eyes wide, hands gripping the armrests of his chair. He was aware there was a lot of dirt and crumbled glass in his lap, and something else as well, but not what the something else was. He was also aware of the wind, blowing more dirt through the Fiesta's broken windows.

Then his vision was blocked by a moving object. The object was a mottle of white skin, brown dirt, raw knuckles, and red blood. It was a fist, and it struck Hogan squarely in the nose. The agony was immediate and intense, as if someone had fired a flare-gun directly up into his brain. For a moment his vision was gone, swallowed in a vast white flash. It had just begun to come back when the kid's hands suddenly clamped around his neck and he could no longer breathe.

The kid, Mr. Bryan Adams from Nowhere, U.S.A., was leaning over the console between the front seats. Blood from perhaps half a dozen different scalp-wounds had flowed over his cheeks and forehead and nose like warpaint. His gray-green eyes stared at Hogan with fixed, lunatic fury.

"Look what you did, you numb fuck!" the kid shouted. *"Look what you did to me!"*

Hogan tried to pull back, and got half a breath when the kid's hold slipped momentarily, but with his seatbelt still buckled — and still locked down, from the feel — there was really nowhere he could go. The kid's hands were back almost at once, and this time his thumbs were pressing into his windpipe, pinching it shut.

Hogan tried to bring his own hands up, but the kid's arms, as rigid as prison bars, blocked him. He tried to knock the kid's arms away, but they wouldn't budge. Now he could hear another wind — a high, roaring wind inside his own head.

"Look what you did, you stupid shit! I'm bleedin'!"

The kid's voice, but further away than it had been.

He's killing me, Hogan thought, and a voice replied: *Right — fuck you, sugar.*

That brought the anger back. He groped in his lap for whatever was there. It was a paper bag. Some bulky object inside it. Hogan closed his hand around it and pistoned his fist upward toward the shelf of the kid's jaw. It connected with a heavy thud. The kid screamed in surprised pain, and his grip on Hogan's throat was suddenly gone as he fell over backward.

Hogan pulled in a deep, convulsive breath and heard a sound like a teakettle howling to be taken off the burner. *Is that me, making that sound? My God, is that me?*

He dragged in another breath. It was full of flying dust, it hurt his throat and made him cough, but it was heaven all the same. He looked down at his fist and saw the shape of the Chattery Teeth clearly outlined against the brown bag.

And suddenly felt them *move.*

There was something so shockingly human in this movement that Hogan shrieked and dropped the bag at once; it was as if he had picked up a human jawbone which had tried to speak to his hand.

The bag hit the kid's back and then tumbled to the van's carpeted floor as "Bryan Adams" pushed himself groggily to his knees. Hogan heard the rubber band snap…and then the unmistakable click and chutter of the teeth themselves, opening and closing.

It's probably just a cog knocked a little off-track, Scooter had said. *I bet a man who was handy could get em walkin' and chompin' again.*

Or maybe just a good knock would do it, Hogan thought. *If I live through this and ever get back that way, I'll have to tell Scooter that all you have to do to fix a pair of malfunctioning Chattery Teeth is roll your van over and then use them to hit a psychotic hitchhiker who's trying to strangle you.*

The Chattery Teeth clattered away inside the torn brown bag; the sides fluttered, making it look like an amputated lung which refused to die. The kid crawled away from the bag without even looking at it — crawled toward the back of the van, shaking his head from side to side, trying to clear it. Blood flew from the clots of his hair in a fine spray.

Hogan found the clasp of his seatbelt and pushed the pop-release. Nothing happened. The square in the center of the buckle did not give even a little and the belt itself was still locked as tight as a cramp, cutting into the middle-aged roll of fat above the waistband of his trousers and pushing a hard diagonal across his chest. He tried rocking back and forth in the seat, hoping that would unlock the belt. The flow of blood from his face increased, and he could feel his cheek flapping back and forth like a strip of dried wallpaper, but that was all. He felt panic struggling to break through amazed shock, and twisted his head over his right shoulder to see what the kid was up to.

The kid was up to no good. He had spotted his knife at the far end of the van, lying atop a litter of instructional manuals and brochures. He grabbed it, flicked his hair away from his face, and peered back over his own shoulder at Hogan. He was grinning, and there was something in that grin that made Hogan's balls simultaneously tighten and shrivel until it felt as if someone had tucked a couple of peach-pits into his Jockey shorts.

Ah, here it is! the kid's grin said. *For a minute or two there I was worried — quite seriously worried — but everything is going to come out all right after all. Things got a little improvisational there for a while, but now we're back to the script.*

"You stuck, Label Dude?" the kid asked over the steady shriek of the wind. "You are, ain't you? Good thing you buckled your belt, right? Good thing for me."

The kid tried to get up, almost made it, and then his knees buckled. An expression of surprise so magnified it would have been comic under other circumstances crossed his face. Then he flicked his blood-greasy hair out of his face again and began to crawl toward Hogan, his left hand wrapped around the imitation bone handle of the knife.

Hogan grasped the seatbelt buckle with both hands and drove his thumbs against the pop-release as enthusiastically as the kid had driven his into Hogan's windpipe. There was absolutely no response. The belt was frozen. He craned his neck to look at the kid again.

The kid had made it as far as the fold-up bed and then stopped. That expression of large, comic surprise had resurfaced on his face. He was staring straight ahead, which meant he was looking at something on the floor, and Hogan suddenly remembered the teeth. They were still chattering away.

He looked down in time to see the Jumbo Chattery Teeth march from the open end of the torn paper bag on their funny orange shoes. The molars and the canines and the incisors chopped rapidly up and down, producing a sound like ice in a cocktail glass. The shoes, dressed up in their tiny white spats, almost seemed to *bounce* along the gray carpet. Hogan found himself thinking of Fred Astaire tap-dancing his way across stage and back again, Fred Astaire with a cane tucked under his arm and a straw boater cocked saucily back on his head.

"Oh shit!" the kid said, half-laughing. "Is *that* what you were dickerin' for? Oh, man! I kill *you,* Label Dude, I'm gonna be doin' the world a favor."

The key, Hogan thought. *The key isn't turning.*

And he suddenly had another of those precognitive flashes; he understood exactly what was going to happen.

The kid is going to reach for them.

The teeth abruptly stopped walking and chattering. They simply stood there on the slightly tilted floor of the van, jaws slightly agape. Eyeless, they still seemed to peer up quizzically at the kid.

"Chattery Teeth," Mr. Bryan Adams, from Nowhere, u.s.a., marvelled. He reached out and curled his right hand around them, just as Hogan had known he would.

"Bite him!" Hogan shrieked. "Bite his fucking fingers *right off!"*

The kid's head snapped up, the gray-green eyes wide with startlement. He gaped at Hogan for a moment — that big expression of totally dumb surprise — and then he began to laugh. His laughter was high and shrieky, a perfect complement to the wind howling through the Fiesta and billowing the curtains like long ghost-hands.

"Bite me! *Bite* me! *Biiiite me!*" the kid chanted, as if it was the punchline to the funniest joke he'd ever heard. "Hey, Label Dude! I thought *I* was the one who bumped my head!"

The kid clamped the handle of the switchblade in his own teeth and stuck the forefinger of his left hand between the Jumbo Chattery Teeth. "Ite ee!" he said around the knife. He giggled and wiggled his finger between the oversized jaws. "Ite ee! O on, ite ee!"

The teeth didn't move. Neither did the orange feet. Hogan's premonition collapsed around him the way dreams do upon waking.

The kid wiggled his finger between the Chattery Teeth one more time, then began to pull his finger free. Suddenly he screamed in pain, and for a moment Hogan's heart leaped in his chest.

"*Oh shit! MotherFUCKER!*" the kid screamed, but he was laughing at the same time, and the teeth, of course, had never moved.

The kid lifted the teeth up for a closer look as he grabbed his knife again. He shook the long blade at the Chattery Teeth like a teacher shaking his pointer at a naughty student. "You shouldn't bite," he said. "That's very bad behav —"

One of the orange feet took a sudden step forward on the grimy palm of the kid's hand. The jaws opened at the same time, and before Hogan was fully aware of what was happening, the Chattery Teeth had closed on the kid's nose.

This time Bryan Adams's scream was real — a thing of agony and ultimate surprise. He flailed at the teeth with his right hand, trying to bat them away, but they were locked on his nose as tightly as Hogan's seatbelt was locked around his middle. Blood and filaments of torn gristle burst out between the canines in red strings. The kid jackknifed backward and for a moment Hogan could see only his flailing body, lashing elbows, and kicking feet. Then he saw the glitter of the knife.

The kid screamed again and bolted into a sitting position. His long hair had fallen over his face in a curtain; the clamped teeth stuck out like the rudder of some strange boat. The kid had somehow managed to insert the blade of his knife between the teeth and what remained of his nose.

"Kill him!" Hogan shouted hoarsely. He had lost his mind; on some level he understood that he *must* have lost his mind, but for the time being, that didn't matter. "*Go on, kill him!*"

The kid shrieked — a long, piercing firewhistle sound — and twisted the knife. The blade snapped, but not before it had managed to pry the disembodied jaws at least partway open. The teeth fell off his face and into his lap. Most of the kid's nose was still impaled on that wide, naked grin.

The kid shook his hair back. His gray-green eyes were crossed, trying to look down at the mangled stump which had once been his nose. His mouth was drawn down in a rictus of pain; the tendons in his neck stood out like pulley-wires.

The kid reached for the teeth. The teeth stepped nimbly backward on their orange cartoon feet. They were nodding up and down, marching in place, grinning at the kid, who was now sitting with his ass on his calves. Blood drenched the front of his T-shirt.

The kid said something then that confirmed Hogan's belief that he, Hogan, had lost his mind; only in a fantasy born of delirium would such words be spoken.

"Give bme bag by *dose,* you sud-of-a-bidtch!"

The kid reached for the teeth again and this time they ran *forward,* under his snatching hand, between his spread legs, and there was a meaty *chump!* sound as they closed on the bulge of faded blue denim just below the place where the zipper of the kid's jeans ended.

Bryan Adams's eyes flew wide open. So did his mouth. His hands rose to the level of his shoulders, springing wide open, as if he meant to conduct the opening movement of some amazing symphony. The switchknife flew over his shoulder to the back of the van.

"*Jesus! Jesus! Jeeeeeee —*"

The orange feet were pumping rapidly, as if doing a Highland Fling. The pink jaws of the Jumbo Chattery Teeth nodded rapidly up and down, as if saying *yes! yes! yes!* and then shook back and forth, just as rapidly as if saying *no! no! no!*

"*— eeeeeeEEEEEEEE —*"

As the cloth of the kid's jeans began to rip — and that was not all that was ripping, by the sound — Bill Hogan passed out.

He came to twice. The first time must have been only a short while later, because the storm was still howling through and around the van, and the light was about the same. He started to turn around, but a monstrous bolt of pain shot up his neck. Whiplash, of course, and probably not as bad as it could have been...or would be tomorrow, for that matter.

Always supposing he lived until tomorrow.

The kid. I have to look and make sure he's dead.

No, you don't. Of course he's dead. If he wasn't, you would be.

Now he began to hear a new sound from behind him — the steady chutter-click-chutter of the teeth.

They're coming for me. They've finished with the kid, but they're still hungry, so they're coming for me.

He placed his hands on the seatbelt buckle again, but the pop-release was still hopelessly jammed, and his hands seemed to have no strength, anyway.

The teeth grew steadily closer — they were right in back of his seat, now, from the sound — and Hogan's confused mind read a rhyme into their ceaseless chomping: *Clickety-clickety-clickety-clack! We are the teeth, and we're coming back! Watch us walk, watch us chew, we ate him, now we'll eat you!*

Hogan closed his eyes.

The clittering sound stopped.

Now there was only the ceaseless whine of the wind and the *spick-spack* of sand striking the dented side of the Fiesta.

Hogan waited. After a long, long time, he heard a single click, followed by the minute sound of tearing fibers. There was a pause, then the click and the tearing sound was repeated.

What's it doing?

The third time the click and the small tearing sound came, he felt the back of his seat moving a little and understood. The teeth were pulling themselves up to where he was. Somehow they were pulling themselves up to him.

Hogan thought of the teeth closing on the bulge of the kid's balls and willed himself to pass out again. Sand flew in through the broken windshield, tickled his cheeks and forehead.

Click...rip. Click...rip. Click...rip.

The last one was very close. Hogan didn't want to look down, but he was unable to help himself. And beyond his right hip, where the seat cushion met the seat's back, he saw a wide white grin. It moved upward with agonizing slowness, pushing with the as-yet-unseen orange feet as it nipped a small fold of gray seat-cover between its incisors...then the jaws let go and it lurched convulsively upward.

This time what the teeth fastened on was the pocket of Hogan's slacks, and he passed out again.

When he came to the second time, the wind had dropped and it was almost dark; the air had taken on a queer purple shade Hogan could not remember ever having seen in the desert before. The swirls of sand running across the desert floor beyond the sagging ruin of the windshield looked like fleeing ghost-children.

For a moment he could remember nothing at all of what had happened to land him here; the last clear memory he could touch was of looking at his gas-gauge, seeing it was down to an eighth, then looking up and seeing a sign at the side of the road which said SCOOTER'S GROCERY & ROADSIDE ZOO GAS SNAX COLD BEER.

SEE LIVE RATLLESNAKE'S!

He understood that he could hold onto this amnesia for a while, if he wanted to; given a little time, his subconscious might even be able to wall off subsequent memories permanently. But it could be *dangerous* not to remember. It could be very dangerous. Because —

The wind gusted. Sand rattled against the badly dented driver's side of the van. It sounded almost like

(teeth! the teeth! the Chattery Teeth!)

The fragile surface of his amnesia shattered, letting everything pour through, and all the heat fell from the surface of Hogan's skin. He uttered a rusty squawk as he remembered the sound

(chump!)

the teeth had made as they closed on the kid's balls, and he closed his hands over his own crotch, eyes rolling fearfully in their sockets as he looked for the runaway teeth.

He didn't see them, but the ease with which his shoulders followed the movement of his hands was new. He looked down at his lap and slowly removed his hands from his crotch. His seatbelt was no longer holding him prisoner. It lay on the gray carpet in two pieces. The metal tongue of the pull-up section was still buried inside the buckle, but beyond it there was only ragged red fabric. The belt had not been cut; it had been gnawed through.

He looked up into the rear-view mirror and saw something else: the back doors of the Fiesta were standing open, and there was only a vague, man-shaped red outline on the gray carpet where the kid had been. Mr. Bryan Adams, from Nowhere, U.S.A., was gone.

And so were the Chattery Teeth.

Hogan got out of the van slowly, like an old man afflicted with a terrible case of arthritis. He found that if he held his head perfectly level, it wasn't too bad... but if he forgot and moved it in any direction, a series of exploding bolts went off in his neck, shoulders, and upper back. Even the thought of allowing his head to roll backward was unbearable.

He walked slowly to the rear of the van, running his hand lightly over the dented, paint-peeled surface, hearing and feeling the glass as it crunched under his feet. He stood at the far end of the driver's side for a long time. He was afraid to turn the corner. He was afraid that, when he did, he would see the kid squatting on his hunkers, holding the knife in his left hand and grinning that empty grin. But he couldn't just stand here, holding his head on top of his strained neck like a big bottle of nitroglycerine, while it got dark around him, so at last Hogan went around.

Nobody. The kid was really gone. Or so it seemed at first.

The wind gusted, blowing Hogan's hair around his bruised face, then dropped away completely. When it did, he heard a harsh scraping noise coming from about twenty yards beyond the van. He looked in that direction and saw the soles of the kid's sneakers just disappearing over the top of a dry-wash. The sneakers were spread in a limp V. They stopped moving for a moment, as if whatever was hauling the kid's body needed a few moments' rest to recoup its strength, and then they began to move again in little jerks.

A picture of terrible, unendurable clarity suddenly rose in Hogan's mind. He saw the jumbo Chattery Teeth standing on their funny orange feet just over the edge of that wash, standing there in spats so cool they made the coolest of the California Raisins look like hicks from Fargo, North Dakota, standing there in the electric purple light which had overspread these empty lands west of Las Vegas. They were clamped shut on a thick wad of the kid's long blonde hair.

The Chattery Teeth were backing up.

The Chattery Teeth were dragging Mr. Bryan Adams away to Nowhere, U.S.A.

Hogan turned in the other direction and walked slowly toward the road, holding his nitro head straight and steady on top of his neck. It took him five minutes to negotiate the ditch and another fifteen to flag a ride, but he eventually managed both things. And during that time, he never looked back once.

Nine months later, on a clear hot summer day in June, Bill Hogan happened by Scooter's Grocery & Roadside Zoo again...except the place had been renamed. NAN'S PLACE, it now said. GAS COLD BEER VIDEO'S. Below the words was a picture of a wolf — or maybe just a Woof — snarling at the moon. Wolf himself, the Amazing Minnesota Coydog, was lying in a cage in the shade of the porch overhang. His back legs were sprawled extravagantly, and his muzzle was on his paws. He did not get up when Hogan got out of his car to fill the tank. Of the rattlesnakes and the tarantula there was no sign.

"Hi, Woof," he said as he went up the steps, and the cage's inmate rolled over on his back, as if hoping to be scratched.

The store looked bigger and cleaner inside. Hogan guessed this was partly because the sky was clear and the air wasn't full of flying dust, but that wasn't all; the windows had been washed, for one thing. The board walls had been replaced with pine-paneling that still smelled fresh and sappy. A snackbar with five stools had been added at the back. The novelty case was still there, but the cigarette loads, the joy-buzzers, and Dr. Wacky's Itching Powder were gone. The case was filled with videotape boxes. A hand-lettered sign read X-RATED IN BACK ROOM "B 18 OR B GONE."

The woman at the cash register was standing in profile to Hogan, looking down at a calculator and running numbers on it. For a moment Hogan was sure this was Mr. and Mrs. Scooter's daughter — the female complement of those three boys Scooter had talked about raising. Then she raised her head and Hogan saw it was Mrs. Scooter herself. It was hard to believe this could be the woman whose mammoth bosom had almost burst the seams of her NEVADA IS GOD'S COUNTRY T-shirt, but it was. Mrs. Scooter had lost at least fifty pounds (most of it in the breastworks, from the look) and dyed her hair a dark walnut brown. Only the sun-wrinkles around the eyes and mouth were the same.

"Getcha gas?" she asked.

"Yep. Fifteen dollars' worth." He handed her a twenty and she rang it up. "Place looks a lot different from the last time I was in."

"Been a lot of changes since Scooter died, all right," she agreed, and pulled a five out of the register. She started to hand it over, really looked at him for the first time, and hesitated. "Say...ain't you the guy who almost got killed the day we had that storm last year?"

He nodded and stuck of his hand. "Bill Hogan."

She didn't hesitate; simply reached over the counter and gave his hand a single strong pump. The death of her husband seemed to have improved her disposition...or maybe it was just that the waiting for it to happen was over.

"I'm sorry about your husband. He seemed like a nice enough sort."

"Scoot? Yeah, he was a good 'nough fella before he took ill," she agreed. "And what about you? You all recovered?"

Hogan nodded. "I wore a neck-brace for about six weeks — not for the first time, either — but I'm okay."

She was looking at the scar which twisted down his right cheek. "He do that? That kid?"

"Yeah."

"Stuck you pretty bad."

"Yeah."

"I heard he got hurt in the crash, crawled out into the desert, and died." She was looking at him shrewdly. "That about right?"

Hogan smiled a little. "Near enough, I guess."

"J. T. — he's the State Bear around these parts — said the animals worked him over pretty good. Desert rats are awful impolite that way."

"I don't know much about that part."

"J. T. said the kid's own mother wouldn't have reckanized him." She put a hand on her reduced bosom and looked at him earnestly. "If I'm lyin', I'm dyin'."

Hogan laughed out loud. In the weeks and months since the day of the storm, this was something he found himself doing more often. He had come, it sometimes seemed to him, to a slightly different arrangement with life since that day.

"Lucky he didn't kill you," Mrs. Scooter said.

"That's right," Hogan agreed. He looked down at the video case. "I see you took out the novelties."

"Them old things? You bet! That was the first thing I did after —" Her eyes suddenly widened. "Oh, say! Jeepers! I got somethin' belongs to you! If I was to forget, I reckon Scooter'd come back and haunt me!"

Hogan frowned, puzzled, but the woman was already going back to the grille area. She went behind the counter, stood on tiptoe, and brought something down from a high shelf above the rack of breakfast cereals. She came back and put the Jumbo Chattery Teeth down beside the cash register.

Hogan stared at them with a deep sense of *déjà vu*...but no real surprise. The oversized teeth stood there on their funny orange shoes, cool as a mountain breeze, grinning up at him as if to say, *Hello, there! Did you forget me? I didn't forget YOU, my friend. Not at all.*

"I found em on the porch the next day, after the storm blew itself out," Mrs. Scooter said. She laughed. "Just like old Scoot to give you somethin' for free, then stick it in a bag with a hole in the bottom. I was gonna throw em out, but he said he give em to you, and I should stick em on a shelf someplace. He said a travelling man who came in once'd most likely come in again...and here you are."

"Yes," Hogan agreed. "Here I am."

He picked up the teeth and slipped his finger between the slightly gaping jaws. He ran the pad of the finger along the molars at the back, and in his mind he heard the kid, Mr. Bryan Adams from Nowhere, U.S.A., chanting *Bite me! Bite me! Biiiiite me!*

Were the back teeth still streaked with some dull rusty color? Hogan thought they were, but perhaps it was only a shadow.

"I saved it because Scooter said you had a boy."

Hogan nodded. "I do." *And,* he thought, *the boy still has a father. I'm holding the reason why. The question is, did they walk all the way back here on their little orange feet because this was home...or because they somehow knew what Scooter knew? That sooner or later, a travelling man always comes back, like a murderer is supposed to come back to the scene of his crime?*

"Well, if you still want em, they're still yours," she said. For a moment she looked solemn...and then she laughed. "Shit, I probably would have throwed em out anyway, except I forgot about em. Course, they're still broken."

Hogan turned the key jutting out of the gum. It went around twice, making little wind-up clicks, then simply turned uselessly in its socket. Broken. Of course they were. And would be until they decided they didn't *want* to be broken for a while. And the question wasn't how they had gotten back here, and the question wasn't even *why* — that was simple. They had been waiting for him, for Mr. William I. Hogan. They had been waiting for the Label Dude.

The question was this: What did they want?

He poked his finger into the white steel grin again and whispered, "Bite me — do you want to?"

The teeth only stood there on their supercool orange feet and grinned.

"They ain't talking, seems like," Mrs. Scooter said.

"No," Hogan said, and suddenly he found himself thinking of the kid. Mr. Bryan Adams, from Nowhere, u.s.a. A lot of kids like him now. A lot of grownups, too, blowing along the highways like tumbleweed, always ready to take your wallet, say *fuck you, sugar,* and run. You could stop picking up hitchhikers (he had), and you could put a burglar alarm system in your home (he'd done that, too), but it was a hard world where planes sometimes fell out of the sky and the crazies were apt to turn up anyplace and there was always room for a little more insurance. He had a wife, after all.

And a son.

He summoned up the memory of the blonde kid's crazy, empty grin, and tried to match it to the one tilted up to him from beside Mrs. Scooter's new NCR register. He didn't think they were the same. Not at all.

He lived in L.A., and he was gone a lot. Someday the blonde kid's spiritual brother might decide to break in, burglar alarm or no burglar alarm — rape the woman, kill the kid, steal whatever wasn't nailed down.

It might be nice if Jack had a set of Jumbo Chattery Teeth sitting on his desk. Just in case something like that happened.

Just in case.

"Thank you for saving them," he said, picking the Chattery Teeth up carefully by the feet. "I think my kid will get a kick out of them even if they are broken."

"Thank Scooter, not me. You want a bag?" She grinned. "I got a plastic one — no holes, guaranteed."

Hogan shook his head and slipped the Chattery Teeth into his sport-coat pocket. "I'll carry them this way," he said, and grinned back at her. "Keep them close to me."

"Suit yourself." As he started for the door, she called after him: "Stop back again! I make a mean cheeseburger!"

"I'll bet you do, and I will," Hogan said. He went out, down the steps, and stood for a moment in the hot desert sunshine, smiling. He felt good — he felt good a lot these days. He had come to think that was just the way to be.

To his left, Woof the Amazing Minnesota Coydog got to his feet, poked his snout through the crisscross of wire on the side of his cage, and barked. In Hogan's pocket, the Chattery Teeth clicked together once. The sound was soft, but Hogan heard it...and felt them move. He patted his pocket. "Down, boy," he said softly.

He walked briskly across the yard, climbed behind the wheel of his new Chevrolet Sprint van, and drove away toward Los Angeles. He had promised Lita and Jack he would be home by seven, eight at the latest, and he was a man who liked to keep his promises.

Lucius Shepard's short fiction has won the Nebula, Hugo, International Horror Guild, National Magazine, Locus, Theodore Sturgeon, and World Fantasy awards. His most recent books are a short fiction collection, *Viator Plus* and a short novel, *The Taborin Scale*. Forthcoming are another short fiction collection, *Five Autobiographies*, and two novels, tentatively titled *The Piercefields* and *The End of Life As We Know It*, and a short novel, *The House of Everything and Nothing*.

Shepard is a stylist who fools around with various genres, often mixing them in entertaining ways in his noirs, fantasies, science fiction, and horror. His characters are rarely nice and rarely successful at their various enterprises, but they're too vital to be true losers, even when they lose in the end.

"A Little Night Music," originally published in 1992, is story about love, obsession, zombies, and music.

A Little Night Music
Lucius Shepard

DEAD MEN CAN'T play jazz.

That's the truth I learned last night at the world premiere performance of the quartet known as Afterlife at Manhattan's Village Vanguard.

Whether or not they can play, period, that's another matter, but it wasn't jazz I heard at the Vanguard, it was something bluer and colder, something with notes made from centuries-old Arctic ice and stones that never saw the light of day, something uncoiling after a long black sleep and tasting dirt in its mouth, something that wasn't the product of creative impulse but of need.

But the bottom line is, it was worth hearing.

As to the morality involved, well, I'll leave that up to you, because that's the real bottom line, isn't it, music lovers? Do you like it enough and will you pay enough to keep the question of morality a hot topic on the Donahue show and out of the courts? Those of you who listened to the simulcast over WBAI have probably already formulated an opinion. The rest of you will have to wait for the CD.

I won't waste your time by talking about the technology. If you don't understand it by now, after all the television specials and the (ohmygodpleasenot-another) in-depth discussions between your local blow-dried news creep and their pet science fiction hack, you must not want to understand it. Nor am I going to wax profound and speculate on just how much of a man is left after reanimation. The only ones who know that aren't able to tell us, because it seems the speech center just doesn't thrive on narcosis. Nor does any fraction of sensibility that cares to communicate itself. In fact, very little seems to thrive on narcosis aside from the desire...no, like I said, the *need* to play music.

And for reasons that God or someone only knows, the *ability* to play music where none existed before.

That may be hard to swallow, I realize, but I'm here to tell you, no matter how weird it sounds, it appears to be true.

For the first time in memory, there was a curtain across the Vanguard's stage. I suppose there's some awkwardness involved in bringing the musicians out. Before the curtain was opened, William Dexter, the genius behind this whole deal, a little bald man with a hearing aid in each ear and the affable, simple face of someone who kids call by his first name, came out and said a few words about the need for drastic solutions to the problems of war and pollution, for a redefinition of our goals and values. Things could not go on as they had been. The words seemed somewhat out of context, though they're always nice to hear. Finally he introduced the quartet. As introductions go, this was a telegram.

"The music you're about to hear," William Dexter said flatly, without the least hint of hype or hyperventilation, "is going to change your lives."

And there they were.

Right on the same stage where Coltrane turned a love supreme into a song, where Miles singed us with the hateful beauty of needles and knives and Watts on fire, where Mingus went crazy in 7/4 time, where Ornette made Kansas City R&B into the art of noise, and a thousand lesser geniuses dreamed and almost died and were changed before our eyes from men into moments so powerful that guys like me can make a living writing about them for people like you who just want to hear that what they felt when they were listening was real.

Two white men, one black, one Hispanic, the racial quota of an all-American TV show, marooned on a radiant island painted by a blue-white spot. All wearing sunglasses.

Ray-Bans, I think.

Wonder if they'll get a commercial.

The piano player was young and skinny, just a kid, with the long brown hair of a rock star and sunglasses that held gleams as shiny and cold as the black surface of his Baldwin. The Hispanic guy on bass couldn't have been more than eighteen, and the horn player, the black man, he was about twenty-five, the oldest. The drummer, a shadow with a crew cut and a pale brow, I couldn't see him clearly but I could tell he was young, too.

Too young, you'd think, to have much to say.

But then maybe time goes by more slowly and wisdom accretes with every measure...in the afterlife.

No apparent signal passed between them, yet as one they began to play. Goodrick reached for his tape recorder, thinking he should listen to the set again before getting into the music, but then he realized that another listen was unnecessary — he could still hear every blessed note. The ocean of dark chords on the piano opening over a snaky, slithering hiss of cymbals and a cluttered rumble plucked from the double bass, and then that sinuous alto line, like snake-charmer music rising out of a storm of thunderheads and scuttling claws, all fusing into a signature as plaintive and familiar and elusive as a muezzin's call. Christ, it stuck with you like a jingle for Burger King...though nothing about it was simple. It seemed to have the freedom of jazz, yet at the same time it had the feel of heavy, ritual music.

Weird shit.

And it sure as hell stuck with you.

He got up from the desk, grabbed his drink and walked over to the window. The nearby buildings ordered the black sky, ranks of tombstones inscribed with a writing of rectangular stars, geometric constellations, and linear rivers of light below, flowing along consecutive chasms through the high country of Manhattan. Usually the view soothed him and turned his thoughts to pleasurable agendas, as if height itself were a form of assurance, an emblematic potency that freed you from anxiety. But tonight he remained unaffected. The sky and the city seemed to have lost their scope and grandeur, to have become merely an adjunct to his living room.

He cast about the apartment, looking for the clock. Couldn't locate it for a second among a chaos of sticks of gleaming chrome, shining black floors, framed prints, and black plush coffins of the sofas. He'd never put it together before, but the place looked like a cross between a Nautilus gym and a goddamn mortuary. Rachel's taste could use a little modification.

Two-thirty A.M.... Damn!

Where the hell was she?

She usually gave him time alone after a show to write his column. Went and had a drink with friends.

Three hours, though.

Maybe she'd found a special friend. Maybe that was the reason she had missed the show tonight. If that was the case, she'd been with the bastard for...what? Almost seven hours now. Screwing her brains out in some midtown hotel.

Bitch! He'd settle her hash when she got home.

Whoa, big fella, he said to himself. Get real. Rachel would be much cooler than that...make that, *had been* much cooler. Her affairs were state of the art, so quietly and elegantly handled that he had been able to perfect denial. This wasn't her style. And even if she were to throw it in his face, he wouldn't do a thing to her. Oh, he'd want to, he'd want to bash her goddamned head in. But he would just sit there and smile and buy her bullshit explanation.

Love, he guessed you'd call it, the kind of love that will accept any insult, any injury...though it might be more accurate to call it pussywhipped. There were times he didn't think he could take it anymore. Times like now when his head felt full of lightning, on the verge of exploding and setting everything around him on fire. But he always managed to contain his anger and swallow his pride, to grin and bear it, to settle for the specious currency of her lovemaking, the price she paid to live high and do what she wanted.

Jesus, he felt strange. Too many pops at the Vanguard, that was likely the problem. But maybe he was coming down with something.

He laughed.

Like maybe middle age? Like the married-to-a-chick-fifteen-years-younger-paranoid flu?

Still, he had felt better in his time. No real symptoms, just out of sorts, sluggish, dulled, some trouble concentrating.

Finish the column, he said to himself, just finish the damn thing, take two aspirin and fall out. Deal with Rachel in the morning.

Right.

Deal with her.

Bring her breakfast in bed, ask how she was feeling, and what was she doing later?

God, he loved her!

Loves her not. Loves. Loves her not.

He tore off a last mental petal and tossed the stem away. Then he returned to the desk and typed a few lines about the music onto the computer and sat considering the screen. After a moment he began to type again.

Plenty of blind men have played the Vanguard, and plenty of men have played there who've had other reasons to hide their eyes, working behind some miracle of modern chemistry that made them sensitive to light. I've never wanted to see their eyes — the fact that they were hidden told me all I need to know about them. But tonight I wanted to see. I wanted to know what the quartet was seeing, what lay behind those sunglasses starred from the white spot.

Darkness: Two Decades of Modern Horror

Shadows, it's said. But what sort of shadows? Shades of gray, like dogs see? Are we shadows to them, or do they see shadows where we see none? I thought if I could look into their eyes, I'd understand what caused the alto to sound like a reedy alarm being given against a crawl of background radiation, why one moment it conjured images of static red flashes amid black mountains moving, and the next brought to mind a livid blue streak pulsing in a serene darkness, a mineral moon in a granite sky.

Despite the compelling quality of the music, I couldn't set aside my curiosity and simply listen. What was I listening to, after all? A clever parlor trick? Sleight of hand on a metaphysical level? Were these guys really playing Death's Top Forty, or had Mr. William Dexter managed to chump the whole world and program four stiffs to make certain muscular reactions to subliminal stimuli?

The funny thing was, Goodrick thought, now he couldn't stop listening to the damn music. In fact, certain phrases were becoming so insistent, circling round and round inside his head, he was having difficulty thinking rationally. He switched the radio on, wanting to hear something else, to get a perspective on the column.

No chance.

Afterlife was playing on the radio, too.

He was stunned, imagining some bizarre *Twilight Zone* circumstance, but then realized that the radio was tuned to WBAI. They must be replaying the simulcast. Pretty unusual for them to devote so much air to one story. Still, it wasn't everyday the dead came back to life and played song stylings for your listening pleasure.

He recognized the passage.

They must have just started the replay. Shit, the boys hadn't even gotten warmed up yet.

Heh, heh.

He followed the serpentine track of the alto cutting across the rumble and clutter of the chords and fills behind it, a bright ribbon of sound etched through thunder and power and darkness.

A moment later he looked at the clock and was startled to discover that the moment had lasted twenty minutes.

Well, so he was a little spaced, so what? He was entitled. He'd had a hard wife…life. Wife. The knifing word he'd wed, the dull flesh, the syrupy blood, the pouty breasts, the painted face he'd thought was pretty. The dead music woman, the woman whose voice caused cancer, whose kisses left damp mildewed stains, whose…

His heart beat flabbily, his hands were cramped, his fingertips were numb, and his thoughts were a whining, glowing crack opening in a smoky sky like slow lightning. Feeling a dark red emotion too contemplative to be anger, he typed a single paragraph and then stopped to read what he had written.

The thing about this music is, it just feels right. It's not art, it's not beauty, it's a meter reading on the state of the soul, of the world. It's the bottom line of all time. A registering of creepy fundamentals, the rendering into music of the crummiest truth, the statement of some meager final tolerance, a universal alpha wave, God's EKG, the least possible music, the absolute minimum of sound, all that's left to say, to be, for them, for us…maybe that's why it feels so damn right. It creates an option to suicide, a place where there is no great trouble, only a trickle of blood through stony flesh and the crackle of a base electric message across the brain.

Well, he thought, now there's a waste of a paragraph. Put that into the column, and he'd be looking for work with a weekly shopping guide. Hey, who knows, it might not be so bad, writing about fabric bargains and turkey raffles and swap meets. Might put him back in touch with his roots.

He essayed a laugh and produced a gulping noise.

Damn, he felt lousy.

Not lousy, really, just…just sort of nothing. Like there was nothing in his head except the music. Music and black dead air. Dead life.

Dead love.

He typed a few more lines.

Maybe Dexter was right, maybe this music will change your life. It sure as hell seems to have changed mine. I feel like shit, my lady's out with some dirtball lowlife and all I can muster by way of a reaction is mild pique. That's a goddamn change, sure enough. I mean, maybe the effect of Afterlife's music is to reduce the emotional volatility of our kind, to diminish us to the level of the stiffs who play it. That might explain Dexter's peace-and-love rap, put it into a cautionary context. People who feel like I do wouldn't have the energy for war, for polluting, for much of anything. They'd probably sit around most of the time, trying to think something, hoping for food to walk in the door...

Jesus, what if the music actually did buzz you like that? Tripped some chemical switch and slowly shut you down, brain cell by brain cell, until you were about three degrees below normal and as lively as a hibernating bear. What if that were true, and right this second it was being broadcast all over hell on WBAI?

This is crazy, man, he told himself, this is truly whacko.

But what if Dexter's hearing aids had been ear plugs, what if the son of a bitch hadn't listened to the music himself? Maybe that speech of his had been more than cautionary. What if he knew how the music would affect the audience, what if he was after turning half of everybody into zombies all in the name of a better world?

And what would be so wrong with that?

Not a thing.

Cleaner air, less war, more food to go around...just stack the dim bulbs in warehouses and let them vegetate, while everyone else cleaned up the mess.

Not a thing wrong with it...as long as you weren't in the half that had listened to the music.

The light was beginning to hurt his eyes. He switched off the lamp and sat in the darkness, staring at the glowing screen. He glanced out the window. Since last he'd looked, it appeared that about three-quarters of the lights in the adjoining buildings had been darkened, making it appear that the remaining lights were some sort of weird code, spelling out a message of golden squares against a black page. He had a crawly feeling along his spine, imagining thousands of other Manhattan nighthawks growing slow and cold and sensitive to light, sitting in their dark rooms, while a whining alto serpent stung them in the brain.

The idea was ludicrous — Dexter had just been shooting off his mouth, firing off more white liberal bullshit. He was no mad scientist, no deviant little monster with a master plan.

Still, Goodrick didn't feel much like laughing.

Maybe, he thought, he should call the police...call someone.

But then he'd have to get up, dial the phone, talk, and it was so much more pleasant just to sit here and listen to the background static of the universe, to the sad song of a next-to-nothing life.

He remembered how peaceful Afterlife had been, the piano man's pale hands flowing over the keys, like white animals gliding, making a rippling track, and the horn man's eyes rolled up, showing all white under the sunglasses, turned inward toward some pacific vision, and the bass man, fingers blurring on the strings, but his head fallen back, gaping, his eyes on the ceiling, as if keeping track of the stars.

This was really happening, he thought, he believed it was happening, he knew it, and yet he couldn't rouse himself to panic. His hands flexed on the arms of the chair, and he swallowed, and he listened. More lights were switched off in the adjoining towers. This was really fucking happening…and he wasn't afraid. As a matter of fact, he was beginning to enjoy the feeling. Like a little vacation. Just turn down the volume and response, sit back and let the ol' brain start to mellow like aging cheese.

Wonder what Rachel would have to say?

Why, she'd be delighted! She hadn't heard the music, after all, and she'd be happy as a goddamn clam to be one of the quick, to have him sit there and fester while she brought over strangers and let them pork her on the living room carpet. I mean, he wouldn't have any objection, right? Maybe dead guys liked to watch. Maybe… His hands started itching, smudged with city dirt. He decided that he had to wash them. It would be a chore, but he figured he'd have to move sometime. Couldn't just sit there and shit himself.

With a mighty effort, feeling like he weighed five hundred pounds, he heaved up to his feet and shuffled toward the bathroom. It took him what seemed a couple of minutes to reach it, to fumble for the wall switch and flick it on. The light almost blinded him, and he reeled back against the wall, shading his eyes. Glints and gleams shattering off porcelain, chrome fixtures, and tiles, a shrapnel of light blowing toward his retinas. "Aw, Jesus," he said. "Jesus!" Then he caught sight of himself in the mirror. Pasty skin, liverish, too-red lips, bruised-looking circles around his eyes. Mr. Zombie, he said to himself, is attired in a charcoal gray suit with Mediterranean lapels by Calvin Swine, his silk rep tie is by Necktie Party, his coral shirt is made of silk and pigeon blood, his shoes are actually layers of filthy dead skin wrinkled into an alligator pattern, and his accessories are by Mr. Mort U. Ary.

At last he managed to look away.

He turned on the faucet. Music ran out along with the bright water, and when he stuck his hands under the flow, he couldn't feel the cold water, just the gloomy notation spidering across his skin.

He jerked his hands back and stared at them, watched them dripping glittering bits of alto and drum, bass and piano. After a moment he switched off the light and stood in the cool, blessed dark, listening to the alto playing in the distance, luring his thoughts down and down into a golden crooked tunnel leading nowhere.

One thing he had to admit, having your vitality turned down to the bottom notch gave you perspective on the whole vital world. Take Rachel, now. She'd come in any minute, all bright and smiling, switching her ass, she'd toss her purse and coat somewhere, give him a perky kiss, ask how the column was going…and all the while her sexual engine would be cooling, ticking away the last degrees of heat like how a car engine ticks in the silence of a garage, some vile juice leaking from her. He could see it clearly, the entire spectrum of her deceit, see it without feeling either helpless rage or frustration, but rather registering it as an untenable state of affairs. Something would have to be done. That was obvious. It was surprising he'd never come to that conclusion before…or maybe not so surprising. He'd been too agitated, too emotional. Now…now change was possible. He would have to talk to Rachel, to work things out differently.

Actually, he thought, a talk wouldn't be necessary.

Just a little listening experience, and she'd get with the program.

He hated to leave the soothing darkness of the bathroom, but he felt he should finish the column…just to tie up loose ends. He went back into the living room and sat in front of the computer. WBAI had finished replaying the simulcast. He must have been in the john a long time. He switched off the radio so he could hear the music in his head.

I'm sitting here listening to a little night music, a reedy little whisper of melody leaking out a crack in death's door, and you know, even though I can't hear or think of much of anything except that shivery sliver of sound, it's become more a virtue than a hindrance, it's beginning to order the world in an entirely new way. I don't have to explain it to those of you who are hearing it with me, but for the rest of you, let me shed some light on the experience. One sees…clearly, I suppose, is the word, yet that doesn't cover it. One is freed from the tangles of inhibition, volatile emotion, and thus can perceive how easy it is to change one's life, and finally, one understands that with a very few changes one can achieve a state of calm perfection. A snip here, a tuck taken there, another snip-snip, and suddenly it becomes apparent that there is nothing left to do, absolutely nothing, and one has achieved utter harmony with one's environment.

The screen was glowing too brightly to look at. Goodrick dimmed it. Even the darkness, he realized, had its own peculiar radiance. B-zarre. He drew a deep breath...or rather tried to, but his chest didn't move. Cool, he thought, very cool. No moving parts. Just solid calm, white, white calm in a black, black shell, and a little bit of fixing up remaining to do. He was almost there.

Wherever *there* was.

A cool alto trickle of pleasure through the rumble of nights.

I cannot recommend the experience too highly. After all, there's almost no overhead, no troublesome desires, no ugly moods, no loathsome habits...

A click — the front door opening, a sound that seemed to increase the brightness in the room. Footsteps, and then Rachel's voice.

"Wade?"

He could feel her. Hot, sticky, soft. He could feel the suety weights of her breasts, the torsion of her hips, the flexing of live sinews, like music of a kind, a lewd concerto of vitality and deceit.

"There you are!" she said brightly, a streak of hot sound, and came up behind him. She leaned down, hands on his shoulders, and kissed his cheek, a serpent of brown hair coiling across his neck and onto his chest. He could hardly smell her perfume, just a hint of it. Perfect. She drenched herself in the stuff, and usually he had big trouble breathing around her, choking on the flowery reek.

"How's the column going?" she asked, moving away.

He cut his eyes toward her. That teardrop ass sheathed in silk, that mind like a sewer running with black bile, that heart like a pound of red raw poisoned hamburger. Those cute little puppies bounding along in front.

He remembered how she'd used to wear her hair up, wear aprons, just like ol' Wilma Flintstone, how he'd come home and pretend to be an adulterous Barney Rubble.

How they'd laughed.

Yabba dabba doo.

And now the fevered temperature of her soiled flesh brightened everything. Even the air was shining. The shadows were black glares.

"Fine," he said. "Almost finished."

...only infinite slow minutes, slow thoughts like curls of smoke, only time, only a flicker of presence, only perfect music that does not exist like smoke...

"So how was the Vanguard?"

He chuckled. "Didn't you catch it on the radio?"

A pause. "No, I was busy."

Busy, uh-huh.

Hips thrusting up from a rumpled sheet, sleek with sweat, mouth full of tongue, breasts rolling fatly, big ass flattening.

"It was good for me," he said.

A nervous giggle.

"Very good," he said. "The best ever."

He examined his feelings. All in order, all under control...what there was of them. A few splinters of despair, a fragment of anger, some shards of love. Not enough to matter, not enough to impair judgment.

"Are you okay? You sound funny."

"I'm fine," he said, feeling a creepy, secretive tingle of delight. "Want to hear the Vanguard set? I taped it."

"Sure...but aren't you sleepy? I can hear it tomorrow."

"I'm fine."

He switched on the recorder. The computer screen was blazing like a white sun.

...the crackling of a black storm, the red thread of a fire on a distant ridge, the whole world irradiated by a mystic vibration, the quickened inches of the flesh becoming cool and easy, the White Nile of the calmed mind flowing everywhere...

"Like it?" he asked.

She had walked over to the window and was standing facing it, gazing out at the city.

"It's...curious," she said. "I don't know if I like it, but it's effective."

Was that a hint of entranced dullness in her voice? Or was it merely distraction?

Open those ears wide, baby, and let that ol' black magic take over.

...just listen, just let it flow in, let it fill the empty spaces in your brain with muttering, cluttering bassy blunders and a crooked wire of brassy red snake fluid, let it cozy around and coil up inside your skull, because it's all you know, America, and all you fucking need to know, Keatsian beauty and truth wrapped up in a freaky little melody...

The column just couldn't hold his interest. Who the hell was going to read it, anyway? His place was with Rachel, helping her through the rough spots of the transition, the confusion, the unsettled feelings. With difficulty, he got to his feet and walked over to Rachel. Put his hands on her hips. She tensed, then relaxed against him. Then she tensed again. He looked out over the top of her head at Manhattan. Only a few lights showing. The message growing simpler and simpler. Dot, dot, dot. Stop. Dot, dot. Stop.

Stop.

"Can we talk, Wade?"

"Listen to the music, baby."

"No...really. We have to talk!"

She tried to pull away from him, but he held her, his fingers hooked on her hipbones.

"It'll keep 'til morning," he said.

"I don't think so." She turned to face him, fixed him with her intricate green eyes. "I've been putting this off too long already." Her mouth opened, as if she were going to speak, but then she looked away. "I'm so sorry," she said after a considerable pause.

He knew what was coming, and he didn't want to hear it. Couldn't she just wait? In a few minutes she'd begin to understand, to know what he knew. Christ, couldn't she wait?

"Listen," he said. "Okay? Listen to the music and then we'll talk."

"God, Wade! What is it with you and this dumb music?"

She started to flounce off, but he caught her by the arm.

"If you give it a chance, you'll see what I mean," he said. "But it takes a while. You have to give it time."

"What are you talking about?"

"The music…it's really something. It does something."

"Oh, God, Wade! This is important!"

She fought against his grip.

"I know," he said, "I know it is. But just do this first. Do it for me."

"All right, all right! If it'll make you happy." She heaved a sigh, made a visible effort at focusing on the music, her head tipped to the side…but only for a couple of seconds.

"I can't listen," she said. "There's too much on my mind."

"You're not trying."

"Oh, Wade," she said, her chin quivering, a catch in her voice. "I've been trying, I really have. You don't know. Please! Let's just sit down and…" She let out another sigh. "Please. I need to talk with you."

He had to calm her, to let his calm generate and flow inside her. He put a hand on the back of her neck, forced her head down onto his shoulder. She struggled, but he kept up a firm pressure.

"Let me go, damn it!" she said, her voice muffled. "Let me go!" Then, after a moment: "You're smothering me."

He let her lift her head.

"What's wrong with you, Wade?"

There was confusion and fright in her face, and he wanted to soothe her, to take away all her anxieties.

"Nothing's wrong," he said with the sedated piety of a priest. "I just want you to listen. Tomorrow morning we…"

"I don't want to listen. Can't you understand that? I don't. Want. To listen. Now let me go."

"I'm doing this for you, baby."

"For me? Are you nuts? Let me go!"

"I can't, baby. I just can't."

She tried to twist free again, but he refused to release her.

"All right, all right! I was trying to avoid a scene, but if that's how you want it!" She tossed back her hair, glared at him defiantly. "I'm leaving…"

He couldn't let her say it and spoil the evening, he couldn't let her disrupt the healing process. Without anger, without bitterness, but rather with the precision and control of someone trimming a hedge, he backhanded her, nailed her flush on the jaw with all his strength, snapping her head about.

She went hard against the thick window glass, the back of her skull impacting with a sharp crack, and then she slumped to the floor, her head twisted at an improbable angle.

Snip, snip.

He stood waiting for grief and fear to flood in, but he felt only a wave of serenity as palpable as a stream of cool water, as a cool golden passage on a distant horn.

Snip.

The shape of his life was perfected.

Rachel's, too.

Lying there, pale, lips parted, face rapt and slack, drained of lust and emotions, she was beautiful. A trickle of blood eeled from her hairline, and Goodrick realized that the pattern it made echoed the alto line exactly, that the music was leaking from her, signalling the minimal continuance of her life. She wasn't dead, she had merely suffered a necessary reduction. He sensed the edgy crackle of her thoughts, like the intermittent popping of a fire gone to embers.

"It's okay, baby. It's okay." He put an arm under her back and lifted her, supporting her about the waist. Then he hauled her over to the sofa. He helped her to sit, and sat beside her, an arm about her shoulders. Her head lolled heavily against his, the softness of her breast pressed into his arm. He could hear the music coming from her, along with the electric wrack and tumble of her thoughts. They had never been closer than they were right now, he thought. Like a couple of high school kids on a couch date. Leaning together, hearing the same music, hearts still, minds tuned to the same wavelength.

He wanted to say something, to tell her how much he loved her, but found that he could no longer speak, his throat muscles slack and useless.

Well, that was okay.

Rachel knew how he felt, anyway.

But if he could speak, he'd tell her that he'd always known they could work things out, that though they'd had their problems, they were made for each other...

Hey, Wilma, he'd say, yabba dabba doo.

And then they would begin to explore this new and calmer life, this purity of music and brightness.

A little too much brightness, if you asked him.

The light was growing incandescent, as if having your life ultimately simplified admitted you to a dimension of blazing whiteness. It was streaming up from everything, from the radio, the television, from Rachel's parted lips, from every surface, whitening the air, the night, whiting out hope, truth, beauty, sadness, joy, leaving room for nothing except the music, which was swelling in volume, stifling thought, becoming a kind of thirsting presence inside him. It was sort of too bad, he said to himself, that things had to be like this, that they couldn't have made it in the usual way, but then he guessed it was all for the best, that this way at least there was no chance of screwing anything up.

Jesus, the goddamn light was killing his eyes!

Might have known, he thought, there'd be some fly in the ointment, that perfection didn't measure up to its rep.

He held onto Rachel tightly, whispering endearments, saying, "Baby, it'll be okay in a minute, just lie back, just take it easy," trying to reassure her, to help her through this part of things. He could tell the light was bothering her as well by the way she buried her face in the crook of his neck.

If this shit kept up, he thought, he was going to have to buy them both some sunglasses.

Poppy Z. Brite's first stories were published in the small press in the early 1990s while she was still in her teens, and she quickly became a major voice in horror fiction with strong contributions to several major anthologies. Her three horror novels, *Lost Souls, Drawing Blood,* and *Exquisite Corpse,* gave Brite a reputation for fearlessness, as she created memorable gay protagonists and never flinched from depicting graphically sexual situations. She subsequently has moved away from horror, writing a series of darkly comedic novels about restaurant life in New Orleans.

"Calcutta, Lord of Nerves" features an India mysterious and fetid, the perfect environment to set a zombie hell on earth. The story was originally published in the anthology *Still Dead,* edited by John Skipp and Craig Spector.

Calcutta, Lord of Nerves

Poppy Z. Brite

I WAS BORN in a North Calcutta hospital in the heart of an Indian midnight just before the beginning of the monsoon season. The air hung heavy as wet velvet over the Hooghly River, offshoot of the holy Ganga, and the stumps of banyan trees on the Upper Chitpur Road were flecked with dots of phosphorus like the ghosts of flames. I was as dark as the new moon in the sky, and I cried very little. I feel as if I remember this, because this is the way it must have been.

My mother died in labor, and later that night the hospital burned to the ground. (I have no reason to connect the two incidents; then again, I have no reason not to. Perhaps a desire to live burned on in my mother's heart. Perhaps the flames were fanned by her hatred for me, the insignificant mewling infant that had killed her.) A nurse carried me out of the roaring husk of the building and laid me in my father's arms. He cradled me, numb with grief.

My father was American. He had come to Calcutta five years earlier, on business. There he had fallen in love with my mother and, like a man who will not pluck a flower from its garden, he could not bear to see her removed from the hot, lush, squalid city that had spawned her. It was part of her exotica. So my father stayed in Calcutta. Now his flower was gone. He pressed his thin chapped lips to the satin of my hair. I remember opening my eyes — they felt tight and shiny, parched by the flames — and looking up at the column of smoke that roiled into the sky, a night sky blasted cloudy pink like a sky full of blood and milk.

There would be no milk for me, only chemical-tasting drops of formula from a plastic nipple. The morgue was in the basement of the hospital and did not burn. My mother lay on a metal table, a hospital gown stiff with her dying sweat pulled up over her red-smeared crotch and thighs. Her eyes stared up through the blackened skeleton of the hospital, up to the milky bloody sky, and ash filtered down to mask her pupils.

My father and I left for America before the monsoon came. Without my mother, Calcutta was a pestilential hellhole, a vast cremation grounds, or so my father thought. In America he could send me to school and movies, ball games and Boy Scouts, secure in the knowledge that someone else would take care of me or I would take care of myself. There were no *thuggees* to rob me and cut my throat, no *goondas* who would snatch me and sell my bones for fertilizer. There were no cows to infect the streets with their steaming sacred piss. My father could give me over to the comparative wholesomeness of American life, leaving himself free to sit in his darkened bedroom and drink whiskey until his long sensitive nose floated hazily in front of his face and the sabre edge of his grief began to dull. He was the sort of man who has only one love in his lifetime, and knows with the sick fervor of a fatalist that this love will be taken from him someday, and is hardly surprised when it happens.

When he was drunk he would talk about Calcutta. My little American mind rejected the place — I was in love with air conditioning, hamburgers and pizza, the free and undiscriminating love that was lavished upon me every time I twisted the TV dial — but somewhere in my Indian heart I longed for it. When I turned eighteen and my father finally failed to wake up from one of his drunken stupors, I returned to the city of my bloody birth as soon as I had the plane fare in my hand.

Calcutta, you will say. What a place to have been when the dead began to walk.

And I reply, what better place to be? What better place than a city where five million people look as if they are already dead — might as well be dead — and another five million wish they were?

I have a friend named Devi, a prostitute who began her work at the age of fifteen from a tarpaper shack on Sudder Street. Sudder is the Bourbon Street of Calcutta, but there is far less of the carnival there, and no one wears a mask on Sudder Street because disguises are useless when shame is irrelevant. Devi works the big hotels now, selling American tourists or British expatriates or German businessmen a taste of exotic Bengal spice. She is gaunt and beautiful and hard as nails. Devi says the world is a whore, too, and Calcutta is the pussy of the world. The world squats and spreads its legs, and Calcutta is the dank sex you see revealed there, wet and fragrant with a thousand odors both delicious and foul. A source of lushest pleasure, a breeding ground for every conceivable disease.

The pussy of the world. It is all right with me. I like pussy, and I love my squalid city.

The dead like pussy too. If they are able to catch a woman and disable her enough so that she cannot resist, you will see the lucky ones burrowing in between her legs as happily as the most avid lover. They do not have to come up for air. I have seen them eat all the way up into the body cavity. The internal female organs seem to be a great delicacy, and why not? They are the caviar of the human body. It is a sobering thing to come across a woman sprawled in the gutter with her intestines sliding from the shredded ruin of her womb, but you do not react. You do not distract the dead from their repast. They are slow and stupid, but that is all the more reason for you to be smart and quick and quiet. They will do the same thing to a man — chew off the soft penis and scrotal sac like choice morsels of squid, leaving only a red raw hole. But you can sidle by while they are feeding and they will not notice you. I do not try to hide from them. I walk the streets and look; that is all I do anymore. I am fascinated. This is not horror, this is simply more of Calcutta.

First I would sleep late, through the sultry morning into the heat of the afternoon. I had a room in one of the decrepit marble palaces of the old city. Devi visited me here often, but on a typical morning I woke alone, clad only in twisted bedsheets and a luxurious patina of sweat. Sun came through the window and fell in bright bars across the floor. I felt safe in my second-story room as long as I kept the door locked. The dead were seldom able to navigate stairs, and they could not manage the sustained cooperative effort to break down a locked door. They were no threat to me. They fed upon those who had given up, those too traumatized to keep running: the senile, abandoned old, the catatonic young women who sat in gutters cradling babies that had died during the night. These were easy prey.

The walls of my room were painted a bright coral and the sills and door were aqua. The colors caught the sun and made the day seem cheerful despite the heat that shimmered outside. I went downstairs, crossed the empty courtyard with its dry marble fountain, and went out into the street. This area was barren in the heat, painfully bright, with parched weeds lining the road and an occasional smear of cow dung decorating the gutter. By nightfall both weeds and dung might be gone. Children collected cow shit and patted it into cakes held together with straw, which could be sold as fuel for cooking fires.

I headed toward Chowringhee Road, the broad main thoroughfare of the city. Halfway up my street, hunched under the awning of a mattress factory, I saw one of the catatonic young mothers. The dead had found her too. They had already taken the baby from her arms and eaten through the soft part at the top of the skull. Vacuous bloody faces rose and dipped. Curds of tender brain fell from slack mouths. The mother sat on the curb nearby, her arms cradling nothing. She wore a filthy green sari that was ripped across the chest. The woman's breasts protruded heavily, swollen with milk. When the dead finished with her baby they would start on her, and she would make no resistance. I had seen it before. I knew how the milk would spurt and then gush as they tore into her breasts. I knew how hungrily they would lap up the twin rivers of blood and milk.

Above their bobbing heads, the tin awning dripped long ropy strands of cotton. Cotton hung from the roof in dirty clumps, caught in the corners of the doorway like spiderweb. Someone's radio blared faintly in another part of the building, tuned to an English-language Christian broadcast. A gospel hymn assured Calcutta that its dead in Christ would rise. I moved on toward Chowringhee.

Most of the streets in the city are positively cluttered with buildings. Buildings are packed in cheek-by-jowl, helter-skelter, like books of different sizes jammed into a rickety bookcase. Buildings even sag over the street so that all you see overhead is a narrow strip of sky crisscrossed by miles of clotheslines. The flapping silks and cottons are very bright against the sodden, dirty sky. But there are certain vantage points where the city opens up and all at once you have a panoramic view of Calcutta. You see a long muddy hillside that has become home to a *bustee*, thousands and thousands of slum dwellings where tiny fires are tended through the night. The dead come often to these slums of tin and cardboard, but the people do not leave the *bustee* — where would they go? Or you see a wasteland of disused factories, empty warehouses, blackened smokestacks jutting into a rust-colored sky. Or a flash of the Hooghly River, steel-gray in its shroud of mist, spanned by the intricate girder-and-wirescape of the Howrah Bridge.

Just now I was walking opposite the river. The waterfront was not considered a safe place because of the danger from drowning victims. Thousands each year took the long plunge off the bridge, and thousands more simply waded into the water. It is easy to commit suicide at a riverfront because despair collects in the water vapor. This is part of the reason for the tangible cloud of despair that hangs over Calcutta along with its veil of humidity.

Now the suicides and the drowned street children were coming out of the river. At any moment the water might regurgitate one, and you would hear him scrabbling up the bank. If he had been in the water long enough he might tear himself to spongy gobbets on the stones and broken bricks that littered the waterfront; all that remained would be a trace of foul brown odor, like the smell of mud from the deep part of the river.

Police had been taking the dead up on the bridge to shoot them. Even from far away I could see spray-patterns of red on the drab girders. Alternately they set the dead alight with gasoline and threw them over the railing into the river. At night it was not uncommon to see several writhing shapes caught in the downstream current, the fiery symmetry of their heads and arms and legs making them into five-pointed human stars.

I stopped at a spice vendor's stand to buy a bunch of red chrysanthemums and a handful of saffron. The saffron I had him wrap in a twist of scarlet silk. "It is a beautiful day," I said to him in Bengali. He stared at me, half amused, half appalled. "A beautiful day for what?"

True Hindu faith calls upon the believer to view all things as sacred. There is nothing profane — no dirty dog picking through the ash bin at a cremation ground, no stinking gangrenous stump thrust into your face by a beggar who seems to hold you personally responsible for all his woes. These things are as sacred as feasting day at the holiest temple. But even for the most devout Hindus it has been difficult to see these walking dead as sacred. They are empty humans. That is the truly horrifying thing about them, more than their vacuous hunger for living flesh, more than the blood caked under their nails or the shreds of flesh caught between their teeth. They are soulless; there is nothing in their eyes; the sounds they make — their farts, their grunts and mewls of hunger — are purely reflexive. The Hindu, who has been taught to believe in the soul of everything, has a particular horror of these drained human vessels. But in Calcutta life goes on. The shops are still open. The confusion of traffic still inches its way up Chowringhee. No one sees any alternatives.

Soon I arrived at what was almost invariably my day's first stop. I would often walk twenty or thirty miles in a day — I had strong shoes and nothing to occupy my time except walking and looking. But I always began at the Kalighat, temple of the Goddess.

There are a million names for her, a million vivid descriptions: Kali the Terrible, Kali the Ferocious, skull-necklace, destroyer of men, eater of souls.

But to me she was Mother Kali, the only one of the vast and colorful pantheon of Hindu gods that stirred my imagination and lifted my heart. She was the Destroyer, but all final refuge was found in her. She was the goddess of the age. She could bleed and burn and still rise again, very awake, beautifully terrible.

I ducked under the garlands of marigolds and strands of temple bells strung across the door, and I entered the temple of Kali. After the constant clamor of the street, the silence inside the temple was deafening. I fancied I could hear the small noises of my body echoing back to me from the ceiling far above. The sweet opium glaze of incense curled around my head. I approached the idol of Kali, the *jagrata*. Her gimlet eyes watched me as I came closer.

She was tall, gaunter and more brazenly naked than my friend Devi even at her best moments. Her breasts were tipped with blood — at least I always imagined them so — and her two sharp fangs and the long streamer of a tongue that uncurled from her open mouth were the color of blood too. Her hair whipped about her head and her eyes were wild, but the third crescent eye in the center of her forehead was merciful; it saw and accepted all.

The necklace of skulls circled the graceful stem of her neck, adorned the sculpted hollow of her throat. Her four arms were so sinuous that if you looked away even for an instant, they seemed to sway. In her four hands she held a noose of rope, a skull-staff, a shining sword, and a gaping, very dead-looking severed head. A silver bowl sat at the foot of the statue just beneath the head, where the blood from the neck would drip. Sometimes this was filled with goat's or sheep's blood as an offering. The bowl was full today. In these times the blood might well be human, though there was no putrid smell to indicate it had come from one of the dead.

I laid my chrysanthemums and saffron at Kali's feet. Among the other offerings, mostly sweets and bundles of spice, I saw a few strange objects. A fingerbone. A shriveled mushroom of flesh that turned out upon closer inspection to be an ear. These were offerings for special protection, mostly wrested from the dead. But who was to say that a few devotees had not lopped off their own ears or finger joints to coax a boon from Kali? Sometimes when I had forgotten to bring an offering, I cut my wrist with a razor blade and let a few drops of my blood fall at the idol's feet.

I heard a shout from outside and turned my head for a moment. When I looked back, the four arms seemed to have woven themselves into a new pattern, the long tongue seemed to loll farther from the scarlet mouth. And — this was a frequent fantasy of mine — the wide hips now seemed to tilt forward, affording me a glimpse of the sweet and terrible petalled cleft between the thighs of the goddess.

I smiled up at the lovely sly face. "If only I had a tongue as long as yours, Mother," I murmured, "I would kneel before you and lick the folds of your holy pussy until you screamed with joy." The toothy grin seemed to grow wider, more lascivious. I imagined much in the presence of Kali.

Outside in the temple yard I saw the source of the shout I had heard. There is a stone block upon which the animals brought to Kali, mostly baby goats, are beheaded by the priests. A gang of roughly dressed men had captured a dead girl and were bashing her head in on the sacrificial block. Their arms rose and fell, ropy muscles flexing. They clutched sharp stones and bits of brick in their scrawny hands. The girl's half-pulped head still lashed back and forth. The lower jaw still snapped, though the teeth and bone were splintered. Foul thin blood coursed down and mingled with the rich animal blood in the earth beneath the block. The girl was nude, filthy with her own gore and waste. The flaccid breasts hung as if sucked dry of meat. The belly was burst open with gases. One of the men thrust a stick into the ruined gouge between the girl's legs and leaned on it with all his weight.

Only in extensive stages of decay can the dead be told from the lepers. The dead are greater in number now, and even the lepers look human when compared to the dead. But that is only if you get close enough to look into the eyes. The faces in various stages of wet and dry rot, the raw ends of bones rubbing through skin like moldy cheesecloth, the cancerous domes of the skulls are the same. After a certain point lepers could no longer stay alive begging in the streets, for most people would now flee in terror at the sight of a rotting face. As a result the lepers were dying, then coming back, and the two races mingled like some obscene parody of incest. Perhaps they actually could breed. The dead could obviously eat and digest, and seemed to excrete at random like everyone else in Calcutta, but I supposed no one knew whether they could ejaculate or conceive.

A stupid idea, really. A dead womb would rot to pieces around a fetus before it could come halfway to term; a dead scrotal sac would be far too cold a cradle for living seed. But no one seemed to know anything about the biology of the dead. The newspapers were hysterical, printing picture upon picture of random slaughter by dead and living alike. Radio stations had either gone off the air or were broadcasting endless religious exhortations that ran together in one long keening whine, the edges of Muslim, Hindu, Christian doctrine beginning to fray and blur.

No one in India could say for sure what made the dead walk. The latest theory I had heard was something about a genetically engineered microbe that had been designed to feed on plastic: a microbe that would save the world from its own waste. But the microbe had mutated and was now eating and "replicating" human cells, causing basic bodily functions to reactivate. It did not much matter whether this was true. Calcutta was a city relatively unsurprised to see its dead rise and walk and feed upon it. It had seen them doing so for a hundred years.

All the rest of the lengthening day I walked through the city. I saw no more dead except a cluster far away at the end of a blocked street, in the last rags of bloody light, fighting each other over the bloated carcass of a sacred cow.

My favorite place at sunset is by the river where I can see the Howrah Bridge. The Hooghly is painfully beautiful in the light of the setting sun. The last rays melt onto the water like hot ghee, turning the river from steel to khaki to nearly golden, a blazing ribbon of light. The bridge rises black and skeletal into the fading orange sky. Tonight an occasional skirl of bright flowers and still-glowing greasy embers floated by, the last earthly traces of bodies cremated farther up the river.

Above the bridge were the burning *ghats* where families lined up to incinerate their dead and cast the ashes into the holy river. Cremation is done more efficiently these days, or at least more hurriedly. People can reconcile in their hearts their fear of strangers' dead, but they do not want to see their own dead rise.

I walked along the river for a while. The wind off the water carried the scent of burning meat. When I was well away from the bridge, I wandered back into the maze of narrow streets and alleyways that lead toward the docks in the far southern end of the city. People were already beginning to settle in for the night, though here a bedroom might mean your own packing crate or your own square of sidewalk. Fires glowed in nooks and corners. A warm breeze still blew off the river and sighed its way through the winding streets. It seemed very late now. As I made my way from corner to corner, through intermittent pools of light and much longer patches of darkness, I heard small bells jingling to the rhythm of my footsteps. The brass bells of rickshaw men, ringing to tell me they were there in case I wished for a ride. But I could see none of the men. The effect was eerie, as if I were walking alone down an empty nighttime street being serenaded by ghostly bells. The feeling soon passed. You are never truly alone in Calcutta.

A thin hand slid out of the darkness as I passed. Looking into the doorway it came from, I could barely make out five gaunt faces, five forms huddled against the night. I dropped several coins into the hand and it slid out of sight again. I am seldom begged from. I look neither rich nor poor, but I have a talent for making myself all but invisible. People look past me, sometimes right through me. I don't mind; I see more things that way. But when I am begged from I always give. With my handful of coins, all five of them might have a bowl of rice and lentils tomorrow.

A bowl of rice and lentils in the morning, a drink of water from a broken standpipe at night.

It seemed to me that the dead were among the best-fed citizens of Calcutta.

Now I crossed a series of narrow streets and was surprised to find myself coming up behind the Kalighat. The side streets are so haphazardly arranged that you are constantly finding yourself in places you had no idea you were even near. I had been to the Kalighat hundreds of times, but I had never approached it from this direction. The temple was dark and still. I had not been here at this hour before, did not even know whether the priests were still here or if one could enter so late. But as I walked closer I saw a little door standing open at the back. The entrance used by the priests, perhaps. Something flickered from within: a candle, a tiny mirror sewn on a robe, the smoldering end of a stick of incense.

I slipped around the side of the temple and stood at the door for a moment. A flight of stone steps led up into the darkness of the temple. The Kalighat at night, deserted, might have been an unpleasant prospect to some. The thought of facing the fierce idol alone in the gloom might have made some turn away from those steps. I began to climb them.

The smell reached me before I ascended halfway. To spend a day walking through Calcutta is to be assailed by thousands of odors both pleasant and foul: the savor of spices frying in ghee, the stink of shit and urine and garbage, the sick-sweet scent of the little white flowers called *mogra* that are sold in garlands and that make me think of the gardenia perfume American undertakers use to mask the smell of their corpses.

Almost everyone in Calcutta is scrupulously clean in person, even the very poor. They will leave their trash and their spit everywhere, but many of them wash their bodies twice a day. Still, everyone sweats under the sodden veil of heat, and at midday any public place will be redolent with the smell of human perspiration, a delicate tang like the mingled juices of lemons and onions. But lingering in the stairwell was an odor stronger and more foul than any I had encountered today. It was deep and brown and moist; it curled at the edges like a mushroom beginning to dry. It was the perfume of mortal corruption. It was the smell of rotting flesh.

Then I came up into the temple, and I saw them.

The large central room was lit only with candles that flickered in a restless draft, first this way, then that. In the dimness the worshippers looked no different from any other supplicants at the feet of Kali. But as my eyes grew accustomed to the candlelight, details resolved themselves. The withered hands, the ruined faces. The burst body cavities where ropy organs could be seen trailing down behind the cagework of ribs.

The offerings they had brought.

By day Kali grinned down upon an array of blossoms and sweetmeats lovingly arranged at the foot of her pedestal. The array spread there now seemed more suited to the goddess. I saw human heads balanced on raw stumps of necks, eyes turned up to crescents of silver-white. I saw gobbets of meat that might have been torn from a belly or a thigh. I saw severed hands like pale lotus flowers, the fingers like petals opening silently in the night.

Most of all, piled on every side of the altar, I saw bones. Bones picked so clean that they gleamed in the candlelight. Bones with smears of meat and long snotty runners of fat still attached. Skinny arm-bones, clubby leg-bones, the pretzel of a pelvis, the beadwork of a spine. The delicate bones of children. The crumbling ivory bones of the old. The bones of those who could not run.

These things the dead brought to their goddess. She had been their goddess all along, and they her acolytes.

Kali's smile was hungrier than ever. The tongue lolled like a wet red streamer from the open mouth. The eyes were blazing black holes in the gaunt and terrible face. If she had stepped down from her pedestal and approached me now, if she had reached for me with those sinuous arms, I might not have been able to fall to my knees before her. I might have run. There are beauties too terrible to be borne.

Slowly the dead began to turn toward me. Their faces lifted and the rotting cavities of their nostrils caught my scent. Their eyes shone iridescent. Faint starry light shimmered in the empty spaces of their bodies. They were like cutouts in the fabric of reality, like conduits to a blank universe. The void where Kali ruled and the only comfort was in death.

They did not approach me. They stood holding their precious offerings and they looked at me — those of them that still had eyes to look — or they looked through me. At that moment I felt more than invisible. I felt empty enough to belong among these human shells.

A ripple seemed to pass through them. Then — in the uncertain candlelight, in the light that shimmered from the bodies of the dead — Kali did move.

The twitch of a finger, the deft turn of a wrist — at first it was so slight as to be nearly imperceptible. But then her lips split into an impossibly wide, toothy grin and the tip of her long tongue curled. She rotated her hips and swung her left leg high into the air. The foot that had trod on millions of corpses made a *pointe* as delicate as a prima ballerina's. The movement spread her sex wide open.

But it was not the petalled mandala-like cleft I had imagined kissing earlier. The pussy of the goddess was an enormous deep red hole that seemed to lead down to the center of the world. It was a gash in the universe, it was rimmed in blood and ash. Two of her four hands beckoned toward it, inviting me in. I could have thrust my head into it, then my shoulders. I could have crawled all the way into that wet crimson eternity, and kept crawling forever.

Then I did run. Before I had even decided to flee I found myself falling down the stone staircase, cracking my head and my knee on the risers. At the bottom I was up and running before I could register the pain. I told myself that I thought the dead would come after me. I do not know what I truly feared was at my back. At times I thought I was running not away from something, but toward it.

I ran all night. When my legs grew too tired to carry me I would board a bus. Once I crossed the bridge and found myself in Howrah, the even poorer suburb on the other side of the Hooghly. I stumbled through desolate streets for an hour or more before doubling back and crossing over into Calcutta again. Once I stopped to ask for a drink of water from a man who carried two cans of it slung on a long stick across his shoulders. He would not let me drink from his tin cup, but poured a little water into my cupped hands. In his face I saw the mingled pity and disgust with which one might look upon a drunk or a beggar. I was a well-dressed beggar, to be sure, but he saw the fear in my eyes.

In the last hour of the night I found myself wandering through a wasteland of factories and warehouses, of smokestacks and rusty corrugated tin gates, of broken windows. There seemed to be thousands of broken windows. After a while I realized I was on the Upper Chitpur Road. I walked for a while in the watery light that fills the sky before dawn. Eventually I left the road and staggered through the wasteland. Not until I saw its girders rising around me like the charred bones of a prehistoric animal did I realize I was in the ruins of the hospital where I had been born.

The hole of the basement had filled up with broken glass and crumbling metal, twenty years' worth of cinders and weeds, all washed innocent in the light of the breaking dawn. Where the building had stood there was only a vast depression in the ground, five or six feet deep. I slid down the shallow embankment, rolled, and came to rest in the ashes. They were infinitely soft; they cradled me. I felt as safe as an embryo. I let the sunrise bathe me. Perhaps I had climbed into the gory chasm between Kali's legs after all, and found my way out again.

Calcutta is cleansed each morning by the dawn. If only the sun rose a thousand times a day, the city would always be clean.

Ashes drifted over me, smudged my hands gray, flecked my lips. I lay safe in the womb of my city, called by its poets Lord of Nerves, city of joy, the pussy of the world. I felt as if I lay among the dead. I was that safe from them: I knew their goddess, I shared their many homes. As the sun came up over the mud and glory of Calcutta, the sky was so full of smoky clouds and pale pink light that it seemed, to my eyes, to burn.

Elizabeth Hand is the multiple-award-winning author of numerous novels and three collections of short fiction. She is also a longtime reviewer for many publications, including the *Washington Post, Salon, Village Voice,* and the *Boston Globe,* and is a columnist for *The Magazine of Fantasy & Science Fiction. Illyria,* her World Fantasy Award-winning novel inspired by Shakespeare's *Twelfth Night,* was recently published for the first time in the U.S. Her most recent novel is *Available Dark,* a sequel to the Shirley Jackson Award-winning novel *Generation Loss,* is forthcoming, as is a young adult novel about Rimbaud.

Hand is one of several writers with stories in this anthology who comfortably glides between science fiction, fantasy, horror, and mainstream. She's a writer who follows her own interests (among them, mythic themes and the cost of creation) and thus over the past two decades has written some of the very best horror stories and novellas, including "The Erl-King," published relatively early in her career.

The Erl-King
Elizabeth Hand

THE KINKAJOU HAD been missing for two days now. Haley feared it was dead, killed by one of the neighborhood dogs or by a fox or wildcat in the woods. Linette was certain it was alive; she even knew where it was.

"Kingdom Come," she announced, pointing a long lazy hand in the direction of the neighboring estate. She dropped her hand and sipped at a mug of tepid tea, twisting so she wouldn't spill it as she rocked back and forth. It was Linette's turn to lie in the hammock. She did so with feckless grace, legs tangled in her long peasant skin, dark hair spilled across the faded canvas. She had more practice at it than Haley, this being Linette's house and Linette's overgrown yard bordering the woods of spindly young pines and birches that separated them from Kingdom Come. Haley frowned, leaned against the oak tree, and pushed her friend desultorily with one foot.

"Then why doesn't your mother call them or something?" Haley loved the kinkajou and justifiably feared the worst. With her friend exotic pets came and went, just as did odd visitors to the tumbledown cottage where Linette lived with her mother, Aurora. Most of the animals were presents from Linette's father, an elderly Broadway producer whose successes paid for the rented cottage and Linette's occasional artistic endeavors (flute lessons, sitar lessons, an incomplete course in airbrushing) as well as the bottles of Tanqueray that lined Aurora's bedroom. And, of course, the animals. An iguana whose skin peeled like mildewed wallpaper, finally lost (and never found) in the drafty dark basement where the girls held annual Hallowe'en seances. An intimidatingly large Moluccan cockatoo that escaped into the trees, terrorizing Kingdom Come's previous owner and his garden-party guests by shrieking at them in Gaelic from the wisteria. Finches and fire weavers small enough to hold in your fist. A quartet of tiny goats, Haley's favorites until the kinkajou.

The cockatoo started to smell worse and worse, until one day it flopped to the bottom of its wrought-iron cage and died. The finches escaped when Linette left the door to their bamboo cage open. The goats ran off into the woods surrounding Lake Muscanth. They were rumored to be living there still. But this summer Haley had come over every day to make certain the kinkajou had enough to eat, that Linette's cats weren't terrorizing it; that Aurora didn't try to feed it crème de menthe as she had the capuchin monkey that had fleetingly resided in her room.

"I don't know," Linette said. She shut her eyes, balancing her mug on her stomach. A drop of tea spilled onto her cotton blouse, another faint petal among faded ink stains and the ghostly impression of eyes left by an abortive attempt at batik. "I think Mom knows the guy who lives there now, she doesn't like him or something. I'll ask my father next time."

Haley prodded the hammock with the toe of her sneaker. "It's almost my turn. Then we should go over there. It'll die if it gets cold at night."

Linette smiled without opening her eyes. "Nah. It's still summer," she said, and yawned.

Haley frowned. She moved her back up and down against the bole of the oak tree, scratching where a scab had formed after their outing to Mandrake Island to look for the goats. It was early August, nearing the end of their last summer before starting high school, the time Aurora had named "the summer before the dark."

"My poor little girls," Aurora had mourned a few months earlier. It had been only June then, the days still cool enough that the City's wealthy fled each weekend to Kamensic Village to hide among the woods and wetlands in their Victorian follies. Aurora was perched with Haley and Linette on an ivied slope above the road, watching the southbound Sunday exodus of limousines and Porsches and Mercedes. "Soon you'll be gone."

"Jeez, Mom," laughed Linette. A plume of ivy tethered her long hair back from her face. Aurora reached to tug it with one unsteady hand. The other clasped a plastic cup full of gin. "No one's going anywhere, I'm going to Fox Lane," — that was the public high school — "you heard what Dad said. Right, Haley?"

Haley had nodded and stroked the kinkajou sleeping in her lap. It never did anything but sleep, or open its golden eyes to half-wakefulness oh so briefly before finding another lap or cushion to curl into. It reminded her of Linette in that, her friend's heavy lazy eyes always ready to shut, her legs quick to curl around pillows or hammock cushions or Haley's own battle-scarred knees.

"Right," said Haley, and she had cupped her palm around the soft warm globe of the kinkajou's head.

Now the hammock creaked noisily as Linette turned onto her stomach, dropping her mug into the long grass. Haley started, looked down to see her hands hollowed as though holding something. If the kinkajou died she'd never speak to Linette again. Her heart beat faster at the thought.

"I think we should go over. If you think it's there. *And —*" Haley grabbed the ropes restraining the hammock, yanked them back and forth so that Linette shrieked, her hair caught between hempen braids — "it's — *my —* turn — *now.*"

They snuck out that night. The sky had turned pale green, the same shade as the crystal globe wherein three ivory-bellied frogs floated, atop a crippled table. To keep the table from falling Haley had propped a broom handle beneath it for a fourth leg — although she hated the frogs, bloated things with prescient yellow eyes. Some nights when she slept over they broke her sleep with their song, high-pitched trilling that disturbed neither Linette snoring in the other bed nor Aurora drinking broodingly in her tiny shed-roofed wing of the cottage. It was uncanny, almost frightening sometimes, how nothing ever disturbed them: not dying pets nor utilities cut off for lack of payment nor unexpected visits from Aurora's small circle of friends, People from the Factory Days she called them. Rejuvenated junkies or pop stars with new careers, or wasted beauties like Aurora Dawn herself. All of them seemingly forever banned from the real world, the adult world Haley's parents and family inhabited, magically free as Linette herself was to sample odd-tasting liqueurs and curious religious notions and lost arts in their dank corners of the City or the shelter of some wealthier friend's up-county retreat. Sleepy-eyed from dope or taut from amphetamines, they lay around the cottage with Haley and Linette, offering sips of their drinks, advice about popular musicians and contraceptives. Their hair was streaked with gray now, or dyed garish mauve or blue or green. They wore high leather boots and clothes inlaid with feathers or mirrors, and had names that sounded like the names of expensive perfumes: Liatris, Coppelia, Electric Velvet. Sometimes Haley felt that she had wandered into a fairy tale, or a movie. *Beauty and the Beast* perhaps, or *The Dark Crystal.* Of course it would be one of Linette's favorites; Linette had more imagination and sensitivity than Haley. The kind of movie Haley would choose to wander into would have fast cars and gunshots in the distance, not aging refugees from another decade passed out next to the fireplace.

She thought of that now, passing the globe of frogs. They went from the eerie interior dusk of the cottage into the strangely aqueous air outside. Despite the warmth of the late summer evening Haley shivered as she gazed back at the cottage. The tiny bungalow might have stood there unchanged for five hundred years, for a thousand. No warm yellow light spilled from the windows as it did at her own house. There was no smell of dinner cooking, no television chattering. Aurora seldom cooked, Linette never. There was no TV. Only the frogs hovering in their silver world, and the faintest cusp of a new moon like a leaf cast upon the surface of the sky.

The main house of the neighboring estate stood upon a broad slope of lawn overlooking the woods. Massive oaks and sycamores studded the grounds, and formal gardens that had been more carefully tended by the mansion's previous owner, a New York fashion designer recently dead. At the foot of the long drive a post bore the placard on which was writ in spidery silver letters KINGDOM COME.

In an upstairs room Lie Vagal perched upon a windowsill. He stared out at the same young moon that watched Haley and Linette as they made their way through the woods. Had Lie known where to look he might have seen them as well; but he was watching the kinkajou sleeping in his lap.

It had appeared at breakfast two days earlier. Lie sat with his grandmother on the south terrace, eating Froot Loops and reading the morning mail, *The Wall Street Journal* and a quarterly royalty statement from BMI. His grandmother stared balefully into a bowl of bran flakes, as though discerning there unpleasant intimations of the future.

"Did you take your medicine, Gram?" asked Lie. A leaf fell from an overhanging branch into his coffee cup. He fished it out before Gram could see it as another dire portent.

"Did you take yours, Elijah?" snapped Gram. She finished the bran flakes and reached for her own coffee, black and laced with chicory. She was eighty-four years old and had outlived all of her other relatives and many of Lie's friends. "I know you didn't yesterday."

Lie shrugged. Another leaf dropped to the table, followed by a hail of bark and twigs. He peered up into the greenery, then pointed.

"Look," he said. "A squirrel or cat or something."

His grandmother squinted, shaking her head peevishly. "I can't see a thing."

The shaking branches parted to show something brown attached to a slender limb. Honey-colored, too big for a squirrel, it clung to a branch that dipped lower and lower, spattering them with more debris. Lie moved his coffee cup and had started to his feet when it fell, landing on top of the latest issue of *New Musical Express*.

For a moment he thought the fall had killed it. It just lay there, legs and long tail curled as though it had been a doodlebug playing dead. Then slowly it opened its eyes, regarded him with a muzzy golden gaze, and yawned, unfurling a tongue so brightly pink it might have been lipsticked. Lie laughed.

"It fell asleep in the tree! It's a — a what-you-call-it, a sloth."

His grandmother shook her head, pushing her glasses onto her nose. "That's not a sloth. They have grass growing on them."

Lie stretched a finger and tentatively stroked its tail. The animal ignored him, closing its eyes once more and folding its paws upon its glossy breast. Around its neck someone had placed a collar, the sort of leather-and-rhinestone ornament old ladies deployed on poodles. Gingerly Lie turned it, until he found a small heart-shaped tab of metal.

KINKAJOU
My name is Valentine
764-0007

"Huh," he said. "I'll be damned. I bet it belongs to those girls next door." Gram sniffed and collected the plates. Next to Lie's coffee mug, the compartmented container holding a week's worth of his medication was still full.

The animal did nothing but sleep and eat. Lie called a pet store in the City and learned that kinkajous ate insects and honey and bananas. He fed it Froot Loops, yogurt and granola, a moth he caught one evening in the bedroom. Tonight it slept once more, and he stroked it, murmuring to himself. He still hadn't called the number on the collar.

From here he could just make out the cottage, a white blur through dark leaves and tangled brush. It was his cottage, really; a long time ago the estate gardener had lived there. The fashion designer had been friends with the present tenant in the City long ago. For the last fourteen years the place had been leased to Aurora Dawn. When he'd learned that, Lie Vagal had given a short laugh, one that the realtor had mistaken for displeasure.

"We could evict her," she'd said anxiously. "Really, she's no trouble, just the town drunk, but once you'd taken possession —"

"I wouldn't *dream* of it." Lie laughed again, shaking his head but not explaining. "Imagine, having Aurora Dawn for a neighbor again.…"

His accountant had suggested selling the cottage, it would be worth a small fortune now, or else turning it into a studio or guest house. But Lie knew that the truth was, his accountant didn't want Lie to start hanging around with Aurora again. Trouble; all the survivors from those days were trouble.

That might have been why Lie didn't call the number on the collar. He hadn't seen Aurora in fifteen years, although he had often glimpsed the girls playing in the woods. More than once he'd started to go meet them, introduce himself, bring them back to the house. He was lonely here. The visitors who still showed up at Aurora's door at four A.M. used to bang around Lie's place in the City. But that was long ago, before what Lie thought of as The Crash and what *Rolling Stone* had termed "the long tragic slide into madness of the one-time *force majeur* of underground rock and roll." And his agent and his lawyer wouldn't think much of him luring children to his woodland lair.

He sighed. Sensing some shift in the summer air, his melancholy perhaps, the sleeping kinkajou sighed as well, and trembled where it lay curled between his thighs. Lie lifted his head to gaze out the open window.

Outside the night lay still and deep over woods and lawns and the little dreaming cottage. A Maxfield Parrish scene, stars spangled across an ultramarine sky, twinkling bit of moon, there at the edge of the grass a trio of cottontails feeding peacefully amidst the dandelions. He had first been drawn to the place because it looked like this, like one of the paintings he collected. "Kiddie stuff," his agent sniffed; "fairy tale porn." Parrish and Rackham and Nielsen and Clarke. Tenniel prints of Alice's trial. The DuFevre painting of the Erl-King that had been the cover of Lie Vagal's second, phenomenally successful album. For the first two weeks after moving he had done nothing but pace the labyrinthine hallways, planning where they all would hang, this picture by this window, that one near another. All day, all night he paced; and always alone.

Because he was afraid his agent or Gram or one of the doctors would find out the truth about Kingdom Come, the reason he had really bought the place. He had noticed it the first time the realtor had shown the house. She'd commented on the number of windows there were —

"South-facing, too, the place is a hundred years old but it really functions as passive solar with all these windows. That flagstone floor in the green room acts as a heat sink —"

She nattered on, but Lie said nothing. He couldn't believe that she didn't notice. No one did, not Gram or his agent or the small legion of people brought in from Stamford who cleaned the place before he moved in.

It was the windows, of course. They always came to the windows first.

The first time he'd seen them had been in Marrakech, nearly sixteen years ago. A window shaped like a downturned heart, looking out onto a sky so blue it seemed to drip; and outside, framed within the window's heavy white curves, Lie saw the crouching figure of a young man, bent over some object that caught the sun and flared so that he'd had to look away. When he'd turned back the young man was staring up in amazement as reddish smoke like dust roiled from the shining object. As Lie watched, the smoke began to take the shape of an immense man. At that point the joint he held burned Lie's fingers and he shouted, as much from panic as pain. When he looked out again the figures were gone.

Since then he'd seen them many times. Different figures, but always familiar, always fleeting, and brightly colored as the tiny people inside a marzipan egg. Sinbad and the Roc; the little mermaid and her sisters; a brave little figure carrying a belt engraved with the words SEVEN AT A BLOW. The steadfast tin soldier and a Christmas tree soon gone to cinders; dogs with eyes as big as teacups, as big as soup plates, as big as millstones. On tour in Paris, London, Munich, L.A., they were always there, as likely (or unlikely) to appear in a hotel room overlooking a dingy alley as within the crystal mullions of some heiress's bedroom. He had never questioned their presence, not after that first shout of surprise. They were the people, *his* people; the only ones he could trust in what was fast becoming a harsh and bewildering world.

It was just a few weeks after the first vision in Marrakech that he went to that fateful party; and a few months after that came the staggering success of *The Erl-King*. And then The Crash, and all the rest of it. He had a confused memory of those years. Even now, when he recalled that time it was as a movie with too much crosscutting and no dialogue. An endless series of women (and men) rolling from his bed; dark glimpses of himself in the studio cutting *Baba Yaga* and *The Singing Bone;* a few overlit sequences with surging crowds screaming soundlessly beneath a narrow stage. During those years his visions of the people changed. At first his psychiatrist was very interested in hearing about them. And so for a few months that was all he'd talk about, until he could see her growing impatient. That was the last time he brought them up to anyone.

But he wished he'd been able to talk to someone about them; about how different they were since The Crash. In the beginning he'd always noticed only how beautiful they were, how like his memories of all those stories from his childhood. The little mermaid gazing adoringly up at her prince; the two children in the cottage made of gingerbread and gumdrops; the girl in her glass coffin awakened by a kiss. It was only after The Crash that he remembered the *other* parts of the tales, the parts that in childhood had made it impossible for him to sleep some nights and which now, perversely, returned to haunt his dreams. The witch shrieking inside the stove as she was burned to death. The wicked queen forced to dance in the red-hot iron shoes until she died. The little mermaid's prince turning from her to marry another, and the mermaid changed to sea foam as punishment for his indifference.

But since he'd been at Kingdom Come these unnerving glimpses of the people had diminished. They were still there, but all was as it had been at the very first, the myriad lovely creatures flitting through the garden like moths at twilight. He thought that maybe it was going off his medication that did it; and so the full prescription bottles were hoarded in a box in his room, hidden from Gram's eyes.

That was how he made sure the people remained at Kingdom Come. Just like in Marrakech: they were in the windows. Each one opened onto a different spectral scene, visual echoes of the fantastic paintings that graced the walls. The bathroom overlooked a twilit ballroom; the kitchen a black dwarf's cave. The dining room's high casements opened onto the Glass Hill. From a tiny window in the third-floor linen closet he could see a juniper tree, and once a flute of pale bone sent its eerie song pulsing through the library.

"You hear that, Gram?" he had gasped. But of course she heard nothing; she was practically deaf.

Lately it seemed that they came more easily, more often. He would feel an itching at the corner of his eyes, Tinkerbell's pixie dust, the Sandman's seed. Then he would turn, and the placid expanse of new-mown lawn would suddenly be transformed into gnarled spooky trees beneath a grinning moon, rabbits holding hands, the grass frosted with dew that held the impressions of many dancing feet. He knew there were others he didn't see, wolves and witches and bones that danced. And the most terrible one of all — the Erl-King, the one he'd met at the party; the one who somehow had set all this in motion and then disappeared. It was Lie's worst fear that someday he would come back.

Now suddenly the view in front of him changed. Lie started forward. The kinkajou slid from his lap like a bolt of silk to lie at his feet, still drowsing. From the trees waltzed a girl, pale in the misty light. She wore a skirt that fetched just above her bare feet, a white blouse that set off a tangle of long dark hair. Stepping onto the lawn she paused, turned back and called into the woods. He could hear her voice but not her words. A child's voice, although the skirt billowed about long legs and he could see where her breasts swelled within the white blouse.

Ah, he thought, and tried to name her. Jorinda, Gretel, Ashputtel?

But then someone else crashed through the brake of saplings. Another girl, taller and wearing jeans and a halter top, swatting at her bare arms. He could hear what *she* was saying; she was swearing loudly while the first girl tried to hush her. He laughed, nudged the kinkajou on the floor. When it didn't respond he bent to pick it up and went downstairs.

"I don't think anyone's home," Haley said. She stood a few feet from the haven of the birch grove, feeling very conspicuous surrounded by all this open lawn. She killed another mosquito and scratched her arm. "Maybe we should just call, or ask your mother. If she knows this guy."

"She doesn't like him," Linette replied dreamily. A faint mist rose in little eddies about them. She lifted her skirts and did a pirouette, her bare feet leaving darker impressions on the gray lawn. "And it would be even cooler if no one was there, we could go in and find Valentine and look around. Like a haunted house."

"Like breaking and entering," Haley said darkly, but she followed her friend tiptoeing up the slope. The dewy grass was cool, the air warm and smelling of something sweet, oranges or maybe some kind of incense wafting down from the immense stone house.

They walked up the lawn, Linette leading the way. Dew soaked the hem of her skirt and the cuffs of Haley's jeans. At the top of the slope stood the great main house, a mock-Tudor fantasy of stone and stucco and oak beams. Waves of ivy and cream-colored roses spilled from the upper eaves; toppling ramparts of hollyhocks grew against the lower story. From here Haley could see only a single light downstairs, a dim green glow from behind curtains of ivy. Upstairs, diamond-paned windows had been pushed open, forcing the vegetation to give way and hang in limp streamers, some of them almost to the ground. The scent of turned earth mingled with that of smoke and oranges.

"Should we go to the front door?" Haley asked. Seeing the back of the house close up like this unnerved her, the smell of things decaying and the darkened mansion's *dishabille*. Like seeing her grandmother once without her false teeth: she wanted to turn away and give the house a chance to pull itself together.

Linette stopped to scratch her foot. "Nah. It'll be easier to just walk in if we go this way. If nobody's home." She straightened and peered back in the direction they'd come. Haley turned with her. The breeze felt good in her face. She could smell the distant dampness of Lake Muscanth, hear the croak of frogs and the rustling of leaves where deer stepped to water's edge to drink. When the girls turned back to the big house each took a step forward. Then they gasped, Linette pawing at the air for Haley's hand.

"Someone's there!"

Haley nodded. She squeezed Linette's fingers and then drew forward.

They had only looked away for an instant. But it had been long enough for lights to go on inside and out, so that now the girls blinked in the glare of spotlights. Someone had thrown open a set of French doors opening onto a sort of patio decorated with tubs of geraniums and very old wicker porch furniture, the wicker sprung in threatening and dangerous patterns. Against the brilliance the hollyhocks loomed black and crimson. A trailing length of white curtain blew from the French doors onto the patio. Haley giggled nervously, and heard Linette breathing hard behind her.

Someone stepped outside, a small figure not much taller than Haley. He held something in his arms, and cocked his head in a way that was, if not exactly welcoming, at least neutral enough to indicate that they should come closer.

Haley swallowed and looked away. She wondered if it would be too stupid just to run back to the cottage. But behind her Linette had frozen. On her face was the same look she had when caught passing notes in class, a look that meant it would be up to Haley, as usual, to get them out of this.

"Hum," Haley said, clearing her throat. The man didn't move. She shrugged, trying to think of something to say.

"Come on up," a voice rang out; a rather high voice with the twangy undercurrent of a Texas accent. It was such a cheerful voice, as though they were expected guests, that for a moment she didn't associate it with the stranger on the patio. "It's okay, you're looking for your pet, right?"

Behind her Linette gasped again, in relief. Then Haley was left behind as her friend raced up the hill, holding up her skirts and glancing back, laughing.

"Come on! He's got Valentine —"

Haley followed her, walking deliberately slowly. Of a sudden she felt odd. The too-bright lights on a patio smelling of earth and mandarin oranges; the white curtain blowing in and out; the welcoming stranger holding Valentine. It all made her dizzy, fairly breathless with anticipation; but frightened, too. For a long moment she stood there, trying to catch her breath. Then she hurried after her friend.

When she got to the top Linette was holding the kinkajou, crooning over it the way Haley usually did. Linette herself hadn't given it this much attention since its arrival last spring. Haley stopped, panting, next to a wicker chair, and bent to scratch her ankle. When she looked up again the stranger was staring at her.

"Hello," he said. Haley smiled shyly and shrugged, then glanced at Linette.

"Hey! You got him back! I told you he was here —"

Linette smiled, settled onto a wicker loveseat with Valentine curled among the folds of her skirt. "Thanks," she said softly, glancing up at the man. "He found him two days ago, he said. This is Haley —"

The man said hello again, still smiling. He was short, and wore a black T-shirt and loose white trousers, like hospital pants only cut from some fancy cloth. He had long black hair, thinning back from his forehead but still thick enough to pull into a ponytail. He reminded her of someone; she couldn't think who. His hands were crossed on his chest and he nodded at Haley, as though he knew what she was thinking.

"You're sisters," he said; then when Linette giggled shook his head, laughing. "No, of course, that's dumb: you're just friends, right? Best friends, I see you all the time together."

Haley couldn't think of anything to say, so she stepped closer to Linette and stroked the kinkajou's head. She wondered what happened now: if they stayed here on the porch with the stranger, or took Valentine and went home, or —

But what happened next was that a very old lady appeared in the French doors that led inside. She moved quickly, as though if she slowed down even for an instant she would be overtaken by one of the things that overtake old people, arthritis maybe, or sleep; and she swatted impatiently at the white curtains blowing in and out.

"Elijah," she said accusingly. She wore a green polyester blouse and pants patterned with enormous orange poppies, and fashionable eyeglasses with very large green frames. Her white hair was carefully styled. As she stood in the doorway her gaze flicked from Linette and the kinkajou to the stranger, then back to Linette. And Haley saw something cross the old woman's face as she looked at her friend, and then at the man again: an expression of pure alarm, terror almost. Then the woman turned and looked at Haley for the first time. She shook her head earnestly and continued to stare at Haley with very bright eyes, as though they knew each other from somewhere, or as though she had quickly sized up the situation and decided Haley was the only other person here with any common sense, which seemed precisely the kind of thing this old lady might think. "I'm Elijah's grandmother," she said at last, and very quickly crossed the patio to stand beside the stranger.

"*Hi,*" said Linette, looking up from beneath waves of dark hair. The man smiled, glancing at the old lady. His hand moved very slightly toward Linette's head, as though he might stroke her hair. Haley desperately wanted to scratch her ankle again, but was suddenly embarrassed lest anyone see her. The old lady continued to stare at her, and Haley finally coughed.

"I'm Haley," she said, then added, "Linette's friend." As though the lady knew who Linette was.

But maybe she did, because she nodded very slightly, glancing again at Linette and then at the man she had said was her grandson. "Well," she said. Her voice was strong and a little shrill, and she too had a Texas accent. "Come on in, girls. *Elijah.* I put some water on for tea."

Now this is too weird, thought Haley. The old lady strode back across the patio and held aside the white curtains, waiting for them to follow her indoors. Linette stood, cradling the kinkajou and murmuring to it. She caught Haley's eye and smiled triumphantly. Then she followed the old lady, her skirt rustling about her legs. That left Haley and the man still standing by the wicker furniture.

"Come on in, Haley," he said to her softly. He extended one hand toward the door, a very long slender hand for such a short man. Around his wrist he wore a number of thin silver- and gold-colored bracelets. There came again that overpowering scent of oranges and fresh earth, and something else too, a smoky musk like incense. Haley blinked and steadied herself by touching the edge of one wicker chair. "It's okay, Haley —"

Is it? she wondered. She looked behind her, down the hill to where the cottage lay sleeping. If she yelled would Aurora hear her? Would anyone? Because she was certain now that something was happening, maybe had already happened and it was just taking a while (as usual) to catch up with Haley. From the woods edging Lake Muscanth came the yapping of the fox again, and the wind brought her the smell of water. For a moment she shut her eyes and pretended she was there, safe with the frogs and foxes.

But even with her eyes closed she could feel the man staring at her with that intent dark gaze. It occurred to Haley then that the only reason he wanted her to come was that he was afraid Linette would go if Haley left. A wave of desolation swept over her, to think she was unwanted, that even here and now it was as it always was: Linette chosen first for teams, for dances, for secrets, and Haley waiting, waiting.

"Haley."

The man touched her hand, a gesture so tentative that for a moment she wasn't even sure it was him: it might have been the breeze, or a leaf falling against her wrist. She looked up and his eyes were pleading, but also apologetic; as though he really believed it wouldn't be the same without her. And she knew that expression — now who stared at her just like that, who was it he looked like?

It was only after she had followed him across the patio, stooping to brush the grass from her bare feet as she stepped over the threshold into Kingdom Come, that she realized he reminded her of Linette.

The tea was Earl Grey, the same kind they drank in Linette's kitchen. But this kitchen was huge: the whole cottage could practically have fit inside it. For all that it was a reassuring place, with all the normal kitchen things where they should be — microwave, refrigerator, ticking cat clock with its tail slicing back and forth, back and forth.

"Cream and sugar?"

The old lady's hands shook as she put the little bowl on the table. Behind her Lie Vagal grinned, opened a cabinet and took out a golden jar.

"I bet she likes *honey,*" he pronounced, setting the jar in front of Linette. She giggled delightedly. "How did you know?"

"Yeah, how did you know?" echoed Haley, frowning a little. In Linette's lap the kinkajou uncurled and yawned, and Linette dropped a spoonful of honey into its mouth. The old lady watched tight-lipped. Behind her glasses her eyes sought Haley's, but the girl looked away, shy and uneasy.

"Just a feeling I had, just a lucky guess," Lie Vagal sang. He took a steaming mug from the table, ignored his grandmother when she pointed meaningfully at the pill bottle beside it. "Now, would you girls like to tour the rest of the house?"

It was an amazing place. There were chairs of brass and ebony, chairs of antlers, chairs of neon tubes. Incense burners shaped like snakes and elephants sent up wisps of sweet smoke. From the living room wall gaped demonic masks, and a hideous stick figure that looked like something that Haley, shuddering, recalled from *Uncle Wiggly.* There was a glass ball that sent out runners of light when you touched it, and a jukebox that played a song about the Sandman.

And everywhere were the paintings. Not exactly what you would expect to find in a place like this: paintings that illustrated fairy tales. Puss in Boots and the Three Billy Goats Gruff. Aladdin and the Monkey King and the Moon saying goodnight. Famous paintings, some of them — Haley recognized scenes from books she'd loved as a child, and framed animation cells from *Pinocchio* and *Snow White* and *Cinderella.*

These were parceled out among the other wonders. A man-high tank seething with piranhas. A room filled with nothing but old record albums, thousands of them. A wall of gold and platinum records and framed clippings from *Rolling Stone* and *NME* and *New York Rocker.* And in the library a series of Andy Warhol silk-screens of a young man with very long hair, alternately colored green and blue, dated 1972.

Linette was entranced by the fairy-tale paintings. She walked right past the Warhol prints to peruse a watercolor of a tiny child and a sparrow, and dreamily traced the edge of its frame. Lie Vagal stared after her, curling a lock of his hair around one finger. Haley lingered in front of the Warhol prints and chewed her thumb thoughtfully.

After a long moment she turned to him and said, "I know who you are. You're, like, this old rock star. Lie Vagal. You had some album that my babysitter liked when I was little."

He smiled and turned from watching Linette. "Yeah, that's me."

Haley rubbed her lower lip, staring at the Warhol prints. "You must've been really famous, to get him to do those paintings. What was that album called? The Mountain King?"

"The Erl-King." He stepped to an ornate ormolu desk adrift with papers. He shuffled through them, finally withdrew a glossy pamphlet. "Let's see —"

He turned back to Haley and handed it to her. A CD catalog, opened to a page headed ROCK AND ROLL ARCHIVES and filled with reproductions of album cover art. He pointed to one, reduced like the others to the size of a postage stamp. The illustration was of a midnight landscape speared by lightning. In the foreground loomed a hooded figure, in the background tiny specks that might have been other figures or trees or merely errors in the printing process. *The Erl-King,* read the legend that ran beneath the picture.

"Huh," said Haley. She glanced up to call Linette, but her friend had wandered into the adjoining room. She could glimpse her standing at the shadowed foot of a set of stairs winding up to the next story. "Awesome," Haley murmured, turning toward Lie Vagal. When he said nothing she awkwardly dropped the catalog onto a chair.

"Let's go upstairs," he said, already heading after Linette. Haley shrugged and followed him, glancing back once at the faces staring from the library wall.

Up here it was more like someone had just moved in. Their footsteps sounded louder, and the air smelled of fresh paint. There were boxes and bags piled against the walls. Amplifiers and speakers and other sound equipment loomed from corners, trailing cables and coils of wire. Only the paintings had been attended to, neatly hung in the corridors and beside windows. Haley thought it was weird, the way they were beside all the windows: not where you usually hung pictures. There were mirrors like that too, beside or between windows, so that sometimes the darkness threw back the night, sometimes her own pale and surprised face.

They found Linette at the end of the long hallway. There was a door there, closed, an ornate antique door that had obviously come from somewhere else. It was of dark wood, carved with hundreds of tiny figures, animals and people and trees, and inlaid with tiny mirrors and bits of glass. Linette stood staring at it, her back to them. From her tangled hair peeked the kinkajou, blinking sleepily as Haley came up behind her.

"Hey," she began. Beside her Lie Vagal smiled and rubbed his forehead.

Without turning Linette asked, "Where does it go?"

"My bedroom," said Lie as he slipped between them. "Would you like to come in?"

No, thought Haley.

"Sure," said Linette. Lie Vagal nodded and opened the door. They followed him inside, blinking as they strove to see in the dimness.

"This is my inner sanctum." He stood there grinning, his long hair falling into his face. "You're the only people who've ever been in it, really, except for me. My grandmother won't come inside."

At first she thought the room was merely dark, and waited for him to switch a light on. But after a moment Haley realized there *were* lights on. And she understood why the grandmother didn't like it. The entire room was painted black, a glossy black like marble. It wasn't a very big room, surely not the one originally intended to be the master bedroom. There were no windows. An oriental carpet covered the floor with purple and blue and scarlet blooms. Against one wall a narrow bed was pushed — such a small bed, a child's bed almost — and on the floor stood something like a tall brass lamp, with snaky tubes running from it.

"Wow," breathed Linette. "A hookah."

"A what?" demanded Haley; but no one paid any attention. Linette walked around, examining the hookah, the paintings on the walls, a bookshelf filled with volumes in old leather bindings. In a corner Lie Vagal rustled with something. After a moment the ceiling became spangled with lights, tiny white Christmas-tree lights strung from corner to corner like stars.

"There!" he said proudly. "Isn't that nice?"

Linette looked up and laughed, then returned to poring over a very old book with a red cover. Haley sidled up beside her. She had to squint to see what Linette was looking at — a garishly tinted illustration in faded red and blue and yellow. The colors oozed from between the lines, and there was a crushed silverfish at the bottom of the page. The picture showed a little boy screaming while a long-legged man armed with a pair of enormous scissors snipped off his thumbs.

"Yuck!" Haley stared open-mouthed, then abruptly walked away. She drew up in front of a carved wooden statue of a troll, child-sized. Its wooden eyes were painted white, with neither pupil nor iris. "Man, this is kind of a creepy bedroom."

From across the room Lie Vagal regarded her, amused. "That's what Gram says." He pointed at the volume in Linette's hands. "I collect old children's books. That's *Struwwelpeter*. German. It means Slovenly Peter."

Linette turned the page. "I love all these pictures and stuff. But isn't it kind of dark in here?" She closed the book and wandered to the far end of the room where Haley stared at a large painting. "I mean, there's no windows or anything."

He shrugged. "I don't know. Maybe. I like it like this."

Linette crossed the room to stand beside Haley in front of the painting. It was a huge canvas, very old, in an elaborate gilt frame. Thousands of fine cracks ran through it. Haley was amazed it hadn't fallen to pieces years ago. A lamp on top of the frame illuminated it, a little too well for Haley's taste. It took her a moment to realize that she had seen it before.

"That's the cover of your album —"

He had come up behind them and stood there, reaching to chuck the kinkajou under the chin. "That's right," he said softly. "The Erl-King."

It scared her. The hooded figure in the foreground hunched towards a tiny form in the distance, its outstretched arms ending in hands like claws. There was a smear of white to indicate its face, and two dark smudges for eyes, as though someone had gouged the paint with his thumbs. In the background the smaller figure seemed to be fleeing on horseback. A bolt of lightning shot the whole scene with splinters of blue light, so that she could just barely make out that the rider held a smaller figure in his lap. Black clouds scudded across the sky, and on the horizon reared a great house with windows glowing yellow and red. Somehow Haley knew the rider would not reach the house in time.

Linette grimaced. On her shoulder the kinkajou had fallen asleep again. She untangled its paws from her hair and asked, "The Erl-King? What's that?"

Lie Vagal took a step closer her.

> "— 'Oh father! My father! And dost thou not see?
> The Erl-King and his daughter are waiting for me?'
> — 'Now shame thee, my dearest! 'Tis fear makes thee blind
> Thou seest the dark willows which wave in the wind.'"

He stopped. Linette shivered, glanced aside at Haley. "Wow. That's creepy — you really like all this creepy stuff...."

Haley swallowed and tried to look unimpressed. "That was a *song?*"

He shook his head. "It's a poem, actually. I just ripped off the words, that's all." He hummed softly. Haley vaguely recognized the tune and guessed it must be from his album.

"'Oh father, my father,'" he sang, and reached to take Linette's hand. She joined him shyly, and the kinkajou drooped from her shoulder across her back.

"Lie!"

The voice made the girls jump. Linette clutched at Lie. The kinkajou squealed unhappily.

"Gram." Lie's voice sounded somewhere between reproach and disappointment as he turned to face her. She stood in the doorway, weaving a little and with one hand on the doorframe to steady herself.

"It's late. I think those girls should go home now."

Linette giggled, embarrassed, and said, "Oh, we don't have —"

"Yeah, I guess so," Haley broke in, and sidled toward the door. Lie Vagal stared after her, then turned to Linette.

"Why don't you come back tomorrow, if you want to see more of the house? Then it won't get too late." He winked at Haley. "And Gram is here, so your parents shouldn't have to worry."

Haley reddened. "They don't care," she lied. "It's just, it's kind of late and all."

"Right, that's right," said the old lady. She waited for them all to pass out of the room, Lie pausing to unplug the Christmas-tree lights, and then followed them downstairs.

On the outside patio the girls halted, unsure how to say goodbye.

"Thank you," Haley said at last. She looked at the old lady. "For the tea."

"Yeah, thanks," echoed Linette. She looked over at Lie Vagal standing in the doorway. The backlight made of him a black shadow, the edges of his hair touched with gold. He nodded to her, said nothing. But as they made their way back down the moonlit hill his voice called after them with soft urgency.

"Come back," he said.

It was two more days before Haley returned to Linette's. After dinner she rode her bike up the long rutted dirt drive, dodging cabbage butterflies and locusts and looking sideways at Kingdom Come perched upon its emerald hill. Even before she reached the cottage she knew Linette wasn't there.

"Haley. Come on in."

Aurora stood in the doorway, her cigarette leaving a long blue arabesque in the still air as she beckoned Haley. The girl leaned her bike against the broken stalks of sunflowers and delphiniums pushing against the house and followed Aurora.

Inside was cool and dark, the flagstones' chill biting through the soles of Haley's sneakers. She wondered how Aurora could stand to walk barefoot, but she did: her feet small and dirty, toenails buffed bright pink. She wore a short black cotton tunic that hitched up around her narrow hips. Some days it doubled as nightgown and daywear; Haley guessed this was one of those days.

"Tea?"

Haley nodded, perching on an old ladderback chair in the kitchen and pretending interest in an ancient issue of *Dairy Goat* magazine. Aurora walked a little unsteadily from counter to sink to stove, finally handing Haley her cup and then sinking into an overstuffed armchair near the window. From Aurora's mug the smell of juniper cut through the bergamot-scented kitchen. She sipped her gin and regarded Haley with slitted eyes.

"So. You met Lie Vagal."

Haley shrugged and stared out the window. "He had Valentine," she said at last.

"He still does — the damn thing ran back over yesterday. Linette went after it last night and didn't come back."

Haley felt a stab of betrayal. She hid her face behind her steaming mug. "Oh," was all she said.

"You'll have to go get her, Haley. She won't come back for me, so it's up to you." Aurora tried to make her voice light, but Haley recognized the strained desperate note in it. She looked at Aurora and frowned.

You're her mother, you bring her back, she thought, but said, "She'll be back. I'll go over there."

Aurora shook her head. She still wore her hair past her shoulders and straight as a needle; no longer blonde, it fell in streaked gray and black lines across her face. "She won't," she said, and took a long sip at her mug. "He's got her now and he won't want to give her back." Her voice trembled and tears blurred the kohl around her eyelids.

Haley bit her lip. She was used to this. Sometimes when Aurora was drunk, she and Linette carried her to bed, covering her with the worn flannel comforter and making sure her cigarettes and matches were out of sight. Linette acted embarrassed, but Haley didn't mind, just as she didn't mind doing the dishes sometimes or making grilled cheese sandwiches or French toast for them all, or riding her bike down to Schelling's Market to get more ice when they ran out. She reached across to the counter and dipped another golden thread of honey into her tea.

"Haley. I want to show you something."

The girl waited as Aurora weaved down the narrow passage into her bedroom. She could hear drawers being thrown open and shut, and finally the heavy thud of the trunk by the bed being opened. In a few minutes Aurora returned, carrying an oversized book.

"Did I ever show you this?"

She padded into the umber darkness of the living room, with its frayed kilims and cracked sitar like some huge shattered gourd leaning against the stuccoed wall. Haley followed, settling beside her. By the door the frogs hung with splayed feet in their sullen globe, their pale bellies turned to amber by the setting sun. On the floor in front of Haley glowed a rhomboid of yellow light. Aurora set the book within that space and turned to Haley. "Have I shown you this?" she asked again, a little anxiously.

"No," Haley lied. She had in fact seen the scrapbook about a dozen times over the years — the pink plastic cover with its peeling Day-Glo flowers hiding newspaper clippings and magazine pages soft as fur beneath her fingers as Aurora pushed it towards her.

"He's in there," Aurora said thickly. Haley glanced up and saw that the woman's eyes were bright red behind their smeared rings of kohl. Tangled in her thin fine hair were hoop earrings that reached nearly to her shoulder, and on one side of her neck, where a love bite might be, a tattoo no bigger than a thumbprint showed an Egyptian Eye of Horus. "Lie Vagal — him and all the rest of them —"

Aurora started flipping through the stiff plastic pages, too fast for Haley to catch more than a glimpse of the photos and articles spilling out. Once she paused, fumbling in the pocket of her tunic until she found her cigarettes.

YOUTHQUAKER! the caption read. Beside it was a black-and-white picture of a girl with long white-blonde hair and enormous, heavily kohled eyes. She was standing with her back arched, wearing a sort of bikini made of playing cards. MODEL AURORA DAWN, BRIGHTEST NEW LIGHT IN POP ARTIST'S SUPERSTAR HEAVEN.

"Wow," Haley breathed. She never got tired of the scrapbooks: it was like watching a silent movie, with Aurora's husky voice intoning the perils that befell the feckless heroine.

"That's not it," Aurora said, almost to herself, and began skipping pages again. More photos of herself, and then others — men with hair long and lush as Aurora's; heavy women smoking cigars; twin girls no older than Haley and Linette, leaning on a naked man's back while another man in a doctor's white coat jabbed them with an absurdly long hypodermic needle. Aurora at an art gallery. Aurora on the cover of *Interview* magazine. Aurora and a radiant woman with shuttered eyes and long, long fishnet-clad legs — the woman was really a man, a transvestite Aurora said; but there was no way you could tell by looking at him. As she flashed through the pictures Aurora began to name them, bursts of cigarette smoke hovering above the pages.

"Fairy Pagan. She's dead.

"Joey Face. He's dead.

"Marletta. She's dead.

"Precious Bane. She's dead.

"The Wanton Hussy. She's dead."

And so on, for pages and pages, dozens of fading images, boys in leather and ostrich plumes, girls in miniskirts prancing across the backs of stuffed elephants at F.A.O. Schwartz or screaming deliriously as fountains of champagne spewed from tables in the back rooms of bars.

"Miss Clancy deWolff. She's dead.

"Dianthus Queen. She's dead.

"Markey French. He's dead."

Until finally the clippings grew smaller and narrower, the pictures smudged and hard to make out beneath curls of disintegrating newsprint — banks of flowers, mostly, and stiff faces with eyes closed beneath poised coffin lids, and one photo Haley wished she'd never seen (but yet again she didn't close her eyes in time) of a woman jackknifed across the top of a convertible in front of the Chelsea Hotel, her head thrown back so that you could see where it had been sheared from her neck neatly as with a razor blade.

"Dead. Dead. Dead," Aurora sang, her finger stabbing at them until flecks of paper flew up into the smoke like ashes; and then suddenly the book ended and Aurora closed it with a soft heavy sound.

"They're all dead," she said thickly; just in case Haley hadn't gotten the point.

The girl leaned back, coughing into the sleeve of her T-shirt. "What happened?" she asked, her voice hoarse. She knew the answers, of course: drugs, mostly, or suicide. One had been recent enough that she could recall reading about it in the *Daily News*.

"What *happened?*" Aurora's eyes glittered. Her hands rested on the scrapbook as on a Ouija board, fingers writhing as though tracing someone's name. "They sold their souls. Every one of them. And they're all dead now. Edie, Candy, Nico, Jackie, Andrea, even Andy. Every single one. They thought it was a joke, but look at it —"

A tiny cloud of dust as she pounded the scrapbook. Haley stared at it and then at Aurora. She wondered unhappily if Linette would be back soon; wondered, somewhat shamefully because for the first time, exactly what had happened last night at Kingdom Come.

"Do you see what I mean, Haley? Do you understand now?" Aurora brushed the girl's face with her finger. Her touch was ice cold and stank of nicotine.

Haley swallowed. "N-no," she said, trying not to flinch. "I mean, I thought they all, like, OD'd or something."

Aurora nodded excitedly. "They did! *Of course* they did — but that was afterward — that was how they *paid —*"

Paid. Selling souls. Aurora and her weird friends talked like that sometimes. Haley bit her lip and tried to look thoughtful. "So they, like, sold their souls to the devil?"

"Of course!" Aurora croaked triumphantly. "How else would they have ever got where they did? Superstars! Rich and famous! And for what reason? None of them had any talent — *none* of them — but they ended up on TV, and in *Vogue,* and in the movies — how else could they have done it?"

She leaned forward until Haley could smell her sickly berry-scented lipstick mingled with the gin. "They all thought they were getting such a great deal, but look how it ended — famous for fifteen minutes, then *pffftttt!* "

"Wow," Haley said again. She had no idea, really, what Aurora was talking about. Some of these people she'd heard of, in magazines or from Aurora and her friends, but mostly their names were meaningless. A bunch of nobodies that nobody but Aurora had ever even cared about.

She glanced down at the scrapbook and felt a small sharp chill beneath her breast. Quickly she glanced up again at Aurora: her ruined face, her eyes; that tattoo like a faded brand upon her neck. A sudden insight made her go *hmm* beneath her breath —

Because maybe that was the point; maybe Aurora wasn't so crazy, and these people really *had* been famous once. But now for some strange reason no one remembered any of them at all; and now they were all dead. Maybe they really were all under some sort of curse. When she looked up Aurora nodded, slowly, as though she could read her thoughts.

"It was at a party. At the Factory," she began in her scorched voice. "We were celebrating the opening of *Scag* — that was the first movie to get real national distribution, it won the Silver Palm at Cannes that year. It was a fabulous party, I remember there was this huge Lalique bowl filled with cocaine and in the bathroom Doctor Bob was giving everyone a pop —

"About three A.M. most of the press hounds had left, and a lot of the neophytes were just too wasted and had passed out or gone on to Max's. But Candy was still there, and Liatris, and Jackie and Lie Vagal — all the core people — and I was sitting by the door, I really was in better shape than most of them, or I thought I was, but then I looked up and there is this *guy* there I've never seen before. And, like, people wandered in and out of there all the time, that was no big deal, but I was sitting right by the door with Jackie, I mean it was sort of a joke, we'd been asking to see people's invitations, turning away the offal, but I swear I never saw this guy come in. Later Jackie said *she'd* seen him come in through the fire escape; but I think she was lying. Anyway, it was weird.

"And so I must have nodded out for a while, because all of a sudden I jerk up and look around and here's this guy with everyone huddled around him, bending over and laughing like he's telling fortunes or something. He kind of looked like that, too, like a gypsy — not that everyone didn't look like that in those days, but with him it wasn't so much like an act. I mean, he had this long curly black hair and these gold earrings, and high suede boots and velvet pants, all black and red and purple, but with him it was like maybe he had *always* dressed like that. He was handsome, but in a creepy sort of way. His eyes were set very close together and his eyebrows grew together over his nose — that's the mark of a warlock, eyebrows like that — and he had this very neat British accent. They always went crazy over anyone with a British accent.

"So obviously I had been missing something, passed out by the door, and so I got up and staggered over to see what was going on. At first I thought he was collecting autographs. He had this very nice leather-bound book, like an autograph book, and everyone was writing in it. And I thought, God, how tacky. But then it struck me as being weird, because a lot of those people — not Candy, she'd sign *anything* — but a lot of the others, they wouldn't be caught dead doing anything so bourgeois as signing autographs. But here just about everybody was passing this pen around — a nice gold Cross pen, I remember that — even Andy, and I thought, Well this I got to see.

"So I edged my way in, and that's when I saw they *were* signing their names. But it wasn't an autograph book at all. It wasn't like anything I'd ever seen before. There was something printed on every page, in this fabulous gold and green lettering, but very official-looking, like when you see an old-fashioned decree of some sort. And they were all signing their names on every page. Just like in a cartoon, you know, 'Sign here!' And, I mean, everyone had done it — Lie Vagal had just finished and when the man saw me coming over he held the book up and flipped through it real fast, so I could see their signatures...."

Haley leaned forward on her knees, heedless now of the smoke and Aurora's huge eyes staring fixedly at the empty air.

"What was it?" the girl breathed. "Was it —?"

"It was *their souls.*" Aurora hissed the last word, stubbing out her cigarette in her empty mug. "Most of them, anyway — because, *get it,* who would ever want *their* souls? It was a standard contract — souls, sanity, first-born children. They all thought it was a joke — but look what happened." She pointed at the scrapbook as though the irrefutable proof lay there.

Haley swallowed. "Did you — did *you* sign?"

Aurora shook her head and laughed bitterly. "Are you crazy? Would I be here now if I had? No, I didn't, and a few others didn't — Viva, Liatris and Coppelia, David Watts. We're about all that's left, now — except for one or two who haven't paid up...."

And she turned and gazed out the window, to where the overgrown apple trees leaned heavily and spilled their burden of green fruit onto the stone wall that separated them from Kingdom Come.

"Lie Vagal," Haley said at last. Her voice sounded hoarse as Aurora's own. "So he signed it, too."

Aurora said nothing, only sat there staring, her yellow hands clutching the thin fabric of her tunic. Haley was about to repeat herself, when the woman began to hum, softly and out of key. Haley had heard that song before — just days ago, where was it? and then the words spilled out in Aurora's throaty contralto:

"— 'Why trembles my darling? Why shrinks she with fear?'
— 'Oh father! My father! The Erl-King is near!
'The Erl-King, with his crown and his hands long and white!'
— 'Thine eyes are deceived by the vapors of night.'"

"That song!" exclaimed Haley. "He was singing it —"

Aurora nodded without looking at her. *"The Erl-King,"* she said. "He recorded it just a few months later.…"

Her gaze dropped abruptly to the book at her knees. She ran her fingers along its edge, then as though with long practice opened it to a page towards the back. "There he is," she murmured, and traced the outlines of a black-and-white photo, neatly pressed beneath its sheath of yellowing plastic.

It was Lie Vagal. His hair was longer, and black as a cat's. He wore high leather boots, and the picture had been posed in a way to make him look taller than he really was. But what made Haley feel sick and frightened was that he was wearing makeup — his face powdered dead white, his eyes livid behind pools of mascara and kohl, his mouth a scarlet blossom. And it wasn't that it made him look like a woman (though it did).

It was that he looked exactly like Linette.

Shaking her head, she turned towards Aurora, talking so fast her teeth chattered. "You — does she — does he — does he know?"

Aurora stared down at the photograph and shook her head. "I don't think so. No one does. I mean, people might have suspected, I'm sure they talked, but — it was so long ago, they all forgot. Except for *him,* of course —"

In the air between them loomed suddenly the image of the man in black and red and purple, heavy gold rings winking from his ears. Haley's head pounded and she felt as though the floor reeled beneath her. In the hazy air the shining figure bowed its head, light gleaming from the unbroken ebony line that ran above its eyes. She seemed to hear a voice hissing to her, and feel cold sharp nails pressing tiny half-moons into the flesh of her arm. But before she could cry out the image was gone. There was only the still dank room, and Aurora saying,

"…for a long time thought he would die, for sure — all those drugs — and then of course he went crazy; but then I realized he wouldn't have made that kind of deal. Lie was sharp, you see; he *did* have some talent, he didn't need this sort of — of *thing* to make him happen. And Lie sure wasn't a fool. Even if he thought it was a joke, he was terrified of dying, terrified of losing his mind — he'd already had that incident in Marrakech — and so that left the other option; and since he never knew, I never told him; well it must have seemed a safe deal to make...."

A deal. Haley's stomach tumbled as Aurora's words came back to her — *A standard contract — souls, sanity, first-born children.* "But how —" she stammered.

"It's time." Aurora's hollow voice echoed through the chilly room. "It's time, is all. Whatever it was that Lie wanted, he got; and now it's time to pay up."

Suddenly she stood, her foot knocking the photo album so that it skidded across the flagstones, and tottered back into the kitchen. Haley could hear the clatter of glassware as she poured herself more gin. Silently the girl crept across the floor and stared for another moment at the photo of Lie Vagal. Then she went outside.

She thought of riding her bike to Kingdom Come, but absurd fears — she had visions of bony hands snaking out of the earth and snatching the wheels as she passed — made her walk instead. She clambered over the stone wall, grimacing at the smell of rotting apples. The unnatural chill of Linette's house had made her forget the relentless late-August heat and breathless air out here, no cooler for all that the sun had set and left a sky colored like the inside of a mussel shell. From the distant lake came the desultory thump of bullfrogs. When she jumped from the wall to the ground a windfall popped beneath her foot, spattering her with vinegary muck. Haley swore to herself and hurried up the hill.

Beneath the ultramarine sky the trees stood absolutely still, each moored to its small circle of shadow. Walking between them made Haley's eyes hurt, going from that eerie dusk to sudden darkness and then back into the twilight. She felt sick, from the heat and from what she had heard. It was crazy, of course, Aurora was always crazy; but Linette *hadn't* come back, and it had been such a creepy place, all those pictures, and the old lady, and Lie Vagal himself skittering through the halls and laughing....

Haley took a deep breath, balled up her T-shirt to wipe the sweat from between her breasts. It was crazy, that's all; but still she'd find Linette and bring her home.

On one side of the narrow bed Linette lay fast asleep, snoring quietly, her hair spun across her cheeks in a shadowy lace. She still wore the pale blue peasant's dress she'd had on the night before, its hem now spattered with candle wax and wine. Lie leaned over her until he could smell it, the faint unwashed musk of sweat and cotton and some cheap drugstore perfume, and over all of it the scent of marijuana. The sticky end of a joint was on the edge of the bedside table, beside an empty bottle of wine. Lie grinned, remembering the girl's awkwardness in smoking the joint. She'd had little enough trouble managing the wine. Aurora's daughter, no doubt about that.

They'd spent most of the day in bed, stoned and asleep; most of the last evening as well, though there were patches of time he couldn't recall. He remembered his grandmother's fury when midnight rolled around and she'd come into the bedroom to discover the girl still with him, and all around them smoke and empty bottles. There'd been some kind of argument then with Gram, Linette shrinking into a corner with her kinkajou; and after that more of their laughing and creeping down hallways. Lie showed her all his paintings. He tried to show her the people, but for some reason they weren't there, not even the three bears drowsing in the little eyebrow window in the attic half-bath. Finally, long after midnight, they'd fallen asleep, Lie's fingers tangled in Linette's long hair, chaste as kittens. His medication had long since leached away most sexual desire. Even before The Crash, he'd always been uncomfortable with the young girls who waited backstage for him after a show, or somehow found their way into the recording studio. That was why Gram's accusations had infuriated him —

"She's a friend, she's just a *friend* — can't I have any friends at all? Can't I?" he'd raged, but of course Gram hadn't understood, she never had. Afterwards had come that long silent night, with the lovely flushed girl asleep in his arms, and outside the hot hollow wind beating at the walls.

Now the girl beside him stirred. Gently Lie ran a finger along her cheekbone and smiled as she frowned in her sleep. She had her mother's huge eyes, her mother's fine bones and milky skin, but none of that hardness he associated with Aurora Dawn. It was so strange, to think that a few days ago he had never met this child; might never have raised the courage to meet her, and now he didn't want to let her go home. Probably it was just his loneliness; that and her beauty, her resemblance to all those shining creatures who had peopled his dreams and visions for so long. He leaned down until his lips grazed hers, then slipped from the bed.

He crossed the room slowly, reluctant to let himself come fully awake. But in the doorway he started.

"Shit!"

Across the walls and ceiling of the hall huge shadows flapped and dove. A buzzing filled the air, the sound of tiny feet pounding against the floor. Something grazed his cheek and he cried out, slapping his face and drawing his hand away sticky and damp. When he gazed at his palm he saw a smear of yellow and the powdery shards of wing.

The hall was full of insects. June bugs and katydids, beetles and lacewings and a Prometheus moth as big as his two hands, all of them flying crazily around the lights blooming on the ceiling and along the walls. Someone had opened all the windows; he had never bothered to put the screens in. He swatted furiously at the air, wiped his hand against the wall and frowned, trying to remember if he'd opened them; then thought of Gram. The heat bothered her more than it did him — odd, considering her seventy-odd years in Port Arthur — but she'd refused his offers to have air conditioning installed. He walked down the corridor, batting at clouds of tiny white moths like flies. He wondered idly where Gram had been all day. It was strange that she wouldn't have looked in on him; but then he couldn't remember much of their argument. Maybe she'd been so mad she took to her own room out of spite. It wouldn't be the first time.

He paused in front of a Kay Nielsen etching from *Snow White*. Inside its simple white frame the picture showed the wicked queen, her face a crimson O as she staggered across a ballroom floor, her feet encased in red-hot iron slippers. He averted his eyes and stared out the window. The sun had set in a wash of green and deep blue; in the east the sky glowed pale gold where the moon was rising. It was ungodly hot, so hot that on the lawn the crickets and katydids cried out only every minute or so, as though in pain. Sighing, he raised his arms, pulling his long hair back from his bare shoulders so that the breath of breeze from the window might cool his neck.

It was too hot to do anything; too hot even to lie in bed, unless sleep had claimed you. For the first time he wished the estate had a pool; then remembered the Jacuzzi. He'd never used it, but there was a skylight in there where he'd once glimpsed a horse like a meteor skimming across the midnight sky. They could take a cool bath, fill the tub with ice cubes. Maybe Gram could be prevailed upon to make some lemonade, or he thought there was still a bottle of champagne in the fridge, a housewarming gift from the realtor. Grinning, he turned and paced back down the hall, lacewings forming an iridescent halo about his head. He didn't turn to see the small figure framed within one of the windows, a fair-haired girl in jeans and T-shirt scuffing determinedly up the hill towards his home; nor did he notice the shadow that darkened another casement, as though someone had hung a heavy curtain there to blot out the sight of the moon.

Outside the evening had deepened. The first stars appeared, not shining so much as glowing through the hazy air, tiny buds of silver showing between the unmoving branches above Haley's head. Where the trees ended Haley hesitated, her hand upon the smooth trunk of a young birch. She felt suddenly and strangely reluctant to go further. Before her, atop its sweep of deep green, Kingdom Come glittered like some spectral toy: spotlights streaming onto the patio, orange and yellow and white gleaming from the window casements, spangled nets of silver and gold spilling from some of the upstairs windows, where presumably Lie Vagal had strung more of his Christmas lights. On the patio the French doors had been flung open. The white curtains hung like loose rope to the ground. In spite of her fears Haley's neck prickled at the sight: it needed only people there moving in the golden light, people and music....

As though in answer to her thought a sudden shriek echoed down the hill, so loud and sudden in the twilight that she started and turned to bolt. But almost immediately the shriek grew softer, resolved itself into music — someone had turned on a stereo too loudly and then adjusted the volume. Haley slapped the birch tree, embarrassed at her reaction, and started across the lawn.

As she walked slowly up the hill she recognized the music. Of course, that song again, the one Aurora had been singing a little earlier. She couldn't make out any words, only the wail of synthesizers and a man's voice, surprisingly deep. Beneath her feet the lawn felt brittle, the grass breaking at her steps and releasing an acrid dusty smell. For some reason it felt cooler here away from the trees. Her T-shirt hung heavy and damp against her skin, her jeans chafed against her bare ankles. Once she stopped and looked back, to see if she could make out Linette's cottage behind its scrim of greenery; but it was gone. There were only the trees, still and ominous beneath a sky blurred with stars.

She turned and went on up the hill. She was close enough now that she could smell that odd odor that pervaded Kingdom Come, oranges and freshly turned earth. The music pealed clear and sweet, an insidious melody that ran counterpoint to the singer's ominous phrasing. She *could* hear the words now, although the singer's voice had dropped to a childish whisper —

"— 'Oh Father! My father! And dost thou not hear
'What words the Erl-King whispers low in mine ear?'
— 'Now hush thee, my darling, thy terrors appease.
'Thou hearest the branches where murmurs the breeze.'"

A few yards in front of her the patio began. She was hurrying across this last stretch of lawn when something made her stop. She waited, trying to figure out if she'd heard some warning sound — a cry from Linette, Aurora shrieking for more ice. Then very slowly she raised her head and gazed up at the house.

There was someone there. In one of the upstairs windows, gazing down upon the lawn and watching her. He was absolutely unmoving, like a cardboard dummy propped against the sill. It looked like he had been watching her forever. With a dull sense of dread she wondered why she hadn't noticed him before. It wasn't Lie Vagal, she knew that; nor could it have been Linette or Gram. So tall it seemed that he must stoop to gaze out at her, his face enormous, perhaps twice the size of a normal man's and a deathly yellow color. Two huge pale eyes stared fixedly at her. His mouth was slightly ajar. That face hung as though in a fog of black, and drawn up against his breast were his hands, knotted together like an old man's — huge hands like a clutch of parsnips, waxy and swollen. Even from here she could see the soft glint of the spangled lights upon his fingernails, and the triangular point of his tongue like an adder's head darting between his lips.

For an instant she fell into a crouch, thinking to flee to the cottage. But the thought of turning her back upon that figure was too much for her. Instead Haley began to run towards the patio. Once she glanced up: and yes, it was still there, it had not moved, its eyes had not wavered from watching her; only it seemed its mouth might have opened a little more, as though it was panting.

Gasping, she nearly fell onto the flagstone patio. On the glass tables the remains of this morning's breakfast sat in congealed pools on bright blue plates. A skein of insects rose and trailed her as she ran through the doors.

"Linette!"

She clapped her hand to her mouth. Of course it would have seen where she entered; but this place was enormous, surely she could find Linette and they could run, or hide —

But the room was so full of the echo of that insistent music that no one could have heard her call out. She waited for several heartbeats, then went on.

Darkness: Two Decades of Modern Horror

She passed all the rooms they had toured just days before. In the corridors the incense burners were dead and cold. The piranhas roiled frantically in their tank, and the neon sculptures hissed like something burning. In one room hung dozens of framed covers of *Interview* magazine, empty-eyed faces staring down at her. It seemed now that she recognized them, could almost have named them if Aurora had been there to prompt her —

Fairy Pagan, Dianthus Queen, Markey French...

As her feet whispered across the heavy carpet she could hear them breathing behind her, *dead, dead, dead.*

She ended up in the kitchen. On the wall the cat-clock ticked loudly. There was a smell of scorched coffee. Without thinking she crossed the room and switched off the automatic coffee maker, its glass carafe burned black and empty. A loaf of bread lay open on a counter, and a half-empty bottle of wine. Haley swallowed: her mouth tasted foul. She grabbed the wine bottle and gulped a mouthful, warm and sour; then coughing, found the way upstairs.

Lie pranced back to the bedroom, singing to himself. He felt giddy, the way he did sometimes after a long while without his medication. By the door he turned and flicked at several buttons on the stereo, grimacing when the music howled and quickly turning the levels down. No way she could have slept through *that.* He pulled his hair back and did a few little dance steps, the rush of pure feeling coming over him like speed.

> *"'If you will, oh my darling, then with me go away,*
> *My daughter shall tend you so fair and so gay...'"*

He twirled so that the cuffs of his loose trousers ballooned about his ankles. "Come, darling, rise and shine, time for little kinkajous to have their milk and honey —" he sang. And stopped.

The bed was empty. On the side table a cigarette — she had taken to cadging cigarettes from him — burned in a little brass tray, a scant half-inch of ash at its head.

"Linette?"

He whirled and went to the door, looked up and down the hall. He would have seen her if she'd gone out, but where could she have gone? Quickly he paced to the bathroom, pushing the door open as he called her name. She would have had to pass him to get there; but the room was empty.

"Linette!"

He hurried back to the room, this time flinging the door wide as he entered. Nothing. The room was too small to hide anyone. There wasn't even a closet. He walked inside, kicking at empty cigarette packs and clothes, one of Linette's sandals, a dangling silver earring. "Linette! Come on, let's go downstairs —"

At the far wall he stopped, staring at the huge canvas that hung there. From the speakers behind him the music swelled, his own voice echoing his shouts.

"'My father! My father! Oh hold me now fast!
He pulls me, he hurts, and will have me at last —'"

Lie's hands began to shake. He swayed a little to one side, swiping at the air as though something had brushed his cheek.

The Erl-King was gone. The painting still hung in its accustomed place in its heavy gilt frame. But instead of the menacing figure in the foreground and the tiny fleeing horse behind it, there was nothing. The yellow lights within the darkly silhouetted house had been extinguished. And where the hooded figure had reared with its extended claws, the canvas was blackened and charred. A hawkmoth was trapped there, its furled antennae broken, its wings shivered to fragments of mica and dust.

"Linette."

From the hallway came a dull crash, as though something had fallen down the stairs. He fled the room while the fairy music ground on behind him.

In the hall he stopped, panting. The insects moved slowly through the air, brushing against his face with their cool wings. He could still hear the music, although now it seemed another voice had joined his own, chanting words he couldn't understand. As he listened he realized this voice did not come from the speakers behind him but from somewhere else — from down the corridor, where he could now see a dark shape moving within one of the windows overlooking the lawn.

"Linette," he whispered.

He began to walk, heedless of the tiny things that writhed beneath his bare feet. For some reason he still couldn't make out the figure waiting at the end of the hallway: the closer he came to it the more insubstantial it seemed, the more difficult it was to see through the cloud of winged creatures that surrounded his face. Then his foot brushed against something heavy and soft. Dazed, he shook his head and glanced down. After a moment he stooped to see what lay there.

It was the kinkajou. Curled to form a perfect circle, its paws drawn protectively about its elfin face. When he stroked it he could feel the tightness beneath the soft fur, the small legs and long tail already stiff.

"Linette," he said again; but this time the name was cut off as Lie staggered to his feet. The kinkajou slid with a gentle thump to the floor.

At the end of the hallway he could see it, quite clearly now, its huge head weaving back and forth as it chanted a wordless monotone. Behind it a slender figure crouched in a pool of pale blue cloth and moaned softly.

"Leave her," Lie choked; but he knew it couldn't hear him. He started to turn, to run the other way back to his bedroom. He tripped once and with a cry kicked aside the kinkajou. Behind him the low moaning had stopped, although he could still hear that glottal voice humming to itself. He stumbled on for another few feet; and then he made the mistake of looking back.

The curved staircase was darker than Haley remembered. Halfway up she nearly fell when she stepped on a glass. It shattered beneath her foot; she felt a soft prick where a shard cut her ankle. Kicking it aside, she went more carefully, holding her breath as she tried to hear anything above that music. Surely the grandmother at least would be about? She paused where the staircase turned, reaching to wipe the blood from her ankle, then with one hand on the paneled wall crept up the next few steps.

That was where she found Gram. At the curve in the stairwell light spilled from the top of the hallway. Something was sprawled across the steps, a filigree of white etched across her face. Beneath Haley's foot something cracked. When she put her hand down she felt the rounded corner of a pair of eyeglasses, the jagged spar where she had broken them.

"Gram," the girl whispered.

She had never seen anyone dead before. One arm flung up and backwards, as though it had stuck to the wall as she fell; her dress raked above her knees so that Haley could see where the blood had pooled onto the next riser, like a shadowy footstep. Her eyes were closed but her mouth was half-open, so that the girl could see how her false teeth had come loose and hung above her lower lip. In the breathless air of the passageway she had a heavy sickly odor, like dead carnations. Haley gagged and leaned back against the wall, closing her eyes and moaning softly.

But she couldn't stay like that. And she couldn't leave, not with Linette up there somewhere; even if that horrible figure was waiting for her. It was crazy: through her mind raced all the movies she had ever seen that were just like this, some idiot kid going up a dark stairway or into the basement where the killer waited, and the audience shrieking *No!* but still she couldn't go back.

The hardest part was stepping over the corpse, trying not to actually *touch* it. She had to stretch across three steps, and then she almost fell but scrabbled frantically at the wall until she caught her balance. After that she ran the rest of the way until she reached the top.

Before her stretched the hallway. It seemed to be lit by some kind of moving light, like a strobe or mirror ball; but then she realized that was because of all the moths bashing against the myriad lamps strung across the ceiling. She took a step, her heart thudding so hard she thought she might faint. There was the doorway to Lie Vagal's bedroom; there all the open windows, and beside them the paintings.

She walked on tiptoe, her sneakers melting into the thick carpeting. At the open doorway she stopped, her breath catching in her throat. But when she looked inside there was no one there. A cigarette burned in an ashtray next to the bed. By the door Lie Vagal's stereo blinked with tiny red and green lights. The music went on, a ringing music like a calliope or glass harp. She continued down the hall.

She passed the first window, then a painting; then another window and another painting. She didn't know what made her stop to look at this one; but when she did her hands grew icy despite the cloying heat.

The picture was empty. A little brass plate at the bottom of the frame read *The Snow Queen;* but the soft wash of watercolors showed only pale blue ice, a sickle moon like a tear on the heavy paper. Stumbling, she turned to look at the frame behind her. *La Belle et La Bête,* it read: an old photograph, a film still, but where two figures had stood beneath an ornate candelabra there was only a whitish blur, as though the negative had been damaged.

She went to the next picture, and the next. They were all the same. Each landscape was empty, as though waiting for the artist to carefully place the principals between glass mountain and glass coffin, silver slippers and seven-league boots. From one to the other Haley paced, never stopping except to pause momentarily before those skeletal frames.

And now she saw that she was coming to the end of the corridor. There on the right was the window where she had seen that ghastly figure; and there beneath it, crouched on the floor like some immense animal or fallen beam, was a hulking shadow. Its head and shoulders were bent as though it fed upon something. She could hear it, a sound like a kitten lapping, so loud that it drowned out even the muted wail of Lie Vagal's music.

She stopped, one hand touching the windowsill beside her. A few yards ahead of her the creature grunted and hissed; and now she could see that there was something pinned beneath it. At first she thought it was the kinkajou. She was stepping backwards, starting to turn to run, when very slowly the great creature lifted its head to gaze at her.

It was the same tallowy face she had glimpsed in the window. Its mouth was open so that she could see its teeth, pointed and dulled like a dog's, and the damp smear across its chin. It seemed to have no eyes, only huge ruined holes where they once had been; and above them stretched an unbroken ridge of black where its eyebrows grew straight and thick as quills. As she stared it moved its hands, huge clumsy hands like a clutch of rotting fruit. Beneath it she could glimpse a white face, and dark hair like a scarf fluttering above where her throat had been torn out.

"Linette!"

Haley heard her own voice screaming. Even much later after the ambulances came she could still hear her friend's name; and another sound that drowned out the sirens: a man singing, wailing almost, crying for his daughter.

Haley started school several weeks late. Her parents decided not to send her to Fox Lane after all, but to a parochial school in Goldens Bridge. She didn't know anyone there and at first didn't care to, but her status as a sort-of celebrity was hard to shake. Her parents had refused to allow Haley to appear on television, but Aurora Dawn had shown up nightly for a good three weeks, pathetically eager to talk about her daughter's murder and Lie Vagal's apparent suicide. She mentioned Haley's name every time.

The nuns and lay people who taught at the high school were gentle and understanding. Counselors had coached the other students in how to behave with someone who had undergone a trauma like that, seeing her best friend murdered and horribly mutilated by the man who turned out to be her father. There was the usual talk about satanic influences in rock music, and Lie Vagal's posthumous career actually was quite promising. Haley herself gradually grew to like her new place in the adolescent scheme of things, half-martyr and half-witch. She even tried out for the school play, and got a small part in it; but that wasn't until spring.

With apologies to Johann Wolfgang von Goethe

Dennis Etchison has been selling stories since the early 1960s and is one of the horror genre's most respected and distinguished practitioners. He is a multiple winner of both the British Fantasy and World Fantasy awards. His short stories are collected in *The Dark Country, Red Dreams, The Blood Kiss,* and *The Death Artist,* plus three retrospectives: *Talking in the Dark, Fine Cuts,* and most recently *Got To Kill Them all.* In addition to having published four novels, he has also edited several acclaimed anthologies, including *Cutting Edge* and *Metahorror.*

Etchison has been a longtime resident of Los Angeles, and this familiarity with its paranoia and obsessions has been put to excellent use in a series of stories that he's written over the years, including "The Dog Park."

The Dog Park
Dennis Etchison

MADDING HEARD THE dogs before he saw them.

They were snarling at each other through the hurricane fence, gums wet and incisors bared, as if about to snap the chain links that held them apart. A barrel-chested boxer reared and slobbered, driving a much smaller Australian kelpie away from the outside of the gate. Spittle flew and the links vibrated and rang.

A few seconds later their owners came running, barking commands and waving leashes like whips.

"Easy, boy," Madding said, reaching one hand out to the seat next to him. Then he remembered that he no longer had a dog of his own. There was nothing to worry about.

He set the brake, rolled the window up all the way, locked the car and walked across the lot to the park.

The boxer was far down the slope by now, pulled along by a man in a flowered shirt and pleated trousers. The Australian sheepdog still trembled by the fence. Its owner, a young woman, jerked a choke chain.

"Greta, sit!"

As Madding neared the gate, the dog growled and tried to stand.

She yanked the chain harder and slapped its hind-quarters back into position.

"Hello, Greta," said Madding, lifting the steel latch. He smiled at the young woman. "You've got a brave little dog there."

"I don't know why she's acting this way," she said, embarrassed.

"Is this her first time?"

"Pardon?"

"At the Dog Park."

"Yes..."

"It takes some getting used to," he told her. "All the freedom. They're not sure how to behave."

"Did you have the same trouble?"

"Of course." He savored the memory, and at the same time wanted to put it out of his mind. "Everybody does. It's normal."

"I named her after Garbo — you know, the actress? I don't think she likes crowds." She looked around. "Where's your dog?"

"Down there, I hope." Madding opened the gate and let himself in, then held it wide for her.

She was squinting at him. "Excuse me," she said, "but you work at Tri-Mark, don't you?"

Madding shook his head. "I'm afraid not."

The kelpie dragged her down the slope with such force that she had to dig her feet into the grass to stop. The boxer was nowhere in sight.

"Greta, heel!"

"You can let her go," Madding said as he came down behind her. "The leash law is only till three o'clock."

"What time is it now?"

He checked his watch. "Almost five."

She bent over and unfastened the leash from the ring on the dog's collar. She was wearing white cotton shorts and a plain, loose-fitting top.

"Did I meet you in Joel Silver's office?" she said.

"I don't think so." He smiled again. "Well, you and Greta have fun."

He wandered off, tilting his face back and breathing deeply. The air was moving, scrubbed clean by the trees, rustling the shiny leaves as it circulated above the city, exchanging pollutants for fresh oxygen. It was easier to be on his own, but without a dog to pick the direction he was at loose ends. He felt the loss tugging at him like a cord that had not yet been broken.

The park was only a couple of acres, nestled between the high, winding turns of a mountain road on one side and a densely overgrown canyon on the other. This was the only park where dogs were allowed to run free, at least during certain hours, and in a few short months it had become an unofficial meeting place for people in the entertainment industry. Where once pitches had been delivered in detox clinics and the gourmet aisles of Westside supermarkets, now ambitious hustlers frequented the Dog Park to sharpen their networking skills. Here starlets connected with recently divorced producers, agents jockeyed for favor with young executives on the come, and actors and screenwriters exchanged tips about veterinarians, casting calls and pilots set to go to series in the fall. All it took was a dog, begged, borrowed or stolen, and the kind of desperate gregariousness that causes one to press business cards into the hands of absolute strangers.

He saw dozens of dogs, expensive breeds mingling shamelessly with common mutts, a microcosm of democracy at work. An English setter sniffed an unshorn French poodle, then gave up and joined the pack gathered around a honey-colored cocker spaniel. A pair of Great Dane puppies tumbled over each other golliwog-style, coming to rest at the feet of a tall, humorless German shepherd. An Afghan chased a Russian wolfhound. And there were the masters, posed against tree trunks, lounging at picnic tables, nervously cleaning up after their pets with long-handled scoopers while they waited to see who would enter the park next.

Madding played a game, trying to match up the animals with their owners. A man with a crewcut tossed a Frisbee, banking it against the setting sun like a translucent UFO before a bull terrier snatched it out of the air. Two fluffed Pekingese waddled across the path in front of Madding, trailing colorful leashes; when they neared the gorge at the edge of the park he started after them reflexively, then stopped as a short, piercing sound turned them and brought them back this way. A bodybuilder in a formfitting T-shirt glowered nearby, a silver whistle showing under his trimmed moustache.

Ahead, a Labrador, a chow and a schnauzer had a silky cornered by a trash bin. Three people seated on a wooden bench glanced up, laughed, and returned to the curled script they were reading. Madding could not see the title, only that the cover was a bilious yellow-green.

"I know," said the young woman, drawing even with him, as her dog dashed off in an ever-widening circle. "It was at New Line. That was you, wasn't it?"

"I've never been to New Line," said Madding.

"Are you sure? The office on Robertson?"

"I'm sure."

"Oh." She was embarrassed once again, and tried to cover it with a self-conscious cheerfulness, the mark of a private person forced into playing the extrovert in order to survive. "You're not an actor, then?"

"Only a writer," said Madding.

She brightened. "I knew it!"

"Isn't everyone in this town?" he said. "The butcher, the baker, the kid who parks your car... My drycleaner says he's writing a script for Tim Burton."

"Really?" she said, quite seriously. "I'm writing a spec script."

Oh no, he thought. He wanted to sink down into the grass and disappear, among the ants and beetles, but the ground was damp from the sprinklers and her dog was circling, hemming him in.

"Sorry," he said.

"That's OK. I have a real job, too. I'm on staff at Fox Network."

"What show?" he asked, to be polite.

"*C.H.U.M.P.* The first episode is on next week. They've already ordered nine more, in case *Don't Worry, Be Happy* gets cancelled."

"I've heard of it," he said.

"Have you? What have you heard?"

He racked his brain. "It's a cop series, right?"

"Canine-Human Unit, Metropolitan Police. You know, dogs that ride around in police cars, and the men and women they sacrifice themselves for? It has a lot of human interest, like *L.A. Law*, only it's told through the dog's eyes."

"*Look Who's Barking*," he said.

"Sort of." She tilted her head to one side and thought for a moment. "I'm sorry," she said. "That was a joke, wasn't it?"

"Sort of."

"I get it." She went on. "But what I really want to write are Movies-of-the-Week. My agent says she'll put my script on Paul Nagle's desk, as soon as I have a first draft."

"What's it about?"

"It's called *A Little-Known Side of Elvis*. That's the working title. My agent says anything about Elvis will sell."

"Which side of Elvis is this one?"

"Well, for example, did you know about his relationship with dogs? Most people don't. '*Hound Dog*' wasn't just a song."

Her kelpie began to bark. A man with inflatable tennis shoes and a baseball cap worn backwards approached them, a clipboard in his hand.

"Hi!" he said, all teeth. "Would you take a minute to sign our petition?"

"No problem," said the young woman. "What's it for?"

"They're trying to close the park to outsiders, except on weekends."

She took his ballpoint pen and balanced the clipboard on her tanned forearm. "How come?"

"It's the residents. They say we take up too many parking places on Mulholland. They want to keep the canyon for themselves."

"Well," she said, "they better watch out, or we might just start leaving our dogs here. Then they'll multiply and take over!"

She grinned, her capped front teeth shining in the sunlight like two chips of paint from a pearly-white Lexus.

"What residents?" asked Madding.

"The homeowners," said the man in the baseball cap, hooking a thumb over his shoulder.

Madding's eyes followed a line to the cliffs overlooking the park, where the cantilevered back-ends of several designer houses hung suspended above the gorge. The undersides of the decks, weathered and faded, were almost camouflaged by the weeds and chaparral.

"How about you?" The man took back the clipboard and held it out to Madding. "We need all the help we can get."

"I'm not a registered voter," said Madding.

"You're not?"

"I don't live here," he said. "I mean, I did, but I don't now. Not anymore."

"Are you registered?" the man asked her.

"Yes."

"In the business?"

"I work at Fox," she said.

"Oh, yeah? How's the new regime? I hear Lili put all the old-timers out to pasture."

"Not the studio," she said. "The network."

"Really? Do you know Kathryn Baker, by any chance?"

"I've seen her parking space. Why?"

"I used to be her dentist." The man took out his wallet. "Here, let me give you my card."

"That's all right," she said. "I already have someone."

"Well, hold on to it anyway. You never know. Do you have a card?"

She reached into a velcro pouch at her waist and handed him a card with a quill pen embossed on one corner.

The man read it. "*C.H.U.M.P.* — that's great! Do you have a dental advisor yet?"

"I don't think so."

"Could you find out?"

"I suppose."

He turned to Madding. "Are you an actor?"

"Writer," said Madding. "But not the kind you mean."

The man was puzzled. The young woman looked at him blankly. Madding felt the need to explain himself.

"I had a novel published, and somebody bought an option. I moved down here to write the screenplay."

"Title?" said the man.

"You've probably never heard of it," said Madding. "It was called *And Soon the Night.*"

"That's it!" she said. "I just finished reading it — I saw your picture on the back of the book!" She furrowed her brow, a slight dimple appearing on the perfectly smooth skin between her eyes, as she struggled to remember. "Don't tell me. Your name is..."

"David Madding," he said, holding out his hand.

"Hi!" she said. "I'm Stacey Chernak."

"Hi, yourself."

"Do you have a card?" the man said to him.

"I'm all out," said Madding. It wasn't exactly a lie. He had never bothered to have any printed.

"What's the start date?"

"There isn't one," said Madding. "They didn't renew the option."

"I see," said the man in the baseball cap, losing interest.

A daisy chain of small dogs ran by, a miniature collie chasing a longhaired dachshund chasing a shivering chihuahua. The collie blurred as it went past, its long coat streaking like a flame.

"Well, I gotta get some more signatures before dark. Don't forget to call me," the man said to her. "I can advise on orthodontics, accident reconstruction, anything they want."

"How about animal dentistry?" she said.

"Hey, why not?"

"I'll give them your name."

"Great," he said to her. "Thanks!"

"Do you think that's his collie?" she said when he had gone.

Madding considered. "More likely the Irish setter."

They saw the man lean down to hook his fingers under the collar of a golden retriever. From the back, his baseball cap revealed the emblem of the New York Yankees. Not from around here, Madding thought. But then, who is?

"Close," she said, and laughed.

The man led his dog past a dirt mound, where there was a drinking fountain, and a spigot that ran water into a trough for animals.

"Water," she said. "That's a good idea. Greta!"

The kelpie came bounding over, eager to escape the attentions of a randy pit bull. They led her to the mound. As Greta drank, Madding read the sign over the spigot.

CAUTION!
WATCH OUT FOR MOUNTAIN LIONS

"What do you think that means?" she said. "It isn't true, is it?"

Madding felt a tightness in his chest. "It could be. This is still wild country."

"Greta, stay with me…"

"Don't worry. They only come out at night, probably."

"Where's your dog?" she said.

"I wish I knew."

She tilted her head, uncertain whether or not he was making another joke.

"He ran away," Madding told her.

"When?"

"Last month. I used to bring him here all the time. One day he didn't come when I called. It got dark, and they closed the park, but he never came back."

"Oh, I'm so sorry!"

"Yeah, me too."

"What was his name?"

"He didn't have one. I couldn't make up my mind, and then it was too late."

They walked on between the trees. She kept a close eye on Greta. Somewhere music was playing. The honey-colored cocker spaniel led the German shepherd, the Irish setter and a Dalmatian to a redwood table. There the cocker's owner, a woman with brassy hair and a sagging green halter, poured white wine into plastic cups for several men.

"I didn't know," said Stacey.

"I missed him at first, but now I figure he's better off. Someplace where he can run free, all the time."

"I'm sorry about your dog," she said. "That's so sad. But what I meant was, I didn't know you were famous."

It was hard to believe that she knew the book. The odds against it were staggering, particularly considering the paltry royalties. He decided not to ask what she thought of it. That would be pressing his luck.

"Who's famous? I sold a novel. Big deal."

"Well, at least you're a real writer. I envy you."

"Why?"

"You have it made."

Sure I do, thought Madding. One decent review in the *Village Voice Literary Supplement*, and some reader at a production company makes an inquiry, and the next thing I know my agent makes a deal with all the money in the world at the top of the ladder. Only the ladder doesn't go far enough. And now I'm back to square one, the option money used up, with a screenplay written on spec that's not worth what it cost me to Xerox it, and I'm six months behind on the next novel. But I've got it made. Just ask the IRS.

The music grew louder as they walked. It seemed to be coming from somewhere overhead. Madding gazed up into the trees, where the late-afternoon rays sparkled through the leaves, gold coins edged in blackness. He thought he heard voices, too, and the clink of glasses. Was there a party? The entire expanse of the park was visible from here, but he could see no evidence of a large group anywhere. The sounds were diffused and unlocalized, as if played back through widely spaced, out-of-phase speakers.

"Where do you live?" she asked.

"What?"

"You said you don't live here anymore."

"In Calistoga."

"Where's that?"

"Up north."

"Oh."

He began to relax. He was glad to be finished with this town.

"I closed out my lease today," he told her. "Everything's packed. As soon as I hit the road, I'm out of here."

"Why did you come back to the park?"

A good question, he thought. He hadn't planned to stop by. It was a last-minute impulse.

"I'm not sure," he said. No, that wasn't true. He might as well admit it. "It sounds crazy, but I guess I wanted to look for my dog. I thought I'd give it one more chance. It doesn't feel right, leaving him."

"Do you think he's still here?"

He felt a tingling in the pit of his stomach. It was not a good feeling. I shouldn't have come, he thought. Then I wouldn't have had to face it. It's dangerous here, too dangerous for there to be much hope.

"At least I'll know," he said.

He heard a sudden intake of breath and turned to her. There were tears in her eyes, as clear as diamonds.

"It's like the end of your book," she said. "When the little girl is alone, and doesn't know what's going to happen next..."

My God, he thought, she did read it. He felt flattered, but kept his ego in check. She's not so tough. She has a heart, after all, under all the bravado. That's worth something — it's worth a lot. I hope she makes it, the Elvis script, whatever she really wants. She deserves it.

She composed herself and looked around, blinking. "What is that?"

"What's what?"

"Don't you hear it?" She raised her chin and moved her head from side to side, eyes closed.

She meant the music, the glasses, the sound of the party that wasn't there.

"I don't know."

Now there was the scraping of steel somewhere behind them, like a rough blade drawn through metal. He stopped and turned around quickly.

A couple of hundred yards away, at the top of the slope, a man in a uniform opened the gate to the park. Beyond the fence, a second man climbed out of an idling car with a red, white and blue shield on the door. He had a heavy chain in one hand.

"Come on," said Madding. "It's time to go."

"It can't be."

"The security guards are here. They close the park at six."

"Already?"

Madding was surprised, too. He wondered how long they had been walking.

He saw the man with the crewcut searching for his frisbee in the grass, the bull terrier at his side. The group on the bench and the woman in the halter were collecting their things. The bodybuilder marched his two ribboned Pekingese to the slope. The Beverly Hills dentist whistled and stood waiting for his dog to come to him. Madding snapped to, as if waking up. It really was time.

The sun had dropped behind the hills and the grass under his feet was darkening. The car in the parking lot above continued to idle; the rumbling of the engine reverberated in the natural bowl of the park, as though close enough to bulldoze them out of the way. He heard a rhythm in the throbbing, and realized that it was music, after all.

They had wandered close to the edge, where the park ended and the gorge began. Over the gorge, the deck of one of the cantilevered houses beat like a drum.

"Where's Greta?" she said.

He saw the stark expression, the tendons outlined through the smooth skin of her throat.

"Here, girl! Over here...!"

She called out, expecting to see her dog. Then she clapped her hands together. The sound bounced back like the echo of a gunshot from the depths of the canyon. The dog did not come.

In the parking lot, the second security guard let a Doberman out of the car. It was a sleek, black streak next to him as he carried the heavy chain to his partner, who was waiting for the park to empty before padlocking the gate.

Madding took her arm. Her skin was covered with gooseflesh. She drew away.

"I can't go," she said. "I have to find Greta."

He scanned the grassy slopes with her, avoiding the gorge until there was nowhere left to look. It was blacker than he remembered. Misshapen bushes and stunted shrubs filled the canyon below, extending all the way down to the formal boundaries of the city. He remembered standing here only a few weeks ago, in exactly the same position. He had told himself then that his dog could not have gone over the edge, but now he saw that there was nowhere else to go.

The breeze became a wind in the canyon and the black liquid eye of a swimming pool winked at him from far down the hillside. Above, the sound of the music stopped abruptly.

"You don't think she went down there, do you?" said Stacey. There was a catch in her voice. "The mountain lions..."

"They only come out at night."

"But it *is* night!"

They heard a high, broken keening.

"Listen!" she said. "That's Greta!"

"No, it's not. Dogs don't make that sound. It's —" He stopped himself.

"What?"

"Coyotes."

He regretted saying it.

Now, without the music, the shuffling of footsteps on the boards was clear and unmistakable. He glanced up. Shadows appeared over the edge of the deck as a line of heads gathered to look down. Ice cubes rattled and someone laughed. Then someone else made a shushing sound and the silhouetted heads bobbed silently, listening and watching.

Can they see us? he wondered.

Madding felt the presence of the Doberman behind him, at the top of the slope. How long would it take to close the distance, once the guard set it loose to clear the park? Surely they would call out a warning first. He waited for the voice, as the seconds ticked by on his watch.

"I have to go get her," she said, starting for the gorge.

"No…"

"I can't just leave."

"It's not safe," he said.

"But she's down there, I know it! Greta!"

There was a giggling from the deck.

They can hear us, too, he thought. Every sound, every word magnified, like a Greek amphitheater. Or a Roman one.

Rover, Spot, Towser? No, Cubby. That's what I was going to call you, if there had been time. I always liked the name. *Cubby.*

He made a decision.

"Stay here," he said, pushing her aside.

"What are you doing?"

"I'm going over."

"You don't have to. It's my dog…"

"Mine, too."

Maybe they're both down there, he thought.

"I'll go with you," she said.

"No."

He stood there, thinking, It all comes down to this. There's no way to avoid it. There never was.

"But you don't know what's there...!"

"Go," he said to her, without turning around. "Get out of here while you can. There's still time."

Go home, he thought, wherever that is. You have a life ahead of you. It's not too late, if you go right now, without looking back.

"Wait...!"

He disappeared over the edge.

A moment later there was a new sound, something more than the breaking of branches and the thrashing. It was powerful and deep, followed immediately by a high, mournful yipping. Then there was only a silence, and the night.

From above the gorge, a series of quick, hard claps fell like rain.

It was the people on the deck.

They were applauding.

Michael Marshall Smith is a bestselling novelist and screenwriter, writing under several different names. His first novel, *Only Forward*, won the August Derleth and Philip K. Dick awards. *Spares* and *One of Us* were optioned for film by DreamWorks and Warner Brothers, and the Straw Men trilogy — *The Straw Men*, *The Lonely Dead*, and *Blood of Angels* — were international bestsellers. His Steel Dagger-nominated novel *The Intruders* is currently in series development with the BBC. His most recent novels are *Bad Things* and *The Servants*, the latter, a short novel published under the new pseudonym M. M. Smith.

He is a three-time winner of the British Fantasy Award for short fiction, and his stories are collected in two volumes — *What You Make It* and *More Tomorrow and Other Stories* (which won the International Horror Guild Award).

Smith is expert at drawing the reader into the seemingly normal existence of his characters while subtly notching up the terror — such as in the following beauty, "Rain Falls."

Rain Falls
Michael Marshall Smith

I SAW WHAT happened. I don't know if anyone else did. Probably not, which worries me. I just happened to see, to be looking in the right directions at the right times. Or the wrong times. But I saw what happened.

I was sitting at one of the tables in The Porcupine, up on the raised level. The Porcupine is a pub on Camden High Street, right on the corner where the smaller of the three markets hangs its hat. At least, there is a pub there, and that's the one I was sitting in. It's not actually called The Porcupine. I've just always called it that for some reason, and I can never remember what its real name is.

On a Saturday night the pub is always crowded with people who've stopped off on the way to the subway after spending the afternoon trawling round the markets. You have to get there very early to score one of the tables up on the raised level: either that or sit and watch like a hawk for when one becomes free. It's an area about ten feet square, with a wooden rail around it, and the windows look out onto the High Street. It's a good place to sit and watch the passing throng, and the couple of feet of elevation gives an impression of looking out over the interior of the pub too.

I didn't get to the pub until about eight o'clock, and when I arrived there wasn't a seat anywhere, never mind on the upper level. The floor was crowded with the usual disparate strands of local color, talking fast and loud. For some reason I always think of them as beatniks, a word which is past its use-by date by about twenty years. I guess it's because the people who hang out in Camden always seem like throwbacks to me. I can't really believe in counterculture in the '90s: not when you know they'll all end up washing their hair some day, and trading the beaten-up Volkswagen for a nice new Ford Sierra.

I angled my way up to the bar and waited for one of the Australians behind it to see me. As I waved some money diffidently around, hoping to catch someone's eye, I flinched at the sound of a sudden shout from behind me.

"Ere, you! Been putting speed in this then 'ave you?"

I half-turned to see that the man standing behind me was shouting at someone behind the bar, gesticulating with a bottle of beer. He was tall, had very short hair and a large ring in his ear, and spoke — or bawled — with a Newcastle accent of compact brutality.

My face hurriedly bland, I turned back to the bar. A ginger-haired bar person was smiling uncertainly at the man with the earring, unsure of how seriously to take the question. The man laughed violently, nudged his mate hard enough to spill his beer, and then shouted again.

"You 'ave, mate. There's drugs in this."

I assume it was some kind of joke relating to how drunk the man felt, but neither I nor the barman were sure. Then a barmaid saw me waiting, and I concentrated on communicating to her my desire for a Budweiser, finding the right change, that sort of thing. When I'd paid I moved away from the bar, carefully skirting the group where the shouting man stood with three or four other men in their mid-twenties. They were all talking very loudly and grinning with vicious good humor, faces red and glistening in the warmth of the crowded pub.

A quick glance around showed that there was still nowhere to sit, so I shuffled my way through the crowd to stand by the long table which runs down the center of the room. By standing in the middle of the pub, and only a few feet away from the steps to the raised area, I would be in a good position to see when a seat became available.

After ten minutes I was beginning to wonder whether I shouldn't just go home instead. I wasn't due to be meeting anyone: I'd spent the day at home working and just fancied being out of doors. I'd brought my current book and was hoping to sit and read for a while, surrounded by the buzz of a Saturday night. The Porcupine's a good pub for that kind of thing. The clientele are quite interesting to watch, the atmosphere is generally good, and if you care to eavesdrop you can learn more about astrology in one evening than you would have believed there was to know.

That night it was different, and it was different because of the group of men standing by the bar. They weren't alone, it seemed. Next to them stood another three, and another five were spread untidily along one side of the long table. They were completely unlike the kind of people you normally find in there, and they changed the feel of the pub. For a start they were all shouting, all at the same time, so that it was impossible to believe that any of them could actually be having a conversation. If they were all talking at the same time, how could they be? They didn't look especially drunk, but relaxed in a hard and tense way. Most of all they looked dangerous.

There's a lot of talk these days about violence to women, and so there should be. In my book, anyone who lays a hand on a woman is breaking the rules. It's simply not done. On the other hand, anyone who gets to their twenties or thirties before they get thumped has had it pretty easy, violence-wise. It's still wrong, but basically what I'm saying is: try being a man. Being a man involves getting hit quite a lot, from a very early age. If you're a teenage girl the physical contact you get tends to be positive: hugs from friends and parents. No one hugs teenage boys. They hit them, fairly often, and quite hard.

Take me, for example. I'm a nice middle-class bloke, and I grew up in a comfortable suburb and went to a good school. It's not like I grew up on an estate or anything. But I took my fair share of knocks, recreational violence that came and went in a meaningless second. I've got a small kink in my nose, for example, which came from it being broken one night. I was walking back from a pub with a couple of friends and three guys behind us simply decided they'd like to push us around. For them the evening clearly wouldn't be complete without a bit of a fight.

We started walking more quickly, but that didn't work. The guys behind us just walked faster. In the end I turned and tried to talk to them, idiot that I was at that age. I said we'd had a good evening and didn't want any trouble. I pointed out that there was a policewoman on the other side of the street. I advanced the opinion that perhaps we could all go our separate ways without any unnecessary unpleasantness. Given that I was more than a little drunk, I think I was probably quite eloquent.

The nearest of them thumped me. He hit me very hard, right on the side of the nose. Suddenly losing faith in reason and the efficacy of a logical discussion, I turned to my friends, to discover that they were already about fifty yards up the road and gaining speed.

I turned to the guys in front of me again. Two of them were grinning, little tight smiles under sparkling eyes. The other was still standing a little closer to me, restlessly shifting his weight from foot to foot. His eyes were blank. I started to recap my previous argument, and he punched me again. I took a clumsy step backwards, in some pain, and he hit me again, a powerful and accurate belt to the cheekbone.

Then, for no evident reason, they drifted off. I turned to see that a police van was sitting at the corner of the road, but I don't think that had made any difference. It was a good eighty yards away, and wasn't coming any closer. My two friends were standing talking to a policeman who was leaning out of the passenger window. There was no sign that any action was going to be taken. There didn't need to be. That's what violence is like, in its most elemental, unnecessary form. It comes, and it goes, like laughter or a cold draught from under a door.

I trotted slowly up the road, and my friends turned and saw me with some relief. The policeman took one look, reached behind into the cab, and passed out a large roll of cotton wool. It was only then that I realized that the lower half of my face, and all of my sweatshirt, was covered in blood.

My face was a little swollen for a couple of days, and my nose never looked quite the same again. But my point is, it was no big deal. The matter-of-fact way in which the policeman handed me something to mop up with said it all. It wasn't important. If you're a man, that kind of thing is going to happen. You wipe your nose and get on.

And that's why when a man walks into a pub, he takes a quick, unconscious look around. He's looking to see if there's any danger, and if so, where it's likely to be located. Similarly, if a fight breaks out, a woman may want to watch, a little breathless with excitement, or she may want to charge fearlessly in and tell them all to stop being silly. Both reasonable reactions, but most men will want to turn the other way, to make themselves invisible. They know that violence isn't a spectator sport: it has a way of reaching out and pulling you in. It won't matter that you don't know anyone involved, that you're just sitting having a quiet drink. These things just happen. There's generally a reason for violence against women. It'll be a very bad reason, don't get me wrong, but there'll be a reason.

Among men violence may be just like an extreme, cold spasm of high spirits. There may not be any reason for it at all, and that's why you have to be very, very careful.

The string of guys standing and sitting near the bar in The Porcupine were giving off exactly the kind of signals that you learn to watch out for. Something about the set of their faces, their restless glances and rabid good humor, said that unreason was at work. The one by the bar was still hollering incomprehensibly at the barman, who was still smiling uncertainly back. Another of the group was leaning across his mate to harangue a couple of nervous-looking girls sitting at a table up against the bar. One of them was wearing a tight sweater, and that's probably all it had taken to kick-start the man's hormones. The look on his face was probably meant to be endearing. It wasn't.

After a couple of minutes the two girls gathered up their stuff and left, but I didn't swoop over to their table. It was too close to the men. Just by being there, by getting too close to their aura, I could have suddenly found myself in trouble. That may sound paranoid, or cowardly: but I've seen it happen. I had every right to sit there, just as a woman has every right to dress the way she wants without attracting unwelcome attention. Rights are nice ideas, a comforting window through which to view the world. But once the glass is broken, you realize they were never really there.

So I remained standing by the long table, sipping my beer and covertly looking around. I couldn't work out what they were doing here. One of them had a woolly hat, which was doing the rounds and getting more and more grubby and beer-stained. I thought it had the letters "FC" on the front somewhere, which would almost certainly stand for Football Club, but I couldn't understand why or how a group of football supporters could have ended up in The Porcupine when it's not near any of the major grounds. One of the groups linked arms to shout some song together at one point, but I couldn't discern any of the words.

I was glancing across to the bar, to see how long the queues were and decide whether it was worth hanging round for another beer, when I saw the first thing. It was very unexceptional, but it's one of the things I saw.

The door onto the main street had been propped open by the staff, presumably in a vain attempt to drop the temperature in the crowded room to something approaching bearable. As I swept the far end of the bar with my gaze, trying to judge the best place to stand if I wanted to get served that evening, a large grey dog came in through the door, and almost immediately disappeared into the throng. I noticed and remembered it because I was sort of expecting its owner to follow him in, but nobody came. I realized he or she must already be in the pub, and the dog had simply popped out for a while. The owner would have to be a he, I decided: no woman would want a dog like that. I only got a very quick sighting of it, but it was very large and slightly odd-looking, a shaggy hound that moved with a speed that was both surprising and somehow oily.

At that moment I saw a couple who were sitting at a table in the raised area reach for their coats, and I forgot about the dog. The couple had been sitting at the best table in the pub, one which is right in the corner of the room, up against the big windows. I immediately started cutting through the mass of people toward it.

Once I'd staked the table out as my territory I went to the bar and bought another beer. It may have been my imagination but it looked to me as if the staff were very aware of the group of men too: though they were all busy, each glanced out into the body of the pub while I was there, keeping half an eye on the long table. I avoided the area completely and got myself served right at the top of the bar, next to the door.

I settled myself back down at the table, glad that the evening was getting on track. I glanced out of the window, though it was mid-evening by then, too late for much to be going on. A few couples strolled by outside in a desultory fashion, dressed with relentless trendiness. Some kind of altercation was taking place in the Kentucky Fried Chicken opposite, and a derelict with dreadlocks was picking through a bin on the pavement near the window. If I can get the window seat early enough I like to sit and watch, but the strong moonlight made the view look distant somehow, unreal.

A fresh surge of noise made me turn away from the window and look out across the pub. One of the men had knocked over his beer, or had it knocked over. Those nearby were shouting and laughing. It didn't look like much was going to come of it. I'd opened my book and was about to start reading when I noticed something else.

There was one more person in the party than there had been before. Now you're probably going to think that I simply hadn't registered him, but that's not true. I'd looked at them hard and long. If I'd seen this man before, I would have remembered it. He was standing with the group nearest the steps which led up to the area where I was sitting. I say "standing with," because there was something about him that set him apart slightly from the other men, though he was right in the middle of them, and had the cocky pub charisma of some-one who's used to respect among his peers. He was wearing jeans and a bulky grey jacket, typical sloppy casual, his dark hair was slightly waved, and his face came to a point in an aquiline nose. He exuded a sort of manic calm, as if it was the result of a bloodstream coursing with equal quantities of heroin and ecstasy, and he was listening to two of the other men with his mouth hanging slackly open, head tilted on one side. When there was another wave of noise from the other part of the group he raised his head slightly, the corners of his mouth creased in a half-smile of anticipation, keen to see what was going on, what new devilry was afoot. He was at home here. This is what he knew, what he was good at. This was where he lived.

He had weird eyes, too. They weren't too big or small, and they weren't a funny color or anything. But they were dead, like two coins pushed into clay. They weren't the kind of eyes you would want to see looking at you across a pub, if you were a woman. If you were a man, they weren't eyes you wanted to see at all. They were not good eyes.

I watched with an odd sort of fascination as the man stood with a loose-limbed solidity, turning from side to side to participate in the various shouting matches going on around him. And all the time he had this half-smile, as if he was enjoying every epic moment. I caught a momentary look on the face of one of his mates, a look of slight puzzlement, but I couldn't interpret it any more closely than that. Not at the time, anyway.

After a while I lost interest and finally started reading my book. The pub was warm, but the window next to me was cool, and I can tune out just about anything when I'm reading. I don't wear a watch, so I don't know how long it was before it all went off.

There was the sudden sound of breaking glass, and the noise level in the pub dipped for a moment, before shooting up into pandemonium. Startled, I looked up, still immersed in my book. Then my head went very clear.

A fight had broken out. That's what they do. They break out, appear like rain from clear April skies. Virtually all of the men around the table seemed to be involved, apart from a pair who were gloatingly watching from the sidelines. The rest of the pub were doing what people always do in these situations. The bar staff were either cowering or gearing themselves up to do something, and the other customers were shifting back in their seats, watching but trying to move out of trouble. I couldn't really see what was going on, but it looked as if the men had taken on another, smaller, group who'd been sitting affably at the bar.

Among the general noise and chaos, I saw that the man with the bulky grey jacket was right in the thick of it. In fact it looked rather as if he'd started the whole thing. Once I'd noticed him again the rest of the action seemed to shade away, and I saw him loop a fist into the mêlée. A couple of the male bar staff emerged into the body of the pub, holding their hands out in a placatory way, trying to look stern. The ginger-haired one in particular looked as if he wished this wasn't his job, that he was a waiter in some nice bistro instead. A couple of men responded by ploughing into them, and the fight immediately leapt up to a new level of intensity. People nearby hurriedly slipped out of their chairs and fled to the sides of the room. A beer bottle was smashed and brandished, and it all looked as if it was going to get very serious indeed.

As everybody was watching the new focus of attention, I happened to glance down toward the other end of the long table. The man in the grey jacket, I was surprised to see, had stopped fighting. He had his arm round the tall man with the earring, who'd been hurt, and was leading him toward the toilets at the back of the pub. I clocked this, and then turned to look back at the other end. The manager, a large man with forearms the size of my thighs, had come out from behind the counter. He was holding a pool cue and looked as if he had every intention of using it.

Luckily, I wasn't the only person who thought so. The man waving the broken bottle faltered, only for a moment, but it was enough. The guy he'd been threatening took a step back, and suddenly the mood dropped. It happened as quickly as that. A gust of wind dispersed the cloud, and sparks stopped arcing through the air. The fight had gone away.

There was a certain amount of jockeying as the two groups of men disentangled and took up their previous positions. The manager kept a firm eye on this, cue still in hand. The other customers gradually relaxed in their seats and slowly, like a fan coming to rest, the evening settled.

When I'd finished my beer I started toward the bar for another, and then elected to go to the toilets first. It was a bit of a struggle getting through the crowd toward the far end of the bar, and my route took me a little closer to the men than I would have liked. When I passed them, however, I relaxed a little. They were still up, still feisty, but the main event of the evening was over. I don't know how, but I could sense that. The mood was different, and something had been satisfied. The funniest joke had been told.

I hesitated for a moment before entering the toilets. As far as I knew, the man with the grey jacket and his wounded colleague were still in there. The Porcupine's toilet is not big, and I'd have to walk quite close to them. But then I thought "fuck it," and pushed the door open. You can be too bloody cautious. Quite apart from anything else, the mood in the aftermath of a fight tends to be one of fierce good humor and comradeship. A nod and a grunt from me would be enough to show I was one of the lads.

I needn't have worried, because it was empty. I took a leak into one of the urinals, and then turned to wash my hands at the minuscule washbasin. There was a certain amount of blood still splattered across the porcelain, the result of a bad nosebleed, by the look of it.

Then I noticed that there were drops of blood on the floor too, leading in the direction of the cubicle. The door was nearly shut, but not actually closed, which was odd. It didn't feel as if anyone was behind the door, and people don't generally pull a cubicle door to when they leave. Not knowing why I was doing so, I carefully pushed it open with my finger.

When it was open a couple of inches I nearly shouted, but stopped myself. When it was open all the way I just stared.

The walls of the cubicle were splattered with blood up to the level of the ceiling, as if someone had loaded dark red paint onto a thick brush and tried to paint the walls as quickly as possible. A couple of lumps of ragged flesh lay behind the bottom of the toilet, and the bowl was full of mottled blood, with a few pale chips of something floating near the top.

My mind balked at what I was seeing, and I simply couldn't understand what might have happened until I saw a large metal ring on the floor, nearly hidden behind one of the lumps.

Moving very quickly, I left the toilet. The pub was still seething with noise and heat, and the way through to the raised area was completely blocked. Suddenly remembering you could do such a thing, I ducked out of the side door. I could walk around the pub and re-enter at the front, much closer to my seat. Or I could just start running. But I didn't think I should. I had to get my book, or people might wonder why it was still there.

The air outside the pub was cool, and I hurried along the wall. After a couple of yards I stopped when I saw a movement on the other side of the road.

The dog was sitting there. Now that it was still, I could see just how large it was. It was much bigger than a normal dog, and bulkier. And it was looking at me, with flat grey eyes.

We stared at each other for a moment. I couldn't move, and just hoped to God it was going to stay where it was. I wanted to sidle along the wall, to get to the bit where the windows started so that people could see me, but I didn't have the courage. If I moved, it might come for me.

It didn't. Still looking directly at me, the dog raised its haunches and then walked slowly away, down toward the dark end of the street where the lamps aren't working. I watched it go, still not trusting. Just before the corner it turned and looked at me again, and then it was gone.

I went back into the pub, grabbed my book and went home. I didn't tell anyone what I'd found. They'd discover it soon enough. As I hurried out of the pub I heard one of the men at the table wonder where Pete was. There was no point me telling him, or showing him what was left. I had to look after myself.

I noticed all of those things. I was looking in those directions, and saw what I saw. I saw the earring on the floor of the cubicle, still attached to the remains of its owner's face. I saw that the man in the grey jacket wasn't there when I left, but that nobody seemed to be asking after him. I saw the look one of the other men had given him, a look of puzzlement, as if he was wondering exactly when he'd met this man with grey eyes, where he knew him from. And I saw the look in the eyes of the dog, and the warning that it held.

I didn't tell anyone anything, but I don't know whether that will be enough. It wasn't my fault I saw things. I wasn't looking for trouble. But I understand enough to realize that makes no difference. Rain will sometimes fall, and I was standing underneath.

I haven't been to The Porcupine in the last month. I've spent a lot of time at home, watching the street. In the last couple of days I've started to wonder if there are as many cats around as usual, and I've heard things outside the window in the night, shufflings. They may not mean anything. It may not be important that the darkness outside my window is becoming paler, as the moon gets fuller every night. All of this may amount to nothing.

But it makes me nervous. It makes me really very nervous.

David J. Schow is known in the horror field for his powerful, award-winning short fiction and for editing *Silver Scream*, arguably the first splatterpunk anthology. But he might be most famous for writing the screenplay to *The Crow*, authoring *The Outer Limits Companion*, and coining the term "splatterpunk" (he is perversely proud of getting that word into the Oxford English Dictionary). He is also the author of the novels *The Kill Riff* and *The Shaft*, and his most recent novel is the hardboiled *Gun Work*. His most recent collection of short stories — the seventh — is *Havoc Swims Jaded*. He can be seen as an expert witness on numerous documentaries and DVD supplements, the two most recent of these being *Famous Monster: Forrest J. Ackerman* and *The Psycho Legacy*.

With "Refrigerator Heaven" Schow is at his edgy best, with crisp language, deft characterizations, and a very dark theme.

Refrigerator Heaven
David J. Schow

THE LIGHT IS beatific. More than beautiful. Garrett sees the light and allows the awe to flow from him.

Garrett can't *not* see the light. His eyelids are slammed tightly shut; tears trickle from aching slits at both corners. The light seeks out the corners and penetrates them. It is so hotly white it obliterates Garrett's view of the thin veinwork on the obverse of his own inadequate eyelids.

He tries to measure time by the beat of his own heart; no good.

The light has always been with him, it seems. It is eternal, omnipotent. Garrett gasps, but not in pain, not *true* pain — no, for the light is a superior force, and he owes it his wonder. It is so much *more* than he is, so intense that he can *hear* it caress his flesh, seeking out his secret places, his organs, his thoughts, illuminating each fissure and furrow in his very brain.

Garrett slams his palms over closed eyes and marvels that the light does not care and offers no quarter. Garrett feels pathetic; the light, he feels, is unequivocal and pure.

Garrett has looked into the light and formulated a new definition of what God must be like. He feels honored that he, among mortals, has been permitted this glimpse of the divine. His mind interprets the light as hot, though he does not feel the anticipated baking of his flesh. So pure, so total…

He has never in his pathetic, mortal life borne witness to a spectacle like it.

Finally, the light is too much. Garrett must avert his gaze, but he cannot. No matter which way he turns his head, the light is there, cleansing away agendas and guilt and human foibles and the mistakes of the past, as well as mistaken notions of the future. The light, forever, there in Garrett's head.

He reaches to find words to offer up to the light, and he can only find limited human conceits, like love.

A woman is in bed with her husband. They are between bouts of lovemaking, and the woman's eyes are hooded and blue in the semidarkness, with that unique glow — a radiance that tells the man he is all she sees, or cares to see right now.

She tells him she loves him. Unnecessarily. The words in the dark do him spiritual good anyway.

She touches his nose with her fingertip and draws it slowly down. *You. I love.*

He knows.

He is about to say something in response, if for no other reason than not to maroon her in their warm, postcoital quiet, stranding her alone with her words of love. He is trying to think of something sexy and witty and genuinely loving, to prove he cares.

He is on his back, and one of her legs, warm and moist on the softest part of the inner thigh, is draped over his. *You are mine*, the embrace says. *You are what I want.*

The man is still struggling with words that won't come. He misses his chance. If you miss the moment, other forces rush in to fill the dead air for you, and rarely does one have control or choice.

Later, the man thinks, if only he had spoken, none of the bad things would have happened.

There are some loud noises. The next thing the man knows, his wife is screaming and he is facedown, cheek bulled roughly against the carpet. His wife is screaming questions that will not be answered in this lifetime.

The man's hands are cuffed behind his back. He is lifted by the cuffs, naked, as lights click on in the bedroom.

He twists his head, tries to see. He is backhanded, very hard, by one of his captors. The image he snatches is of his wife, also naked, held by her throat against the bedroom wall, by a man in a tight business suit. With his free hand the suit is holding an automatic an inch from her nose and telling her in no uncertain verbiage to shut up if she knows what is good for her.

Like a bad gangster movie, thinks the man.

He sees all this in an eighth of a second. Then, *bang*. He hits the floor again, feeling the wetness of fresh blood oozing from a split eyebrow.

His ankles are ziplocked together — one of those vinyl slipknot cuffs used by police. Then he is hoisted bodily, penis dangling, and carried out of his own bedroom like a roast on a spit.

Darkness: Two Decades of Modern Horror

He fights to see his wife before his captors have him out the door. In this moment, seeing her one last time becomes the most important imperative ever to burn in his mind.

As he is hauled away, he says he loves her. He has no way of knowing whether she hears. He cannot see her as he speaks the words. In the end, the words come easily.

He never sees his wife again.

Donnelly regarded the box with a funny expression tilting his face to starboard. He took a long draw on his smoke, which made a quarter inch of ash, then shrugged the way a comedian does when he *knows* he's just delivered a knee-slapper...and the audience is too stupid to appreciate it.

"So what did this guy *do?*" he said with artificial levity.

"That's classified," said Cambreaux. "That's none of your beeswax. That, Chester, is a dumb question, and you oughta know better."

"Just testing," said Donnelly. "I'm supposed to jump-quiz smartasses like you to make sure there are no security leaks. So what did he do?"

"He's a reporter, from what I gather. He was in the wrong place at the right time with a camera and a tape recorder, neither of which we can find. They sent down orders to scoop him."

"Very funny."

"Scoop him up, I mean." Cambreaux popped four codeine-coated aspirin like M&Ms. "Do you have any more questions?"

"What did he see? What did he hear?"

"Let me ask *you* a question: Do you want to keep your job? Do you want me to lose *my* job?"

"That's two questions." Donnelly was having fun.

"You asked two questions first."

"Yeah, but your answers are cooler. You want a cigarette?"

"No." Cambreaux really wanted the smoke, but thought this was a habit over which he should exert more control. There was a definite lack of things to do with one's hands down in this little, secure room, and he was grateful for Donnelly's company, this shift. "They locked this guy in a cell for four days, your basic sweat-out. No phone calls. No go. So then Human Factors beats the crap out of him; still nothing. They used one of those canvas tubes filled with iron filings."

"Mm." Donnelly finished his cigarette and looked around for an ashtray. Finally he ground out the butt on the sole of his shoe. "No exterior marks, except for a bruise or two, and your organs get pureed."

"Yeah. They used a phone book, too."

"And he read the phone book and said, 'This has got a lot of great characters, but the plot sucks.'"

"Boy, you got a million of 'em. And they all stink."

"Thanks." Donnelly patted himself down for a fresh smoke. It was a habit he swore he needed to quit. The pat-down, not the smoking. "Then what?"

"Then what. They brought in Medical Assist. They tried sodium pentothal; no dice. Then psychedelics, then electroshock. Still zero. So here we be."

Donnelly looked twice. Yes, that *was* a kitchen timer on top of Cambreaux's console. Donnelly's wife had one just like it — round clock face, adjustable for sixty minutes. She used it to brew coffee precisely; she was fastidious about things like perfect coffee. Donnelly indicated the timer, then the big box. "You baking him in there?"

"Yeah. He's not done yet."

The box was about five feet square and resembled an industrial refrigerator. It was enameled white, steel-reinforced, and featureless except for a big screw-down hatch lock like the ones Donnelly had seen while touring an aircraft carrier. Thick 220-volt cables snaked from the box to Cambreaux's console.

"You got gypped," said Donnelly. "No ice-maker."

Cambreaux made the face he always made at Donnelly's jokes. Donnelly noticed — not for the first time — that Cambreaux's head seemed perfectly round, a moon head distinguished by a perfect crescent of hair at eyebrow level, punctuated by round mad-scientist specs with flecks of blue and gold in the rims.

"New glasses?"

"Yeah, the old ones were too tight on my head. Torture. Gave me the strokes, right here." Cambreaux indicated his temples. "Pure fucking torture. Man, you ever need any info out of me, just make me wear my old glasses and I'll kill my children for you."

Donnelly strolled around the box, one full circuit. "What do we call this?"

"The refrigerator. What else?"

"A *reporter*? Funny. Most journalists don't have the spine or the sperm for this sort of marathon."

"If he'd talked, he wouldn't be here."

"Point. Agreed."

"What are you *staring* at, Chester?"

"I love to watch a man who enjoys his work."

Cambreaux gave him the finger. "You going to stand around admiring me all afternoon, or can I talk you into setting up a fresh pot on the machine?"

Cambreaux's timer went *ding*.

"I was waiting to see what happens when our reporter is done basting," said Donnelly.

"What happens is this." Cambreaux lifted the timer and cranked it back to sixty minutes.

Donnelly squinted at him. "Jesus. How long have you been here today?"

"Six hours. New regs call for eight hours up."

"Oh. Cream and sugar?"

"Just a spot of each. Just enough cream to discolor the coffee."

"You're starting to sound like my wife."

"Grope me and I'll shoot you in the balls."

"This is probably a stupid question —"

"Guaranteed, from you," Cambreaux overrode.

"— but can I get anything for our pal the reporter?"

Cambreaux pushed back from the console, the racketing of his chair casters loud and hollow in the room, like the too harsh ticking of the appliance timer. He winnowed his fingers beneath his glasses and rubbed his eyes until they were pink.

"Did I say this guy is a reporter? Scratch that. He *was* a reporter. When he comes out of the fridge, he won't need anything except maybe a padded cell. Or a casket."

Donnelly kept staring at the box. It was just weird enough, the sort of anomaly you can't take your eye from.

"How about I just bring him a shot of good ole government-issue cyanide?"

"Not just yet," said Cambreaux, touching his timer as if for inspiration, then jotting a note on a gray legal pad. "Not just yet, my friend."

Elapsed time has ceased to have meaning, and this is good for Garrett.

A relief. He has been released from what were once boundaries, and the mundane of the day-to-day. There is no day here, no night, no time. He has been liberated. Elemental input and the limitations of his physical form have become his sole realities. He had once read that the next step in human evolution might be to a formless intellect, eternal, almost cosmic, undying, immortal, transcendent.

If the light had been God, then the cold is Sleep. New rules, new deities.

He is curled into a fetal ball like a beaten animal, shuddering uncontrollably while his lit-up mind wrestles with the problems of how to properly pay obeisance to this latest god.

His *bones* feel cold; his hands and feet, distant and insensate. Respiration is a knife of ice, boring in to pierce his lungs in tandem. He shallows his breath and prays that his rawed esophagus might lend the air a mote of metabolic heat before it plunges mercilessly into his lung tissue.

He is still merely tissue.

He knows the cold will not steal more than a few critical degrees of his core heat. The cold will not murder him; it is testing him, inviting him to discover his own extremes. To kill Garrett would be too easy, and pointless. He would not have survived the light only to perish by the cold. The cold cares about him, as the light had, as an uncaring god is said to care for the flock that is crippled, tormented, and killed…only to profess renewed faith.

The cold is intimate in a way that surpasses his mere flesh.

His fingers and toes are now remote tributaries of forgotten feeling. Garrett curls on his right side, then his left, to spell each of his lungs in turn, to stave off the workload of chilly pain by reducing it to processable fragments.

He allows the sub-zero ambience to flow *through*, not batter against, the inadequate walls of his skin. He thinks of the felled tree in the forest. He is here so the cold will have a purpose. He is the proof of sound in the silent, snowbound woodland; the freezing air needed him as much as he needed it to verify his own existence.

Huddled, then, and shivering, still naked, his blood retarded to a thick crawl in unthawed veins, Garret permits the cold to have him. He welcomes its forward nature, its brashness.

Garrett closes his eyes. Feels bliss. Smiling, with clenched teeth, he sleeps.

On the dirty coffee table in front of Alvarado there were several items of interest: a bottle of Laphroaig scotch, a big camera, a snubnosed gun, and an unopened letter.

The camera was an autofocusing rig with flashless 1600 ASA color film and a blimped speedwinder, for silent work. Twenty-one exposures had been recorded in scant seconds. The Laphroaig was very mellow and half gone. The gun was a Charter Arms .44 Bulldog, no shots used yet.

Whenever the building made a slight nighttime noise around him, Alvarado tensed, his heart thudding briskly with anticipation. Moment to moment, he was safe...though the next moment might bring last call.

He had driven all the way into the San Fernando Valley to mail his preaddressed packets, copies of his precious tapes and photos. Now his backstop was secure, his evidence was damning, and the only reason he could think of for still hanging around his apartment was because he, too, felt damned. Soiled somehow.

New evidence waited inside his camera. Rawer, more toxic, dangerously good stuff to reinforce his already strong case.

Alvarado lifted the envelope and read the address for the thousandth time. It was a cable TV bill for Garrett, his next-door neighbor. Once upon a time, the gods running computerized mailing lists had hiccuped, fouled their numbers. Rather than rectify the irritant with fruitless phone calls, Alvarado and Garrett had beer, trading mail for nearly a year now, sliding it beneath each other's respective doors when they were out. They both traveled a lot. The mail thing had become an after-hours joke between them.

Garrett was an ad agent for a publishing company. He toured his turf with a folio of new releases and pitched store to store. Alvarado had been staff at the *Los Angeles Times* until he was let go in a seasonal pruning, followed by a hiring freeze blamed on the latest recession. He made do as a freelancer until his time rolled around again; he had made his living professionally long enough to believe in karmic work rhythms. Freelancing had propelled him into some very odd new places. Alternative papers. Tabloids. Pop magazines.

Investigative journalism, self-motivated.

Now, if his backstop allies made proper use of the duplicate tapes and photos now safely in postal transit, Alvarado would be back on the map, big time. The waiting was not the worst part, though it *had* made his life pretty suspenseful during the past few hellish days.

Sometimes reporters got assassinated for their reportage. It happened, though the public rarely heard about it. Thus, Alvarado had emplaced his elaborate backstop network.

Sometimes reporters got *worse* than killed. Thus the gun, yes, loaded, and this quiet vigil in a dark room.

It had happened four or five days ago. Say a week. Alvarado's schedule and sleeptime had become totally bollixed, of combat necessity.

A week ago, he had heard a noisy commotion in the night. His damning photos and tapes had not yet been copied or mailed. He was awake from his snooze on the sofa in a silent instant, fully alert. At first he thought the disturbance was a simple domestic — Garrett and his wife or girlfriend having some temporary and loud disagreement in tire middle of the night, as lovers sometimes do.

Alvarado's mind decoded the noises he heard. This was no argument.

He remembered grabbing his camera and moving to the balcony. After a second of hesitation he had stepped around to Garrett's adjoining balcony, and recognized immediately that very bad shit was going on inside.

He witnessed most of it through his viewfinder, focusing on the slit of light permitted by the curtains on Garrett's sliding door. He saw Garrett naked, trussed and manhandled by an efficiently fast goon squad in the very best JC Penney's Secret Service wash-and-wear. Garrett's wife or girlfriend, also naked, was being abused and threatened on the far side of the bedroom. The men moved like they had a purpose.

Twenty-one rapid-fire exposures later, Garrett was out, abducted, gone... and Alvarado was off to the mailbox with older, no less scary business. He had his own future to protect.

Now, tonight, Alvarado sat staring at the cable bill addressed to Garrett. He had received it. And Garrett had received a late-night visit intended for his neighbor.

Intended for *me*, Alvarado knew.

It was a coincidence almost divine, winning Alvarado the time to get his material to safety. Garrett had picked up the check, and perhaps that was why Alvarado was still hanging around.

Just like that, his life had become bad film noir. Here he was, drinking, fondling his gun, and fantasizing about the inevitable confrontation. *Blam, blam*, and in a blaze of glory *everybody* gets to be in the papers.

Post-mortem.

Provided the bad guys got the address right this time.

If the light was God, and the cold Sleep, then the sound was Love.

Garrett decides he is being tempered and refined for some very special purpose, duty, or chosen destiny. He feels proud and fulfilled. He cannot be the recipient of so many revelations for some nothing purpose…and so he pays very close attention to the lessons the sound brings him.

He is quite the attentive little godling in training.

The extremes he withstands are the signposts of his own evolution. He began as a normal man. He is becoming more.

It is exhilarating.

He eagerly awaits Heat, and Silence, and Darkness, and whatever he needs beyond them.

"You want to hear a funny?" said Cambreaux.

Donnelly felt he was not going to walk away amused. "I do the jokes in this toilet."

"Not as boffo as this: Our reporter? Janitorial collected him at three o'clock this morning. We've had the wrong guy in the refrigerator for a week."

Donnelly did not laugh. He never laughed when he could feel his stomach dropping away like a clipped elevator, skimming his balls enroute to Hell. "You mean this guy is *innocent?*"

Cambreaux's style did not admit of sheepishness, or comeback. "I wouldn't say that."

"Everybody's guilty of something, is that it?"

"No. I wouldn't say that our friend in the box is innocent. Not anymore."

They both stared at the refrigerator. Locked inside was a man who had been subjected to stresses and extremes known to fracture the toughest operatives going. His brain had to be string cheese by now. And he hadn't *done* anything… except be innocent.

"Fucking Janitorial," Donnelly snorted. "They're always screwing up the work orders."

"Bunch of gung-ho bullet boys," Cambreaux agreed. Better to fault another department, always.

"So…you going to let him out?"

"Not my call." Both he and Donnelly knew that the man in the box had to be released, but neither of them would budge until the right documents dropped down the correct chute.

"What's he on now?"

"High-frequency sound. Metered for — oh, *shit!*"

Donnelly saw Cambreaux rocket from his chair to grab the kitchen timer and hurl it across the chamber. It disintegrated into frags. Then Cambreaux was frantically snapping off switches, cranking dials down.

"Goddamn timer froze! It stopped!"

Donnelly immediately looked at the fridge.

"It was on too high for too long, Chet! Goddamn timer!"

Both of them wondered what they would see when the lid was finally opened.

Garrett feels at last that he is being pushed too far, that he must extract too high a price from himself.

He endures, because he must. He hovers on the brink of a human millennium. He is the first. He must experience the change with his eyes open.

The sound removed everything from Garrett's world.

Not too late at last, Garrett says *I love you*.

He has to scream it. Not too late.

Then his eardrums burst.

Cambreaux was drinking coffee in the lounge, shoulders sagging, elbows planted on knees, penitent.

"Ever hear the one about the self-protecting fuse?" said Donnelly. "The one that protects itself by blowing up your whole stereo?" No reaction. "I saw the fridge open. When did they take our boy?"

"This morning. I was on the console when the orders finally came down."

"Hey — your hands are shaking."

"Chet, I feel like I have to cry, almost. I saw that guy come out of the fridge. I've never seen anything like it."

Donnelly sat down beside Cambreaux. "Bad?"

"Bad." A poisonous laugh escaped him. It was more like a cough, or a bark. "We opened the box. And that guy looked at us like we'd just stolen his soul. He had blood all over him, mostly from his ears. He started hollering. Chet, he didn't want us to take him out."

This didn't sound good, spilling from a professional like Cambreaux. Donnelly let out a measured breath, leavening his own racing metabolism.

"But you took him out."

"Yes sir, we did. Orders. And when we got him out, he broke, and clawed his own eyes out, and choked to death on his tongue."

Darkness: Two Decades of Modern Horror

"Jesus Christ…"

"Janitorial took him."

"Disposal's the one thing those bozos are good at."

"You got a cigarette?"

Donnelly handed it over and lit it for him. He lit himself one.

"Chet, did you ever read 'The Pit and the Pendulum'?"

"I saw the movie."

"The story is basically about a guy who gets tortured for days by the Inquisition. Right before he makes his final fall into the pit, he gets rescued by the French army."

"Fiction."

"Yeah, happy endings and all. We did the same thing. Except the guy didn't want to leave. He *found* something in there, Chet. Something you or I don't ever have a chance at. And we took him out, away from the thing he discovered…"

"And he died."

"Yeah."

They were silent together for a few minutes. Neither of them was very spiritual; they were men who were paid for their ability to do their jobs. Yet neither could resist the idea of what Garrett might have seen in the box.

Neither of them would ever climb into the box to find out. Too many reasons not to. Thousands.

"I got you a present," Donnelly said.

He handed over a factory-fresh appliance timer. This one came with a warranty and guarantee. That made Cambreaux smile. A bit.

"Take it slow, old buddy. Duty calls. We'll have a drink later."

Cambreaux nodded and accepted Donnelly's fraternal pat on the shoulder. He had just done his job. No sin in that.

Donnelly walked along the fluorescent-lit corridor, very consciously avoiding the route that would take him past the room where the refrigerator was. He did not want to see it hanging open just now.

He made a mental note to look up the Poe story. He loved a good read.

Joyce Carol Oates is one of the most prolific and respected writers in the United States today. Oates has written fiction in almost every genre and medium. Her keen interest in the Gothic and psychological horror has spurred her to write dark suspense novels under the name Rosamond Smith, to write enough stories in the genre to have published five collections of dark fiction, the most recent being *The Museum of Dr. Moses: Tales of Mystery and Suspense* and *Wild Nights!: Stories about the Last Days of Poe, Dickinson, Twain, James, and Hemingway*, and to edit *American Gothic Tales*. Oates's short novel *Zombie* won the Bram Stoker Award, and she has been honored with a Life Achievement Award by the Horror Writers Association.

Oates's most recent novels are *Blood Mask, The Gravedigger's Daughter,* and *My Sister, My Love: The Intimate Story of Skyler Rampike.* She teaches creative writing at Princeton and with her late husband, Raymond J. Smith, ran the small press and literary magazine *The Ontario Review* for many years.

████████████████ can be read literally and/or symbolically. But either way this is one of Oates's most chilling stories.

Joyce Carol Oates

It was the most beautiful house I had ever seen up close. Or was ever to enter. Three stories high, broad, and gleaming pale pink, made of sandstone, Uncle Rebhorn said, custom-designed and *his* design of course. They came to get me — Uncle Rebhorn, Aunt Elinor, my cousin Audrey, who was my age, and my cousin Darren, who was three years older — one Sunday in July 1969. How excited I was, how special I felt, singled out for a visit to Uncle Rebhorn's house in Grosse Pointe Shores. I see the house shimmering before me and then I see emptiness, a strange rectangular blackness, and nothing.

For at the center of what happened on that Sunday many years ago is blackness.

I can remember what led to the blackness and what followed after it — not clearly, but to a degree, as, waking vague and stunned from a powerful dream, we retain shreds of the dream though we remain incapable of making them coalesce into a whole; nor can we "see" them as we'd seen them during the dream. So I can summon back a memory of the black rectangle and I can superimpose depth upon it — for it could not be flat, like a canvas — but I have to admit defeat, I can't "see" anything inside it. And this black rectangle is at the center of that Sunday in July 1969, and at the center of my girlhood.

Unless it was the end of my girlhood.

But how do I know, if I can't remember?

I was eleven years old. It was to be my first time ever — and it was to be the last time, too, though I didn't know it then — that I was brought by my father's older stepbrother, Uncle Rebhorn, to visit his new house and to go sailing on Lake St. Clair. Because of my cousin Audrey, who was like a sister of mine though I saw her rarely — I guessed this was why Mommy told me, in a careful, neutral voice, that of course Audrey didn't have any friends, or Darren either. I asked why and Mommy said they just didn't, that's all. That's the price you pay for *moving up* too quickly in the world.

All our family lived in the Detroit suburb of Hamtramck and had lived there for a long time. Uncle Rebhorn too, until the age of eighteen when he left and now, how many years later, he was a rich man — president of Rebhorn Auto Supply, Inc., and he'd married a well-to-do Grosse Pointe woman — and built his big, beautiful new house on Lake St. Clair everybody in the family talked about but nobody had actually seen. (Unless they'd seen the house from the outside? Not my parents, who were too proud to stoop to such a maneuver, but other relatives were said to have driven all the way to Grosse Pointe Shores to gape at Uncle Rebhorn's pink mansion, as much as they could see of it from Buena Vista Drive. Uninvited, they dared not ring the buzzer at the wrought-iron gate, shut and presumably locked at the foot of the drive.) Uncle Rebhorn, whom I did not know at all, had left Hamtramck far behind and was said to "scorn" his upbringing and his own family. There was a good deal of jealousy of course, and envy, but since everybody hoped secretly to be remembered by him sometime, and invited to share in his amazing good fortune — imagine, a millionaire in the family! — they were always sending cards, wedding invitations, announcements of births and christenings and confirmations; sometimes even telegrams, since Uncle Rebhorn's telephone number was unlisted and even his brothers didn't know what it was. Daddy said, with that heavy, sullen droop to his voice we tried never to hear, "If he wants to keep to himself that's fine, I can respect that. We'll keep to ourselves, too."

Then, out of nowhere, the invitation came to *me*. Just a telephone call from Aunt Elinor.

Mommy, who'd taken the call, of course, and made the arrangements, didn't want me to stay overnight. Aunt Elinor had suggested this for it was a long drive, between forty-five minutes and an hour, and she'd said that Audrey would be disappointed, but Mommy said no and that was that.

So, that Sunday, how vividly I can remember! — Uncle Rebhorn, Aunt Elinor, Audrey, and Darren came to get me in Uncle Rebhorn's shiny black Lincoln Continental, which rolled like a hearse up our street of woodframe asphalt-sided bungalows and drew stares from our neighbors. Daddy was gone — Daddy was not going to hang around, he said, on the chance of saying hello and maybe getting to shake hands with his stepbrother — but Mommy was with me, waiting at the front door when Uncle Rebhorn pulled up; but there were no words exchanged between Mommy and the Rebhorns, for Uncle Rebhorn merely tapped the car horn to signal their arrival, and Aunt Elinor, though she waved and smiled at Mommy, did not get out of the car, and made not the slightest gesture inviting Mommy to come out to speak with *her*. I ran breathless to the curb — I had a panicky vision of Uncle Rebhorn starting the big black car up and leaving me behind in Hamtramck — and climbed into the back seat, to sit beside Audrey. "Get in, hurry, we don't have all day," Uncle Rebhorn said in that gruff jovial cartoon voice some adults use with children, meant to be playful — or maybe not. Aunt Elinor cast me a frowning sort of smile over her shoulder and put her finger to her lips as if to indicate that I take Uncle Rebhorn's remark in silence, as naturally I would. My heart was hammering with excitement just to be in such a magnificent automobile!

How fascinating the drive from our familiar neighborhood into the city of Detroit where there were so many black people on the streets and many of them, glimpsing Uncle Rebhorn's Lincoln Continental, stared openly. We moved swiftly along Outer Drive and so to Eight Mile Road and east to Lake St. Clair where I had never been before, and I could not believe how beautiful everything was once we turned onto Lakeshore Drive. Now it was my turn to stare and stare. Such mansions on grassy hills facing the lake! So many tall trees, so much leafy space! So much sky! (The sky in Hamtramck was usually low and overcast and wrinkled like soiled laundry.) And Lake St. Clair, which was a deep rich aqua, like a painted lake! During most of the drive, Uncle Rebhorn was talking, pointing out the mansions of wealthy, famous people — I only remember "Ford" — "Dodge" — "Fisher" — "Wilson" — and Aunt Elinor was nodding and murmuring inaudibly, and in the back seat, silent and subdued, Audrey and Darren and I sat looking out the tinted windows. I was a little hurt and disappointed that Audrey seemed to be ignoring me, and sitting very stiffly beside me; though I guessed that, with Uncle Rebhorn talking continuously, and addressing his remarks to the entire car, Audrey did not want to seem to interrupt him. Nor did Darren say a word to anyone.

At last, in Grosse Pointe Shores, we turned off Lakeshore Drive onto a narrow, curving road called Buena Vista, where the mansions were smaller, though still mansions; Buena Vista led into a cul-de-sac bordered by tall, massive oaks and elms. At the very end, overlooking the lake, was Uncle Rebhorn's house — as I've said, the most beautiful house I had ever seen up close, or would ever enter. Made of that pale pink glimmering sandstone, with a graceful portico covered in English ivy, and four slender columns, and dozens of latticed windows reflecting the sun like smiles, the house looked like a storybook illustration. And beyond was the sky, a pure cobalt blue except for thin wisps of cloud. Uncle Rebhorn pressed a button in the dashboard of his car, and the wrought-iron gate swung open — like nothing I'd ever seen before in real life. The driveway too was like no driveway I knew, curving and dipping, and comprised of rosy-pink gravel, exquisite as miniature seashells. Tiny pebbles flew up beneath the car as Uncle Rebhorn drove in and the gate swung miraculously shut behind us.

How lucky Audrey was to live here, I thought, gnawing at my thumbnail as Mommy had told me a thousand times not to do. Oh I would die to live in such a house, I thought.

Uncle Rebhorn seemed to have heard me. "We think so, yes indeed," he said. To my embarrassment, he was watching me through the rearview mirror and seemed to be winking at me. His eyes glittered bright and teasing. Had I spoken out loud without meaning to? — I could feel my face burn.

Darren, squeezed against the farther armrest, made a sniggering, derisive noise. He had not so much as glanced at me when I climbed into the car and had been sulky during the drive so I felt that he did not like me. He was a fattish, flaccid-skinned boy who looked more like twelve than fourteen; he had Uncle Rebhorn's lard-colored complexion and full, drooping lips, but not Uncle Rebhorn's shrewd-glittering eyes; his were damp and close-set and mean. Whatever Darren meant by his snigger, Uncle Rebhorn heard it above the hum of the air conditioner — was there anything Uncle Rebhorn could not hear? — and said in a low, pleasant, warning voice, "Son, mind your manners! Or somebody else will mind them for you."

Darren protested, "I didn't say anything, sir. I —"

Quickly, Aunt Elinor intervened, "Darren."

"— I'm sorry, sir. I won't do it again."

Uncle Rebhorn chuckled as if he found this very funny and in some way preposterous. But by this time he had pulled the magnificent black car up in front of the portico of the house and switched off the ignition. "Here we are!"

But to enter Uncle Rebhorn's sandstone mansion, it was strange, and a little scary how we had to crouch. And push and squeeze our shoulders through the doorway. Even Audrey and me, who were the smallest. As we approached the big front door which was made of carved wood, with a beautiful gleaming brass American eagle, its dimensions seemed to shrink; the closer we got, the smaller the door got, reversing the usual circumstances where of course as you approach an object it increases size, or gives that illusion. "Girls, watch your heads," Uncle Rebhorn cautioned, wagging his forefinger. He had a brusque laughing way of speaking as if most subjects were jokes or could be made to seem so by laughing. But his eyes, bright as chips of glass, were watchful and without humor.

How could this be? — Uncle Rebhorn's house that was so spacious-seeming on the outside was so cramped, and dark, and scary on the inside?

"Come on, come on! It's Sunday, it's the Sabbath, we haven't got all day!" Uncle Rebhorn cried, clapping his hands.

We were in a kind of tunnel, crowded together. There was a strong smell of something sharp and hurtful like ammonia; at first I couldn't breathe, and started to choke. Nobody paid any attention to me except Audrey who tugged at my wrist, whispering, "This way, June — don't make Daddy mad." Uncle Rebhorn led the way, followed by Darren, then Aunt Elinor, Audrey, and me, walking on our haunches in a squatting position; the tunnel was too low for standing upright and you couldn't crawl on your hands and knees because the floor was littered with shards of glass. Why was it so dark? Where were the windows I'd seen from the outside? "Isn't this fun! We're so glad you could join us today, June!" Aunt Elinor murmured. How awkward it must have been for a woman like Aunt Elinor, so prettily dressed in a tulip-yellow summer knit suit, white high-heeled pumps, and stockings, to make her way on her haunches in such a cramped space! — yet she did it uncomplaining, and with a smile.

Strands of cobweb brushed against my face. I was breathing so hard and in such a choppy way it sounded like sobbing, which scared me because I knew Uncle Rebhorn would be offended. Several times Audrey squeezed my wrist so hard it hurt, cautioning me to be quiet; Aunt Elinor poked at me, too. Uncle Rebhorn was saying, cheerfully, "Who's hungry? — I'm starving," and again, in a louder voice, "Who's hungry?" and Darren echoed, "I'm starving!" and Uncle Rebhorn repeated bright and brassy as a TV commercial, *"Who's hungry?"* and this time Aunt Elinor, Darren, Audrey, and I echoed in a chorus, *"I'm starving!"* Which was the correct reply, Uncle Rebhorn accepted it with a happy chuckle.

Now we were in a larger space, the tunnel had opened out onto a room crowded with cartons and barrels, stacks of lumber and tar pots, workmen's things scattered about. There were two windows in this room but they were small and square and crudely criss-crossed by strips of plywood; there were no windowpanes, only fluttering strips of cheap transparent plastic that blocked out most of the light. I could not stop shivering though Audrey pinched me hard, and cast me an anxious, angry look. Why, when it was a warm summer day outside, was it so cold inside Uncle Rebhorn's house? Needles of freezing air rose from the floorboards. The sharp ammonia odor was mixed with a smell of food cooking which made my stomach queasy. Uncle Rebhorn was criticizing Aunt Elinor in his joky angry way, saying she'd let things go a bit, hadn't she? — and Aunt Elinor was frightened, stammering and pressing her hand against her bosom, saying the interior decorator had promised everything would be in place by now. "Plenty of time for Christmas, eh?" Uncle Rebhorn said sarcastically. For some reason, both Darren and Audrey giggled.

Uncle Rebhorn had a thick, strong neck and his head swiveled alertly and his eyes swung onto you before you were prepared — those gleaming, glassy-glittering eyes. There was a glisten to the whites of Uncle Rebhorn's eyes I had never seen in anyone before and his pupils were dilated and very black. He was a stocky man; he panted and made a snuffling noise, his wide nostrils flattened with deep, impatient inhalations. His pale skin was flushed, especially in the cheeks; there was a livid, feverish look to his face. He was dressed for Sunday in a red-plaid sport coat that fitted him tightly in the shoulders, and a white shirt with a necktie, and navy blue linen trousers that had picked up some cobwebs on our way in. Uncle Rebhorn had a glowing bald spot at the crown of his head over which he had carefully combed wetted strands of hair; his cheeks were bunched like muscles as he smiled. And smiled. How hard it was to look at Uncle Rebhorn, his eyes so glittering, and his *smile*—! When I try to remember him now miniature slices of blindness skid toward me ▮▮▮▮▮▮▮▮▮ in my vision, I have to blink carefully to regain my full sight. And why am I shivering, I must put an end to such neurotic behavior, what other purpose to this memoir? — what other purpose to any effort of the retrieval of memory that gives such pain?

Uncle Rebhorn chuckled deep in his throat and wagged a forefinger at me, "Naughty girl, I know what *you're* thinking," he said, and at once my face burned, I could feel my freckles standing out like hot inflamed pimples, though I did not know what he meant. Audrey, beside me, giggled again nervously, and Uncle Rebhorn shook his forefinger at her, too, "And you, honeybunch

— for sure, Daddy knows *you*." He made a sudden motion at us the way one might gesture at a cowering dog to further frighten it, or to mock its fear; when, clutching at each other, Audrey and I flinched away, Uncle Rebhorn roared with laughter, raising his bushy eyebrows as if he was puzzled, and hurt. "Mmmmm girls, you don't think I'm going to hit you, do you?"

Quickly Audrey stammered, "Oh no, Daddy — *no*."

I was so frightened I could not speak at all. I tried to hide behind Andrey who was shivering as badly as I was.

"You *don't* think I'm going to hit you, eh?" Uncle Rebhorn said, more menacingly; he swung his fist playfully in my direction and a strand of hair caught in his signet ring and I squealed with pain which made him laugh, and relent a little. Watching me, Darren and Audrey and even Aunt Elinor laughed. Aunt Elinor tidied my hair and again pressed a finger to her lips as if in warning.

I am not a naughty girl I wanted to protest and now too *I am not to blame.*

For Sunday dinner we sat on packing cases and ate from planks balanced across two sawhorses. A dwarfish olive-skinned woman with a single fierce eyebrow waited on us, wearing a white rayon uniform and a hairnet. She set plates down before us sulkily, though, with Uncle Rebhorn, who kept up a steady teasing banter with her, calling her "honey" and "sweetheart," she did exchange a smile. Aunt Elinor pretended to notice nothing, encouraging Audrey and me to eat. The dwarf-woman glanced at me with a look of contempt, guessing I was a poor relation I suppose, her dark eyes raked me like a razor.

Uncle Rebhorn and Darren ate hungrily. Father and son hunched over the improvised table in the same posture, bringing their faces close to their plates and, chewing, turning their heads slightly to the sides, eyes moist with pleasure. "Mmmmm! — good," Uncle Rebhorn declared. And Darren echoed, "— *good*." Aunt Elinor and Audrey were picking at their food, managing to eat some of it, but I was nauseated and terrified of being sick to my stomach. The food was lukewarm, served in plastic containers. There were coarse slabs of tough, bright pink meat curling at the edges and leaking blood, and puddles of corn pudding, corn kernels, and slices of onion and green pepper in a runny pale sauce like pus. Uncle Rebhorn gazed up from his plate, his eyes soft at first, then regaining some of their glassy glitter when he saw how little his wife and daughter and niece had eaten. "Say, what's up? 'Waste not, want not.'

Remember" — here he reached over and jabbed my shoulder with his fork — "this is the Sabbath, and keep it holy. Eh?"

Aunt Elinor smiled encouragingly at me. Her lipstick was crimson pink and glossy, a permanent smile; her hair was a shining pale blond like a helmet. She wore pretty pale-pink pearls in her ears and a matching necklace around her neck. In the car, she had seemed younger than my mother, but now, close up, I could see hairline creases in her skin, or actual cracks, as in glazed pottery; there was something out of focus in her eyes though she was looking directly at me. "June, dear, there is a hunger beyond hunger," she said softly, "and this is the hunger that must be reached."

Uncle Rebhorn added, emphatically, "And we're Americans. Remember *that.*"

Somehow, I managed to eat what was on my plate. *I am not a naughty girl but a good girl: see!*

For dessert, the dwarf-woman dropped bowls in front of us containing a quivering amber jelly. I thought it might be apple jelly, apple jelly with cinnamon, and my mouth watered in anticipation. We were to eat with spoons but my spoon wasn't sharp enough to cut into the jelly; and the jelly quivered harder, and wriggled in my bowl. Seeing the look on my face, Uncle Rebhorn asked pleasantly, "What's wrong now, Junie?" and I mumbled, "I don't know, sir," and Uncle Rebhorn chuckled, and said, "Hmmmm! You don't think your dessert is a *jellyfish,* do you?" — roaring with delight, as the others laughed, less forcefully, with him.

For that was exactly what it was: a jellyfish. Each of us had one, in our bowls. Warm and pulsing with life and fear radiating from it like raw nerves. ▆▆▆▆▆ ▆▆▆▆▆▆▆▆▆ flicking toward me, slivers of blindness. Unless fissures in the air itself? — fibrillations like those at the onset of sleep the way dreams begin to skid toward you — at you — into you — and there is no escape for the dream *is* you.

Yes I would like to cease my memoir here. I am not accustomed to writing, to selecting words with such care. When I speak, I often stammer but there is a comfort in that — nobody knows, what comfort! — for you hold back what you must say, hold it back until it is fully your own and cannot surprise you. *I am not to blame, I am not deserving of hurt neither then nor now* but do I believe this, even if I cannot succeed in having you believe it.

How can an experience belong to you if you cannot remember it? That is the extent of what I wish to know. If I cannot remember it, how then can

I summon it back to comprehend it, still less to change it. *And why am I shivering, when the sun today is poison-hot burning through the foliage dry and crackling as papier-mâché yet I keep shivering shivering shivering if there is a God in heaven please forgive me.*

After Sunday dinner we were to go sailing. Uncle Rebhorn had a beautiful white sailboat bobbing at the end of a dock, out there in the lake, which was a rich deep aqua blue scintillating with light. On Lake St. Clair on this breezy summer afternoon there were many sailboats, speedboats, yachts. I had stared at them in wondering admiration as we'd driven along the Lakeshore Drive. What a dazzling sight like nothing in Hamtramck!

First, though, we had to change our clothes. All of us, said Uncle Rebhorn, have to change into bathing suits.

Audrey and I changed in a dark cubbyhole beneath a stairway. This was Audrey's room and nobody was supposed to come inside to disturb us but the door was pushing inward and Audrey whimpered, "No, no Daddy," laughing nervously and trying to hold the door shut with her arm. I was a shy child; when I had to change for gym class at school I turned my back to the other girls and changed as quickly as I could. Even showing my panties to another girl was embarrassing to me, my face burned with a strange wild heat. Uncle Rebhorn was on the other side of the door, we could hear his harsh labored breathing. His voice was light, though, when he asked, "Hmmmm — d'you naughty little girls need any help getting your panties down? Or your bathing suits on?" "No, Daddy, please," Audrey said. Her eyes were wide and stark in her face and she seemed not aware of me any longer but in a space of her own, trembling, hunched over. I was scared, too, but thinking why don't we joke with Uncle Rebhorn, he wants us to joke with him, that's the kind of man he is, what harm could he do us? — the most any adult had ever done to me by the age of eleven was Grandpa tickling me a little too hard so I'd screamed with laughter and kicked but that was years ago when I'd been a baby practically, and while I had not liked being tickled it was nothing truly painful or scary — was it? I tried to joke with my uncle through the door, I was giggling saying, "No no no, you stay out of here, Uncle Rebhorn! We don't need your help no we don't!" There was a moment's silence, then Uncle Rebhorn chuckled appreciatively, but there came then suddenly the sound of Aunt Elinor's raised voice, and we heard a sharp slap, and a cry, a female cry immediately cut off. And the door ceased its inward movement, and Audrey shoved me whispering, "Hurry up! You dumb dope, hurry up!" So quickly — safely — we changed into our bathing suits.

It was a surprise, how by chance Audrey's and my bathing suits looked alike, and us like twin sisters in them: both were pretty shades of pink, with elasticized tops that fitted tight over our tiny, flat breasts. Mine had emerald green seahorses sewn onto the bodice and Audrey's had little ruffles, the suggestion of a skirt.

Seeing my face, which must have shown hurt, Audrey hugged me with her thin, cold arms. I thought she would say how much she liked me, I was her favorite cousin, she was happy to see me — but she didn't say anything at all.

Beyond the door Uncle Rebhorn was shouting and clapping his hands.

"C'mon move your sweet little asses! Chop-chop! Time's a-wastin'! There'll be hell to pay if we've lost the sun!"

Audrey and I crept out in our bathing suits and Aunt Elinor grabbed us by the hands making an annoyed "tsking" sound and pulling us hurriedly along. We had to push our way out of a small doorway — no more than an opening, a hole, in the wall — and then we were outside, on the back lawn of Uncle Rebhorn's property. What had seemed like lush green grass from a distance was synthetic grass, the kind you see laid out in flat strips on pavement. The hill was steep down to the dock, as if a giant hand was lifting it behind us, making us scramble. Uncle Rebhorn and Darren were trotting ahead, in matching swim trunks — gold trimmed in blue. Aunt Elinor had changed into a single-piece white satin bathing suit that exposed her bony shoulders and sunken chest; it was shocking to see her. She called out to Uncle Rebhorn that she wasn't feeling well — the sun had given her a migraine headache — sailing would make the headache worse — could she be excused? — but Uncle Rebhorn shouted over his shoulder, "You're coming with us, goddamn you! Why did we buy this frigging sailboat except to enjoy it?" Aunt Elinor winced, and murmured, "Yes, dear," and Uncle Rebhorn said, snorting, with a wink at Audrey and me, "Hmmm! It better be 'yes, dear,' you stupid cow-cunt."

By the time we crawled out onto the deck of the sailboat a chill wind had come up, and in fact the sun was disappearing like something being sucked down a drain. It was more like November than July, the sky heavy with clouds like stained concrete. Uncle Rebhorn said suddenly, "— bought this frigging sailboat to enjoy it for God's sake — for the family and that means *all the family*." The sailboat was lurching in the choppy water like a living, frantic thing as Uncle Rebhorn loosed us from the dock and set sail. "First mate! Look sharp! Where the hell are you, boy? Move your ass!" — Uncle Rebhorn kept up a constant barrage of commands at poor Darren who scampered to obey them, yanking at ropes that slipped from his fingers, trying to swing the heavy, sodden mainsail around. The wind seemed to come from several directions at once and the sails flapped and whipped helplessly. Darren did his best but he was clumsy and ill-coordinated and terrified of his father. His pudgy face had turned ashen, and his eyes darted wildly about; his gold swim trunks, which were made of a shiny material like rayon, fitted him so tightly a loose belt of fat protruded over the waistband and jiggled comically as, desperate to follow Uncle Rebhorn's instructions, Darren fell to one knee, pushed himself up, slipped and fell again, this time onto his belly on the slippery deck. Uncle Rebhorn, naked but for his swimming trunks and a visored sailor's cap jammed onto his head, shouted mercilessly, "Son, get *up*. Get that frigging sail to the wind or it's *mutiny!*"

The sailboat was now about thirty feet from the safety of the dock, careening and lurching in the water, which was nothing like the painted aqua water I had seen from shore; it was dark, metallic gray, and greasy, and very cold. Winds howled about us. There was no cabin in the sailboat, all was exposed, and Uncle Rebhorn had taken the only seat. I was terrified the sailboat would sink, or I would be swept off to drown in the water by wild, frothy waves washing across the deck. I had never been in any boat except rowboats with my parents in the Hamtramck Park lagoon. "Isn't this fun? Isn't it! Sailing is the most exciting —" Aunt Elinor shouted at me, with her wide fixed smile, but Uncle Rebhorn, seeing my white, pinched face, interrupted, "Nobody's going to drown today, least of all *you*. Ungrateful little brat!"

Aunt Elinor poked me, and smiled, pressing a finger to her lips. Of course, Uncle Rebhorn was just teasing.

For a few minutes it seemed as if the winds were filling our sails in the right way for the boat moved in a single unswerving direction. Darren was holding for dear life to a rope, to keep the mainsail steady. Then suddenly a dazzling white yacht sped by us, three times the size of Uncle Rebhorn's boat, dreamlike out of the flying spray, and in its wake Uncle Rebhorn's boat shuddered and lurched; there was a piercing, derisive sound of a horn — too late; the prow of the sailboat went under, freezing waves washed across the deck, the boat rocked crazily. I'd lost sight of Audrey and Aunt Elinor and was clutching a length of frayed rope with both hands, to keep myself from being swept overboard. How I whimpered with fear and pain! *This is your punishment, now you know you must be bad.* Uncle Rebhorn crouched at the prow of the boat, his eyes glittering in his flushed face, screaming commands at Darren who couldn't move fast enough to prevent the mainsail from suddenly swinging around, skimming over my head, and knocking Darren into the water.

Uncle Rebhorn yelled, "Son! Son!" With a hook at the end of a long wooden pole he fished about in the sudsy waves for my cousin, who sank like a bundle of sodden laundry; then surfaced again as a wave struck him from beneath and buoyed him upward; then sank again, this time beneath the lurching boat, his arms and legs flailing. I stared aghast, clutching at my rope. Audrey and Aunt Elinor were somewhere behind me, crying, "Help! Help!" Uncle Rebhorn ignored them, cursing as he scrambled to the other side of the boat, and swiping with the hook in the water until he snagged something and, blood vessels prominent as angry worms in his face, hauled Darren out of the water and onto the swaying deck. The hook had caught my cousin in the armpit, and streams of blood ran down his side. Was Darren alive? — I stared, I could not tell. Aunt Elinor was screaming hysterically. With deft, rough hands Uncle Rebhorn laid his son on his back, like a fat, pale fish, and stretched the boy's arms and legs out, and straddled Darren's hips and began to rock in a quickened rhythmic movement and to squeeze his rib cage, *squeeze and release! squeeze and release!* until driblets of foamy water and vomit began to be expelled from Darren's mouth, and, gasping and choking, the boy was breathing again. Tears of rage and sorrow streaked Uncle Rebhorn's flushed face. "You disappoint me, son! Son, you disappoint me! I, your dad who gave you life — you disappoint me!"

A sudden prankish gust of wind lifted Uncle Rebhorn's sailor cap off his head and sent it flying and spinning out into the misty depths of Lake St. Clair.

I have been counseled not to retrieve the past where it is ▮▮▮▮▮▮ blocked by ▮▮▮▮▮▮ like those frequent attacks of "visual impairment" (*not* blindness, the neurologist insists) but have I not a right to my own memories? to my own past? Why should that right be taken from me?

What are you frightened of, Mother, my children ask me, sometimes in merriment, what are *you* frightened of? — as if anything truly significant, truly frightening, could have happened, or could have been imagined to have happened, to me.

So I joke with them, I tease them saying, "Maybe — *you!*"

For in giving birth to them I suffered ████████ slivers of ████████ too, which for the most part I have forgotten ████████ as all wounds heal and pain is lost in time — isn't it?

What happened on that lost Sunday in July 1969 in Uncle Rebhorn's house in Grosse Pointe Shores is a true mystery never comprehended by the very person (myself) who experienced it. For at the center of it is an emptiness ████████ black rectangular emptiness ██████ skidding toward me like a fracturing of the air *and it is ticklish too, my shivering turns convulsive on the brink of wild leaping laughter.* I recall the relief that my cousin Darren did not drown and I recall the relief that we returned to the dock which was swaying and rotted but did not collapse, held firm as Uncle Rebhorn cast a rope noose to secure the boat. I know that we returned breathless and excited from our outing on Lake St. Clair and that Aunt Elinor said it was too bad no snapshots had been taken to commemorate my visit, and Uncle Rebhorn asked where the Polaroid camera was, why did Aunt Elinor never remember it for God's sake, their lives and happy times flying by and nobody recording them. I know that we entered the house and once again in the dark cubbyhole that was my cousin Audrey's room beneath the stairs we were changing frantically from our bathing suits which were soaking wet into our dry clothes and this time Aunt Elinor, still less Audrey, could not prevent the door from pushing open crying ████████ ████████ "Daddy, no!" and "No, please, Daddy!" until I was crying too and laughing screaming as a man's rough fingers ████ ran over my bare ribs bruising ████ the frizzy-wiry hairs of his chest and belly tickling my face ████ until what was beneath us which I had believed to be a floor fell away suddenly ████ dissolving like ████ water *I was not crying, I was not fighting I was a good girl: see?* ████████

Neil Gaiman is the Newbery Medal-winning author of *The Graveyard Book* and a *New York Times* bestseller, whose books have been made into major motion pictures including the recent *Coraline*. He is also famous for the "Sandman" graphic novel series, and for numerous other books and comics for adult, young adult, and younger readers. He has won the Hugo, Nebula, Mythopoeic, World Fantasy, and other awards. He is also the author of powerful short stories and poems. What he is *not* known for is visceral horror, although during his long, productive career, he has certainly written some, including this harrowing prose poem first published in 1996.

Eaten (Scenes from a Moving Picture)
Neil Gaiman

INT. WEBSTER'S OFFICE. DAY
As WEBSTER sits
reading the *LA Times*, MCBRIDE walks in
and tells in

FLASHBACK
how his SISTER came
to Hollywood eleven months ago
to make her fortune, and to meet the stars.
Of how he'd heard from friends that she'd "gone strange."
Imagining the needle, or far worse,
he travels out to Hollywood himself
and finds her standing underneath a bridge.
Her skin is pale. She screams at him "Get lost!"
and sobs and runs. A TALL MAN DRESSED IN BLACK
grabs hold his sleeve, tells him to let it drop
"Forget your sister," but of course he can't…

(IN SEPIA
we see the two as teens,
a YOUNG MCBRIDE and SISTER way back when,
giggles beneath the porch, "I'll show you mine,"
closer perhaps than siblings ought to be…
PAN UP
to watch a passing butterfly.
We hear them breathe and fumble in the dark:
IN CLOSE-UP now he spurts into her hand,

she licks her palm: first makes a face, then smiles...
HOLD on her lips and teeth and on her tongue).

END FLASHBACK
WEBSTER says he'll take the case,
says something flip and hard about LA,
like how it eats young girls and spits them out,
and takes a hundred dollars on account.

CUT TO
THE PURPLE PUSSY. INT. A DIVE,
THREE NAKED WOMEN dance for dollar bills.
WEBSTER comes in, and talks to one of them,
slips her a twenty, shows a photograph,
the stripper — standing close enough that he
could touch her (but they've bouncers on patrol,
weird steroid cases who will break your wrists) —
admits she thinks she knows the girl he means.
Then WEBSTER leaves.

INT. WEBSTER'S CONDO. NIGHT.
A video awaits him at his home.
It shows A WOMAN lovelier than life
Shot from the rib cage up (her breasts exposed)
Advising him to "let this whole thing drop,
forget it," promising she'll see him soon...

DISSOLVE TO
INT. MCBRIDE'S HOTEL ROOM. NIGHT.
MCBRIDE'S alone and lying on the bed,
He's watching soft-core porn on pay-per-view.
Naked. He rubs his cock with Vaseline,
lazy and slow, he doesn't want to come.
A BANG upon the window. He sits up,
flaccid and scared (he's on the second floor)
and opens up the window of his room.

HIS SISTER enters, looking almost dead,
implores him to forget her. He says no.
THE SISTER shambles over to the door.
A WOMAN DRESSED IN BLACK waits in the hall.
Brunette in leather, kinky as all hell,
who steps over the threshold with a smile.
And they have sex.

THE SISTER stands alone.
She watches as THE BRUNETTE takes MCBRIDE
(her skin's necrotic blue. She's fully dressed).
THE BRUNETTE gestures curtly with her hand,
off come THE SISTER'S clothes. She looks a mess.
Her skin's all scarred and scored; one nipple's gone.
She takes her gloves off and we see her hands:
Her fingers look like ribs, or chicken wings,
well chewed, and rescued from a garbage can —
dry bones with scraps of flesh and cartilage.
She puts her fingers in THE BRUNETTE'S mouth…
AND FADE TO BLACK.

INT. WEBSTER'S OFFICE. DAY.
THE PHONE RINGS. It's MCBRIDE. "Just drop the case.
I've found my sister, and I'm going home.
You've got five hundred dollars, and my thanks."
PULL BACK on WEBSTER, puzzled and confused.

MONTAGE of WEBSTER here. A week goes by,
we see him eating, pissing, drinking, drunk.
We watch him throw HIS GIRLFRIEND out of bed.
We see him play the video again…
The VIDEO GIRL stares at him and says
she'll see him soon. "I promise, Webster, soon."

CUT TO
THE PLACE OF EATERS, UNDERGROUND.

Pale people stand like cattle in a pen.
We see MCBRIDE. The flesh is off his chest.
White meat is good. We're looking through his ribs:
his heart is still. His lungs, however, breathe,
inflate, deflate. And tears of pus run down
his sunken cheeks. He pisses in the muck.
It doesn't steam. He wishes he were dead.
A DREAM:
As WEBSTER tosses in his bed.
He sees MCBRIDE, a corpse beneath a bridge,
all INTERCUT with lots of shots of food,
to make our theme explicit: this is art.

EXT. LA. DAY.
WEBSTER'S become obsessed.
He has to find the woman from the screen.
He beats somebody up, fucks someone else,
fixated on "I'll see you, Webster, soon."

He's thrown in prison. And they come for him,
THE MAN IN BLACK attending THE BRUNETTE.
Open his cell with keys, escort him out,
and leave the prison building. Through a door.
They walk him to the car park. They go down,
below the car park, deep beneath the town,
past shadowed writhing things that suck and hiss
and glossy things that laugh, and things that scream.
Now other feeder-folk are walking past...
They handcuff WEBSTER to A TINY MAN
who's covered with vaginas and with teeth,
and escorts WEBSTER to

THE QUEEN'S SALON.

(An interjection here: my wife awoke,
scared by an evil dream. "You hated me.

You brought these women home I didn't know,
but they knew me, and then we had a fight,
and after we had shouted you stormed out.
You said you'd find a girl to fuck and eat."

This scares me just a little. As we write
we summon little demons. So I shrug.)

The handcuffs are removed. He's left alone.
The hangings are red velvet, then they lift,
reveal THE QUEEN. We recognize her face,
the woman we saw on the VCR.
"The world divides so sweetly, neatly up
into the feeder-folk, into their prey."
That's what she says. Her voice is soft and sweet.
Imagine honey ants: the tiny head,
the chest, the tiny arms, the tiny hands,
and after that the bloat of honey-swell,
the abdomen enormous as it hangs
translucent, made of honey, sweet as lust.

THE QUEEN has quite a perfect little face,
her breasts are pale, blue-veined; her nipples pink;
her hands are white. But then, below her breasts
the whole swells like a whale or like a shrine,
a human honey ant, she's huge as rooms,
as elephants, as dinosaurs, as love.
Her flesh is opalescent, and she calls
poor WEBSTER to her. And he nods and comes.
(She must be over twenty-five feet long.)
She orders him to take off all his clothes.
His cock is hard. He shivers. He looks lost.
He moans "I'm harder than I've ever been."
Then, with her mouth, she licks and tongues his cock…

We linger here. The language of the eye

becomes a bland, unflinching, blowjob porn,
(her lips are glossy, and her tongue is red)
HOLD on her face. We hear him gasping "Oh.
Oh, baby. Yes. Oh. Take it in your mouth."
And then she opens up her mouth, and grins,
and bites his cock off.

Spurting blood pumps out
into her mouth. She hardly spills a drop.
We never do pan up to see his face,
just her. It's what they call the money shot.

Then, when his cock's gone down, and blood's congealed,
we see his face. He looks all dazed and healed.
Some feeders come and take him out of there.
Down in the pens he's chained beside MCBRIDE.
Deep in the mud lie carcasses picked clean
who grin at them and dream of being soup.

Poor things.

We're almost done.

We'll leave them there.

CUT to some lonely doorway, where A TRAMP
has three cold fingers up ANOTHER TRAMP,
they're starving but they fingerfuck like hell,
and underneath the layers of old clothes
beneath the cardboard, newspaper and cloth,
their genders are impossible to tell.

PAN UP

to watch a butterfly go past.
(ENDS)

Kelly Link is the author of three collections, *Stranger Things Happen*, *Magic for Beginners*, and *Pretty Monsters* (the last, for young adults). Her short stories have recently been published in *Tin House*, *Firebirds Rising*, *Noisy Outlaws*, *The Restless Dead*, *The Starry Rift*, and *Troll's Eye View*. Her work has won three Nebula Awards, as well as the Hugo, Locus, British Science Fiction, and World Fantasy awards. She once won a free trip around the world by answering the question "Why do you want to go around the world?" ("Because you can't go through it.") She and her husband Gavin J. Grant run Small Beer Press, and twice-yearly produce the 'zine *Lady Churchill's Rosebud Wristlet*.

Some people seem to believe that Link is an "overnight sensation," when, in fact, her science fiction, fantasy, horror, and sometimes unclassifiable stories have been published since 1988 and began attracting notice from the mid-'90s on. She is a consummate stylist, and over time, has attained remarkable control over structure.

"The Specialist's Hat," appearing herein, was published in 1998, winning the World Fantasy Award in 1999.

The Specialist's Hat
Kelly Link

"WHEN YOU'RE DEAD," Samantha says, "you don't have to brush your teeth…"

"When you're Dead," Claire says, "you live in a box, and it's always dark, but you're not ever afraid."

Claire and Samantha are identical twins. Their combined age is twenty years, four months, and six days. Claire is better at being Dead than Samantha.

The babysitter yawns, covering up her mouth with a long white hand. "I said to brush your teeth and that it's time for bed," she says. She sits crosslegged on the flowered bedspread between them. She has been teaching them a card game called Pounce, which involves three decks of cards, one for each of them. Samantha's deck is missing the Jack of Spades and the Two of Hearts, and Claire keeps on cheating. The babysitter wins anyway. There are still flecks of dried shaving cream and toilet paper on her arms. It is hard to tell how old she is — at first they thought she must be a grownup, but now she hardly looks older than them. Samantha has forgotten the babysitter's name.

Claire's face is stubborn. "When you're Dead," she says, "you stay up all night long."

"When you're dead," the babysitter snaps, "it's always very cold and damp, and you have to be very, very quiet or else the Specialist will get you."

"This house is haunted," Claire says.

"I know it is," the babysitter says. "I used to live here."

> Something is creeping up the stairs,
> Something is standing outside the door,
> Something is sobbing, sobbing in the dark;
> Something is sighing across the floor.

Claire and Samantha are spending the summer with their father, in the house called Eight Chimneys. Their mother is dead. She has been dead for exactly 282 days.

Their father is writing a history of Eight Chimneys and of the poet Charles Cheatham Rash, who lived here at the turn of the century, and who ran away to sea when he was thirteen, and returned when he was thirty-eight. He married, fathered a child, wrote three volumes of bad, obscure poetry, and an even worse and more obscure novel, *The One Who Is Watching Me Through the Window*, before disappearing again in 1907, this time for good. Samantha and Claire's father says that some of the poetry is actually quite readable and at least the novel isn't very long.

When Samantha asked him why he was writing about Rash, he replied that no one else had, and why didn't she and Samantha go play outside. When she pointed out that she was Samantha, he just scowled and said how could he be expected to tell them apart when they both wore blue jeans and flannel shirts, and why couldn't one of them dress all in green and the other in pink?

Claire and Samantha prefer to play inside. Eight Chimneys is as big as a castle, but dustier and darker than Samantha imagines a castle would be. There are more sofas, more china shepherdesses with chipped fingers, fewer suits of armor. No moat.

The house is open to the public, and, during the day, people — families — driving along the Blue Ridge Parkway will stop to tour the grounds and the first story; the third story belongs to Claire and Samantha. Sometimes they play explorers, and sometimes they follow the caretaker as he gives tours to visitors. After a few weeks, they have memorized his lecture, and they mouth it along with him. They help him sell postcards and copies of Rash's poetry to the tourist families who come into the little gift shop.

When the mothers smile at them and say how sweet they are, they stare back and don't say anything at all. The dim light in the house makes the mothers look pale and flickery and tired. They leave Eight Chimneys, mothers and families, looking not quite as real as they did before they paid their admissions, and of course Claire and Samantha will never see them again, so maybe they aren't real. Better to stay inside the house, they want to tell the families, and if you must leave, then go straight to your cars.

The caretaker says the woods aren't safe.

Their father stays in the library on the second story all morning, typing, and in the afternoon he takes long walks. He takes his pocket recorder along with him and a hip flask of Gentleman Jack, but not Samantha and Claire.

The caretaker of Eight Chimneys is Mr. Coeslak. His left leg is noticeably shorter than his right. He wears one stacked heel. Short black hairs grow out of his ears and his nostrils and there is no hair at all on top of his head, but he's given Samantha and Claire permission to explore the whole of the house. It was Mr. Coeslak who told them that there are copperheads in the woods, and that the house is haunted. He says they are all, ghosts and snakes, a pretty badtempered lot, and Samantha and Claire should stick to the marked trails, and stay out of the attic.

Mr. Coeslak can tell the twins apart, even if their father can't; Claire's eyes are grey, like a cat's fur, he says, but Samantha's are *gray*, like the ocean when it has been raining.

Samantha and Claire went walking in the woods on the second day that they were at Eight Chimneys. They saw something. Samantha thought it was a woman, but Claire said it was a snake. The staircase that goes up to the attic has been locked. They peeked through the keyhole, but it was too dark to see anything.

And so he had a wife, and they say she was real pretty. There was another man who wanted to go with her, and first she wouldn't, because she was afraid of her husband, and then she did. Her husband found out, and they say he killed a snake and got some of this snake's blood and put it in some whiskey and gave it to her. He had learned this from an island man who had been on a ship with him. And in about six months snakes created in her and they got between her meat and the skin. And they say you could just see them running up and down her legs. They say she was just hollow to the top of her body, and it kept on like that till she died. Now my daddy said he saw it.

— An Oral History of Eight Chimneys

Eight Chimneys is over two hundred years old. It is named for the eight chimneys that are each big enough that Samantha and Claire can both fit in one fireplace. The chimneys are red brick, and on each floor there are eight fireplaces, making a total of twenty-four. Samantha imagines the chimney stacks stretching like stout red tree trunks, all the way up through the slate roof of the house. Beside each fireplace is a heavy black firedog, and a set of wrought iron pokers shaped like snakes. Claire and Samantha pretend to duel with the snake-pokers before the fireplace in their bedroom on the third floor. Wind rises up the back of the chimney. When they stick their faces in, they can feel the air rushing damply upwards, like a river. The flue smells old and sooty and wet, like stones from a river.

Their bedroom was once the nursery. They sleep together in a poster bed which resembles a ship with four masts. It smells of mothballs, and Claire kicks in her sleep. Charles Cheatham Rash slept here when he was a little boy, and also his daughter. She disappeared when her father did. It might have been gambling debts. They may have moved to New Orleans. She was fourteen years old, Mr. Coeslak said. What was her name, Claire asked. What happened to her mother, Samantha wanted to know. Mr. Coeslak closed his eyes in an almost wink. Mrs. Rash had died the year before her husband and daughter disappeared, he said, of a mysterious wasting disease. He can't remember the name of the poor little girl, he said.

Eight Chimneys has exactly one hundred windows, all still with the original wavery panes of handblown glass. With so many windows, Samantha thinks, Eight Chimneys should always be full of light, but instead the trees press close against the house, so that the rooms on the first and second story — even the third-story rooms — are green and dim, as if Samantha and Claire are living deep under the sea. This is the light that makes the tourists into ghosts. In the morning, and again towards evening, a fog settles in around the house. Sometimes it is grey like Claire's eyes, and sometimes it is gray, like Samantha's eyes.

I met a woman in the wood,
Her lips were two red snakes.
She smiled at me, her eyes were lewd
And burning like a fire.

A few nights ago, the wind was sighing in the nursery chimney. Their father had already tucked them in and turned off the light. Claire dared Samantha to stick her head into the fireplace, in the dark, and so she did. The cold wet air licked at her face and it almost sounded like voices talking low, muttering. She couldn't quite make out what they were saying.

Their father has mostly ignored Claire and Samantha since they arrived at Eight Chimneys. He never mentions their mother. One evening they heard him shouting in the library, and when they came downstairs, there was a large sticky stain on the desk, where a glass of whiskey had been knocked over. It was

Darkness: Two Decades of Modern Horror

looking at me, he said, through the window. It had orange eyes.

Samantha and Claire refrained from pointing out that the library is on the second story.

At night, their father's breath has been sweet from drinking, and he is spending more and more time in the woods, and less in the library. At dinner, usually hot dogs and baked beans from a can, which they eat off of paper plates in the first floor dining room, beneath the Austrian chandelier (which has exactly 632 leaded crystals shaped like teardrops), their father recites the poetry of Charles Cheatham Rash, which neither Samantha nor Claire cares for.

He has been reading the ship diaries that Rash kept, and he says that he has discovered proof in them that Rash's most famous poem, "The Specialist's Hat," is not a poem at all, and in any case, Rash didn't write it. It is something that one of the men on the whaler used to say, to conjure up a whale. Rash simply copied it down and stuck an end on it and said it was his.

The man was from Mulatuppu, which is a place neither Samantha nor Claire has ever heard of. Their father says that the man was supposed to be some sort of magician, but he drowned shortly before Rash came back to Eight Chimneys. Their father says that the other sailors wanted to throw the magician's chest overboard, but Rash persuaded them to let him keep it until he could be put ashore, with the chest, off the coast of North Carolina.

> *The specialist's hat makes a noise like an agouti;*
> *The specialist's hat makes a noise like a collared peccary;*
> *The specialist's hat makes a noise like a white-lipped peccary;*
> *The specialist's hat makes a noise like a tapir;*
> *The specialist's hat makes a noise like a rabbit;*
> *The specialist's hat makes a noise like a squirrel;*
> *The specialist's hat makes a noise like a curassow;*
> *The specialist's hat moans like a whale in the water;*
> *The specialist's hat moans like the wind in my wife's hair;*
> *The specialist's hat makes a noise like a snake;*
> *I have hung the hat of the specialist upon my wall.*

The reason that Claire and Samantha have a babysitter is that their father met a woman in the woods. He is going to see her tonight, and they are going to have a picnic supper and look at the stars. This is the time of year when the Perseids can be seen, falling across the sky on clear nights. Their father said that he has been walking with the woman every afternoon. She is a distant relation of Rash and besides, he said, he needs a night off and some grownup conversation.

Mr. Coeslak won't stay in the house after dark, but he agreed to find someone to look after Samantha and Claire. Then their father couldn't find Mr. Coeslak, but the babysitter showed up precisely at seven o'clock. The babysitter, whose name neither twin quite caught, wears a blue cotton dress with short floaty sleeves. Both Samantha and Claire think she is pretty in an old-fashioned sort of way.

They were in the library with their father, looking up Mulatuppu in the red leather atlas, when she arrived. She didn't knock on the front door, she simply walked in and then up the stairs, as if she knew where to find them.

Their father kissed them goodbye, a hasty smack, told them to be good and he would take them into town on the weekend to see the Disney film. They went to the window to watch as he walked into the woods. Already it was getting dark and there were fireflies, tiny yellow-hot sparks in the air. When their father had entirely disappeared into the trees, they turned around and stared at the babysitter instead. She raised one eyebrow. "Well," she said. "What sort of games do you like to play?"

Widdershins around the chimneys,
Once, twice, again.
The spokes click like a clock on the bicycle;
They tick down the days of the life of a man.

First they played Go Fish, and then they played Crazy Eights, and then they made the babysitter into a mummy by putting shaving cream from their father's bathroom on her arms and legs, and wrapping her in toilet paper. She is the best babysitter they have ever had.

At nine-thirty, she tried to put them to bed. Neither Claire nor Samantha wanted to go to bed, so they began to play the Dead game. The Dead game is a let's pretend that they have been playing every day for 274 days now, but never in front of their father or any other adult. When they are Dead, they are allowed to do anything they want to. They can even fly by jumping off the nursery bed, and just waving their arms. Someday this will work, if they practice hard enough.

The Dead game has three rules.

One. Numbers are significant. The twins keep a list of important numbers in a green address book that belonged to their mother. Mr. Coeslak's tour has been a good source of significant amounts and tallies: they are writing a tragical history of numbers.

Two. The twins don't play the Dead game in front of grownups. They have been summing up the babysitter, and have decided that she doesn't count. They tell her the rules.

Three is the best and most important rule. When you are Dead, you don't have to be afraid of anything. Samantha and Claire aren't sure who the Specialist is, but they aren't afraid of him.

To become Dead, they hold their breath while counting to thirty-five, which is as high as their mother got, not counting a few days.

"You never lived here," Claire says. "Mr. Coeslak lives here."

"Not at night," says the babysitter. "This was my bedroom when I was little."

"Really?" Samantha says. Claire says, "Prove it."

The babysitter gives Samantha and Claire a look, as if she is measuring them: how old, how smart, how brave, how tall. Then she nods. The wind is in the flue, and in the dim nursery light they can see the milky strands of fog seeping out of the fireplace. "Go stand in the chimney," she instructs them. "Stick your hand as far up as you can, and there is a little hole on the left side, with a key in it."

Samantha looks at Claire, who says, "Go ahead." Claire is fifteen minutes and some few uncounted seconds older than Samantha, and therefore gets to tell Samantha what to do. Samantha remembers the muttering voices and then reminds herself that she is Dead. She goes over to the fireplace and ducks inside.

When Samantha stands up in the chimney, she can only see the very edge of the room. She can see the fringe of the mothy blue rug, and one bed leg, and beside it, Claire's foot, swinging back and forth like a metronome. Claire's shoelace has come undone and there is a Band-Aid on her ankle. It all looks very pleasant and peaceful from inside the chimney, like a dream, and for a moment she almost wishes she didn't have to be Dead. But it's safer, really.

She sticks her left hand up as far as she can reach, trailing it along the crumbly wall, until she feels an indentation. She thinks about spiders and severed fingers, and rusty razorblades, and then she reaches inside. She keeps her eyes lowered, focused on the corner of the room and Claire's twitchy foot.

Inside the hole, there is a tiny cold key, its teeth facing outward. She pulls it out, and ducks back into the room. "She wasn't lying," she tells Claire.

"Of course I wasn't lying," the babysitter says. "When you're Dead, you're not allowed to tell lies."

"Unless you want to," Claire says.

> *Dreary and dreadful beats the sea at the shore.*
> *Ghastly and dripping is the mist at the door.*
> *The clock in the hall is chiming one, two, three, four.*
> *The morning comes not, no, never, no more.*

Samantha and Claire have gone to camp for three weeks every summer since they were seven. This year their father didn't ask them if they wanted to go back and, after discussing it, they decided that it was just as well. They didn't want to have to explain to all their friends how they were half-orphans now. They are used to being envied, because they are identical twins. They don't want to be pitiful.

It has not even been a year, but Samantha realizes that she is forgetting what her mother looked like. Not her mother's face so much as the way she smelled, which was something like dry hay, and something like Chanel No. 5, and like something else too. She can't remember whether her mother had gray eyes, like her, or grey eyes, like Claire. She doesn't dream about her mother anymore, but she does dream about Prince Charming, a bay whom she once rode in the horse show at her camp. In the dream, Prince Charming did not smell like a horse at all. He smelled like Chanel No. 5. When she is Dead, she can have all the horses she wants, and they all smell like Chanel No. 5.

"Where does the key go to?" Samantha says.

The babysitter holds out her hand. "To the attic. You don't really need it, but taking the stairs is easier than the chimney. At least the first time."

"Aren't you going to make us go to bed?" Claire says.

The babysitter ignores Claire. "My father used to lock me in the attic when I was little, but I didn't mind. There was a bicycle up there and I used to ride it around and around the chimneys until my mother let me out again."

Do you know how to ride a bicycle?"

"Of course," Claire says.

"If you ride fast enough, the Specialist can't catch you."

"What's the Specialist?" Samantha says. Bicycles are okay, but horses can go faster.

"The Specialist wears a hat," says the babysitter. "The hat makes noises." She doesn't say anything else.

> *When you're dead, the grass is greener*
> *Over your grave. The wind is keener.*
> *Your eyes sink in, your flesh decays. You*
> *Grow accustomed to slowness; expect delays.*

The attic is somehow bigger and lonelier than Samantha and Claire thought it would be. The babysitter's key opens the locked door at the end of the hallway, revealing a narrow set of stairs. She waves them ahead and upwards.

It isn't as dark in the attic as they had imagined. The oaks that block the light and make the first three stories so dim and green and mysterious during the day, don't reach all the way up. Extravagant moonlight, dusty and pale, streams in the angled dormer windows. It lights the length of the attic, which is wide enough to hold a softball game in, and lined with trunks where Samantha imagines people could sit, could be hiding and watching. The ceiling slopes down, impaled upon the eight thickwaisted chimney stacks. The chimneys seem too alive, somehow, to be contained in this empty, neglected place; they thrust almost angrily through the roof and attic floor. In the moonlight they look like they are breathing. "They're so beautiful," she says.

"Which chimney is the nursery chimney?" Claire says.

The babysitter points to the nearest righthand stack. "That one," she says. "It runs up through the ballroom on the first floor, the library, the nursery."

Hanging from a nail on the nursery chimney is a long black object. It looks lumpy and heavy, as if it were full of things. The babysitter takes it down, twirls it on her finger. There are holes in the black thing and it whistles mournfully as she spins it. "The Specialist's hat," she says.

"That doesn't look like a hat," says Claire. "It doesn't look like anything at all." She goes to look through the boxes and trunks that are stacked against the far wall.

"It's a special hat," the babysitter says. "It's not supposed to look like anything. But it can sound like anything you can imagine. My father made it."

"Our father writes books," Samantha says.

"My father did too." The babysitter hangs the hat back on the nail. It curls blackly against the chimney. Samantha stares at it. It nickers at her. "He was a bad poet, but he was worse at magic."

Last summer, Samantha wished more than anything that she could have a horse. She thought she would have given up anything for one — even being a twin was not as good as having a horse. She still doesn't have a horse, but she doesn't have a mother either, and she can't help wondering if it's her fault. The hat nickers again, or maybe it is the wind in the chimney.

"What happened to him?" Claire asks.

"After he made the hat, the Specialist came and took him away. I hid in the nursery chimney while it was looking for him, and it didn't find me."

"Weren't you scared?"

There is a clattering, shivering, clicking noise. Claire has found the babysitter's bike and is dragging it towards them by the handlebars. The babysitter shrugs. "Rule number three," she says.

Claire snatches the hat off the nail. "I'm the Specialist!" she says, putting the hat on her head. It falls over her eyes, the floppy shapeless brim sewn with little asymmetrical buttons that flash and catch at the moonlight like teeth. Samantha looks again and sees that they are teeth. Without counting, she suddenly knows that there are exactly fifty-two teeth on the hat, and that they are the teeth of agoutis, of curassows, of white-lipped peccaries, and of the wife of Charles Cheatham Rash. The chimneys are moaning, and Claire's voice booms hollowly beneath the hat. "Run away, or I'll catch you and eat you!"

Samantha and the babysitter run away, laughing as Claire mounts the rusty, noisy bicycle and pedals madly after them. She rings the bicycle bell as she rides, and the Specialist's hat bobs up and down on her head. It spits like a cat. The bell is shrill and thin, and the bike wails and shrieks. It leans first towards the right and then to the left. Claire's knobby knees stick out on either side like makeshift counterweights.

Claire weaves in and out between the chimneys, chasing Samantha and the babysitter. Samantha is slow, turning to look behind. As Claire approaches, she keeps one hand on the handlebars and stretches the other hand out towards Samantha. Just as she is about to grab Samantha, the babysitter turns back and plucks the hat off Claire's head.

"Shit!" the babysitter says, and drops it. There is a drop of blood forming on the fleshy part of the babysitter's hand, black in the moonlight, where the Specialist's hat has bitten her.

Claire dismounts, giggling. Samantha watches as the Specialist's hat rolls away. It picks up speed, veering across the attic floor, and disappears, thumping down the stairs. "Go get it," Claire says. "You can be the Specialist this time."

"No," the babysitter says, sucking at her palm. "It's time for bed."

When they go down the stairs, there is no sign of the Specialist's hat. They brush their teeth, climb into the ship-bed, and pull the covers up to their necks. The babysitter sits between their feet. "When you're Dead," Samantha says, "do you still get tired and have to go to sleep? Do you have dreams?"

"When you're Dead," the babysitter says, "everything's a lot easier. You don't have to do anything that you don't want to. You don't have to have a name, you don't have to remember. You don't even have to breathe."

She shows them exactly what she means.

When she has time to think about it (and now she has all the time in the world to think), Samantha realizes with a small pang that she is now stuck indefinitely between ten and eleven years old, stuck with Claire and the babysitter. She considers this. The number 10 is pleasing and round, like a beach ball, but all in all, it hasn't been an easy year. She wonders what 11 would have been like. Sharper, like needles maybe. She has chosen to be Dead, instead. She hopes that she's made the right decision. She wonders if her mother would have decided to be Dead, instead of dead, if she could have.

Last year they were learning fractions in school, when her mother died. Fractions remind Samantha of herds of wild horses, piebalds and pintos and palominos. There are so many of them, and they are, well, fractious and unruly. Just when you think you have one under control, it throws up its head and tosses you off. Claire's favorite number is 4, which she says is a tall, skinny boy. Samantha doesn't care for boys that much. She likes numbers. Take the number 8 for instance, which can be more than one thing at once. Looked at one way, 8 looks like a bent woman with curvy hair. But if you lay it down on its side, it looks like a snake curled with its tail in its mouth. This is sort of like the difference between being Dead and being dead. Maybe when Samantha is tired of one, she will try the other.

On the lawn, under the oak trees, she hears someone calling her name. Samantha climbs out of bed and goes to the nursery window. She looks out through the wavy glass. It's Mr. Coeslak. "Samantha, Claire!" he calls up to her. "Are you all right? Is your father there?" Samantha can almost see the moonlight shining through him. "They're always locking me in the tool room. Goddamn spooky things," he says. "Are you there, Samantha? Claire? Girls?"

The babysitter comes and stands beside Samantha. The babysitter puts her finger to her lip. Claire's eyes glitter at them from the dark bed. Samantha doesn't say anything, but she waves at Mr. Coeslak. The babysitter waves too. Maybe he can see them waving, because after a little while he stops shouting and goes away. "Be careful," the babysitter says. "*He'll* be coming soon. It will be coming soon."

She takes Samantha's hand, and leads her back to the bed, where Claire is waiting. They sit and wait. Time passes, but they don't get tired, they don't get any older.

Who's there?
Just air.

The front door opens on the first floor, and Samantha, Claire, and the babysitter can hear someone creeping, creeping up the stairs. "Be quiet," the babysitter says. "It's the Specialist."

Samantha and Claire are quiet. The nursery is dark and the wind crackles like a fire in the fireplace.

"Claire, Samantha, Samantha, Claire?" The Specialist's voice is blurry and wet. It sounds like their father's voice, but that's because the hat can imitate any noise, any voice. "Are you still awake?"

"Quick," the babysitter says. "It's time to go up to the attic and hide."

Claire and Samantha slip out from under the covers and dress quickly and silently. They follow her. Without speech, without breathing, she pulls them into the safety of the chimney. It is too dark to see, but they understand the babysitter perfectly when she mouths the word, *Up.* She goes first, so they can see where the finger-holds are, the bricks that jut out for their feet. Then Claire. Samantha watches her sister's foot ascend like smoke, the shoelace still untied.

"Claire? Samantha? Goddammit, you're scaring me. Where are you?" The

Specialist is standing just outside the half-open door. "Samantha? I think I've been bitten by something. I think I've been bitten by a goddamn snake." Samantha hesitates for only a second. Then she is climbing up, up, up the nursery chimney.

Gene Wolfe is best known for his Book of the New Sun series and his tetralogy *The Book of the Long Sun*. He also wrote the trilogy *The Book of the Short Sun*, and many stand alone novels including *Pirate Freedom* and *An Evil Guest*. He has won the World Fantasy Award, the Nebula Award, and the Locus Award multiple times for his work, and also won the World Fantasy Life Achievement Award.

He has also written some amazing shorter fiction, including the inter-connected trio of novellas called *The Fifth Head of Cerberus* and the stories in his several collections, the most recent being *The Best of Gene Wolfe: A Definitive Retrospective of His Finest Short Fiction*.

"The Tree Is My Hat," originally published in the anthology *999* edited by Al Sarrantonio, shows off Wolfe's imaginative short fiction at its most exotic and perhaps its strangest.

The Tree Is My Hat
Gene Wolfe

30 JAN. I saw a strange stranger on the beach this morning. I had been swimming in the little bay between here and the village; that may have had something to do with it, although I did not feel tired. Dived down and thought I saw a shark coming around the big staghorn coral. Got out fast. The whole swim cannot have been more than ten minutes. Ran out of the water and started walking.

There it is. I have begun this journal at last. (Thought I never would.) So let us return to all the things I ought to have put in and did not. I bought this the day after I came back from Africa.

No, the day I got out of the hospital — I remember now. I was wandering around, wondering when I would have another attack, and went into a little shop on Forty-second Street. There was a nice-looking woman in there, one of those good-looking black women, and I thought it might be nice to talk to her, so I had to buy something. I said, "I just got back from Africa."

She: "Really. How was it?" Me: "Hot."

Anyway, I came out with this notebook and told myself I had not wasted my money because I would keep a journal, writing down my attacks, what I had been doing and eating, as instructed; but all I could think of was how she looked when she turned to go to the back of the shop. Her legs and how she held her head. Her hips.

After that I planned to write down everything I remember from Africa, and what we said if Mary returned my calls. Then it was going to be about this assignment.

31 JAN. Setting up my new Mac. Who would think this place would have phones? But there are wires to Kololahi, and a dish. I can chat with people all over the world, for which the agency pays. (Talk about soft!) Nothing like this in Africa. Just the radio, and good luck with that.

I was full of enthusiasm. "A remote Pacific island chain." Wait…

P. D.: "Baden, we're going to send you to the Takanga Group."

No doubt I looked blank.

"It's a remote Pacific island chain." She cleared her throat and seemed to have swallowed a bone. "It's not going to be like Africa, Bad. You'll be on your own out there."

Me: "I thought you were going to fire me."

P. D.: "No, no! We wouldn't do that."

"Permanent sick leave."

"No, no, no! But, Bad." She leaned across her desk and for a minute I was afraid she was going to squeeze my hand. "This will be rough. I'm not going to try to fool you."

Hah!

Cut to the chase. This is nothing. This is a bungalow with rotten boards in the floors that has been here since before the British pulled out, a mile from the village and less than half that from the beach, close enough that the Pacific-smell is in all the rooms. The people are fat and happy, and my guess is not more than half are dumb. (Try and match that around Chicago.) Once or twice a year one gets yaws or some such, and Rev. Robbins gives him arsenic. *Which cures it.* Pooey!

There are fish in the ocean, plenty of them. Wild fruit in the jungle, and they know which you can eat. They plant yams and breadfruit, and if they need money or just want something, they dive for pearls and trade them when Jack's boat comes. Or do a big holiday boat trip to Kololahi.

There are coconuts too, which I forgot. They know how to open them. Or perhaps I am just not strong enough yet. (I look in the mirror, and ugh.) I used to weigh two hundred pounds.

"You skinny," the king says. "Ha, ha, ha!" He is really a good guy, I think. He has a primitive sense of humor, but there are worse things. He can take a jungle chopper (we said *upanga* but they say *heletay*) and open a coconut like a pack of gum. I have coconuts and a heletay but I might as well try to open them with a spoon.

1 Feb. Nothing to report except a couple of wonderful swims. I did not swim at all for the first couple of weeks. There are sharks. I know they are really out there because I have seen them once or twice. According to what I was told,

there are saltwater crocs, too, up to fourteen feet long. I have never seen any of those and am skeptical, although I know they have them in Queensland. Every so often you hear about somebody who was killed by a shark, but that does not stop the people from swimming all the time, and I do not see why it should stop me. Good luck so far.

2 Feb. Saturday. I was supposed to write about the dwarf I saw on the beach that time, but I never got the nerve. Sometimes I used to see things in the hospital. Afraid it may be coming back. I decided to take a walk on the beach. All right, did I get sunstroke?

Pooey.

He was just a little man, shorter even than Mary's father. He was too small for any adult in the village. He was certainly not a child, and was too pale to have been one of the islanders at all.

He cannot have been here long; he was whiter than I am.

Rev. Robbins will know — ask tomorrow.

3 Feb. Hot and getting hotter. Jan. is the hottest month here, according to Rob Robbins. Well, I got here the first week in Jan. and it has never been this hot.

Got up early while it was still cool. Went down the beach, to the village. (Stopped to have a look at the rocks where the dwarf disappeared.) Waited around for the service to begin but could not talk to Rob, he was rehearsing the choir — "Nearer My God to Thee."

Half the village came, and the service went on for almost two hours. When it was over I was able to get Rob alone. I said if he would drive us into Kololahi I would buy our Sunday dinner. (He has a jeep.) He was nice, but no — too far and the bad roads. I told him I had personal troubles I wanted his advice on, and he said, "Why don't we go to your place, Baden, and have a talk? I'd invite you for lemonade, but they'd be after me every minute."

So we walked back. It was hotter than hell, and this time I tried not to look. I got cold Cokes out of my rusty little fridge, and we sat on the porch (Rob calls it the veranda) and fanned ourselves. He knew I felt bad about not being able to do anything for these people, and urged patience. My chance would come.

I said, "I've given up on that, Reverend."

(That was when he told me to call him Rob. His first name is Mervyn.) "Never give up, Baden. Never." He looked so serious I almost laughed.

"All right, I'll keep my eyes open, and maybe someday the Agency will send me someplace where I'm needed."

"Back to Uganda?"

I explained that the A.O.A.A. almost never sends anyone to the same area twice. "That wasn't really what I wanted to talk to you about. It's my personal life. Well, really two things, but that's one of them. I'd like to get back together with my ex-wife. You're going to advise me to forget it, because I'm here and she's in Chicago; but I can send E-mail, and I'd like to put the bitterness behind us."

"Were there children? Sorry, Baden. I didn't intend it to hurt."

I explained how Mary had wanted them and I had not, and he gave me some advice. I have not E-mailed yet, but I will tonight after I write it out here.

"You're afraid that you were hallucinating. Did you feel feverish?" He got out his thermometer and took my temperature, which was nearly normal. "Let's look at it logically, Baden. This island is a hundred miles long and about thirty miles at the widest point. There are eight villages I know of. The population of Kololahi is over twelve hundred."

I said I understood all that.

"Twice a week, the plane from Cairns brings new tourists."

"Who almost never go five miles from Kololahi."

"Almost never, Baden. Not never. You say it wasn't one of the villagers. All right, I accept that. Was it me?"

"Of course not."

"Then it was someone from outside the village, someone from another village, from Kololahi, or a tourist. Why shake your head?"

I told him.

"I doubt there's a leprosarium nearer than the Marshalls. Anyway, I don't know of one closer. Unless you saw something else, some other sign of the disease, I doubt that this little man you saw had leprosy. It's a lot more likely that you saw a tourist with pasty white skin greased with sun blocker. As for his disappearing, the explanation seems pretty obvious. He dived off the rocks into the bay."

"There wasn't anybody there. I looked."

"There wasn't anybody there you saw, you mean. He would have been up to his neck in water, and the sun was glaring on the water, wasn't it?"

"I suppose so."

"It must have been. The weather's been clear." Rob drained his Coke and pushed it away. "As for his not leaving footprints, stop playing Sherlock Holmes.

That's harsh, I realize, but I say it for your own good. Footprints in soft sand are shapeless indentations at best."

"I could see mine."

"You knew where to look. Did you try to backtrack yourself? I thought not. May I ask a few questions? When you saw him, did you think he was real?"

"Yes, absolutely. Would you like another one? Or something to eat?"

"No, thanks. When was the last time you had an attack?"

"A bad one? About six weeks."

"How about a not-bad one?"

"Last night, but it didn't amount to much. Two hours of chills, and it went away."

"That must have been a relief. No, I see it wasn't. Baden, the next time you have an attack, severe or not, I want you to come and see me. Understand?"

I promised.

"This is Bad. I still love you. That's all I have to say, but I want to say it. I was wrong, and I know it. I hope you've forgiven me." And sign off.

4 FEB. Saw him again last night, and he has pointed teeth. I was shaking under the netting, and he looked through the window and smiled. Told Rob, and said I read somewhere that cannibals used to file their teeth. I know these people were cannibals three or four generations back, and I asked if they had done it. He thinks not but will ask the king.

"I have been very ill, Mary, but I feel better now. It is evening here, and I am going to bed. I love you. Good night. I love you." Sign off.

5 FEB. Two men with spears came to take me to the king: I asked if I was under arrest, and they laughed. No ha, ha, ha from His Majesty this time, though. He was in the big house, but he came out and we went some distance among hardwoods the size of office buildings smothered in flowering vines, stopping in a circle of stones: the king, the men with spears, and an old man with a drum. The men with spears built a fire, and the drum made soft sounds like waves while the king made a speech or recited a poem, mocked all the while by invisible birds with eerie voices.

When the king was finished, he hung this piece of carved bone around my neck. While we were walking back to the village, he put his arm around me, which surprised me more than anything. He is bigger than a tackle in the NFL, and must weigh four hundred pounds. It felt like I was carrying a calf.

Horrible, *horrible* dreams! Swimming in boiling blood. Too scared to sleep anymore. Logged on and tried to find something on dreams and what they mean. Stumbled onto a witch in L.A. — her home page, then the lady herself. (I'll get you and your little dog too!) Actually, she seemed nice.

Got out the carved bone thing the king gave me. Old, and probably ought to be in a museum, but I suppose I had better wear it as long as I stay here, at least when I go out. Suppose I were to offend him? He might sit on me! Seems to be a fish with pictures scratched into both sides. More fish, man in a hat, etc. Cord through the eye. Wish I had a magnifying glass.

6 FEB. Still haven't gone back to bed, but my watch says Wednesday. Wrote a long E-mail, typing it in as it came to me. Told her where I am and what I'm doing, and begged her to respond. After that I went outside and swam naked in the moonlit sea. Tomorrow I want to look for the place where the king hung this fish charm on me. Back to bed.

Morning, and beautiful. Why has it taken me so long to see what a beautiful place this is? (Maybe my heart just got back from Africa.) Palms swaying forever in the trade winds, and people like heroic bronze statues. How small, how stunted and pale we have to look to them!

Took a real swim to get the screaming out of my ears. Will I laugh in a year when I see that I said my midnight swim made me understand these people better? Maybe I will. But it did. They have been swimming in the moon like that for hundreds of years.

E-mail! God bless E-mail and whoever invented it! Just checked mine and found I had a message. Tried to guess who it might be. I wanted Mary, and was about certain it would be from the witch, from Annys. Read the name and it was "Julius R. Christmas." Pops! Mary's Pops! Got up and ran around the room, so excited I could not read it. Now I have printed it out, and I am going to copy it here.

"She went to Uganda looking for you, Bad. Coming back tomorrow, Kennedy,

AA 47 from Heathrow. I'll tell her where you are. Watch out for those hula-hula girls."

SHE WENT TO UGANDA LOOKING FOR ME

7 Feb. More dreams — little man with pointed teeth smiling through the window. I doubt that I should write it all down, but I knew (in the dream) that he hurt people, and he kept telling me he would not hurt me. Maybe the first time was a dream too. More screams.

Anyway, I talked to Rob again yesterday afternoon, although I had not planned on it. By the time I got back here I was too sick to do anything except lie on the bed. The worst since I left the hospital, I think.

Went looking for the place the king took me to. Did not want to start from the village, kids might have followed me, so I tried to circle and come at it from the other side. Found two old buildings, small and no roofs, and a bone that looked human. More about that later. Did not see any marks, but did not look for them either. It was black on one end like it had been in a fire, though.

Kept going about three hours and wore myself out. Tripped on a chunk of stone and stopped to wipe off the sweat, and Blam! I was there! Found the ashes and where the king and I stood. Looked around wishing I had my camera, and there was Rob, sitting up on four stones that were still together and looking down at me. I said, "Hey, why didn't you say something?"

And he said, "I wanted to see what you would do." So he had been spying on me; I did not say it, but that was what it was.

I told him about going there with the king, and how he gave me a charm. I said I was sorry I had not worn it, but anytime he wanted a Coke I would show it to him.

"It doesn't matter. He knows you're sick, and I imagine he gave you something to heal you. It might even work, because God hears all sorts of prayers. That's not what they teach in the seminary, or even what it says in the Bible. But I've been out in the missions long enough to know. When somebody with good intentions talks to the God who created him, he's heard. Pretty often the answer is yes. Why did you come back here?"

"I wanted to see it again, that's all. At first I thought it was just a circle of rocks, then when I thought about it, it seemed like it must have been more."

Rob kept quiet; so I explained that I had been thinking of Stonehenge.

Stonehenge was a circle of big rocks, but the idea had been to look at the positions of certain stars and where the sun rose. But this could not be the same kind of thing, because of the trees. Stonehenge is out in the open on Salisbury Plain. I asked if it was some kind of temple.

"It was a palace once, Baden." Rob cleared his throat. "If I tell you something about it in confidence, can you keep it to yourself?"

I promised.

"These are good people now. I want to make that clear. They seem a little childlike to us, as all primitives do. If we were primitives ourselves — and we were, Bad, not so long ago — they wouldn't. Can you imagine how they'd seem to us if they didn't seem a little childlike?"

I said, "I was thinking about that this morning before I left the bungalow."

Rob nodded. "Now I understand why you wanted to come back here. The Polynesians are scattered all over the South Pacific. Did you know that? Captain Cook, a British naval officer, was the first to explore the Pacific with any thoroughness, and he was absolutely astounded to find that after he'd sailed for weeks his interpreter could still talk to the natives. We know, for example, that Polynesians came down from Hawaii in sufficient numbers to conquer New Zealand. The historians hadn't admitted it the last time I looked, but it's a fact, recorded by the Maori themselves in their own history. The distance is about four thousand miles."

"Impressive."

"But you wonder what I'm getting at. I don't blame you. They're supposed to have come from Malaya originally. I won't go into all the reasons for thinking that they didn't, beyond saying that if it were the case they should be in New Guinea and Australia, and they're not."

I asked where they had come from, and for a minute or two he just rubbed his chin; then he said, "I'm not going to tell you that either. You wouldn't believe me, so why waste breath on it? Think of a distant land, a mountainous country with buildings and monuments to rival ancient Egypt's, and gods worse than any demon Cotton Mather could have imagined. The time…" He shrugged. "After Moses but before Christ."

"Babylon?"

He shook his head. "They developed a ruling class, and in time those rulers, their priest and warriors, became something like another race, bigger and stronger than the peasants they treated like slaves. They drenched the altars of their gods with blood, the blood of enemies when they could capture enough, and the blood of peasants when they couldn't. Their peasants rebelled and drove them from the mountains to the sea, and into the sea."

I think he was waiting for me to say something; but I kept quiet, thinking over what he had said and wondering if it were true.

"They sailed away in terror of the thing they had awakened in the hearts of the nation that had been their own. I doubt very much if there were more than a few thousand, and there may well have been fewer than a thousand. They learned seamanship, and learned it well. They had to. In the ancient world they were the only people to rival the Phoenicians, and they surpassed even the Phoenicians."

I asked whether he believed all that, and he said, "It doesn't matter whether I believe it, because it's true."

He pointed to one of the stones. "I called them primitives, and they are. But they weren't always as primitive as they are now. This was a palace, and there are ruins like this all over Polynesia, great buildings of coral rock falling to pieces. A palace and thus a sacred place, because the king was holy, the gods' representative. That was why he brought you here."

Rob was going to leave, but I told him about the buildings I found earlier and he wanted to see them. "There is a temple, too, Baden, although I've never been able to find it. When it was built, it must have been evil beyond our imagining…." He grinned then, surprising hell out of me. "You must get teased about your name."

"Ever since elementary school. It doesn't bother me." But the truth is it does, sometimes.

More later.

Well, I have met the little man I saw on the beach, and to tell the truth (what's the sense of one of these if you are not going to tell the truth?) I like him. I am going to write about all that in a minute.

Rob and I looked for the buildings I had seen when I was looking for the palace but could not find them. Described them, but Rob did not think they were the temple he has been looking for since he came. "They know where it is. Certainly the older people do. Once in a while I catch little oblique references to it. Not jokes. They joke about the place you found, but not about that."

I asked what the place I had found had been.

"A Japanese camp. The Japanese were here during World War Two."

I had not known that.

"There were no battles. They built those buildings you found, presumably, and they dug caves in the hills from which to fight. I've found some of those myself. But the Americans and Australians simply bypassed this island, as they did many other islands. The Japanese soldiers remained here, stranded. There must have been about a company, originally."

"What happened to them?"

"Some surrendered. Some came out of the jungle to surrender and were killed. A few held out, twenty or twenty-five, from what I've heard. They left their caves and went back to the camp they had built when they thought Japan would win and control the entire Pacific. That was what you found, I believe, and that's why I'd like to see it."

I said I could not understand how we could have missed it, and he said, "Look at this jungle, Baden. One of those buildings could be within ten feet of us."

After that we went on for another mile or two and came out on the beach. I did not know where we were, but Rob did. "This is where we separate. The village is that way, and your bungalow the other way, beyond the bay."

I had been thinking about the Japs, and asked if they were all dead, and he said they were. "They were older every year and fewer every year, and a time came when the rifles and machine guns that had kept the villages in terror no longer worked. And after that, a time when the people realized they didn't. They went to the Japanese camp one night with their spears and war clubs. They killed the remaining Japanese and ate them, and sometimes they make sly little jokes about it when they want to get my goat."

I was feeling pretty rocky and knew I was in for a bad time, so I came back here. I was sick the rest of the afternoon and all night, chills, fever, headache, the works. I remember watching the little vase on the bureau get up and walk to the other side, and sit back down, and seeing an American in a baseball cap float in. He took off his cap and combed his hair in front of the mirror, and floated back out. It was a Cardinals cap.

Now about Hanga, the little man I see on the beach.

After I wrote all that about the palace, I wanted to ask Rob a couple of questions and tell him Mary was coming. All right, no one has actually said she was, and so far I have heard nothing from her directly, only the one E-mail from Pops. But she went to Africa, so why not here? I thanked Pops and told him where I am again. He knows how much I want to see her. If she comes, I am going to ask Rob to re-marry us, if she will.

Started down the beach, and I saw him; but after half a minute or so he seemed to melt into the haze. I told myself I was still seeing things, and I was still sick; and I reminded myself that I promised to go by Rob's mission next time I felt bad. But when I got to the end of the bay, there he was, perfectly real, sitting in the shade of one of the young palms. I wanted to talk to him, so I said, "Okay if I sit down, too? This sun's frying my brains."

He smiled (the pointed teeth are real) and said, "The tree is my hat."

I thought he just meant the shade, but after I sat he showed me, biting off a palm frond and peeling a strip from it, then showing me how to peel them and weave them into a rough sort of straw hat, with a high crown and a wide brim.

We talked a little, although he does not speak English as well as some of the others. He does not live in the village, and the people who do, do not like him although he likes them. They are afraid of him, he says, and give him things because they are. They prefer he stay away. "No village, no boat."

I said it must be lonely, but he only stared out to sea. I doubt that he knows the word.

He wanted to know about the charm the king gave me. I described it and asked if it brings good luck. He shook his head. "No *malhoi.*" Picking up a single palm fiber, "This *malhoi.*" Not knowing what *malhoi* meant, I was in no position to argue.

That is pretty much all, except that I told him to visit when he wants company; and he told me I must eat fish to restore my health. (I have no idea who told him I am ill sometimes, but I never tried to keep it a secret.) Also that I would never have to fear an attack (I think that must have been what he meant) while he was with me.

His skin is rough and hard, much lighter in color than the skin of my forearm, but I have no idea whether that is a symptom or a birth defect. When I got up to leave, he stood too, and came no higher than my chest. Poor little man.

One more thing. I had not intended to put it down, but after what Rob said maybe I should. When I had walked some distance toward the village, I turned back to wave to Hanga, and he was gone. I walked back, thinking that the shade of the palm had fooled me; he was not there. I went to the bay, thinking he was in the water as Rob suggested. It is a beautiful little cove, but Hanga was not there, either. I am beginning to feel sympathy for the old mariners. These islands vanished when they approached.

At any rate, Rob says that *malhoi* means "strong." Since a palm fiber is not as strong as a cotton thread, there must be something wrong somewhere. (More likely, something I do not understand.) Maybe the word has more than one meaning.

Hanga means "shark," Rob says, but he does not know my friend Hanga. Nearly all the men are named for fish.

More E-mail, this time the witch. "There is danger hanging over you. I feel it and know some higher power guided you to me. Be careful. Stay away from places of worship, my tarot shows trouble for you there. Tell me about the fetish you mentioned."

I doubt that I should, and that I will E-mail her again.

9 FEB. I guess I wore myself out on writing Thursday. I see I wrote nothing yesterday. To tell the truth, there was nothing to write about except my swim in Hanga's bay. And I cannot write about that in a way that makes sense. Beautiful beyond description. That is all I can say. To tell the truth, I am afraid to go back. Afraid I will be disappointed. No spot on earth, even under the sea, can be as lovely as I remember it. Colored coral, and the little sea-animals that look like flowers, and schools of blue and red and orange fish like live jewels.

Today when I went to see Rob (all right, Annys warned me; but I think she is full of it) I said he probably likes to think God made this beautiful world so we could admire it; but if He had, He would have given us gills.

"Do I also think that He made the stars for us, Baden? All those flaming suns hundreds and thousands of light-years away? Did God create whole galaxies so that once or twice in our lives we might chance to look up and glimpse them?"

When he said that I had to wonder about people like me, who work for the federal government. Would we be driven out someday, like the people Rob talked about? A lot of us do not care any more about ordinary people than they did. I know P. D. does not.

A woman who had cut her hand came in about then. Rob talked to her in her own language while he treated her, and she talked a good deal more, chattering away. When she left I asked whether he had really understood everything she said. He said, "I did and I didn't. I knew all the words she used, if that's what you mean. How long have you been here now, Baden?"

I told him and he said, "About five weeks? That's perfect. I've been here about five years. I don't speak as well as they do. Sometimes I have to stop to think of the right word, and sometimes I can't think of it at all. But I understand when I hear them. It's not an elaborate language. Are you troubled by ghosts?"

I suppose I gawked.

"That was one of the things she said. The king has sent for a woman from another village to rid you of them, a sort of witch-doctress, I imagine. Her name is Langitokoua."

I said the only ghost bothering me was my dead marriage's, and I hoped to resuscitate it with his help.

He tried to look through me and may have succeeded; he has that kind of eyes. "You still don't know when Mary's coming?"

I shook my head.

"She'll want to rest a few days after her trip to Africa. I hope you're allowing for that."

"And she'll have to fly from Chicago to Los Angeles, from Los Angeles to Melbourne, and from there to Cairns, after which she'll have to wait for the next plane to Kololahi. Believe me, Rob, I've taken all that into consideration."

"Good. Has it occurred to you that your little friend Hanga might be a ghost? I mean, has it occurred to you since you spoke to him?"

Right then, I had that "what am I doing here" feeling I used to get in the bush. There I sat in that bright, flimsy little room with the medicine smell, and a jar of cotton balls at my elbow, and the noise of the surf coming in the window, about a thousand miles from anyplace that matters; and I could not remember the decisions I had made and the plans that had worked or not worked to get me there:

"Let me tell you a story, Baden. You don't have to believe it. The first year I was here, I had to go to town to see about some building supplies we were buying. As things fell out, there was a day there when I had nothing to do, and I decided to drive up to North Point. People had told me it was the most scenic part of the island, and I convinced myself I ought to see it. Have you ever been there?"

I had not even heard of it.

"The road only goes as far as the closest village. After that there's a footpath that takes two hours or so. It really is beautiful, rocks standing above the waves, and dramatic cliffs overlooking the ocean. I stayed there long enough to get the lovely, lonely feel of the place and make some sketches. Then I hiked back to the village where I'd left the jeep and started to drive back to Kololahi. It was almost dark.

"I hadn't gone far when I saw a man from our village walking along the road. Back then I didn't know everybody, but I knew him. I stopped, and we chatted for a minute. He said he was on his way to see his parents, and I thought they must live in the place I had just left. I told him to get into the jeep, and drove back, and let him out. He thanked me over and over, and when I got out to look at one of the tires I was worried about, he hugged me and kissed my eyes. I've never forgotten that."

I said something stupid about how warmhearted the people here are.

"You're right, of course. But, Baden, when I got back, I learned that North Point is a haunted place. It's where the souls of the dead go to make their farewell to the land of the living. The man I'd picked up had been killed by a shark the day I left, four days before I gave him a ride."

I did not know what to say, and at last I blurted out, "They lied to you. They had to be lying."

"No doubt — or I'm lying to you. At any rate, I'd like you to bring your friend Hanga here to see me if you can."

I promised I would try to bring Rob to see Hanga, since Hanga will not go into the village.

Swimming in the little bay again. I never thought of myself as a strong swimmer, never even had much chance to swim, but have been swimming like a dolphin, diving underwater and swimming with my eyes open for what has got to be two or two and a half minutes if not longer. Incredible! My God, wait till I show Mary!

You can buy scuba gear in Kololahi. I'll rent Rob's jeep or pay one of the men to take me in his canoe.

11 Feb. I let this slide again, and need to catch up. Yesterday was very odd. So was Saturday.

After I went to bed (still full of Rob's ghost story and the new world underwater) and *crash!* Jumped up scared as hell, and my bureau had fallen on its face. Dry rot in the legs, apparently. A couple of drawers broke, and stuff scattered all over.

I propped it back up and started cleaning up the mess, and found a book I never saw before, *The Light Garden of the Angel King,* about traveling through Afghanistan. In front is somebody's name and a date, and "American Overseas Assistance Agency." None of it registered right then.

But there it was, spelled out for me. And here is where he was, Larry Scribble. He was an Agency man, had bought the book three years ago (when he was posted to Afghanistan, most likely) and brought it with him when he was sent here. I only use the top three drawers, and it had been in one of the others and got overlooked when somebody (who?) cleared out his things.

Why was he gone when I got here? He should have been here to brief me, and stayed for a week or so. No one has so much as mentioned his name, and there must be a reason for that.

Intended to go to services at the mission and bring the book, but was sick again. Hundred and nine. Took medicine and went to bed, too weak to move, and had this very strange dream. Somehow I knew somebody was in the house. (I suppose steps, although I cannot remember any.) Sat up, and there was Hanga smiling by my bed. "I knock. You not come."

I said, "I'm sorry. I've been sick." I felt fine. Got up and offered to get him a Coke or something to eat, but he wanted to see the charm. I said sure, and got it off the bureau.

He looked at it, grunting and tracing the little drawings on its sides with his forefinger. "No tie? You take loose?" He pointed to the knot.

I said there was no reason to, that it would go over my head without untying the cord.

"Want friend?" He pointed to himself, and it was pathetic. "Hanga friend? Bad friend?"

"Yes," I said. "Absolutely."

"Untie."

I said I would cut the cord if he wanted me to.

"Untie, please. Blood friend." (He took my arm then, repeating, "Blood friend!")

I said all right and began to pick at the knot, which was complex; and at that moment, I swear, I heard someone else in the bungalow, some third person who pounded on the walls. I believe I would have gone to see who it was then, but Hanga was still holding my arm. He has big hands on those short arms, with a lot of strength in them.

In a minute or two I got the cord loose and asked if he wanted it, and he said eagerly that he did. I gave it to him, and there was one of those changes you get in dreams. He straightened up, and was at least as tall as I am. Holding my arm, he cut it quickly and neatly with his teeth and licked the blood, and seemed to grow again. It was as if some sort of defilement had been wiped away. He looked intelligent and almost handsome.

Then he cut the skin of his own arm just like mine. He offered it to me, and I licked his blood like he had licked mine. For some reason I expected it to taste horrible, but it did not; it was as if I had gotten seawater in my mouth while I was swimming.

"We are blood friends now, Bad," Hanga told me. "I shall not harm you, and you must not harm me."

That was the end of the dream. The next thing I remember is lying in bed and smelling something sweet, while something tickled my ear. I thought the mosquito netting had come loose, and looked to see, and there was a woman with a flower in her hair lying beside me. I rolled over; and she, seeing that I was awake, embraced and kissed me.

She is Langitokoua, the woman Rob told me the king had sent for, but I call her Langi. She says she does not know how old she is, and is fibbing. Her size (she is about six feet tall, and must weigh a good two-fifty) makes her look older than she is, I feel sure. Twenty-five, maybe. Or seventeen. I asked her about ghosts, and she said very matter-of-factly that there is one in the house but he means no harm.

Pooey.

After that, naturally I asked her why the king wanted her to stay with me; and she solemnly explained that it is not good for a man to live by himself, that a man should have someone to cook and sweep, and take care of him when he is ill. That was my chance, and I went for it. I explained that I am expecting a woman from America soon, that American women are jealous, and that I would have to tell the American woman Langi was there to nurse me. Langi agreed without any fuss.

What else?

Hanga's visit was a dream, and I know it; but it seems I was sleepwalking.

(Perhaps I wandered around the bungalow delirious.) The charm was where I left it on the dresser, but the cord was gone. I found it under my bed and tried to put it back through the fish's eye, but it will not go.

E-mail from Annys: "The hounds of hell are loosed. For heaven's sake be careful. Benign influences rising, so have hope." Crazy if you ask me.

E-mail from Pops: "How are you? We haven't heard from you. Have you found a place for Mary and the kids? She is on her way."

What kids? Why, the old puritan!

Sent a long E-mail back saying I had been very ill but was better, and there were several places where Mary could stay, including this bungalow, and I would leave the final choice to her. In fairness to Pops, he has no idea where or how I live, and may have imagined a rented room in Kololahi with a monkish cot. I should send another E-mail asking about her flight from Cairns; I doubt he knows, but it may be worth a try.

Almost midnight, and Langi is asleep. We sat on the beach to watch the sunset, drank rum-and-Coke and rum-and-coconut-milk when the Coke ran out, looked at the stars, talked, and made love. Talked some more, drank some more, and made love again.

There. I had to put that down. Now I have to figure out where I can hide this so Mary never sees it. I will not destroy it and I will not lie. (Nothing is worse than lying to yourself. *Nothing*. I ought to know.)

Something else in the was-it-a-dream category, but I do not think it was. I was lying on my back in the sand, looking up at the stars with Langi beside me asleep; and I saw a UFO. It was somewhere between me and the stars, sleek, dark, and torpedo-shaped, but with a big fin on the back, like a rocket ship in an old comic. Circled over us two or three times, and was gone. Haunting, though.

It made me think. Those stars are like the islands here, only a million billion times bigger. Nobody really knows how many islands there are, and there are probably a few to this day that nobody has ever been on. At night they look up at the stars and the stars look down on them, and they tell each other, "They're coming!"

Langi's name means "sky sister" so I am not the only one who ever thought like that.

Found the temple!!! Even now I cannot believe it. Rob has been looking for it for five years, and I found it in six weeks. God, but I would love to tell him!

Which I cannot do. I gave Langi my word, so it is out of the question.

We went swimming in the little bay. I dove down, showing her corals and things that she has probably been seeing since she was old enough to walk, and she showed the temple to me. The roof is gone if it ever had one, and the walls are covered with coral and the sea creatures that look like flowers; you can hardly see it unless somebody shows you. But once you do it is all there, the long straight walls, the main entrance, the little rooms at the sides, everything. It is as if you were looking at the ruins of a cathedral, but they were decked in flowers and bunting for a fiesta. (I know that is not clear, but it is what it was like, the nearest I can come.) They built it on land, and the water rose; but it is still there. It looks hidden, not abandoned. Too old to see, and too big.

I will never forget this: How one minute it was just rocks and coral, and the next it was walls and altar, with a fifty-foot branched coral like a big tree growing right out of it. Then an enormous gray-white shark with eyes like a man's came out of the shadow of the coral tree to look at us, worse than a lion or a leopard. My god, was I ever scared!

When we were both back up on the rocks, Langi explained that the shark had not meant to harm us, that we would both be dead if it had. (I cannot argue with that.) Then we picked flowers, and she made wreaths out of them and threw them in the water and sang a song. Afterward she said it was all right for me to know, because we are us; but I must never tell other *mulis*. I promised faithfully that I would not.

She has gone to the village to buy groceries. I asked her whether they worshipped Rob's God in the temple underwater. (I had to say it like that for her to understand.) She laughed and said no, they worshiped the shark god so the sharks would not eat them. I have been thinking about that.

It seems to me that they must have brought other gods from the mountains where they lived, a couple of thousand years ago, and they settled here and built that temple to their old gods. Later, probably hundreds of years later, the sea came up and swallowed it. Those old gods went away, but they left the sharks to guard their house. Someday the water will go down again. The ice will grow thick and strong on Antarctica once more, the Pacific will recede, and those murderous old mountain gods will return. That is how it seems to me, and if it is true I am glad I will not be around to see it.

I do not believe in Rob's God, so logically I should not believe in them either. But I do. It is a new millennium, but we are still playing by the old rules. They are going to come to teach us the new ones, or that is what I am afraid of.

Valentine's Day. Mary passed away. That is how Mom would have said it, and I have to say it like that, too. Print it. I cannot make these fingers print the other yet.

Can anybody read this?

Langi and I had presented her with a wreath of orchids, and she was wearing them. It was so fast, so crazy.

So much blood, and Mary and kids screaming.

I had better backtrack or give this up altogether.

There was a boar hunt. I did not go, remembering how sick I had been after tramping through the jungle with Rob, but Langi and I went to the pig roast afterward. Boar hunting is the men's favorite pastime; she says it is the only thing that the men like better than dancing. They do not have dogs and do not use bows and arrows. It is all a matter of tracking, and the boars are killed with spears when they find them, which must be really dangerous. I got to talk to the king about this hunt, and he told me how they get the boar they want to a place where it cannot run away anymore. It turns then and defies them, and may charge; but if it does not, four or five men all throw their spears at once. It was the king's spear, he said, that pierced the heart of this boar.

Anyway it was a grand feast with pineapples and native beer, and my rum, and lots of pork. It was nearly morning by the time we got back here, where Mary was asleep with Mark and Adam.

Which was a very good thing, since it gave us a chance to swim and otherwise freshen up. By the time they woke up, Langi had prepared a fruit tray breakfast and woven the orchids, and I had picked them for her and made coffee. Little boys, in my experience, are generally cranky in the morning (could it be because we do not allow them coffee?) but Adam and Mark were sufficiently overwhelmed by the presence of a brown lady giant and a live skeleton that conversation was possible. They are fraternal twins, and I think they really are mine; certainly they look very much like I did at their age. The wind had begun to rise, but we thought nothing of it.

"Were you surprised to see me?" Mary was older than I remembered, and had the beginnings of a double chin.

"Delighted. But Pops told me you'd gone to Uganda, and you were on your way here."

"To the end of the earth." (She smiled, and my heart leaped.) "I never realized the end would be as pretty as this."

I told her that in another generation the beach would be lined with condos.

"Then let's be glad that we're in this one." She turned to the boys. "You have to take in everything as long as we're here. You'll never get another chance like this."

I said, "Which will be a long time, I hope."

"You mean that you and...?"

"Langitokoua." I shook my head. (Here it was, and all my lies had melted away.) "Was I ever honest with you, Mary?"

"Certainly. Often."

"I wasn't, and you know it. So do I. I've got no right to expect you to believe me now. But I'm going to tell you, and myself, God's own truth. It's in remission now. Langi and I were able to go to a banquet last night, and eat, and talk to people, and enjoy ourselves. But when it's bad, it's horrible. I'm too sick to do anything but shake and sweat and moan, and I see things that aren't there. I —"

Mary interrupted me, trying to be kind. "You don't look as sick as I expected."

"I know how I look. My mirror tells me every morning while I shave. I look like death in a microwave oven, and that's not very far from the truth. It's liable to kill me this year. If it doesn't, I'll probably get attacks on and off for the rest of my life, which is apt to be short."

There was a silence that Langi filled by asking whether the boys wanted some coconut milk. They said they did, and she got my heletay and showed them how to open a green coconut with one chop. Mary and I stopped talking to watch her, and that's when I heard the surf. It was the first time that the sound of waves hitting the beach had ever reached as far inland as my bungalow.

Mary said, "I rented a Range Rover at the airport." It was the tone she used when she had to bring up something she really did not want to bring up.

"I know. I saw it."

"It's fifty dollars a day, Bad, plus mileage. I won't be able to keep it long."

I said, "I understand."

"We tried to phone. I had hoped you would be well enough to come for us, or send someone."

I said I would have had to borrow Rob's jeep if I had gotten her call.

"I wouldn't have known where you were, but we met a native, a very handsome man who says he knows you. He came along to show us the way." (At that point, the boys' expressions told me something was seriously wrong.) "He wouldn't take any money for it. Was I wrong to offer to pay him? He didn't seem angry."

"No," I said, and would have given anything to get the boys alone. But would it have been different if I had? When I read this, when I really get to where I can face it, the thing I will miss on was how fast it was — how fast the whole thing went. It cannot have been an hour between the time Mary woke up and the time Langi ran to the village to get Rob.

Mark lying there whiter than the sand. So thin and white, and looking just like me.

"He thought you were down on the beach, and wanted us to look for you there, but we were too tired," Mary said.

That is all for now, and in fact it is too much. I can barely read this left-handed printing, and my stump aches from holding down the book. I am going to go to bed, where I will cry, I know, and Langi will cuddle me like a kid.

Again tomorrow.

17 FEB. Hospital sent its plane for Mark, but no room for us. Doctor a lot more interested in my disease than my stump. "Dr. Robbins" did a fine job there, he said. We will catch the Cairns plane Monday.

I should catch up. But first: I am going to steal Rob's jeep tomorrow. He will not lend it, does not think I can drive. It will be slow, but I know I can.

19 FEB. Parked on the tarmac, something wrong with one engine. Have I got up nerve enough to write about it now? We will see.

Mary was telling us about her guide, how good-looking, and all he told her about the islands, lots I had not known myself. As if she were surprised she had not seen him sooner, she pointed and said, "Here he is now."

There was nobody there. Or rather, there was nobody Langi and I or the boys could see. I talked to Adam (to my son Adam, I have to get used to that) when it was over, while Rob was working on Mark and Mary. I had a bunch of surgical gauze and had to hold it as tight as I could. There was no strength left in my hand.

Adam said Mary had stopped and the door opened, and she made him get in back with Mark. *The door opened by itself.* That is the part he remembers most clearly, and the part of his story I will always remember, too. After that Mary seemed to be talking all the time to somebody he and his brother could not see or hear.

She screamed, and there, for just an instant, was the shark. He was as big as a boat, and the wind was like a current in the ocean, blowing us down to the water. I really do not see how I can ever explain this.

No takeoff yet, so I have to try. It is easy to say what was not happening. What is hard is saying what was, because there are no words. The shark was not swimming in air. I know that is what it will sound like, but it (he) was not. We were not under the water, either. We could breathe and walk and run just as he could swim, although not nearly so fast, and even fight the current a little.

The worst thing of all was he came and went and came and went, so that it seemed almost that we were running or fighting him by flashes of lightning, and sometimes he was Hanga, taller than the king and smiling at me while he herded us.

No. The most worst thing was really that he was herding everybody but me. He drove them toward the beach the way a dog drives sheep, Mary, Langi, Adam, and Mark, and he would have let me escape. (I wonder sometimes why I did not. This was a new me, a me I doubt I will ever see again.)

His jaws were real, and sometimes I could hear them snap when I could not see him. I shouted, calling him by name, and I believe I shouted that he was breaking our agreement, that to hurt my wives and my sons was to hurt me. To give the devil his due, I do not think he understood. The old gods are very wise, as the king told me today; still, there are limits to their understanding.

I ran for the knife, the heletay Langi opened coconuts with. I thought of the boar, and by God I charged them. I must have been terrified. I do not remember, only slashing at something and someone huge that was and was not there, and in an instant was back again. The sting of the wind-blown sand,

and then up to my arms in foaming water, and cutting and stabbing, and the hammerhead with my knife and my hand in its mouth.

We got them all out, Langi and I did. But Mark has lost his leg, and jaws three feet across had closed on Mary. That was Hanga himself, I feel sure.

Here is what I think. I think he could only make one of us see him at a time, and that was why he flashed in and out. He is real. (God knows he is real!) Not really physical the way a stone is, but physical in other ways that I do not understand. Physical like and unlike light and radiation. He showed himself to each of us, each time for less than a second.

Mary wanted children, so she stopped the pill and did not tell me. That was what she told me when I drove Rob's jeep out to North Point. I was afraid. Not so much afraid of Hanga (though there was that, too) but afraid she would not be there. Then somebody said "Banzai!" It was exactly as if he were sitting next to me in the jeep, except that there was nobody there. I said "Banzai" back, and I never heard him again; but after that I knew I would find her, and I waited for her at the edge of the cliff.

She came back to me when the sun touched the Pacific, and the darker the night and the brighter the stars, the more real she was. Most of the time it was as if she were really in my arms. When the stars got dim and the first light showed in the east, she whispered, "I have to go," and walked over the edge, walking north with the sun to her right and getting dimmer and dimmer.

I got dressed again and drove back and it was finished. That was the last thing Mary ever said to me, spoken a couple of days after she died.

She was not going to get back together with me at all; then she heard how sick I was in Uganda, and she thought the disease might have changed me. (It has. What does it matter about people at the "end of the earth" if you cannot be good to your own people, most of all to your own family?)

Taking off.
We are airborne at last. Oh, Mary! Mary starlight!

Langi and I will take Adam to his grandfather's, then come back and stay with Mark (Brisbane or Melbourne) until he is well enough to come home.

The stewardess is serving lunch, and for the first time since it happened, I think I may be able to eat more than a mouthful. One stewardess, twenty or thirty people, which is all this plane will hold. News of the shark attack is driving tourists off the island.

As you see, I can print better with my left hand. I should be able to write eventually. The back of my right hand itches, even though it is gone. I wish I could scratch it.

Here comes the food.

An engine has quit. Pilot says no danger.

He is out there, swimming beside the plane. I watched him for a minute or more until he disappeared into a thunderhead. "The tree is my hat." Oh, God.

Oh my God!

My blood brother.

What can I do?

Steve Rasnic Tem has had recent stories in *Asimov's*, *Interzone*, and *Postscripts*. His latest novel, written in collaboration with wife Melanie Tem, is *The Man on the Ceiling*, built around their award-winning novella of the same title. A collection of all his story collaborations with Melanie Tem, *In Concert*, is forthcoming from Centipede Press. Also, Speaking Volumes (www.speakingvolumes.us) is bringing out *Invisible*, a six CD audio collection of some of his relatively recent stories, most of which are previously uncollected.

Tem is a prolific and inspired short story writer who is always finding new ways to pierce the mystery and sometimes pain of familial relationships. In "Heat" a terrible loss foments obsession.

Heat
Steve Rasnic Tem

IGNITION POINT, THE minimum temperature for burning. She knew the temperature at which paper would burn because of that book by Bradbury. She did not know the right temperature for the combustion of flesh. Whenever she asked her doctor he just shook his head, patted her shoulder. For her part, she did not tell him about the things she saw when she looked out his window. Or the way his office smelled of char.

"Just tell me about whatever pops into your head," he said, smiling. She found herself wondering how much internal body heat was used to make a smile.

But "a calorie is the amount of heat required to raise the temperature of one gram of water one degree Centigrade," is what she replied.

He looked at her appraisingly. She wondered how much heat he used to suppress his initial reaction and to reconsider his words. "And that is a fact which is important to you?" he asked, obviously knowing the answer.

"Cotton batting ignites at four hundred forty-six degrees Fahrenheit," she replied. "Wool blankets at four hundred one, fiberboard at four twenty-one."

"Try this on for size," he said, softly. "Sometimes knowing the facts and figures makes what we fear seem more comprehensible. They present the possibility that this might, after all, be dealt with."

She gazed out his window without speaking. In the middle distance smoke had appeared. Dozens of fires moved through the streets. With their blazing heads and torsos and two or more legs, she could not tell if they were people on fire writhing in agony or a new form of fiery life performing an ecstatic dance.

Eventually she tore her eyes away long enough to look at the doctor. "Did you know, Doctor," she asked, "that the world was without fire until Prometheus brought it down to us? He'd stolen it from heaven."

It was one of those hot, shimmering days so common in Arizona this time of year. Or so Sandra had been told. She'd been here for two of those years, leaving Colorado in almost frantic haste the third summer after the plane went down and burned up her ex-husband along with their only child.

David. He would have been thirteen in another month. Hair a runaway blaze of copper. He would have hated Arizona, but then she would never have lived here if he'd been alive. He'd liked it cool, sought it out in swimming pools and shade trees and ski runs, fall evenings curled up on the porch swing with his mom just like a little kid, his babyish face in the moonlight a pale antidote to his dazzle of hair.

The heated air shuddered over the car lot beyond her balcony, or maybe it was her eyesight going from grief held adamantly at bay. If she started crying now she wouldn't stop for a week, and she'd had a few weeks like that back in Colorado before the move.

Don't get me started! she'd say to David when he used to question her, question everything with an energetic resentment only a child that full of life could maintain. Just don't get me started, not today. I have to get dressed, get to work. I can't start crying today.

One of the legs of her pantyhose developed a run under her shaking hands. Dammit. She hurried around the apartment, bumping into things and cursing. She'd had to settle for a smaller place than they'd owned in Colorado, but the thought of finding something to do with all that room was terrifying in any case. *Smaller, hell — we had a house! Big shade trees in the back yard and flowers everywhere, orange and red like scattered matchheads...* She found another pair of hose with only a couple of snags, willed herself to slip them on carefully, easing them over her raw-feeling legs like a second skin. Her friends at the bank teased her over this insistence of hers that she wear pantyhose every day, whatever the heat. And makeup — she couldn't go outside without makeup. She couldn't bear to look people in the face if she wasn't wearing makeup. They might see too much.

Outside in the black asphalt lot a child screamed. Sandra stamped shoeless out onto the balcony. Down below a father held the crying child, mother frantically brushing at the little one's bare feet as if she could clean the pain away. Their shiny white car had Indiana plates. Sandra closed her eyes and swore. Every summer some tourist permitted his child to walk barefoot on the asphalt. And if the child was a toddler, reaction times being slow at that age, the burns could be...

Sandra felt heat on her eyelids, saw the fire licking at the edges of the shutters she'd made to keep the world out, saw dancing flames through closed eyes.

She managed to get herself back inside before the attack subsided, fireworms leading her, racing ahead over the tops of bookcases and trailing across the back of the charcoal-upholstered couch. This wasn't an unfamiliar sensation — she'd had the experience several times since the hot weather began. Something was wrong with her eyes, of course, but she just couldn't bring herself to see her doctor about it, to describe the phenomenon and be questioned about her diet, her habits, her losses. She kept thinking she should be shaking this off, calling an ambulance for those poor people outside. But she could hear the sounds of excited conversation now, other people in the complex coming out to help. It probably wasn't very serious anyway, just a little burn, and she would have embarrassed everyone with her hysterical overreaction. It wouldn't have taken much, perhaps just a glance from the hurt child, and she'd have fallen down on that hot asphalt, burning herself, burning herself all over and not even caring.

She looked around — she was on the couch although she couldn't remember sitting down. With a feeling surprisingly akin to disappointment she noted that the flames were gone from her apartment. But still a hint of smoke in the air. Not that that was confirmation of anything; this time of year, people said, it always smelled like smoke.

She gradually became aware of an ache in her lower extremities. Then saw that she was kicking her right foot over and over in anxious rhythm, against the coffee table leg, against some book wedged beneath the couch, the stocking toe torn as if chewed. She made herself stop, reached down and freed the leather-bound volume.

Her fingers trembled over the cover. She thought she'd gotten rid of it, then remembered she couldn't figure out how: throw it away and someone might find it, trace it back to her, ask her embarrassing questions about herself, her life without David. Her face suffused with heat visualizing the look on the questioners' faces. At one point she'd actually thought she'd burn it, had even brought the matches up out of the jumble at the back of the drawer where she'd banished them, but could not will them to strike.

She opened the scrapbook for the terrible reassurance that the clippings were still there: glued to the pages in no particular order or alignment: a chronicle of human disaster, a catalog of all the myriad ways a human body might lose warmth, color, thought and urgency. A narrative chronicling the departure of heat from human life. All the ways a life might discorporate. A collage of suicides, murder, fatal activity, accident (in which she found it increasingly difficult to believe), disease, earth, wind, water, and especially fire.

And included among these clippings, but with no special handling or delineation, were the stories about the one particular fire, the singular plane crash which had changed her life forever. Her own audacity in this one aspect of this book of disasters still did not fail to take her breath away.

She'd never shown the book to her doctor; she'd never shown it to anyone. She would have been ashamed. For the whole purpose of this tome was to keep other people, their lives, their messy tragedies, at bay. She'd discovered simply too much pain out there. And if anyone else were to read this scrapbook they would know what she had discovered about herself: she didn't really care what happened to them, not really. She couldn't afford to.

"It's a charter," her ex-husband had said. "I'm not going to tell you how much, but it's worth it. We'll fly up for two days of skiing, the prettiest snow country David's ever seen, then back in time for school on Monday. He'll love it."

And he did, of course. David had told her so himself when he called, thirty minutes before boarding the return flight.

She fingered the strips of newsprint carefully, as if handling brittle historic documents. They were unexpectedly yellowed — it hadn't been that long ago, after all. But the clippings looked so old, and the chronicle — of how the ice had weighed heavy on one wing, resulting in a loss of control after take-off, the plane rolling, the search for survivors, and finally the list of names, David's name — read like a piece of history, too far away to touch her.

But the evidence of how much she had been touched, changed, transformed was here in abundance, in the very existence of such a scrapbook, and the jumble of hundreds of notations and extended commentary, scribblings in a tiny, intense handwriting inserted among the clippings, using up every bit of available space, added to daily before she'd managed to free herself and move away from Colorado. Forty killed. A hundred twenty killed. Chemical oxidation is a common source of heat. Pilot error. Class B fires are fires in flammable petroleum products. Wreckage scattered over ten square miles. The emperor Augustus instituted a night patrol of slaves to watch out for fire. Varnished fabrics are prone to spontaneous ignition. The Wilson family, who missed the flight, expressed their sympathy. The five stages of combustion, free-burning, smoldering, and total loss, total involvement.

But she'd brought the book with her, hadn't she? Once she'd made it, it almost seemed too dangerous to be gotten rid of. And now, after slipping into shoes to cover the tears in her stocking, pulling on a suit jacket — "in *this heat*, Sandra?" — she unaccountably tucked the scrapbook under her arm for the long, hot drive to work.

The couple sitting across from Sandra's desk smiled fiercely. *What is it with all the smiling people in my life?* she thought, and imagined a fire under their feet, the heat radiating up through their bodies forcing the lips to stretch into an impossibly wide line before evolving further into a grimace. What else could such a smile mean? The man occasionally glanced at the coffee maker on the credenza behind Sandra, no doubt wondering why she hadn't offered them any. He probably felt entitled — that's what the coffee was for, for loan department employees to offer to the customers and he had certainly seen other customers get their share so where was his? Sandra could hear the machine bubbling away behind her, liquid dripping and sizzling down the hot sides. She never went near that death machine; no way was she going to start today. You never saw an open flame, but that was the worst, the absolute worst. The heat was still there, disguised, waiting for you to make a mistake.

The man smiled anyway. As did his wife. A fact which made Sandra profoundly uncomfortable as they'd come in so that she might tell them *in person* that there was no way Southwest was going to give them a loan, a loan which might allow them to keep their home. The reason she had to deliver this bad news in person was because Southwest was the Bank with the Personal Touch.

The idea of touching these people made her shudder. They were probably good people, they probably worked hard and were great neighbors to have around, decent company. But a truck was about to run them down, smear them across the hot asphalt, and Sandra desperately did not want to be there when it happened.

The more they smiled the more Sandra fidgeted. Maybe they always smiled like this, whatever the news. "I'm sorry," she repeated. Even more smiles, as if they couldn't help themselves. Only the small child sitting between them seemed unhappy, seemed to understand exactly what Sandra was trying to tell them, and Sandra found herself peering over at that child more and more, as if appealing for help.

But the child, a little girl with luxurious wavy brown hair, looked elsewhere. Under the desk, by Sandra's feet, where Sandra had quickly hid the scrapbook when the couple came in ten minutes early for their appointment. Sandra glanced nervously between her legs: the book had fallen open, several rather graphic photos of car crashes displayed themselves. Her handwriting looked large and crazy on these pages; she worried that the little girl might be able to read the words. She should never have left it out — she should have stuck it into a drawer. Now this child might be damaged by what she had done. The central picture on the exposed page was of a burned-out vehicle: a large one, she thought it might be a van. In blocky lettering by the picture, her emphatic writing: OXYGEN. Underneath that was an observation she thought she remembered.

Human beings breathe in oxygen. Burning is a rapid oxidation. If there were no nitrogen in the air to retard oxygen, all fires would burn uncontrolled. Perhaps they would burn forever.

Across from her, as if in answer, the woman breathed heavily. The little girl looked up at Sandra with an annoyed expression. The man continued to smile, but Sandra could detect the beginnings of an unraveling at the corners of his mouth. "Well, perhaps you could try again sometime, when your credit history improves," Sandra began, looking for a way to initiate the goodbyes and head the family toward the door. Someone had a radio on their desk, listening to the news. Something about a fire downtown. Sandra glanced down at her scrapbook of disasters, her purse. It was almost lunchtime; she could reach the site of the fire in less than ten minutes. If only these two would stop smiling. If they'd just stop smiling she might be able to get them to leave. Perhaps their English wasn't very good, although nothing on the application had suggested immigration. She looked from the man to the woman — maybe if she could bring herself to go to the coffee machine, and brought the man back a cup, then he would leave. She could give him a styrofoam cupful, something he could take with him. Hell, she could give him one of those complementary thermoses they had for people opening new savings accounts, the ones with the bank logo embossed in red on the side.

She looked at the little girl again, asleep in her mother's arms now. Face so still, pale. Children that age could sleep so deeply it seemed more akin to hibernation than to normal slumber. Barely breathing, almost no perceptible signs of life. Terrifying. The cheeks and forehead appeared so cool, all heat color gone from the face. More than once she had wrestled David out of just such a sleep to make sure he was still alive.

The bubbling from the coffee maker was louder behind her now, an anxious sizzle from the cherry wood credenza top. The couple's eyes appeared to widen in alarm, but the smiles held.

She looked down at the little girl, who held Sandra's scrapbook in her lap, turning the pages, playing with the brittle yellow flaps of newsprint. She looked up at Sandra and laughed. The mother tilted her head toward the scrapbook and began to read.

"Oh you really don't want to see that!" Sandra exclaimed, reaching over the desk and snatching one edge of the book. The pages fluttered, clippings dangling precariously as she pulled, the little girl resisting, then finally letting go so suddenly Sandra stumbled backwards. She clasped the book to her chest, a sick panic growing in her stomach when she saw that some of the clippings had fallen out, littering the carpet around her desk like soiled underwear. She looked around to see who among her co-workers might be watching, suddenly convinced she wouldn't be able to work here anymore. She turned back to the family and tried stammering an apology.

A yellow finger of flame tapped the man's right shoulder, grew into a hand reaching for his high, stiff collar, pouted its lips to kiss, then whisper into his ear. Unless she was mistaken, his smile grew even more, engorged with warmth, his eyes shiny with reflected heat.

Flame spread its legs and leapt from husband to wife, a nimbus behind their heads, so that they were two saints smiling beneficently at her. Their clothing began to glow as if wrapping hot coals.

"So…please try us again," she said, her purse and scrapbook ready in her hands. She set her purse on the desk and reached out to shake whatever hand might be offered, then pulled back when hands enveloped in blue flame floated up from the other side. She grabbed her purse again and clutched it with the scrapbook in front of her, turning her head away from the fiery pupa the little girl had become in her mother's arms, and racing out the door.

Downtown, Sandra drove through layered soot and falling debris, so much smoke, so much ash floating through the air. There were fire trucks everywhere, and road blocks. A police officer stopped her a block from the fire. "You can't go this way, ma'am."

"But I have to get closer. I have to see."

The policeman waved his arms in irritation. Car horns pierced the overheated air behind her. Beyond the officer, where she wanted to be, great white hoses like prehistoric snakes meandered down the street, over curbs and sidewalks, slipped into ragged, darkened cavities seeking to drink the fire. "Lady, back this vehicle up *now* if you don't want to spend the night in jail!"

She turned her car around jerkily, backing it against one of the great hoses, which sent the cop cursing, chasing after her. She stepped on the gas, nearly sideswiping several parked cars as she made a quick right into the next alley. She pulled behind some battered trashcans, got out with her scrapbook and ran toward the other end where she saw firefighters running past, their giant beetle-like forms fleeing the conflagration.

She burst out of the mouth of the alley into heavy black smoke and sparking air. She felt small and helpless, an insect chased from a burning log. Up and down the street empty windows full of fire, black rectangular spaces alive with flames. Across the street, paramedics attended to several firefighters with their masks off, faces black-caked and androgynous. A few feet away, a dead fireman wrapped in a gray blanket, another bending over him, face scarred by fire and tears. She stepped back, anxious to keep her distance. She worried about being seen, of a policeman confiscating her scrapbook, reading it, and arresting her for its contents. She thought of the newspaper stories that would be appearing tomorrow, the picture of this dead fireman on the front page. She thought about where that clipping might go into her scrapbook.

Small groups of firefighters charged several doorways, long axes in hand. Sandra knew then why she envied them, why her admiration of them was never compromised. Their job was clear: they put out fires. An army of good against a nebulous evil.

An explosion over the rooftops, and Sandra gazed up to see fire wrapping the buildings like a giant woman's hair, like tornadoes devouring the firefighters who struggled there. Falling hot cinders beat her to the pavement. She crawled over to a Dumpster whose lid had been spread open like a wing. There she cowered, opening the scrapbook to one article and then to another, gazing at the pictures, trying to visualize the burned bodies the newspapers refused to show. They would not tell the truth. No one wanted to tell her the truth.

She read how fire was like any living thing: it ate, it breathed. Sometimes the fire would leave a room and go into the walls in search of air. Sometimes it was like an animal, hiding wherever it found the right place, then attacking when it was cornered.

When fire came into you it ate up everything: all memory, all hope, all that had made you a presence when you were in the world.

And yet when fire left you it left you empty and cold, the spark and the gleam gone, so that those who'd loved you would find nothing there.

"I had a wonderful time," David said, his voice distorted by distance and static. In the dark she could feel the embers of every word her sweet child had ever said to her burning through her clothes.

Sandra awakened into a land of disintegration. Black shadows of furniture leered out of vanished walls, their shapes stark and distinctive.

Firemen stalked through this gray other world, killing the bright creatures wherever they showed themselves.

Beneath her trembling hands the scrapbook crumbled to ash.

Sssss, a doll's melted face whispered.

"Here, let me help you," the fireman said softly at her side. "Here, try not to move."

She looked up into his mask. "I love you," she whispered through burning lips.

The masked head nodded silently, flames dancing in the bright plastic where there might have been eyes, heat warping the lips into well-intentioned smile.

Ramsey Campbell has been described as "Britain's most respected living horror writer" and he has been given more awards than any other writer in the field, including the Grand Master Award of the World Horror Convention, the Lifetime Achievement Award of the Horror Writers Association, and the Living Legend Award of the International Horror Guild. His most recent novels are *Secret Story*, *The Grin of the Dark*, and *Thieving Fear*. Forthcoming are *Creatures of the Pool* and *The Seven Days of Cain*. His short fiction has been collected in *Waking Nightmares*, *Alone with the Horrors*, *Ghosts and Grisly Things*, *Told by the Dead*, and *Just Behind You*, and his nonfiction is collected in *Ramsey Campbell, Probably*. His novels *The Nameless* and *Pact of the Fathers* have been filmed in Spain. His regular columns appear in *All Hallows*, *Dead Reckonings*, and *Video Watchdog*. He is the President of the British Fantasy Society and of the Society of Fantastic Films.

Campbell is a writer whose work has been consistently excellent, despite its quantity. His influence has been felt over the several decades since he started publishing (once he left behind the Lovecraftian mantle he donned when very young) and his current output hasn't faltered. Most of his short fiction takes place in England. He has written so many excellent stories that it's impossible to choose one quintessential, or even one favorite. But here is one I quite like.

No Strings
Ramsey Campbell

"GOOD NIGHT TILL tomorrow," Phil Linford said, having faded the signature tune of *Linford Till Midnight* up under his voice, "and a special good night to anyone I've been alone with." As he removed his headphones, imitated by the reverse of himself in the dark beyond the inner window, he felt as if he was unburdening himself of all the voices he'd talked to during the previous two hours. They'd been discussing the homeless, whom most of the callers had insisted on describing as beggars or worse, until Linford had declared that he respected anyone who did their best to earn their keep, to feed themselves and their dependants. He hadn't intended to condemn those who only begged, if they were capable of nothing else, but several of his listeners did with increasing viciousness. After all that, the very last caller had hoped aloud that nobody homeless had been listening. Maybe Linford oughtn't to have responded that if they were homeless they wouldn't have anywhere to plug in a radio, but he always tried to end with a joke.

There was no point in leaving listeners depressed: that wasn't the responsibility he was paid for. If he'd given them a chance to have their say and something to carry on chewing over, he'd done what was expected of him. If he weren't doing a good job he wouldn't still be on the air. At least it wasn't television — at least he wasn't making people do no more than sit and gawk. As the second hand of the clock above the console fingered midnight he faded out his tune and gave up the station to the national network.

The news paced him as he walked through the station, killing lights. This year's second war, another famine, a seaboard devastated by a hurricane, a town buried by a volcano — no room for anything local, not even the people who'd been missing for weeks or months. In the deserted newsroom computer terminals presented their blank bulging profiles to him. Beyond the unstaffed reception desk a solitary call was flashing like a warning on the switchboard.

Its glow and its insect clicking died as he padded across the plump carpet of the reception area. He was reaching for the electronic latch to let him into the street when he faltered. Beyond the glass door, on the second of the three concrete steps to the pavement, a man was seated with his back to him.

Had he fallen asleep over the contents of his lap? He wore a black suit a size too large, above which peeked an inch of collar gleaming white as a vicar's beneath the neon streetlights, not an ensemble that benefited from being topped by a dark green baseball cap pulled as low as it would stretch on the bald neck. If he was waiting for anyone it surely couldn't be Linford, who nonetheless felt as if he had attracted the other somehow, perhaps by having left all the lights on while he was alone in the station. The news brought itself to an end with a droll anecdote about a music student who had almost managed to sell a forged manuscript before the buyer had noticed the composer's name was spelled Beathoven, and Linford eased the door open. He was on the way to opening enough of a gap to sidle through, into the stagnant July heat beneath the heavy clouds, when *Early Morning Moods* commenced with a rush of jaunty flourishes on a violin. At once the figure on the steps jerked to his feet as though tugged by invisible strings and joined in.

So he was a busker, and the contents of his lap had been a violin and its bow, but the discovery wasn't the only reason why Linford pulled the door wide. The violinist wasn't merely imitating the baroque solo from the radio; he was copying every nuance and intonation, an exact echo no more than a fraction of a second late. Linford felt as though he'd been selected to judge a talent show. "Hey, that's good," he said. "You ought —"

He had barely started speaking when the violinist dodged away with a movement that, whether intentionally or from inability, was less a dance than a series of head-to-toe wriggles that imparted a gypsy swaying to the violin and bow. Perhaps to blot out the interference Linford's voice represented, he began to play louder, though as sweetly as ever. He halted in the middle of the pedestrianised road, between the radio station and a department store lit up for the night. Linford stayed in the doorway until the broadcast melody gave way to the presenter's voice, then closed the door behind him, feeling it lock. "Well done," he called. "Listen, I wonder —"

He could only assume the musician was unable to hear him for playing. No sooner had the melody ended than it recommenced while the player moved away as though guided by his bunch of faint shadows that gave him the appearance of not quite owning up to the possession of several extra limbs. Linford was growing frustrated with the behaviour of someone he only wanted to help. "Excuse me," he said, loud enough for the plate glass across the street to fling his voice back at him. "If it's an audition you need I can get you one. No strings. No commission."

The repetition of the melody didn't falter, but the violinist halted in front of a window scattered with wire skeletons sporting flimsy clothes. When the player didn't turn to face him, Linford followed. He knew talent when he heard it, and local talent was meant to be the point of local radio, but he also didn't mind feeling like the newsman he'd been until he'd found he was better at chatting between his choices of music too old to be broadcast by anyone except him. Years of that had landed him the late-night phone-in, where he sometimes felt he made less of a difference than he had in him. Now here was his chance to make one, and he wasn't about to object if putting the violinist on the air helped his reputation too, not when his contract was due for renewal. He was almost alongside the violinist — close enough to glimpse a twitching of the pale smooth cheek, apparently in time with a mouthing that accompanied the music — when the other danced, if it could be called a dance, away from him.

Unless he was mute — no, even if he was — Linford was determined to extract some sense from him. He supposed it was possible that the musician wasn't quite right in some way, but then it occurred to him that the man might already be employed and so not in need of being discovered. "Do you play with anyone?" he called at the top of his voice.

That seemed to earn him a response. The violinist gestured ahead with his bow, so tersely that Linford heard no break in the music. If the gesture hadn't demonstrated that the player was going Linford's way, he might have sought clarification of whatever he was meant to have understood. Instead he went after the musician, not running or even trotting, since he would have felt absurd, and so not managing to come within arm's length.

The green glow of a window display — clothed dummies exhibiting price tags or challenging the passer-by to guess their worth, their blank-eyed faces immobile and rudimentary as death-masks moulded by a trainee — settled on the baseball cap as the player turned along the side street that led to the car park, and the cap appeared to glisten like moss. A quarter of a mile away down the main road, Linford saw a police car crested with lights speed across a junction, the closest that traffic was allowed to approach. Of course the police could drive anywhere they liked, and their cameras were perched on roofs: one of his late-night partners in conversation had declared that these days the cameras were the nearest things to God. While Linford felt no immediate need of them, there was surely nothing wrong with knowing you were watched. Waving a hand in front of his face to ward off a raw smell the side street had enclosed, he strode after the musician.

The street led directly into the car park, a patch of waste ground about two hundred yards square, strewn with minor chunks of rubble, empty bottles, squashed cans. Only the exit barrier and the solitary presence of Linford's Peugeot indicated that the square did any work. Department stores backed onto its near side, and to its right were restaurants whose bins must be responsible for the wafts of a raw smell. To the left a chain fence crowned with barbed wire protected a building site, while the far side was overlooked by three storeys of derelict offices. The musician was prancing straight for these beneath arc-lights that set his intensified shadows scuttling around him.

He reached the building as Linford came abreast of the car. Without omitting so much as a quaver from the rapid eager melody, the violinist lifted one foot in a movement that suggested the climax of a dance and shoved the back door open. The long brownish stick of the bow jerked up as though to beckon Linford. Before he had time to call out, if indeed he felt obliged to, he saw the player vanish into a narrow oblong black as turned earth.

He rested a hand on the tepid roof of the car and told himself he'd done enough. If the musician was using the disused offices as a squat he was unlikely to be alone, and perhaps his thinness was a symptom of addiction. The prospect of encountering a roomful of drug addicts fell short of appealing to Linford. He was fishing out his keys when an abrupt silence filled the car park. The music, rendered hollow by the dark interior, had ceased in the midst of a phrase, but it hadn't entirely obscured a shrill cry from within — a cry, Linford was too sure to be able to ignore it, for help.

Five minutes — less if he surprised himself by proving to be in a condition to run — would take him back to the radio station to call the police. The main street might even feature a phone booth that accepted coins rather than cards. Less than five minutes could be far too long for whoever needed help, and so Linford stalked across the car park, waving his arms at the offices as he raised his face to mouth for help at the featureless slate sky. He was hoping some policeman was observing him and would send reinforcements — he was hoping to hear a police car raise its voice on its way to him. He'd heard nothing but his own dwarfed isolated footsteps by the time he reached the ajar door.

Perhaps someone had planned to repaint it and given up early in the process. Those patches of old paint that weren't flaking were blistered. The largest blister had split open, and he saw an insect writhe into hiding inside the charred bulge as he dealt the door a slow kick to shove it wide. A short hall with two doors on each side led to a staircase that turned its back on itself halfway up. The widening glare from the car park pressed the darkness back towards the stairs, but only to thicken it on them and within the doorways. Since all the doors were open, he ventured as far as the nearest pair and peered quickly to either side of him.

Random shapes of light were stranded near the windows, all of which were broken. The floorboards of both rooms weren't much less rubbly than the car park. In the room to his left two rusty filing cabinets had been pulled fully open, though surely there could have been nothing to remove from them, let alone to put in. To his right a single office desk was leaning on a broken leg and grimacing with both the black rectangles that used to contain drawers. Perhaps it was his tension that rendered these sights unpleasant, or perhaps it was the raw smell. His will to intervene was failing as he began to wonder if he had really heard any sound except music — and then the cry was repeated above him. It could be a woman's voice or a man's grown shrill with terror, but there was no mistaking its words. "Help," it pleaded. "Oh God."

No more than a couple of streets away a nightclub emitted music and loud voices, followed by an outburst of the slamming of car doors. The noises made Linford feel less alone: there must be at least one bouncer outside the nightclub, within earshot of a yell. Perhaps that wasn't as reassuring as he allowed it to seem, but it let him advance to the foot of the stairs and shout into the dimness that was after all not quite dark. "Hello? What's happening up there? What's wrong?"

His first word brought the others out with it. The more of them there were, the less sure he was how advisable they might be. They were met by utter silence except for a creak of the lowest stair, on which he'd tentatively stepped. He hadn't betrayed his presence, he told himself fiercely: whoever was above him had already been aware of him, or there would have been no point to the cry for help. Nevertheless once he seized the splintered banister it was on tiptoe that he ran upstairs. He was turning the bend when an object almost tripped him — the musician's baseball cap.

The banister emitted a groan not far short of vocal as he leaned on it to steady himself. The sound was answered by another cry of "Help," or most of it before the voice was muffled by a hand over the mouth. It came from a room at the far end of the corridor ahead. He was intensely aware of the moment, of scraps of light that clung like pale bats to the ceiling of the corridor, the rats' tails of the flexes that had held sockets for light bulbs, the blackness of the doorways that put him in mind of holes in the ground, the knowledge that this was his last chance to retreat. Instead he ran almost soundlessly up the stairs and past two rooms that a glance into each appeared to show were empty save for rubble and broken glass. Before he came abreast of the further left-hand room he knew it was where he had to go. For a moment he thought someone had hung a sign on the door.

It was a tattered office calendar dangling from a nail. Dates some weeks apart on it — the most recent almost a fortnight ago — were marked with ovals that in daytime might have looked more reddish. He was thinking that the marks couldn't be fingerprints, since they contained no lines, as he took a step into the room.

A shape lay on the area of the floor least visited by daylight, under the window amid shards of glass. A ragged curtain tied at the neck covered all of it except the head, which was so large and bald and swollen it reminded him of the moon. The features appeared to be sinking into it: the unreadably shadowed eyes and gaping whitish lips could have passed for craters, and its nostrils were doing without a nose. Despite its baldness, it was a woman's head, since Linford distinguished the outline of breasts under the curtain — indeed, enough bulk for an extra pair. The head wobbled upright to greet him, its scalp springing alight with the glare from the car park, and large hands whose white flesh was loose as oversized gloves groped out from beneath the curtain. He could see no nails on them. The foot he wasn't conscious of holding in mid-air trod on a fragile object he'd failed to notice — a violinist's bow. It snapped and pitched him forward to see more of the room.

Four desk drawers had been brought into it, one to a corner. Each drawer contained a nest of newspapers and office scrap. Around the drawers were strewn crumpled sheets of music, stained dark as though — Linford thought and then tried not to — they had been employed to wipe mouths. Whatever had occurred had apparently involved the scattering about the bare floor of enough spare bows to equip a small string orchestra. By no means anxious to understand any of the contents of the room until he was well clear of it, Linford was backing away when the violin recommenced its dance behind him.

He swung around and at once saw far too much. The violinist was as bald as the figure under the window, but despite the oddly temporary nature of the bland smooth face, particularly around the nose, it was plain that the musician was female too. The long brown stick she was passing back and forth over the instrument had never been a bow — not that one would have made a difference, since the cracked violin was stringless. The perfect imitation of the broadcast melody was streaming out of her wide toothless mouth, the interior of which was at least as white as the rest of her face. Despite her task she managed a smile, though he sensed it wasn't for him but about him. She was blocking the doorway, and the idea of going closer to her — to the smell of rawness, some of which was certainly emerging from her mouth — almost crushed his mind to nothing. He had to entice her away from the doorway, and he was struggling to will himself to retreat into the room — struggling to keep his back to it — when a voice cried "Help."

It was the cry he'd come to find: exactly the cry, and it was behind him in the room. He twisted half around and saw the shape under the window begin to cover her mouth, then let her hand fall. She must have decided there was no longer any reason to cut the repetition short. "Oh God," she added, precisely as she had before, and rubbed her curtained stomach.

It wasn't just a trick, it was as much of an imitation as the music had been. He had to make more of an effort than he could remember ever having used to swallow the sound the realisation almost forced out of his mouth. For years he'd earned his living by not letting there be more than a second of silence, but could staying absolutely quiet now save him? He was unable to think what else to do, not that he was anything like sure of being capable of silence. "Help, oh God," the curtained shape repeated, more of a demand now, and rubbed her stomach harder. The player dropped the violin and the other item, and before their clatter faded she came at Linford with a writhing movement that might have been a jubilant dance — came just far enough to continue to block his escape.

His lips trembled, his teeth chattered, and he couldn't suppress his words, however idiotic they might be. "My mistake. I only —"

"My mistake. I only." Several voices took up his protest at once, but he could see no mouths uttering it, only an agitation of the lower half of the curtain. Then two small forms crawled out from underneath, immediately followed by two more, all undisguised by any kind of covering. Their plump white bodies seemed all the more wormlike for the incompleteness of the faces on the bald heads — no more than nostrils and greedily dilated mouths. Just the same they wriggled straight to him, grabbing pointed fragments of glass. He saw the violinist press her hands over her ears, and thought that she felt some sympathy for him until he grasped that she was ensuring she didn't have to imitate whatever sound he made. The window was his only chance now: if the creature beneath it was as helpless as she seemed, if he could bear to step over or on her so as to scream from the window for somebody out there to hear — But when he screamed it was from the floor where, having expertly tripped him, the young were swarming up his legs, and he found he had no interest in the words he was screaming, especially when they were repeated in chorus to him.

Terry Dowling is one of Australia's most awarded, versatile, and respected writers of science fiction, dark fantasy, and horror. In addition to having written the internationally acclaimed Tom Rynosseros saga and *Wormwood*, a collection of linked sf stories, he is the author of several excellent collections of horror fiction including *An Intimate Knowledge of the Night*, *Blackwater Days*, and the retrospective *Basic Black: Tales of Appropriate Fear*. This last won the 2007 International Horror Guild Award for Best Collection. Dowling's stories have appeared in *The Year's Best Science Fiction*, *The Year's Best SF*, *The Year's Best Fantasy*, *Best New Horror*, and many times in *The Year's Best Fantasy and Horror*, as well as in the anthologies *Dreaming Down Under*, *Wizards*, *The Dark*, *Inferno*, and *Dreaming Again*.

I first became aware of Dowling's work through his science fiction stories, which can be quite powerful. But I fell in love with his consistently disturbing supernatural and psychological horror fiction. In fact, more of his horror stories appeared in *The Year's Best Fantasy and Horror* during its twenty-one-year run than any other writer.

Stitch
Terry Dowling

SOON BELLA WOULD find the nerve to go upstairs. Soon she would be able to excuse herself from her uncle and aunt and climb the familiar old stairs, counting every one, enter the toilet in the alcove of the upstairs bathroom, and confront Mr. Stitch.

She couldn't leave without seeing him. Not this time. It was Auntie Inga's birthday, occasion enough, yes, but this time Mr. Stitch *was* the reason for being here. Bella had always tried to see him once or twice a year, just to make sure he was still there, shut tight behind the glass, locked in his frame. This time it had to be more.

"Your boyfriend couldn't make it, Bel?" Auntie Inga asked, but gently, in case there was a point of delicacy involved.

"Roger? No. He had to work, like I said." Bella knew she had said. It had been the third or fourth line out of her mouth when she arrived. "Sends his best wishes though. 'Manniest happiest returns' — quote, unquote. His exact words." What he would have said anyway. "He has to work every second Saturday."

Bluff and hearty as ever, but it's what you often had to do where Roger was concerned. Maybe it would have been better if he *were* here. Having someone to be with her through it. Through this. Bella couldn't remember feeling such dread.

But this time she had to be alone. This time she wanted more.

"This photo of your mom was always my favorite," Auntie Inga said, returning to the page in the old album, going through them as she always did when Bella visited. Possibly when anyone visited.

Bella ignored the mention of her mother, concentrated instead on what Uncle Sal was doing. He smiled kindly at them both and poured more coffee. Bella couldn't remember him any other way. It was as if at some point in his life he had discovered the word "avuncular" and had resolved to be precisely that for the rest of his days. With Mr. Stitch upstairs, it made him seem positively sinister, a gleefully distracting conspirator. An avuncular usher, Bella thought, then was reminded of the old witch in the story of Hansel and Gretel. And witch rhymed with stitch, so back she went, into the panic loop again, with both hands steadying her coffee cup, her heart hammering and her feet flexing inside her shoes, itching to run. If only Roger *could* have been here, could have at least made an effort to understand what this meant. Stayed close. That would have made all the difference.

Though alone, alone. Some things had to be done alone. And today had to be different. Today she had to change it all.

"Auntie Inga, do you still have that old sampler on the wall in the upstairs toilet? The one with the two Dutch children in the street?" Bright voice. Light voice. Smiling all the while. No big deal. As if she hadn't been up there in years, hadn't *made* herself go up and see it on each and every one of those terrifying visits.

"What's that dear?" Auntie Inga said. "Dutch children?"

Summoned by name, the rosy-cheeked sixty-seven-year-old came tracking across the years from where the photographs had taken her. Smile for smile, here she was: Auntie Inga, always Hansel and Gretel witch (stitch!) friendly. She'd never been any different. But forgetful today. Mentioning her mother.

What *was* the female form of avuncular? Bella wondered. Because here it was, tidied up, presented and displayed: more in terms of velour and Hush Puppies than gingham and gingerbread, but just as real.

"The sampler?" her aunt added, as if only a few words ever got through at a time, drip-feed fashion. "That old thing! Of course. Been there forever."

This was the moment. "Of all your cross-stitch pieces, that's my favorite." Bold and direct. Tell a big enough lie and people will believe. Could she pull it off?

"Really, Bel? I would have done that when I was thirty-one. Just before you were born. Landscapes. Street scenes. I suppose they are Dutch children when I think of it. I did so many. Gave them as gifts too." She considered the framed pieces on the walls of the cozy living-room. "I did a lot of these pieces then."

Bella dutifully let herself be seen to be admiring the embroideries. Yes, and both you and Uncle Sal are so like the smarmy, neighbourly, *avuncular* people in them. Made up of so many tiny squares, a neat and orderly mosaic. Four stitches in the aida backing to give a really good square. Four to make each black square of Mr. Stitch. But, yes, neat and tidy like that, Inga and Sal. Chock full of smarm. Terminal avuncular.

Though one of the cliched pieces did charm Bella, she had to admit: the road leading off from the open door towards a sunset, with words set in the doorway, picked out vividly against the light.

> *Westering home,*
> *And a song in the air,*
> *Light in the eye,*
> *And it's good-bye to care;*
> *Laughter o'Love,*
> *And a welcoming there;*
> *Isle of my heart,*
> *My own one!*

The door, the setting sun, the sentiments, the sheer belonging: such precious things. It brought her parents' faces, always did, but she was skilled at pushing those aside. She'd dealt with that, and so could almost let herself go there, through that door. But no bidding care good-bye today. And that door, pulled right back, inviting in, inviting out, showing the road and the setting sun, was the absolute opposite of her own dark green front door, always locked these past ten, fifteen years. Double locked. Triple locked. Because of Stitch. Mr. Stitch. Because of all that her life had ended up being.

Even as Bella pulled back, accepting how the world was, there was Auntie Inga. A new thought, that thought, had occurred to her.

"Funny that you like it now. You were frightened of it as a girl."

Frightened. An understatement in the ratio of Hitler being misguided, or the atomic bomb at Hiroshima causing collateral damage.

"Oh?" Said calmly enough. Interested. This was the part Bella had to get through.

Auntie Inga was looking off up the stairs, as if a part of herself had been sent off to check the piece or, better yet, was running replays of a tinier, younger Bella Dillon sobbing, yelling, refusing to use *that* bathroom, *that* toilet. "You hated going into that bathroom. Lise — your mother — we always noticed it. That cross-stitch upset you. Two little kids in a street and you'd run away screaming."

Her mother again. Aunt Inga *was* forgetting.

Can't stop. Can't stop. Can't stop now. Bella pretended to be easy. Pretended to remember. "They were facing away, looking off up the street," Bella said, feet wanting to run. *Don't mention Mr. Stitch.*

"It wasn't that I couldn't do faces," Auntie Inga insisted, some old point of pique and a welcome show of larger humanity, a blemish on the sugar rose. "It's how the picture came in the kit. I liked doing faces. Look at *The Man in the Golden Helmet* there."

Bella glanced briefly, dutifully, but stayed on track. "Well, I'm very fond of it now. Just being sentimental, I guess. That one in the bathroom." Bella added the last remark to keep Auntie Inga on the piece upstairs. Even Uncle Sal stayed with her. He was nodding: Uncle Sal on Avuncular Setting #3.

"You're welcome to go up and see," he said. "It's still there."

At one level, Bella would never need to see it again. She knew it intimately. Two children holding hands seen from behind, looking off up a street. The boy in long-sleeved blue top and white pants, long brown hair, a brown Dutch or Flemish hat — soft, shaped like a bucket, definitely a hat worn by boys from another time and place; the little girl in a dark red dress with a white lace collar, long blonde hair. Two houses foreshortened, leading off up the street, then a wall and a tree beyond; an old-style lamp-post in the middle distance on the footpath just at the edge of the road.

And the face of a woman, probably their mother, looking down at them from a partly opened leadlight window as if reminding them what to get at the village shop, possibly warning them to beware of strangers.

And that had been the crux of it.

For along that foreshortened street, off in its tidy, converging cross-stitch distances near where the wall met the tree, was just such a stranger. A pedestrian on the sidewalk, stylized, minimalist, no doubt meant to be a token figure to fill out the scene, sketched in, stitched in with exactly seventy and a half black cross-stitch squares. Small, yet large enough, exactly seventy and a half squares big in fact, each set of four making a bold black larger square, squares set oddly so he was jagged and jigsawed down one side. A jigsaw man.

Bella could never forget that figure beyond the lamp-post, beyond the houses, small and sketchy, jagged with distance. Give her a pen and she could draw him, could tell his bits like marking squares in a hopscotch rhyme. It had been the mantra of her years.

Four in a true square
Then eight more in two lines
Four in another square
And four for shoulders fine
Six in a body line
Then six to get it right
Five more make it odd one out
Like someone took a bite.
Six more in a body line
Then six to keep it strong
Five again is odd one out
Like someone got it wrong
Three begins to give him legs
Then three and a half — it's true!
Four in a line is almost there
But not like me and you.
One and a half — space — a half and one
One and a half — space — a half and one
Now Mr. Stitch can run run run!

It was all in *how* they were set together. A man in a thick-brimmed black hat (or with a hideously deformed head), with two bites out of his left side, ruining his body, a third snipped out of his legs. A lopsided, jigsaw man.

And here was Bella about to confront him again. The figure who stood behind her days, who determined things like the extra locks on her big green front door, on the inner doors as well, the green Keep Away doors, because she'd read somewhere that dark green kept demons and devils at bay.

"I will go up and take a look, if you don't mind," Bella said. "Guess I'm sentimental like you, Auntie Inga."

"Sentimental is good, dear," her aunt said. "Too much nastiness in the world. Too many bad people. Old values are best."

"Why don't I keep you company, Bel?" Uncle Sal said, totally unexpected. "I have to get something upstairs. Inga, we could sure use some of that new Darjeeling you bought. I'm sure Bella would."

Bella was surprised, pleased, shocked all in an instant. When had Uncle Sal ever initiated anything? When had he shown such strategic thinking too, any kind of thinking that put him at odds with the Inga and Sal show?

There had to be a reason.

And before Inga could veto it, ask him to help with the tea — it was her birthday, after all — Sal was out of his chair and leading the way.

Another first.

Bella was after him in a flash, ready for that climb to that landing and that bathroom. But there had to be a reason.

"Uncle Sal," she said at the foot of the stairs. "You really don't have to."

"Nonsense, Bel. When do I ever get to do anything for myself?"

Again he'd surprised her. So why now? Why this? Bella decided to be direct.

"So why this time?" Sharp and hard, considering, and he blinked at her as she took the first few steps ahead of him.

"Just wanted to see you were okay," he said, following her up the staircase. "That cross-stitch bothers me too."

Bella could have stumbled and fallen in amazement. What had he said?

"What's that, Uncle Sal?" She heard the tremble in her voice.

"Bothers me. Bothers you," he said from behind. "Always hated it. Figure in the distance. Small and wrong."

Exactly! Exactly that! Small and wrong. Jagged and incomplete.

They were halfway to the landing when Bella slowed, hearing his breathing, laboured, agitated somehow.

For it had dawned on her.

He's serving me up. Making sure I get there. They're in collusion.

Bella stopped on the stairs.

It made terrible sense. The *new* Uncle Sal, the odd behaviour.

Bring her to me!

Bella turned, pressed her back hard against the wall.

"Don't think I will," she said.

"What, Bel? What is it?"

"This." *You.* "I can't do this today." *You're different.*

"Bel, I'm being brave. I'm doing it right. Should have done it years ago."

"What?" She gasped the word and so said it again. "What?"

"Should have told you. Said something about Benny."

"Benny? What's Benny got to do with anything?"

But it was all there in the instant. Benny in his stupid blue-plaid shirt. Benny eight years older, surprising her in the bathroom. In the toilet. Benny and Stitch.

Time was frozen on the stairs: Bella against the wall, Uncle Sal two steps lower, back to the rail, Aunt Inga lost in the impossibly far reaches of the kitchen.

"We know what he did, Bel. Your aunt won't have it. A mother can't. But we know. I know."

Part of Bella stayed on the old safe track.

What's he going on about? They haven't seen Benny in years. Benny went from their lives. Upped and went, just like that. Just like anyone can.

Part of Bella was in the other fork of that eternal moment. Benny against her. The smell of his blue-plaid shirt. The hand over her mouth. And Stitch. Mr. Stitch urging him on. Stitch behind it all, looming on the wall, waiting off along the street, there but not all there. Jagged. Dark man-thing in a funny thick hat or with a big cross-shaped hammer head. Benny breathing hard. "My word against yours! No one believes a kid!" Hard against her. Then inspired, worried, improvising. "That's Stitch! Mr. Stitch! He'll get you. It was his idea. He's coming for you, see! He'll get you if you tell!"

Both tracks running, playing out on the stairs, Uncle Sal's eyes catching hers at last, pulling her back, but the walls pounding, drumming, thundering with the mighty secret heartbeat of the house.

"You're safe now, Bel. We're all safe. You can go see."

Bella was back with him, five steps from the top. Blue-plaid Benny was gone and Uncle Sal was here and Bella was back and doing what she still had to do, always had to do.

"Thanks for knowing," she said.

"You can't go home again. Had to be said."

"I can do it alone."

"Never doubted it. I'll be outside."

"Th-Thanks."

And into the bathroom she went. The door to the toilet was ajar. She couldn't see the back wall, of course, just the strip of dim blue wall through the crack.

You can't go home again.

The truth in those words.

But I keep trying. Keep coming here.

She couldn't see the back wall, or the frame, or the children.

A warning to the Dutch children. *You can't go home again! You'll never see your mother!*

That word.

Bella had closed the bathroom door behind her. Old habit. But she hadn't locked it. Hadn't locked it then, hadn't now.

Put on your blue-plaid shirt, Sal, and bring her to me!

But she could lock the toilet door. Lock it this time. Just in case. Though that would be locking her in. And Benny, something of Benny, might be off in the cross-stitch distance. Two of them now, along that terrible, too tidy street.

She had to know. Had to act. Now or never.

She grabbed the door-knob and pushed back the door.

There was the old patterned lino, so well known, the old toilet and cistern, the air freshener in its container, the two frosted window panes on the right, the pale blue walls. There — letting her gaze move up — was the frame, brown wood, the neatly braided world forming, the children and the street, the lamppost in the middle distance, the wall and the tree.

The black ragged form.

Hello, Bella.

"Bastard!" She said it quietly.

Sal's putting on his blue-plaid shirt.

"Bastard! Bastard!"

Like father, like son. He's bigger. Older but bigger.

"Bastard! Bastard! Bastard!"

Put your hands on the cistern like before. There's a good girl.

"Bastard! Bastard! Bastard!"

You could ask for me. Take me home. Get me through your Green Door.

Reading her mind. "Bastard!"

Language, Bel. Get a needle and thread then. Make me complete.

Tears were hot and brimming, running down her cheeks.

"Bastard! Bastard!"

Mr. Stitch was moving in her tears. Her tears were making him run.

You like me jagged. Ragged. Here I come!

Bella wiped her eyes with the back of her hand, freed herself from him. Steadied herself. Her hands were on the cistern.

"Bastard! Bastard!"

She snatched them away.

You want it! You were ready!

"No! No! Bastard!"

Scaredy cat! Ready cat!

"Bastard!"

And Sal was pushing at the toilet door. "Bella! What's wrong? What is it?" She hadn't locked it! Meant to. Thought to. Hadn't.

Says it all, Bel!

Stitch was running in her tears. Jigging. Jagging. Running.

"Bel, what's wrong?"

Sal pushing at the door. Stitch running.

One hand was on the cistern, but to steady her, so she could turn. Nothing like before.

"You bastard!"

"What, Bel? What is it?" Sal's voice.

And the door was finally open far enough and Sal was there and no blue-plaid shirt.

Bella stole a final glance. Stitch was back along the street, back by the wall and the tree. The children were safe. *All* the children were safe.

"Oh, Uncle Sal! I thought — for a moment, I just thought — it's all right. It's fine now!"

"What happened?"

"You know. Old memories. Dealing with old memories. Would Aunt Inga let me have this?"

Yes! Take me home!

Sal, bless him, understood.

"Bel, just take it. Sneak it out. I'll distract her."

It was beyond all expectation, Uncle Sal saying this.

"But —"

"You mightn't have noticed, but your aunt — she's getting forgetful. Repeating herself, things like that. We can say she gave it to you. I'll put another one in here. She won't remember, won't — be certain."

"Uncle Sal, it's not — you know?"

"Can't be sure yet. But Alzheimer's is a possibility, the doctor says. The thing is, she doesn't come in here much. She uses the en suite. So take it. She's got so many. It's never been a favorite."

Yes! Bella thought, so relieved, so grateful, then hesitated.

Too easy. Too easy. What if Sal were an accomplice after all?

Get me through the Green Door, Stitch had said.

And was quiet now, down by the tree all jagged and waiting. With not a word.

It was what she wanted too — crazily, what they both wanted. Unless this impulse came from Stitch via her mind, via Sal's. Stitch using them all.

He never said a word. Just stood off in the real, never-real, cross-stitch world, just seventy and a half stitches himself, but trying to be more, embroidering back.

How could she know? How could she be sure of anything now?

"Probably shouldn't," she said.

"Your choice, hon," Sal said.

They stood in the bathroom, Bella staring in at the piece in its frame, waiting for some reply. Stitch would be thwarted if she went without him. Furious. Bella laughed at the word-play. *Cross* Stitch. But he would still *be here*, in this blue-plaid, hands-on-the-cistern place. And she'd be back again and again because of it.

Her need was as great as his, that's what it came down to. And this was her chance to be free of it. To move it along. Stop it being something here and now. Now and then.

"Sal, why don't you bring it over tomorrow? Tell Auntie Inga she promised it. See if she goes along with it."

"Bel, one more thing."

"Yes?"

"You mom and dad —"

"Uncle Sal, let it go, please!"

"Has to be said, darlin'. Now that we're talking, just let me —"

"No!"

"Bel, you've managed this much. Go the rest of the way. They weren't to blame. They couldn't protect you —"

"Listen, Uncle Sal —"

"It wasn't their fault. None of it. What happened on *Sea Spray*. The explosion. Of course you feel responsible —"

No! No! No! No! No!

Bella actually had her hands over her ears. "Uncle Sal!"

"It was an accident! If we'd found their bodies, maybe that would've made a difference. They didn't leave you with this! Didn't desert you!"

Stitch hadn't said a word.

"You promised, Uncle Sal! You promised!"

Stitch was out there, up there, back there, listening.

"Okay. Okay. Enough. But it had to be said. I'm sorry!"

Bastard, bastard, Uncle Sal.

Or Stitch was putting his words in Sal's mouth. Had a thin, jagged, cross-stitch arm up Sal's back, working Sal's jaws.

But Bella saw the resignation in the eyes, the strain on the old face.

This wasn't Stitch. This was Sal, torn loose from avuncular, reinventing himself second by second for this desperate task, with only a few known aces up his sleeve. Known cards every one.

"I'm sorry, Uncle Sal," she said into the silence, the terrible end-time silence of these haunted upstairs.

Stitch was nowhere to be found. Back on the wall. Back in his frame. Seventy and a half meager twists of black. Barely made.

"It's just — hon, you couldn't do anything. They didn't fail you."

Again. Bella added the word. *Get it right, Uncle Sal. You meant to say didn't fail me again.*

"We'll play it your way," Sal said then, saving what he could. "We'll come over tomorrow. I'll tell your aunt we promised. We'll bring the cross-stitch."

Better. Much better.

"Can't guarantee that your aunt — you know — won't mention certain things. Won't —"

"Listen, Uncle Sal, let's take it over now! You said Auntie Inga forgets things. Let's just do it! Tell her we arranged it. A special outing for her birthday. It's a surprise! I'll take you over in my car, bring you back. You said Auntie Inga's always wanted to see — mom's place again. What I've done with it. This is her birthday treat!"

"I don't know, hon. It's so sudden. Your aunt —"

"I'll have you back inside the hour, two at the most. Say it's important to me. Important that she sees where I'm going to hang it! We can do it, Sal!"

Panic was driving her, determination to do it before her courage failed, before Stitch came back.

"I'll go see, okay?" Sal turned towards the stairs.

"We can do it, Uncle Sal. It'll really help."

He looked back, smiled his old safe smile. "Anything for closure, they say."

Stitch was too quiet. It had been too long.

"Anything. Look, I'll come down with you now. Tell her I've got a birthday cake or something. We can get one on the way."

Pride, vanity and panic of another kind helped. Auntie Inga wasn't about to admit that she had forgotten their outing, or that she couldn't remember promising the cross-stitch. Bella felt a stab of guilt and shame at the duplicity, using such a desperate condition against the person suffering from it, but her own need was greater. Having the person who had created Stitch carry him across the threshold, through the green door; now that was perfect. Suddenly important. Closure, Sal had said. This would do it.

They left the pot of new Darjeeling cooling on the kitchen bench. While Bella jollied Aunt Inga along, helped her into the front passenger seat of the Lexus, got the seatbelt done up, Sal fetched Stitch, brought him down swathed in an old towel and put him in the back.

Bella could never have done it. She felt a giddiness, an intense, irrational joy, a sudden certainty. This was right in every sense. Inga doing the honors. Inga bringing Stitch. All so perfect.

Bella couldn't remember what she said as she drove, just that she was babbling happily all the while, going on about a special birthday treat and how important it all was. Aunt Inga blossomed under the attention. This was her day, her outing. Bella was being, well, avuncular.

Stitch never said a word.

He was there in the back next to Sal, hidden under his towel. This was what he wanted too, no doubt, staying close like this, but at least he was out of the upstairs bathroom, *that* place.

They stopped for a birthday cake as Sal and she had agreed: a store-bought mudcake with *Happy Birthday* in white looping letters. Then, in another two minutes, they were at Eltham Street, tree-lined and shady, and there was the big white house with the green door.

"It looks wonderful, dear," Aunt Inga said. "Your mother liked the white with the green trimming. It's nice that you've kept it. She'd be very proud, Bel."

Bella endured it, forced herself to say thanks, again half-expecting a refrain from Stitch: *She'd be very proud*. But nothing came. Again nothing. Perhaps he thought he could still win. Perhaps he was saving his best till last. Perhaps — it suddenly occurred to her — being out in a *real* day on a *real* street was simply too much. Either way, she'd prepared. She was ready for him.

Bella swung into the sheltered driveway, opened the garage with the remote and drove in. A wink and a smile at Sal in the rear-view mirror, then more fussing over Auntie Inga, helping her out, drawing her attention to the marigolds and geraniums in the big planters while Sal hauled Stitch out after him. Who would have thought that it could go so smoothly?

Then they were through the first green door and in the hall, then through the second and in the sitting room at last.

Inga and Sal never expected it. Even as their noses twitched at the odd smell, even as their eyes widened, making sense of what they saw, Bella had the stiletto off the sideboard and into Inga's throat. Had it in before her aunt knew it had happened, before her little shard of a scream died in a gurgle. Then Bella had the blade out and into Sal's neck at the exact moment he dropped the shrouded frame and managed: "Bella, what on earth —?"

But he saw what it was and had to know. His eyes were wide as they glazed, as the light in them died. He'd know. He had seen the figures — Bella's mother and father, and Benny and Roger — sitting upright in their chairs, had seen them totally stitched over with black, head to toe, every surface covered with precious dark thread, protected forever from the jagged man.

Bella closed and locked the door, old instinct, old habit, then reached down and removed the towel from the frame with its broken glass and tiny helpless figure. She wiped the stiletto clean, then sat cross-legged on the floor and began the unpicking. Seventy and a half stitches, then they would be safe. All the children.

Glen Hirshberg's novelette, "The Janus Tree," won the 2008 Shirley Jackson Award, and both of his collections, *American Morons* and *The Two Sams,* won the International Horror Guild Award. He is also the author of a novel, *The Snowman's Children.* His new novel, *The Book of Bunk,* is due out from Earthling in late 2010. He co-founded, with Dennis Etchison and Peter Atkins, the Rolling Darkness Revue, a traveling ghost story performance troupe that tours the West Coast of the United States each October. His fiction has been published in numerous magazines and anthologies, including *Inferno, Dark Terrors 6, Trampoline,* and *Cemetery Dance,* and has appeared several times in *The Year's Best Fantasy and Horror, The Mammoth Book of Best New Horror,* and *Best Horror of the Year.*

I've found "Dancing Men" to be one of his most chilling stories, since I first published it in *The Dark.* The novelette won the International Horror Guild Award in 2003.

![decorative rule]

Dancing Men
Glen Hirshberg

These are the last days of our lives so we give a signal maybe there still will be relatives or acquaintances of these persons.... They were tortured and burnt good-bye....
— Testimonial found at Chelmno

I

WE'D BEEN ALL afternoon in the Old Jewish Cemetery, where green light filters through the trees and lies atop the tumbled tombstones like algae. Mostly I think the kids were tired. The two-week Legacy of the Holocaust tour I had organized had taken us to Zeppelin Field in Nuremberg, where downed electrical wires slither through the brittle grass, and Bebelplatz in East Berlin, where ghost-shadows of burned books flutter in their chamber in the ground like white wings. We'd spent our nights not sleeping on sleeper trains east to Auschwitz and Birkenau and our days on public transport, traipsing through the fields of dead and the monuments to them, and all seven high-school juniors in my care had had enough.

From my spot on a bench alongside the roped-off stone path that meandered through the grounds and back out to the streets of Josefov, I watched six of my seven charges giggling and chattering around the final resting place of Rabbi Loew. I'd told them the story of the rabbi, and the clay man he'd supposedly created and then animated, and now they were running their hands over his tombstone, tracing Hebrew letters they couldn't read, chanting *"Emet,"* the word I'd taught them, in low voices and laughing. As of yet, nothing had risen from the dirt. The Tribe, they'd taken to calling themselves, after I told them that the Wandering Jews didn't really work, historically, since the essential characteristic of the Wanderer himself was his solitude.

There are teachers, I suppose, who would have been considered members of the Tribe by the Tribe, particularly on a summer trip, far from home and school and television and familiar language. But I had never been that sort of teacher.

Nor was I the only excluded member of our traveling party. Lurking not far from me, I spotted Penny Berry, the quietest member of our group and the only Goy, staring over the graves into the trees with her expressionless eyes half closed and her lipstickless lips curled into the barest hint of a smile. Her auburn hair sat cocked on the back of her head in a tight, precise ponytail. When she saw me watching, she wandered over, and I swallowed a sigh. It wasn't that I didn't like Penny, exactly. But she asked uncomfortable questions, and she knew how to wait for answers, and she made me nervous for no reason I could explain.

"Hey, Mr. Gadeuszki," she said, her enunciation studied, perfect. She'd made me teach her how to say it right, grind the s and z and k together into that single, Slavic snarl of sound. "What's with the stones?"

She gestured at the tiny gray pebbles placed across the tops of several nearby tombstones. Those on the slab nearest us glinted in the warm, green light like little eyes. "In memory" I said. I thought about sliding over on the bench to make room for her, then thought that would only make both of us even more awkward.

"Why not flowers?" Penny said.

I sat still, listening to the clamor of new-millennium Prague just beyond the stone wall that enclosed the cemetery. "Jews bring stones."

A few minutes later, when she realized I wasn't going to say anything else, Penny moved off in the general direction of the Tribe. I watched her go and allowed myself a few more peaceful seconds. Probably, I thought, it was time to move us along. We had the astronomical clock left to see today, puppet-theater tickets for tonight, the plane home to Cleveland in the morning. And just because the kids were tired didn't mean they would tolerate loitering here much longer. For seven summers in a row, I had taken students on some sort of exploring trip. "Because you've got nothing better to do," one member of the Tribe cheerfully informed me one night the preceding week. Then he'd said, "Oh my God, I was just kidding, Mr. G."

And I'd had to reassure him that I knew he was, I always looked like that. "That's true. You do," he'd said, and returned to his tripmates.

Now, I rubbed my hand over the stubble on my shaven scalp, stood, and blinked as my family name — in its original Polish spelling — flashed behind my eyelids again, looking just the way it had this morning amongst all the other names etched into the Pinkas Synagogue wall. The ground went slippery underneath me, the tombstones slid sideways in the grass, and I teetered and sat down hard.

When I lifted my head and opened my eyes, the Tribe had swarmed around me, a whirl of backwards baseball caps and tanned legs and Nike symbols. "I'm fine," I said quickly, stood up, and to my relief I found I did feel fine. I had no idea what had just happened. "Slipped."

"Kind of," said Penny Berry from the edges of the group, and I avoided looking her way.

"Time to go, gang. Lots more to see."

It has always surprised me when they do what I say, because mostly, they do. It's not me, really. The social contract between teachers and students may be the oldest mutually accepted enacted ritual on this earth, and its power is stronger than most people imagine.

We passed between the last of the graves and through a low stone opening. The dizziness or whatever it had been was gone, and I felt only a faint tingling in my fingertips as I drew my last breath of that too-heavy air, thick with loam and grass springing from bodies stacked a dozen deep in the ground.

The side street beside the Old-New Synagogue was crammed with tourists, their purses and backpacks open like the mouths of grotesquely overgrown chicks. Into those open mouths went wooden puppets and embroidered kipot and Chamsa hands from the rows of stalls that lined the sidewalk; the walls, I thought, of an all-new, much more ingenious sort of ghetto. In a way, this place had become exactly what Hitler had meant for it to be: a Museum of a Dead Race, only the paying customers were descendants of the Race, and they spent money in amounts he could never have dreamed. The ground had begun to roll under me again, and I closed my eyes. When I opened them, the tourists had cleared in front of me, and I saw the stall, a lopsided wooden hulk on bulky brass wheels. It tilted toward me, the puppets nailed to its side leering and chattering while the gypsy leaned out from between them, nose studded with a silver star, grinning.

He touched the toy nearest him, set it rocking on its terrible, thin wire. *"Loh-oot-kovay deevahd-low,"* he said, and then I was down, flat on my face in the street.

I don't know how I wound up on my back. Somehow, somebody had rolled me over. I couldn't breathe. My stomach felt squashed, as though there was something squatting on it, wooden and heavy, and I jerked, gagged, opened my eyes, and the light blinded me.

"I didn't," I said, blinking, brain flailing. I wasn't even sure I'd been all the way unconscious, couldn't have been out more than a few seconds. But the way the light affected my eyes, it was as though I'd been buried for a month.

"Doh-bree den, doh-bree den," said a voice over me, and I squinted, teared up, blinked into the gypsy's face, the one from the stall, and almost screamed. Then he touched my forehead, and he was just a man, red Manchester United cap on his head, black eyes kind as they hovered around mine. The cool hand he laid against my brow had a wedding ring on it, and the silver star in his nose caught the afternoon light.

I meant to say I was okay, but what came out was "I didn't" again.

The gypsy said something else to me. The language could have been Czech or Slovakian or Romani. I didn't know enough to tell the difference, and my ears weren't working right. In them I could feel a painful, persistent pressure.

The gypsy stood, and I saw my students clustered behind him like a knot I'd drawn taut. When they saw me looking, they burst out babbling, and I shook my head, tried to calm them, and then I felt their hands on mine, pulling me to a sitting position. The world didn't spin. The ground stayed still. The puppet stall I would not look at kept its distance.

"Mr. G., are you all right?" one of them asked, her voice shrill, slipping toward panic.

Then Penny Berry knelt beside me and looked straight into me, and I could see her formidable brain churning behind those placid eyes, the silvery color of Lake Erie when it's frozen.

"Didn't what?" she asked.

And I answered, because I had no choice. "Kill my grandfather."

2

They propped me at my desk in our pension not far from the Charles Bridge and brought me a glass of "nice water," which was one of our traveling jokes. It was what the too-thin waitress at Terezin — the "town presented to the Jews by the Nazis," as the old propaganda film we saw at the museum proclaimed — thought we were saying when we asked for ice.

For a while, the Tribe sat on my bed and talked quietly to each other and refilled my glass for me. But after thirty minutes or so, when I hadn't keeled over again and wasn't babbling and seemed my usual sullen, solid, bald self, they started shuffling around, playing with my curtains, ignoring me. One of them threw a pencil at another. For a short while, I almost forgot about the nausea churning in my stomach, the trembling in my wrists, the puppets bobbing on their wires in my head.

"Hey," I said. I had to say it twice more to get their attention. I usually do.

Finally, Penny noticed and said, "Mr. Gadeuszki's trying to say something," and they slowly quieted down.

I put my quivering hands on my lap under the desk and left them there. "Why don't you kids get back on the metro and go see the astronomical clock?"

The Tribe members looked at each other uncertainly. "Really," I told them. "I'm fine. When's the next time you're going to be in Prague?"

They were good kids, and they looked unsure for a few seconds longer. In the end, though, they started trickling toward the door, and I thought I'd gotten them out until Penny Berry stepped in front of me.

"You killed your grandfather," she said.

"Didn't," I snarled, and Penny blinked, and everyone whirled to stare at me. I took a breath, almost got control of my voice. "I said I didn't kill him."

"Oh," Penny said. She was on this trip not because of any familial or cultural heritage but because this was the most interesting experience she could find to devour this month. She was pressing me now because she suspected I had something more startling to share than Prague did at the moment. And she was always hungry.

Or maybe she was just lonely, confused about the kid she had never quite been and the world she didn't quite feel part of. Which would make her more than a little like me, and might explain why she had always annoyed me as much as she did.

"It's stupid," I said. "It's nothing."

Penny didn't move. In my memory, the little wooden man on his black pine branch quivered, twitched, and began to rock, side to side.

"I need to write it down," I said, trying to sound gentle. Then I lied. "Maybe I'll show you when I'm done."

Five minutes later, I was alone in my room with a fresh glass of nice water and there was sand on my tongue and desert sun on my neck and that horrid, gasping breathing like a snake rattle in my ears, and for the first time in many, many years, I was home.

3

In June 1978, on the day after school let out, I was sitting in my bedroom in Albuquerque, New Mexico, thinking about absolutely nothing when my dad came in and sat down on my bed and said, "I want you to do something for me."

In my nine years of life, my father had almost never asked me to do anything for him. As far as I could tell, he had very few things that he wanted. He worked at an insurance firm and came home at exactly 5:30 every night and played an hour of catch with me before dinner or, sometimes, walked me to the ice-cream shop. After dinner, he sat on the black couch in the den reading paperback mystery novels until 9:30. The paperbacks were all old, with bright yellow or red covers featuring men in trench coats and women with black dresses sliding down the curves in their bodies like tar. It made me nervous, sometimes, just watching my father's hands on the covers. I asked him once why he liked those kinds of books, and he just shook his head. "All those people," he said, sounding, as usual, as though he was speaking to me through a tin can from a great distance. "Doing all those things." At exactly 9:30, every single night I can remember, my father clicked off the lamp next to the couch and touched me on the head if I was up and went to bed.

"What do you want me to do?" I asked that June morning, though I didn't much care. This was the first weekend of summer vacation, and I had months of free time in front of me, and I never knew quite what to do with it anyway.

"What I tell you, okay?" my father said.

Without even thinking, I said, "Sure."

And he said, "Good. I'll tell Grandpa you're coming." Then he left me gaping on the bed while he went into the kitchen to use the phone.

My grandfather lived seventeen miles from Albuquerque in a red adobe hut in the middle of the desert. The only sign of humanity anywhere around him was the ruins of a small pueblo maybe half a mile away. Even now, what I remember most about my grandfather's house is the desert rolling up to and through it in an endless red tide that never receded. From the back steps, I could see the pueblo honeycombed with caves like a giant beehive tipped on its side, empty of bees but buzzing as the wind whipped through it.

Four years before, my grandfather had told my parents to knock off the token visits. Then he'd had his phone shut off. As far as I knew, none of us had seen him since.

All my life, he'd been dying. He had emphysema and some kind of weird allergic condition that turned swatches of his skin pink. The last time I'd been with him, he'd just sat in a chair in a tank top breathing through a tube. He'd looked like a piece of petrified wood.

The next morning, a Sunday, my father packed my green camp duffel bag with a box of new, unopened wax packs of baseball cards and the transistor radio my mother had given me for my birthday the year before, then loaded it and me into the grimy green Datsun he always meant to wash and never did. "Time to go," he told me in his mechanical voice, and I was still too baffled by what was happening to protest as he led me outside. Moments before, a morning thunderstorm had rocked the whole house, but now the sun was up, searing the whole sky orange. Our street smelled like creosote and green chili and adobe mud.

"I don't want to go," I said to my father.

"I wouldn't either, if I were you," he told me, and started the car.

"You don't even like him," I said.

My father just looked at me, and for an astonishing second, I thought he was going to hug me. But he looked away instead, dropped the car into gear, and drove us out of town.

All the way to my grandfather's house, we followed the thunderstorm. It must have been traveling at exactly our speed, because we never got any closer, and it never got farther away. It just retreated before us, a big black wall of nothing, like a shadow the whole world cast, and every now and then streaks of lightning flew up the clouds like signal flares and illuminated the sand and mountains and rain.

"Why are we doing this?" I asked when my dad started slowing, studying the sand on his side of the car for the dirt track that led to my grandfather's.

"Want to drive?" He gestured to me to slide across the seat into his lap.

Again, I was surprised. My dad always seemed willing enough to play catch with me. But he rarely generated ideas on his own for things we could do together. And the thought of sitting in his lap with his arms around me was too alien to fathom. I waited too long, and the moment passed. My father didn't ask again. Through the windshield, I looked at the wet road already drying in patches in the sun. The whole day felt distant, like someone else's dream.

"You know he was in the war, right?" my father said, and despite our crawling speed he had to jam on the brakes to avoid passing the turnoff. No one, it seemed to me, could possibly have intended this to be a road. It wasn't dug or flattened or marked, just a rumple in the earth.

"Yeah," I said.

That he'd been in the war was pretty much the only thing I knew about my grandfather. Actually, he'd been in the camps. After the war, he'd been in other camps in Israel for almost five years while Red Cross workers searched for living relatives and found none, and finally turned him loose to make his way as best he could.

As soon as we were off the highway, sand ghosts rose around the car, ticking against the trunk and hood as we passed. Thanks to the thunderstorm, they left a wet, red residue like bug smear on the hood and windshield.

"You know, now that I think about it," my father said, his voice flat as ever but the words clearer, somehow, and I found myself leaning closer to him to make sure I heard him over the churning wheels. "He was even less of a grandfather to you than a father to me." He rubbed a hand over the bald spot just beginning to spread over the top of his head like an egg yolk being squashed. I'd never seen him do that before. It made him look old.

My grandfather's house rose out of the desert like a druid mound. There was no shape to it. It had exactly one window, and that couldn't be seen from the road. No mailbox. Never in my life, I realized abruptly, had I had to sleep in there.

"Dad, please don't make me stay," I said as he stopped the car fifteen feet or so from the front door.

He looked at me, and his mouth turned down a little, and his shoulders tensed. Then he sighed. "Three days," he said, and got out.

"*You* stay," I said, but I got out, too.

When I was standing beside him, looking past the house at the distant pueblo, he said, "Your grandfather didn't ask for me, he asked for you. He won't hurt you. And he doesn't ask for much from us, or from anyone."

"Neither do you."

After a while, and very slowly, as though remembering how, my father smiled. "And neither do you, Seth."

Neither the smile nor the statement reassured me.

"Just remember this, son. Your grandfather has had a very hard life, and not just because of the camps. He worked two jobs for twenty-five years to provide for my mother and me. He never called in sick. He never took vacations. And he was ecstatic when you were born."

That surprised me. "Really? How do you know?"

For the first time I could remember, my father blushed, and I thought maybe I'd caught him lying, and then I wasn't sure. He kept looking at me. "Well, he came to town, for one thing. Twice."

For a little longer, we stood together while the wind rolled over the rocks and sand. I couldn't smell the rain anymore, but I thought I could taste it, a little. Tall, leaning cacti prowled the waste around us like stick figures who'd escaped from one of my doodles. I was always doodling, then, trying to get the shapes of things.

Finally, the thin, wooden door to the adobe clicked open, and out stepped Lucy, and my father straightened and put his hand on his bald spot again and put it back down.

She didn't live there, as far as I knew. But I'd never been to my grandfather's house when she wasn't in it. I knew she worked for some foundation that provided care to Holocaust victims, though she was Navajo, not Jewish, and that she'd been coming out here all my life to make my grandfather's meals, bathe him, keep him company. I rarely saw them speak to each other. When I was little and my grandmother was still alive and we were still welcome, Lucy used to take me to the pueblo after she'd finished with my grandfather and watch me climb around on the stones and peer into the empty caves and listen to the wind chase thousand-year-old echoes out of the walls.

There were gray streaks now in the black hair that poured down Lucy's shoulders, and I could see semicircular lines like tree rings in her dark, weathered cheeks. But I was uncomfortably aware, this time, of the way her breasts pushed her plain white denim shirt out of the top of her jeans while her eyes settled on mine, black and still.

"Thank you for coming," she said, as if I'd had a choice. When I didn't answer, she looked at my father. "Thank you for bringing him. We're set up out back."

I threw one last questioning glance at my father as Lucy started away, but he just looked bewildered or bored or whatever he generally was. And that made me angry. "'Bye," I told him, and moved toward the house.

"Good-bye," I heard him say, and something in his tone unsettled me; it was too sad. I shivered, turned around, and my father said, "He want to see me?"

He looked thin, I thought, just another spindly cactus, holding my duffel bag out from his side. If he'd been speaking to me, I might have run to him. I wanted to. But he was watching Lucy, who had stopped at the edge of the square of patio cement outside the front door.

"I don't think so," she said, and came over to me and took my hand.

Without another word, my father tossed my duffel bag onto the miniature patio and climbed back in his car. For a moment, his eyes caught mine through the windshield, and I said, "Wait," but my father didn't hear me. I said it louder, and Lucy put her hand on my shoulder.

"This has to be done, Seth," she said.

"What does?"

"This way." She gestured toward the other side of the house, and I followed her there and stopped when I saw the hogan.

It sat next to the squat gray cactus I'd always considered the edge of my grandfather's yard. It looked surprisingly solid, its mud walls dry and gray and hard, its pocked, stumpy wooden pillars firm in the ground, almost as if they were real trees that had somehow taken root there.

"You live here now?" I blurted, and Lucy stared at me.

"Oh, yes, Seth. Me sleep-um ground. *How.*" She pulled aside the hide curtain at the front of the hogan and ducked inside, and I followed.

I thought it would be cooler in there, but it wasn't. The wood and mud trapped the heat but blocked the light. I didn't like it. It reminded me of an oven, of Hansel and Gretel. And it reeked of the desert: burnt sand, hot wind, nothingness.

"This is where you'll sleep," Lucy said. "It's also where we'll work." She knelt and lit a beeswax candle and placed it in the center of the dirt floor in a scratched glass drugstore candlestick. "We need to begin right now."

"Begin what?" I asked, fighting down another shudder as the candlelight played over the room. Against the far wall, tucked under a miniature canopy constructed of metal poles and a tarpaulin, were a sleeping bag and a pillow. My bed, I assumed. Beside it sat a low, rolling table, and on the table were another candlestick, a cracked ceramic bowl, some matches, and the Dancing Man.

In my room in the pension in the Czech Republic, five thousand miles and twenty years removed from that place, I put my pen down and swallowed the entire glass of lukewarm water my students had left me. Then I got up and went to the window, staring out at the trees and the street. I was hoping to see my kids returning like ducks to a familiar pond, flapping their arms and jostling each other and squawking and laughing. Instead, I saw my own face, faint and featureless, too white in the window glass. I went back to the desk and picked up the pen.

The Dancing Man's eyes were all pupil, carved in two perfect ovals in the knottiest wood I had ever seen. The nose was just a notch, but the mouth was enormous, a giant O, like the opening of a cave. I was terrified of the thing even before I noticed that it was moving.

Moving, I suppose, is too grand a description. It...leaned. First one way, then the other, on a bent black pine branch that ran straight through its belly. In a fit of panic, after a nightmare, I described it to my college roommate, a physics major, and he shrugged and said something about perfect balance and pendulums and gravity and the rotation of the earth. For the first and only time, right in that first moment, I lifted the branch off the table, and the Dancing Man leaned a little faster, weaving to the beat of my blood. I put the branch down fast.

"Take the drum," Lucy said behind me, and I ripped my eyes away from the Dancing Man.

"What?" I said.

She gestured at the table, and I realized she meant the ceramic bowl. I didn't understand, and I didn't want to go over there. But I didn't know what else to do, and I felt ridiculous under Lucy's stare.

The Dancing Man was at the far end of its branch, leaning, mouth open. Trying to be casual, I snatched the bowl from underneath it and retreated to where Lucy knelt. The water inside the bowl made a sloshing sound but didn't splash out, and I held it away from my chest in surprise and noticed the covering stitched over the top. It was hide of some kind, moist when I touched it.

"Like this," said Lucy, and she leaned close and tapped on the skin of the drum. The sound was deep and tuneful, like a voice. I sat down next to Lucy. She tapped again, in a slow, repeating pattern. I put my hands where hers had been, and when she nodded at me, I began to play.

"Okay? I said.

"Harder." Lucy reached into her pocket and pulled out a long wooden stick. The candlelight flickered across the stick, and I saw the carving. A pine tree, and underneath it, roots that bulged along the base of the stick like thick black veins.

"What is that?" I asked.

"A rattle stick. My grandmother made it. I'm going to rattle it while you play. So if you would. Like I showed you."

I beat on the drum, and the sound came out dead in that airless space.

"For God's sake," Lucy snapped. "Harder!" She had never been exceptionally friendly to me. But she'd been friendlier than this.

I slammed my hands down harder, and after a few beats, Lucy leaned back and nodded and watched. Not long after, she lifted her hand, stared at me as though daring me to stop her, and shook the stick. The sound it made was less rattle than buzz, as though it had wasps inside it. Lucy shook it a few more times, always at the same halfpause in my rhythm. Then her eyes rolled back in her head, and her spine arched, and my hand froze over the drum and Lucy snarled, "Don't stop."

After that, she began to chant. There was no tune to it, but a pattern, the pitch sliding up a little, down some, up a little more. When Lucy reached the top note, the ground under my crossed legs seemed to tingle, as though there were scorpions sliding out of the sand, but I didn't look down. I thought of the wooden figure behind me, but I didn't turn around. I played the drum and I watched Lucy, and I kept my mouth shut.

We went on for a long, long time. After that first flush of fear, I was too mesmerized to think. My bones were tingling, too, and the air in the hogan was heavy. I couldn't get enough of it in my lungs. Tiny tidepools of sweat had formed in the hollow of Lucy's neck and under her ears and at the throat of her shirt. Under my palms, the drum was sweating, too, and the skin got slippery and warm. Not until Lucy stopped chanting did I realize that I was rocking side to side. Leaning.

"Want lunch?" Lucy said, standing and brushing the earth off her jeans.

I put my hands out perpendicular, felt the skin prickle and realized my wrists had gone to sleep even as they pounded out the rhythm Lucy had taught me. When I stood, the floor of the hogan seemed unstable, like the bottom of one of those balloon-tents my classmates sometimes had at birthday parties. I didn't want to look behind me, and then I did. The Dancing Man rocked slowly in no wind.

I turned around again, but Lucy had left the hogan. I didn't want to be alone in there, so I leapt through the hide curtain and winced against the sudden blast of sunlight and saw my grandfather.

He was propped up in his wheelchair, positioned dead center between the hogan and the back of his house. He must have been there the whole time, I thought, and somehow I'd managed not to notice him when I came in, because unless he'd gotten a whole lot better in the years since I'd seen him last, he couldn't have wheeled himself out. And he looked worse.

For one thing, his skin was falling off. At every exposed place on him, I saw flappy folds of yellow-pink. What was underneath was uglier still, not red or bleeding, just not skin. Too dry. Too colorless. He looked like a corn husk. An empty one.

Next to him, propped on a rusty blue dolly, was a cylindrical silver oxygen tank. A clear tube ran from the nozzle at the top of the tank to the blue mask over my grandfather's nose and mouth. Above the mask, my grandfather's heavy-lidded eyes watched me, though they didn't seem capable of movement, either. Leave him out here, I thought, and those eyes would simply fill up with sand.

"Come in, Seth," Lucy told me, without any word to my grandfather or acknowledgment that he was there.

I had my hand on the screen door, was halfway into the house when I realized I'd heard him speak. I stopped. It had to have been him, I thought, and couldn't have been. I turned around and saw the back of his head tilting toward the top of the chair. Retracing my steps — I'd given him a wide berth — I returned to face him. The eyes stayed still, and the oxygen tank was silent. But the mask fogged, and I heard the whisper again.

"Ruach," he said. It was what he always called me, when he called me anything.

In spite of the heat, I felt goosebumps spring from my skin, all along my legs and arms. I couldn't move. I couldn't answer. I should say hello, I thought. Say something.

I waited instead. A few seconds later, the oxygen mask fogged again. *"Trees,"* said the whisper-voice. *"Screaming. In the trees."* One of my grandfather's hands raised an inch or so off the arm of the chair and fell back into place.

"Patience," Lucy said from the doorway. "Come on, Seth." This time, my grandfather said nothing as I slipped past him into the house.

Lucy slid a bologna sandwich and a bag of Fritos and a plastic glass of apple juice in front of me. I lifted the sandwich, found that I couldn't imagine putting it in my mouth, and dropped it on the plate.

"Better eat," Lucy said. "We have a long day yet."

I ate, a little. Eventually, Lucy sat down across from me, but she didn't say anything else. She just gnawed a celery stick and watched the sand outside change color as the sun crawled west. The house was silent, the countertops and walls bare.

"Can I ask you something?" I finally asked.

Lucy was washing my plate in the sink. She didn't turn around, but she didn't say no.

"What are we doing? Out there, I mean."

No answer. Through the kitchen doorway, I could see my grandfather's living room, the stained wood floor and the single brown armchair lodged against a wall across from the TV. My grandfather had spent every waking minute of his life in this place for fifteen years or more, and there was no trace of him in it.

"It's a Way, isn't it?" I said, and Lucy shut off the water.

When she turned, her expression was the same as it had been all day, a little mocking, a little angry. She took a step toward the table.

"We learned about them at school," I said.

"Did you?"

"We're studying lots of Indian things."

The smile that spread over Lucy's face was cruel. Or maybe just tired. "Good for you," she said. "Come on. We don't have much time."

"Is this to make my grandfather better?"

"Nothing's going to make your grandfather better." Without waiting for me, she pushed through the screen door into the heat.

This time, I made myself stop beside my grandfather's chair. I could just hear the hiss of the oxygen tank, like steam escaping from the boiling ground. When no fog appeared in the blue mask and no words emerged from the hiss, I followed Lucy into the hogan and let the hide curtain fall shut.

All afternoon and into the evening, I played the water drum while Lucy chanted. By the time the air began to cool outside, the whole hogan was vibrating, and the ground, too. Whatever we were doing, I could feel the power in it. I was the beating heart of a living thing, and Lucy was its voice. Once, I found myself wondering just what we were setting loose or summoning here, and I stopped, for a single beat. But the silence was worse. The silence was like being dead. And

I thought I could hear the Dancing Man behind me. If I inclined my head, stopped playing for too long, I almost believed I'd hear him whispering.

When Lucy finally rocked to her feet and left without speaking to me, it was evening, and the desert was alive. I sat shaking as the rhythm spilled out of me and the sand soaked it up. Then I stood, and that unsteady feeling came over me again, stronger this time, as if the air were wobbling, too, threatening to slide right off the surface of the earth. When I emerged from the hogan, I saw black spiders on the wall of my grandfather's house, and I heard wind and rabbits and the first coyotes yipping somewhere to the west. My grandfather sat slumped in the same position he had been in hours and hours ago, which meant he had been baking out here all afternoon. Lucy was on the patio, watching the sun melt into the horizon's open mouth. Her skin was slick, and her hair was wet where it touched her ear and neck.

"Your grandfather's going to tell you a story," she said, sounding exhausted. "And you're going to listen."

My grandfather's head rolled upright, and I wished we were back in the hogan, doing whatever it was we'd been doing. At least there, I was moving, pounding hard enough to drown sound out. Maybe. The screen door slapped shut, and my grandfather looked at me. His eyes were deep, deep brown, almost black, and horribly familiar. Did my eyes look like that?

"Ruach," he whispered, and I wasn't sure, but his whisper seemed stronger than it had before. The oxygen mask fogged and stayed fogged. The whisper kept coming, as though Lucy had turned a spigot and left it open. *"You will know... Now... Then the world...won't be yours...anymore."* My grandfather shifted like some sort of giant, bloated sand-spider in the center of its web, and I heard his ruined skin rustle. Above us, the whole sky went red.

"At war's end..." my grandfather hissed. *"Do you...understand?"* I nodded, transfixed. I could hear his breathing, now, the ribs rising, parting, collapsing. The tank machinery had gone strangely silent. Was he breathing on his own, I wondered? Could he, still?

"A few days. Do you understand? Before the Red Army came..." He coughed. Even his cough sounded stronger. *"The Nazis took...me. And the Gypsies. From...our camp. To Chelmno."*

I'd never heard the word before. I've almost never heard it since. But as my grandfather said it, another cough roared out of his throat, and when it was gone, the tank was hissing again. Still, my grandfather continued to whisper.

"To die. Do you understand?" Gasp. Hiss. Silence. *"To die. But not yet. Not...right away"* Gasp. *"We came...by train, but open train. Not cattle car. Wasteland. Farmland. Nothing. And then trees."* Under the mask, the lips twitched, and above it, the eyes closed completely. *"That first time. Ruach. All those...giant...green...trees. Unimaginable. To think anything...on the Earth we knew...could live that long."*

His voice continued to fade, faster than the daylight. A few minutes more, I thought, and he'd be silent again, just machine and breath, and I could sit out here in the yard and let the evening wind roll over me.

"When they took...us off the train," my grandfather said, *"for one moment...I swear I smelled...leaves. Fat, green leaves...the new green...in them. Then the old smell... The only smell. Blood in dirt. The stink...of us. Piss. Shit. Open... sores. Skin on fire. Hnnn."*

His voice trailed away, hardly-there air over barely moving mouth, and still he kept talking. *"Prayed for...some people...to die. They smelled...better. Dead. That was one prayer...always answered.*

"They took us...into the woods. Not to barracks. So few of them. Ten. Maybe twenty. Faces like...possums. Stupid. Blank. No thoughts. We came to...ditches. Deep. Like wells. Half full, already. They told us 'Stand still'... 'Breathe in.'"

At first, I thought the ensuing silence was for effect. He was letting me smell it. And I did smell it, the earth and the dead people, and there were German soldiers all around us, floating up out of the sand with black uniforms and white, blank faces. Then my grandfather crumpled forward, and I screamed for Lucy.

She came fast but not running and put a hand on my grandfather's back and another on his neck. After a few seconds, she straightened. "He's asleep," she told me. "Stay here." She wheeled my grandfather into the house, and she was gone a long time.

Sliding to a sitting position, I closed my eyes and tried not to hear my grandfather's voice. After a while I thought I could hear bugs and snakes and something larger padding out beyond the cacti. I could feel the moonlight, too, white and cool on my skin. The screen door banged, and I opened my eyes to find Lucy moving toward me, past me, carrying a picnic basket into the hogan.

"I want to eat out here," I said quickly, and Lucy turned with the hide curtain in her hand.

"Why don't we go in?" she said, and the note of coaxing in her voice made me nervous. So did the way she glanced over her shoulder into the hogan, as though something in there had spoken.

I stayed where I was, and eventually Lucy shrugged and let the curtain fall and dropped the basket at my feet. From the way she was acting, I thought she might leave me alone out there, but she sat down instead and looked at the sand and the cacti and the stars.

Inside the basket, I found warmed canned chili in a plastic Tupperware container and fry bread with cinnamon sugar and two cellophane-wrapped broccoli stalks that reminded me of uprooted miniature trees. In my ears, my grandfather's voice murmured, and to drown out the sound, I began to eat.

As soon as I was finished, Lucy began to stack the containers inside the basket, but she stopped when I spoke. "Please. Just talk to me a little."

She looked at me. The same look. As though we'd never even met. "Get some sleep. Tomorrow...well, let's just say tomorrow's a big day."

"For who?"

Lucy pursed her lips, and all at once, inexplicably, she seemed on the verge of tears. "Go to sleep."

"I'm not sleeping in the hogan," I told her.

"Suit yourself."

She was standing, and her back was to me now. I said, "Just tell me what kind of Way we're doing."

"An Enemy Way."

"What does it do?"

"It's nothing, Seth. God's sake. It's silly. Your grandfather thinks it will help him talk. He thinks it will sustain him while he tells you what he needs to tell you. Don't worry about the goddamn Way. Worry about your grandfather, for once."

My mouth flew open, and my skin stung as though she'd slapped me. I started to protest, then found I couldn't, and didn't want to. All my life, I'd built my grandfather into a figure of fear, a gasping, grotesque monster in a wheelchair. And my father had let me. I started to cry.

"I'm sorry," I said.

"Don't apologize to me." Lucy walked to the screen door.

"Isn't it a little late?" I called after her, furious at myself, at my father, at Lucy. Sad for my grandfather. Scared and sad.

One more time, Lucy turned around, and the moonlight poured down the white streaks in her hair like wax through a mold. Soon, I thought, she'd be made of it.

"I mean for my grandfather's Enemies," I said. "The Way can't really do anything to the Nazis. Right?"

"His Enemies are inside him," Lucy said, and left me.

For hours, it seemed, I sat in the sand, watching constellations explode out of the blackness, one after another, like firecrackers. In the ground, I heard night creatures stirring. I thought about the tube in my grandfather's mouth, and the unspeakable hurt in his eyes — because that's what it was, I thought now, not boredom, not hatred — and the enemies inside him. And then, slowly, exhaustion overtook me. The taste of fry bread lingered in my mouth, and the starlight got brighter still. I leaned back on my elbows. And finally, at God knows what hour, I crawled into the hogan, under the tarpaulin canopy Lucy had made me, and fell asleep.

When I awoke, the Dancing Man was leaning over me on its branch, and I knew, all at once, where I'd seen eyes like my grandfather's, and the old fear exploded through me all over again. How had he done it, I wondered? The carving on the wooden man's face was basic, the features crude. But the eyes were his. They had the same singular, almost oval shape, with identical little notches right near the tear ducts. The same too-heavy lids. Same expression, or lack of any.

I was transfixed, and I stopped breathing. All I could see were those eyes dancing above me. When the Dancing Man was perfectly perpendicular, it seemed to stop momentarily, as though studying me, and I remembered something my dad had told me about wolves. "They're not trial-and-error animals," he'd said. "They wait and watch, wait and watch, until they're sure they know how the thing is done. And then they do it."

The Dancing Man went on weaving. First to one side, then the other, then back. Slower and slower. If it gets itself completely still, I thought — I *knew* — I would die. Or I would change. That was why Lucy was ignoring me. She had lied to me about what we were doing here. That was the reason they hadn't let my father stay. Leaping to my feet, I grabbed the Dancing Man around its clunky wooden base, and it came off the table with the faintest little suck, as though I'd yanked a weed out of the ground. I wanted to throw it, but I didn't dare. Instead, bent double, not looking at my clenched fist, I crab-walked to the entrance of the hogan, brushed back the hide curtain, slammed the Dancing Man down in the sand outside, and flung the curtain closed again. Then I squatted in the shadows, panting. Listening.

I crouched there a long time, watching the bottom of the curtain, expecting to see the Dancing Man slithering beneath it. But the hide stayed motionless, the hogan shadowy but still. I let myself sit back, and eventually, I slid into my sleeping bag again. I didn't expect to sleep anymore, but I did.

The smell of fresh fry bread woke me, and when I opened my eyes, Lucy was laying a tray of breads and sausage and juice on a woven red blanket on the floor of the hogan. My lips tasted sandy, and I could feel grit in my clothes and between my teeth and under my eyelids, as though I'd been buried overnight and dug up again.

"Hurry," Lucy told me, in the same chilly voice as yesterday.

I threw back the sleeping bag and started to sit up and saw the Dancing Man tilting on its branch, watching me. My whole body clenched, and I glared at Lucy and shouted, "How did that get back here?" Even as I said it, I realized that wasn't what I wanted to ask. More than how, I needed to know *when*. Exactly how long had it been hovering there without my knowing?

Without raising an eyebrow or even looking at me, Lucy shrugged and sat back. "Your grandfather wants you to have it," she said.

"I don't want it."

"Grow up."

Edging as far from the nightstand as possible, I shed the sleeping bag and sat down on the blanket and ate. Everything tasted sweet and sandy. My skin prickled with the intensifying heat. I still had a piece of fry bread and half a sausage left when I put my plastic fork down and looked at Lucy, who was arranging a new candle, settling the water drum near me, tying her hair back with a red rubber-band.

"Where did it come from?" I asked.

For the first time that day, Lucy looked at me, and this time, there really were tears in her eyes. "I don't understand your family," she said.

I shook my head. "Neither do I."

"Your grandfather's been saving that for you, Seth."

"Since when?"

"Since before you were born. Before your father was born. Before he ever imagined there could be a you."

This time, when the guilt came for me, it mixed with my fear rather than chasing it away, and I broke out sweating, and I thought I might be sick.

"You have to eat. Damn you," said Lucy.

I picked up my fork and squashed a piece of sausage into the fry bread and put it in my mouth. My stomach convulsed, but accepted what I gave it.

I managed a few more bites. As soon as I pushed the plate back, Lucy shoved the drum onto my lap. I played while she chanted, and the sides of the hogan seemed to breathe in and out, very slowly. I felt drugged. Then I wondered if I had been. Had they sprinkled something on the bread? Was that the next step? And toward what? Erasing me, I thought, almost chanted. Erasing me, and my hands flew off the drum, and Lucy stopped.

"Alright," she said. "That's probably enough." Then, to my surprise, she actually reached out and tucked some of my hair behind my ear, then touched my face for a second as she took the drum from me. "It's time for your Journey," she said.

I stared at her. The walls, I noticed, had stilled. I didn't feel any less strange, but a little more awake, at least. "Journey where?"

"You'll need water. And I've packed you a lunch." She slipped through the hide curtain, and I followed, dazed, and almost walked into my grandfather, parked right outside the hogan with a black towel on his head, so that his eyes and splitting skin were in shadow. He wore black leather gloves. His hands, I thought, must be on fire.

Right at the moment I noticed that Lucy was no longer with us, the hiss from the oxygen tank sharpened, and my grandfather's lips moved beneath the mask. *"Ruach."* This morning, the nickname sounded almost affectionate.

I waited, unable to look away. But the oxygen hiss settled again, like leaves after a gust of wind, and my grandfather said nothing more. A few seconds later, Lucy came back carrying a red backpack, which she handed to me.

"Follow the signs," she said, and turned me around until I was facing straight out from the road into the empty desert.

Struggling to life, I shook her hand off my shoulder. "Signs of what? What am I supposed to be doing?"

"Finding. Bringing back."

"I won't go."

"You'll go," Lucy said coldly. "The signs will be easily recognizable, and easy to locate. I have been assured of that. All you have to do is pay attention."

"'Assured' by who?"

"The first sign, I am told, will be left by the tall flowering cactus."

She pointed, which was unnecessary. A hundred yards or so from my grandfather's house, a spiky green cactus poked out of the rock and sand, supported on either side by two miniature versions of itself. A little cactus family, staggering in out of the waste.

I glanced at my grandfather under his mock-cowl, Lucy with her ferocious black eyes trained on me. Tomorrow, I thought, my father would come for me, and with any luck, I would never have to come out here again.

Then, suddenly, I felt ridiculous, and sad, and guilty once more.

Without even realizing what I was doing, I stuck my hand and touched my grandfather's arm. The skin under his thin cotton shirt depressed beneath my fingers like the squishy center of a misshapen pillow. It wasn't hot. It didn't feel alive at all. I yanked my hand back, and Lucy glared at me. Tears sprang to my eyes.

"Get out of here," she said, and I stumbled away into the sand.

I don't really think the heat intensified as soon as I stepped away from my grandfather's house. But it seemed to. Along my bare arms and legs, I could feel the little hairs curling as though singed. The sun had scorched the sky white, and the only place to look that didn't hurt my eyes was down. Usually, when I walked in the desert, I was terrified of scorpions, but not that day. It was impossible to imagine anything scuttling or stinging or even breathing out there. Except me.

I don't know what I expected to find. Footprints, maybe, or animal scat, or something dead. Instead, stuck to the stem by a cactus needle, I found a yellow Post-It note. It said: "Pueblo."

Gently, avoiding the rest of the spiny needles, I removed the note. The writing was black and blocky. I glanced toward my grandfather's house, but he and Lucy were gone. The ceremonial hogan looked silly from this distance, like a little kid's pup tent.

Unlike the pueblo, I thought. I didn't even want to look that way, let alone go there. Already I could hear it, calling for me in a whisper that sounded far too much like my grandfather's. I could head for the road, I thought. Start toward town instead of the pueblo, and wait for a passing truck to carry me home. There would have to be a truck, sooner or later.

I did go to the road. But when I got there, I turned in the direction of the pueblo. I don't know why. I didn't feel as if I had choice.

The walk, if anything, was too short. No cars passed. No road signs sprang from the dirt to point the way back to the world I knew. I watched the asphalt rise out of itself and roll in the heat, and I thought of my grandfather in the woods of Chelmno, digging graves in long green shadows. Lucy had put ice in the thermos she gave me, and the cubes clicked against my teeth when I drank.

I walked, and I watched the desert, trying to spot a bird or a lizard. Even a scorpion would have been welcome. What I saw was sand, distant, colorless mountains, and white sky, a world as empty of life and its echoes as the surface of Mars, and just as red.

Even the lone road sign pointing to the pueblo was rusted through, crusted with sand, the letters so scratched away that the name of the place was no longer legible. I'd never seen a tourist here, or another living soul. Even calling it a pueblo seemed grandiose.

It was two sets of caves dug into the side of a cliff face, the top one longer than the bottom, so that together they formed a sort of gigantic cracked harmonica for the desert wind to play. The roof and walls of the top set of caves had fallen in. The whole structure seemed more monument than ruin, a marker of a people who no longer existed, rather than a place they had lived.

The bottom stretch of caves was largely intact, and as I stumbled toward them along the cracking macadam, I could feel their pull in my ankles. They seemed to be sucking the desert inside them, bit by bit. I stopped in front and listened.

I couldn't hear anything. I looked at the cracked, nearly square window openings, the doorless entryways leading into what had once been living spaces, the low, shadowed caves of dirt and rock. The whole pueblo just squatted there, inhaling sand through its dozens of dead mouths in a mockery of breath. I waited a while longer, but the open air didn't feel any safer, just hotter. If my grandfather's Enemies were inside him, I suddenly wondered, and if we were calling them out, then where were they going? Finally I ducked through the nearest entryway and stood in the gloom.

After a few seconds, my eyes adjusted. But there was nothing to see. Along the window openings, blown sand lay in waves and mounds, like miniature relief maps of the desert outside. At my feet lay tiny stones, too small to hide scorpions, and a few animal bones, none of them larger than my pinky, distinguishable primarily by their curves, their stubborn whiteness.

Then, as though my entry had triggered some sort of mechanical magic show, sound coursed into my ears. In the walls, tiny feet and bellies slithered and scuttled. Nothing rattled a warning. Nothing hissed. And the footsteps, when they came, came so softly that at first I mistook them for sand shifting along the sills and the cool clay floor.

I didn't scream, but I staggered backward, lost my footing, slipped down, and I had the thermos raised and ready to swing when my father stepped out of the shadows and sat down cross-legged across the room from me.

"What —" I said, tears flying down my face, my heart thudding.

My father said nothing. From the pocket of his plain yellow button-up shirt, he pulled a packet of cigarette papers and a pouch of tobacco, then rolled a cigarette in a series of quick, expert motions.

"You don't smoke," I said, and my father lit the cigarette and dragged air down his lungs with a rasp.

"Far as you know," he answered. The orange glow from the tip looked like an open sore on his lips. Around us, the pueblo lifted, settled.

"Why does Grandpa call me '*Ruach*'?" I snapped. And still, my father only sat and smoked. The smell tickled unpleasantly in my nostrils. "God, Dad. What's going on? What are you doing here, and —"

"Do you know what *ruach* means?" he said.

I shook my head.

"It's a Hebrew word. It means ghost."

Hearing that was like being slammed to the ground. I couldn't get my lungs to work.

My father went on. "Sometimes, that's what it means. It depends what you use it with, you see? Sometimes, it means spirit, as in the spirit of God. Spirit of life. What God gave to his creations." He stubbed his cigarette in the sand, and the orange glow winked out like an eye blinking shut. "And sometimes it just means wind."

By my sides, I could feel my hands clutch as breath returned to my body. The sand felt cool and soft against my palms. "You don't know Hebrew, either," I said.

"I made a point of knowing that."

"Why?"

"Because that's what he called me, too," my father said, and rolled a second cigarette, but didn't light it. For a while, we sat. Then my father said, "Lucy called me two weeks ago. She told me it was time, and she said she needed a partner for your...ceremony. Someone to hide this, then help you find it. She said it was essential to the ritual." Reaching behind him, he produced a brown paper grocery bag with the top rolled down and tossed it to me. "I didn't kill it," he said.

I stared at him, and more tears stung my eyes. Sand licked along the skin of my legs and arms and crawled up my shorts and sleeves, as though seeking pores, points of entry. Nothing about my father's presence here was reassuring. Nothing about him had ever been reassuring, or anything else, I thought furiously, and the fury felt good. It helped me move. I yanked the bag to me.

The first thing I saw when I ripped it open was an eye. It was yellow-going-gray, almost dry. Not quite, though. Then I saw the folded, ridged black wings. A furry, broken body, twisted into a J. Except for the smell and the eye, it could have been a Halloween decoration.

"Is that a bat?" I whispered. Then I shoved the bag away and gagged.

My father glanced around at the walls, back at me. He made no move toward me. He was part of it, I thought wildly, he knew what they were doing, and then I pushed the thought away. It couldn't be true. "Dad, I don't understand," I pleaded.

"I know you're young," my father said. "He didn't do this to me until I left for college. But there's no more time, is there? You've seen him."

"Why do I have to do this at all?"

At that, my father's gaze swung down on me. He cocked his head and pursed his lips, as though I'd asked something completely incomprehensible. "It's your birthright," he said, and stood up.

We drove back to my grandfather's adobe in silence. The trip lasted less than five minutes. I couldn't even figure out what else to ask, let alone what I might do. I glanced at my father, wanting to scream at him, pound on him until he told me why he was acting this way.

Except that I wasn't sure he was acting anything but normal, for him. He didn't speak when he walked me to the ice-cream shop, either. When we arrived at the adobe, he leaned across me to push my door open, and I grabbed his hand.

"Dad. At least tell me what the bat is for."

My father sat up, moved the air-conditioning lever right, then hard back to the left, as though he could surprise it into working. He always did this. It never worked. My father and his routines. "Nothing," he said. "It's a symbol."

"For what?"

"Lucy will tell you."

"But you know." I was almost snarling at him now.

"Only what Lucy told me. It stands for the skin at the tip of the tongue. It's the Talking God. Or associated with it. Or something. It goes where nothing else can go. Or helps someone else go there. I think. I'm sorry."

Gently, hand on my shoulder, he eased me out of the car before it occurred to me to wonder what he was apologizing for. But he surprised me by calling after me. "I promise you this, Seth. This is the last time in your life that you'll have to come here. Shut the door."

Too stunned and confused and scared to do anything else, I shut it, then watched as my father's car disintegrated into the first, far-off shadows of twilight. Already, too soon, I felt the change in the air, the night chill seeping through the gauze-dry day like blood through a bandage.

My grandfather and Lucy were waiting on the patio. She had her hand on his shoulder, her long hair gathered on her head, and without its dark frame, her face looked much older. And his — fully exposed now, without its protective shawl — looked like a rubber mask on a hook, with no bones inside to support it.

Slowly, my grandfather's wheelchair squeaked over the patio onto the hard sand as Lucy propelled it. I could do nothing but watch. The wheelchair stopped, and my grandfather studied me.

"*Ruach,*" he said. There was still no tone in his voice. But there were no holes in it, either, no gaps where last night his breath had failed him. "*Bring it to me.*"

It was my imagination, surely, or the first hint of breeze, that made the bag seem to squirm in my hands. This would be the last time, my father had said. I stumbled forward and dropped the paper bag in my grandfather's lap.

Faster than I'd ever seen him move, but still not fast, my grandfather crushed the bag against his chest. His head tilted forward, and I had the insane idea that he was about to sing to it, like a baby. But all he did was close his eyes and hold it.

"Alright, that's enough, I told you it doesn't work like that," Lucy said, and took the bag from him. She touched him gently on the back but didn't look at me.

"What did he just do?" I challenged her. "What did the bat do?"

Once more, Lucy smiled her slow, nasty smile. "Wait and see."

Then she was gone, and my grandfather and I were alone in the yard. The dark came drifting down the distant mountainsides like a fog bank, but faster. When it reached us, I closed my eyes and felt nothing except an instantaneous chill. I opened my eyes, and my grandfather was still watching me, head cocked a little on his neck. A wolf indeed.

"Digging," he said. *"All we did, at first. Making pits deeper. The dirt so black. So soft. Like sticking your hands...inside an animal. All those trees leaning over us. Pines. Great white birches. Bark, smooth as baby skin. The Nazis gave... nothing to drink. Nothing to eat. But they paid...no attention, either. I sat next to the gypsy I had slept beside all...through the war. On a single slab of rotted wood. We had shared body heat. Blood from...each other's wounds. Infections. Lice.*

"I never...even knew his name. Four years six inches from each other...never knew it. Couldn't understand each other. Never really tried. He'd saved —" a cough rattled my grandfather's entire body, and his eyes got wilder, began to bulge, and I thought be wasn't breathing and almost yelled for Lucy again, but he gathered himself and went on. *"Buttons,"* he said. *"You understand? From somewhere. Rubbed their edges on rocks. Posts. Anything handy. Until they were...sharp. Not to kill. Not as a weapon."* More coughing. *"As a tool. To whittle."*

"Whittle," I said automatically, as though talking in my sleep.

"When he was starving. When he...woke up screaming. When we had to watch children's...bodies dangle from gallows...until the first crows came for their eyes. When it was snowing, and...we had to march...barefoot...or stand outside all night. The gypsy whittled."

Again, my grandfather's eyes ballooned in their sockets as though they would burst. Again came the cough, shaking him so hard that he almost fell from the chair. And again, he fought his body to stillness.

"Wait," he gasped. *"You will wait. You must."*

I waited. What else could I do?

A long while later, he said, *"Two little girls."*

I stared at him. His words wrapped me like strands of a cocoon. "What?"

"Listen. Two girls. The same ones, over and over. That's what...the gypsy... whittled."

Dimly, in the part of my brain that still felt alert, I wondered how anyone could tell if two figures carved in God knows what with the sharpened edge of a button were the same girls.

But my grandfather just nodded. *"Even at the end. Even at Chelmno. In the woods. In the moments...when we weren't digging, and the rest of us...sat. He went straight for the trees. Put his hands on them like they were warm. Wept. First time, all war. Despite everything we saw. Everything we knew...no tears from him, until then. When he came back, he had...strips of pine bark in his hands. And while everyone else slept...or froze...or died...he worked. All night. Under the trees.*

"Every few hours...shipments came. Of people, you understand? Jews. We heard trains. Then, later, we saw creatures...between tree trunks. Thin. Awful. Like dead saplings walking. When the Nazis...began shooting...they fell with no sound. Poppoppop from the guns. Then silence. Things lying in leaves. In the wet.

"The killing wasn't...enough fun...for the Nazis, of course. They made us roll bodies...into the pits, with our hands. Then bury them. With our hands. Or our mouths. Sometimes our mouths. Dirt and blood. Bits of person in your teeth. A few of us lay down. Died on the ground. The Nazis didn't have...to tell us. We just...pushed anything dead...into the nearest pit. No prayers. No last look to see who it was. It was no one. Do you see? No one. Burying. Or buried. No difference.

"And still, all night, the gypsy whittled.

"For the dawn...shipment...the Nazis tried...something new. Stripped the newcomers...then lined them up...on the lip of a pit...twenty, thirty at a time. Then they played...perforation games. Shoot up the body...down it...see if you could get it...to flap apart...before it fell. Open up, like a flower.

"All through the next day. And all the next night. Digging. Waiting. Whittling. Killing. Burying. Over and over. Sometime...late second day, maybe...I got angry. Not at the Nazis. For what? Being angry at human beings...for killing...for cruelty...like being mad at ice, for freezing. It's just... what to expect. So I got angry...at the trees. For standing there. For being green, and alive. For not falling when bullets hit them.

"I started...screaming. Trying to. In Hebrew. In Polish. The Nazis looked up, and I thought they would shoot me. They laughed instead. One began to clap. A rhythm. See?"

Somehow, my grandfather lifted his limp hands from the arms of the wheelchair and brought them together. They met with a sort of crackle, like dry twigs crumbling.

"The gypsy...just watched. Still weeping. But also...after a while... nodding."

All this time, my grandfather's eyes had seemed to swell, as though there was too much air being pumped into his body. But now, the air went out of him in a rush, and the eyes went dark, and the lids came down. I thought maybe he'd fallen asleep again, the way he had last night. But I still couldn't move. Dimly, I realized that the sweat from my long day's walking had cooled on my skin, and that I was freezing.

My grandfather's lids opened, a little. He seemed to be peering at me from inside a trunk, or a coffin.

"I don't know how the gypsy knew...that it was ending. That it was time. Maybe just because...it had been hours...half a day...between shipments. The world had gone...quiet. Us. Nazis. Trees. Corpses. There had been worse places...I thought...to stop living. Despite the smell.

"Probably, I was sleeping. I must have been, because the gypsy shook me... by the shoulder. Then held out...what he'd made. He had it...balanced...on a stick he'd bent. So the carving moved. Back and forth. Up and down."

My mouth opened and then hung there. I was rock, sand, and the air moved through me and left me nothing.

"'Life,' the gypsy said to me, in Polish. First Polish I ever heard him speak. 'Life. You see?'

"I shook...my head. He said it again. 'Life.' And then...I don't know how... but I did...see.

"I asked him...'Why not you?' He took...from his pocket...one of his old carvings. The two girls. Holding hands. I hadn't noticed...the hands before. And I understood.

"'My girls,' he said. Polish, again. 'Smoke. No more. Five years ago.' I understood that, too.

"I took the carving from him. We waited. We slept, side by side. One last time. Then the Nazis came.

"They made us stand. Hardly any of them, now. The rest gone. Fifteen of us. Maybe less. They said something. German. None of us knew German. But to me...at least...the word meant...run.

"The gypsy…just stood there. Died where he was. Under the trees. The rest…I don't know. The Nazi who caught me…laughing…a boy. Not much… older than you. Laughing. Awkward with his gun. Too big for him. I looked at my hand. Holding…the carving. The wooden man. 'Life,' I found myself chanting…instead of Shema. 'Life.' Then the Nazi shot me in the head. Bang."

And with that single word, my grandfather clicked off, as though a switch had been thrown. He slumped in his chair. My paralysis lasted a few more seconds, and then I started waving my hands in front of me, as if I could ward off what he'd told me, and I was so busy doing that that I didn't notice, at first, the way my grandfather's torso heaved and rattled. Whimpering, I lowered my hands, but by then, my grandfather wasn't heaving anymore, and he'd slumped forward farther, and nothing on him was moving.

"Lucy!" I screamed, but she was already out of the house, wrestling my grandfather out of his chair to the ground. Her head dove down on my grandfather's as she shoved the mask up his face, but before their mouths even met, my grandfather coughed, and Lucy fell back, sobbing, tugging the mask back into place.

My grandfather lay where he'd been thrown, a scatter of bones in the dirt. He didn't open his eyes. The oxygen tank hissed, and the blue tube stretching to his mask filled with wet fog.

"How?" I whispered.

Lucy swept tears from her eyes. "What?"

"He said he got shot in the head." And even as I said that, I felt it for the first time, that cold slithering up my intestines into my stomach, then my throat.

"Stop it," I said. But Lucy slid forward so that her knees were under my grandfather's head and ignored me. Overhead, I saw the moon half-embedded in the ridged black of the sky like the lidded eye of a Gila monster. I stumbled around the side of the house, and without thinking about it, slipped into the hogan.

Once inside, I jerked the curtain down to block out the sight of Lucy and my grandfather and that moon, then drew my knees tight against my chest to pin that freezing feeling where it was. I stayed that way a long while, but whenever I closed my eyes, I saw people splitting open like peeled bananas, limbs strewn across bare black ground like tree branches after a lightning storm, pits full of naked dead people.

I'd wished him dead, I realized. At the moment he tumbled forward in his chair, I'd hoped he was dead. And for what, exactly? For being in the camps? For telling me about it? For getting sick, and making me confront it?

But with astonishing, disturbing speed, the guilt over those thoughts passed. And when it was gone, I realized that the cold had seeped down my legs and up to my neck. It clogged my ears, coated my tongue like a paste, sealing the world out. All I could hear was my grandfather's voice, like blown sand against the inside of my skull. *Life*. He was inside me, I thought. He had absorbed me, taken my place. He was becoming me.

I threw my hands over my ears, which had no effect. My thoughts flashed through the last two days, the drumming and chanting, the dead Talking God-bat in the paper bag, my father's good-bye, while that voice beat in my ears, attaching itself to my pulse. *Life*. And finally, I realized that I'd trapped myself. I was alone in the hogan in the dark. When I turned around, I would see the Dancing Man. It would be floating over me with its mouth wide open. And then it would be over, too late. It might already be.

Flinging my hands behind me, I grabbed the Dancing Man around its thin black neck. I could feel it bob on its branch, and I half-expected it to squirm as I fought to my feet. It didn't, but its wooden skin gave where I pressed it, like real skin. Inside my head, the new voice kept beating.

At my feet on the floor lay the matches Lucy had used to light her ceremonial candles. I snatched up the matchbook, then threw the carved thing to the ground, where it smacked on its base and tipped over, face up, staring at me. I broke a match against the matchbox, then another. The third match lit.

For one moment, I held the flame over the Dancing Man. The heat felt wonderful crawling toward my fingers, a blazing, living thing, chasing back the cold inside me. I dropped the match, and the Dancing Man disintegrated in a spasm of white orange flame.

And then, abruptly, there was nothing to be done. The hogan was a dirt-and-wood shelter, the night outside the plain old desert night, the Dancing Man a puddle of red and black ash I scattered with my foot. Still cold, but mostly tired, I staggered back outside and sat down hard against the side of the hogan and closed my eyes.

Footsteps woke me, and I sat up and found, to my amazement, that it was daylight. I waited, tense, afraid to look up, and then I did.

My father was kneeling beside me on the ground.

"You're here already?" I asked.

"Your grandpa died, Seth," he said. In his zombie-Dad voice, though he touched my hand the way a real father would. "I've come to take you home."

4

The familiar commotion in the hallway of the pension alerted me to my students' return. One of them, but only one, stopped outside my door. I waited, holding my breath, wishing I'd snapped out the light. But Penny didn't knock, and after a few seconds, I heard her careful, precise footfall continuing toward her room. And so I was alone with my puppets and my memories and any horrible suspicions, the way I have always been.

The way I am now, one month later, in my plain, posterless Ohio apartment with its cableless television and nearly bare cupboards and single shelf stacked with textbooks, on the eve of the new school year. I'm remembering rousing myself out of the malaise I couldn't quite seem to shake — have never, for one instant, shaken since — during that last ride home from my grandfather's. "I killed him," I told my father, and when he glanced at me, expressionless, I told him all of it, my grandfather's gypsy and the Dancing Man and the Way and the thoughts I'd had.

My father didn't laugh. He also didn't touch me. All he said was, "That's silly, Seth." And for a while, I thought it was.

But today, I am thinking of Rabbi Loew and his golem, the creature he infected with a sort of life. A creature that walked, talked, thought, saw, but couldn't taste. Couldn't feel. I'm thinking of my father, the way he always was. If I'm right, then of course it had been done to him, too. And I'm thinking of the way I only seem all the way real, even to me, when I see myself in the vividly reflective faces of my students.

It's possible, I realize, that nothing happened to me those last days at my grandfather's. It could have happened years before I was born. The gypsy had offered what he offered, and my grandfather had accepted, and as a result became what he was. Might have been. If that was true, then my father and I were unexceptional, in a way. Natural progeny. We'd simply inherited our natures, and our limitations, the way all earthly creatures do.

But I can't help thinking about the graves I saw on this summer's trip, and the millions of people in them. And the millions more without graves. The ones who are smoke.

And I find that I can feel it, at last. Or that I've always felt it, without knowing what it was: the Holocaust, roaring down the generations like a wave of radiation, eradicating, in everyone it touches, the ability to trust people, experience joy, fall in love, believe in love when you see it in others.

And I wonder what difference it makes, in the end, whether it really was my grandfather, or the golem-grandfather that the gypsy made, who finally crawled out of the woods of Chelmno.

Joe Hill's short stories have been published in the magazines *Postscripts*, *Subterranean*, *The Third Alternative*, and *Crimewave*, and in the anthology *The Many Faces of Van Helsing*. Those stories and several new ones comprise his excellent debut collection, *20th Century Ghosts*, winner of the William L. Crawford Award for first fantasy book, and the Bram Stoker Award, the World Fantasy Award, the International Horror Guild Award, and the British Fantasy Award for Best Collection. His stories have been reprinted in *The Mammoth Book of Best New Horror* and in *The Year's Best Fantasy and Horror*. His first novel, *Heart-Shaped Box*, was published in 2007. He is a past recipient of the Ray Bradbury Fellowship and the A. E. Coppard Long Fiction Prize.

Hill often writes about parent-child relationships and uses some of the places he's lived in as settings. His fertile imagination transforms them into weird, often very creepy tales, as in "My Father's Mask," a story that has stayed with me since I first read it.

My Father's Mask
Joe Hill

ON THE DRIVE to Big Cat Lake, we played a game. It was my mother's idea. It was dusk by the time we reached the state highway, and when there was no light left in the sky, except for a splash of cold, pale brilliance in the west, she told me they were looking for me.

"They're playing card people," she said. "Queens and kings. They're so flat they can slip themselves under doors. They'll be coming from the other direction, from the lake. Searching for us. Trying to head us off. Get out of sight whenever someone comes the other way. We can't protect you from them — not on the road. Quick, get down. Here comes one of them now."

I stretched out across the backseat and watched the headlights of an approaching car race across the ceiling. Whether I was playing along, or just stretching out to get comfortable, I wasn't sure. I was in a funk. I had been hoping for a sleepover at my friend Luke Redhill's, ping-pong and late night TV with Luke (and Luke's leggy older sister Jane, and her lush-haired friend Melinda), but had come home from school to find suitcases in the driveway and my father loading the car. That was the first I heard we were spending the night at my grandfather's cabin on Big Cat Lake. I couldn't be angry at my parents for not letting me in on their plans in advance, because they probably hadn't made plans in advance. It was very likely they had decided to go up to Big Cat Lake over lunch. My parents didn't have plans. They had impulses and a thirteen-year-old son and they saw no reason to ever let the latter upset the former.

"Why can't you protect me?" I asked.

My mother said, "Because there are some things a mother's love and a father's courage can't keep you safe from. Besides, who could fight them? You know about playing card people. How they all go around with little golden hatchets and little silver swords. Have you ever noticed how well-armed most good hands of poker are?"

"No accident the first card game everyone learns is War," my father said, driving with one wrist slung across the wheel. "They're all variations on the same plot. Metaphorical kings fighting over the world's limited supplies of wenches and money."

My mother regarded me seriously over the back of her seat, her eyes luminous in the dark.

"We're in trouble, Jack," she said. "We're in terrible trouble."

"Okay," I said.

"It's been building for a while. We kept it from you at first, because we didn't want to scare you. But you have to know. It's right for you to know. We're — well, you see — we don't have any money anymore. It's the playing card people. They've been working against us, poisoning investments, tying assets up in red tape. They've been spreading the most awful rumors about your father at work. I don't want to upset you with the crude details. They make menacing phone calls. They call me up in the middle of the day and talk about the awful things they're going to do to me. To you. To all of us."

"They put something in the clam sauce the other night, and gave me wicked runs," my father said. "I thought I was going to die. And our dry cleaning came back with funny white stains on it. That was them too."

My mother laughed. I've heard that dogs have six kinds of barks, each with a specific meaning: *intruder, let's play, I need to pee.* My mother had a certain number of laughs, each with an unmistakable meaning and identity, all of them wonderful. This laugh, convulsive and unpolished, was the way she responded to dirty jokes; also to accusations, to being caught making mischief.

I laughed with her, sitting up, my stomach unknotting. She had been so wide-eyed and solemn, for a moment I had started to forget she was making it all up.

My mother leaned toward my father and ran her finger over his lips, miming the closing of a zipper.

"You let me tell it," she said. "I forbid you to talk anymore."

"If we're in so much financial trouble, I could go and live with Luke for a while," I said. *And Jane,* I thought. "I wouldn't want to be a burden on the family."

She looked back at me again. "The money I'm not worried about. There's an appraiser coming by tomorrow. There are some wonderful old things in that house, things your great-grandfather left us. We're going to see about selling them."

My great-grandfather, Upton, had died the year before, in a way no one liked to discuss, a death that had no place in his life, a horror movie conclusion tacked on to a blowsy, Capra-esque comedy. He was in New York, where he kept a condo on the fifth floor of a brownstone on the Upper East Side, one of many places he owned. He called the elevator and stepped through the doors when they opened — but there was no elevator there, and he fell four stories. The fall did not kill him. He lived for another day, at the bottom of the elevator shaft. The elevator was old and slow and complained loudly whenever it had to move, not unlike most of the building's residents. No one heard him screaming.

"Why don't we sell the Big Cat Lake house?" I asked. "Then we'd be rolling in the loot."

"Oh, we couldn't do that. It isn't ours. It's held in trust for all of us, me, you, Aunt Blake, the Greenly twins. And even if it did belong to us, we couldn't sell it. It's always been in our family."

For the first time since getting into the car, I thought I understood why we were *really* going to Big Cat Lake. I saw at last that my weekend plans had been sacrificed on the altar of interior decoration. My mother loved to decorate. She loved picking out curtains, stained-glass lamp-shades, unique iron knobs for the cabinets. Someone had put her in charge of redecorating the cabin on Big Cat Lake — or, more likely, she had put herself in charge — and she meant to begin by getting rid of all the clutter.

I felt like a chump for letting her distract me from my bad mood with one of her games.

"I wanted to spend the night with Luke," I said.

My mother directed a sly, knowing look at me from beneath half-lowered eyelids, and I felt a sudden scalp-prickle of unease. It was a look that made me wonder what she knew and if she had guessed the true reasons for my friendship with Luke Redhill, a rude but good-natured nose-picker I considered intellectually beneath me.

"You wouldn't be safe there. The playing card people would've got you," she said, her tone both gleeful and rather too-coy.

I looked at the ceiling of the car. "Okay."

We rode for a while in silence.

"Why are they after me?" I asked, even though by then I was sick of it, wanted done with the game.

"It's all because we're so incredibly superlucky. No one ought to be as lucky as us. They hate the idea that anyone is getting a free ride. But it would all even out if they got ahold of you. I don't care how lucky you've been, if you lose a kid, the good times are over."

We were lucky, of course, maybe even superlucky, and it wasn't just that we were well off, like everyone in our extended family of trust-fund ne'er-do-wells. My father had more time for me than other fathers had for their boys. He went to work after I left for school, and was usually home by the time I got back, and if I didn't have anything else going on, we'd drive to the golf course to whack a few. My mother was beautiful, still young, just thirty-five, with a natural instinct for mischief that had made her a hit with my friends. I suspected several of the kids I hung out with, Luke Redhill included, had cast her in a variety of masturbatory fantasies, and that indeed, their attraction to her explained most of their fondness for me.

"And why is Big Cat Lake so safe?" I said.

"Who said it's safe?"

"Then why are we going there?"

She turned away from me. "So we can have a nice cozy fire in the fireplace, and sleep late, and eat egg pancake, and spend the morning in our pajamas. Even if we are in fear for our lives, that's no reason to be miserable all weekend."

She put her hand on the back of my father's neck and played with his hair. Then she stiffened, and her fingernails sank into the skin just below his hairline.

"Jack," she said to me. She was looking past my father, through the driver's side window, at something out in the dark. "Get down, Jack, get down."

We were on Route 16, a long straight highway, with a narrow grass median between the two lanes. A car was parked on a turnaround between the lanes, and as we went by it, its headlights snapped on. I turned my head and stared into them for a moment before sinking down out of sight. The car — a sleek silver Jaguar — turned onto the road and accelerated after us.

"I told you not to let them see you," my mother said. "Go faster, Henry. Get away from them."

Our car picked up speed, rushing through the darkness. I squeezed my fingers into the seat, sitting up on my knees to peek out the rear window. The other car stayed exactly the same distance behind us no matter how fast we went, clutching the curves of the road with a quiet, menacing assurance.

Sometimes my breath would catch in my throat for a few moments before I remembered to breathe. Road signs whipped past, gone too quickly to be read.

The Jag followed for three miles, before it swung into the parking lot of a roadside diner. When I turned around in my seat my mother was lighting a cigarette with the pulsing orange ring of the dashboard lighter. My father hummed softly to himself, easing up on the gas. He swung his head a little from side to side, keeping time to a melody I didn't recognize.

I ran through the dark, with the wind knifing at me and my head down, not looking where I was going. My mother was right behind me, the both of us rushing for the porch. No light lit the front of the cottage by the water. My father had switched car and headlights off, and the house was in the woods, at the end of a rutted dirt road where there were no streetlamps. Just beyond the house I caught a glimpse of the lake, a hole in the world, filled with a heaving darkness.

My mother let us in and went around switching on lights. The cabin was built around a single great room with a lodge-house ceiling, bare rafters showing, log walls with red bark peeling off them. To the left of the door was a dresser, the mirror on the back hidden behind a pair of black veils. Wandering, my hands pulled into the sleeves of my jacket for warmth, I approached the dresser. Through the semi-transparent curtains I saw a dim, roughly formed figure, my own obscured reflection, coming to meet me in the mirror. I felt a tickle of unease at the sight of the reflected me, a featureless shadow skulking behind black silk, someone I didn't know. I pushed the curtain back, but saw only myself, cheeks stung into redness by the wind.

I was about to step away when I noticed the masks. The mirror was supported by two delicate posts, and a few masks hung from the top of each, the sort, like the Lone Ranger's, that only cover the eyes and a little of the nose. One had whiskers and glittery spackle on it and would make the wearer look like a jeweled mouse. Another was of rich black velvet, and would have been appropriate dress for a courtesan on her way to an Edwardian masquerade.

The whole cottage had been artfully decorated in masks. They dangled from doorknobs and the backs of chairs. A great crimson mask glared furiously down from the mantle above the hearth, a surreal demon made out of lacquered papier-mâché, with a hooked beak and feathers around the eyes — just the thing to wear if you had been cast as the Red Death in an Edgar Allan Poe revival.

The most unsettling of them hung from a lock on one of the windows. It was made of some distorted but clear plastic, and looked like a man's face molded out of an impossibly thin piece of ice. It was hard to see, dangling in front of the glass, and I twitched nervously when I spotted it from the corner of my eye. For an instant I thought there was a man, spectral and barely-there, hovering on the porch, gaping in at me.

The front door crashed open and my father came in dragging luggage. At the same time, my mother spoke from behind me.

"When we were young, just kids, your father and I used to sneak off to this place to get away from everyone. *Wait.* Wait, I know. Let's play a game. You have until we leave to guess which room you were conceived in."

She liked to try and disgust me now and then with intimate, unasked-for revelations about herself and my father. I frowned and gave what I hoped was a scolding look, and she laughed again, and we were both satisfied, having played ourselves perfectly.

"Why are there curtains over all the mirrors?"

"I don't know," she said. "Maybe whoever stayed here last hung them up as a way to remember your grandfather. In Jewish tradition, after someone dies, the mourners cover the mirrors, as a warning against vanity."

"But we aren't Jewish," I said.

"It's a nice tradition though. All of us could stand to spend less time thinking about ourselves."

"What's with all the masks?"

"Every vacation home ought to have a few masks lying around. What if you want a vacation from your own face? I get awfully sick of being the same person day in, day out. What do you think of that one, do you like it?"

I was absent-mindedly fingering the glassy, blank-featured mask hanging from the window. When she brought my attention to what I was doing, I pulled my hand back. A chill crawled along the thickening flesh of my forearms.

"You should put it on," she said, her voice breathy and eager. "You should see how you look in it."

"It's awful," I said.

"Are you going to be okay sleeping in your own room? You could sleep in bed with us. That's what you did the last time you were here. Although you were much younger then."

"That's all right. I wouldn't want to get in the way, in case you feel like conceiving someone else."

"Be careful what you wish for," she said. "History repeats."

The only furniture in my small room was a camp cot dressed in sheets that smelled of mothballs and a wardrobe against one wall, with paisley drapes pulled across the mirror on the back. A half-face mask hung from the curtain rod. It was made of green silk leaves, sewn together and ornamented with emerald sequins, and I liked it until I turned the light off. In the gloom, the leaves looked like the horny scales of some lizard-faced thing, with dark gaping sockets where the eyes belonged. I switched the light back on and got up long enough to turn it face-to the wall.

Trees grew against the house and sometimes a limb batted the side of the cottage, making a knocking sound that always brought me awake with the idea someone was at the bedroom door. I woke, dozed, and woke again. The wind built to a thin shriek and from somewhere outside came a steady, metallic ping-ping-ping, as if a wheel were turning in the gale. I went to the window to look, not expecting to see anything. The moon was up, though, and as the trees blew, moonlight raced across the ground, through the darkness, like schools of those little silver fish that live in deep water and glow in the dark.

A bicycle leaned against a tree, an antique with a giant front wheel, and a rear wheel almost comically too small. The front wheel turned continuously, ping-ping-ping. A boy came across the grass toward it, a chubby boy with fair hair, in a white nightgown, and at the sight of him I felt an instinctive rush of dread. He took the handlebars of the bike, then cocked his head as if at a sound, and I mewed, shrank back from the glass. He turned and stared at me with silver eyes and silver teeth, dimples in his fat cupid cheeks, and I sprang awake in my mothball-smelling bed, making unhappy sounds of fear in my throat.

When morning came, and I finally struggled up out of sleep for the last time, I found myself in the master bedroom, under heaped quilts, with the sun slanting across my face. The impression of my mother's head still dented the pillow beside me. I didn't remember rushing there in the dark and was glad. At thirteen, I was still a little kid, but I had my pride.

I lay like a salamander on a rock — sun-dazed and awake without being conscious — until I heard someone pull a zipper on the other side of the room.

I peered around and saw my father, opening the suitcase on top of the bureau. Some subtle rustling of the quilts caught his attention, and he turned his head to look at me.

He was naked. The morning sunshine bronzed his short, compact body. He wore the clear plastic mask that had been hanging in the window of the great room, the night before. It squashed the features beneath, flattening them out of their recognizable shapes. He stared at me blankly, as if he hadn't known I was lying there in the bed, or perhaps as if he didn't know me at all. The thick length of his penis rested on a cushion of gingery hair. I had seen him naked often enough before, but with the mask on he was someone different, and his nakedness was disconcerting. He looked at me and did not speak — and that was disconcerting too.

I opened my mouth to say hello and good morning, but there was a wheeze in my chest. The thought crossed my mind that he was, really and not metaphorically, a person I didn't know. I couldn't hold his stare, looked away, then slipped from under the quilts and went into the great room, willing myself not to run.

A pot clanked in the kitchen. Water hissed from a faucet. I followed the sounds to my mother, who was at the sink, filling a tea kettle. She heard the pad of my feet, and glanced back over her shoulder. The sight of her stopped me in my tracks. She had on a black kitten mask, edged in rhinestones, and with glistening whiskers. She was not naked, but wore a MILLER LITE T-shirt that came to her hips. Her legs, though, were bare, and when she leaned over the sink to shut off the water I saw a flash of strappy black panties. I was reassured by the fact that she had grinned to see me, and not just stared at me as if we had never met.

"Egg pancake in the oven," she said.

"Why are you and dad wearing masks?"

"It's Halloween isn't it?"

"No," I said. "Try next Thursday."

"Any law against starting early?" she asked. Then she paused by the stove, an oven mitt on one hand, and shot another look at me. "Actually. *Actually.*"

"Here it comes. The truck is backing up. The back end is rising. The bullshit is about to come sliding out."

"In this place it's always Halloween. It's called Masquerade House. That's our secret name for it. It's one of the rules of the cottage, while you're staying here you have to wear a mask. It's always been that way."

"I can wait until Halloween."

She pulled a pan out of the oven and cut me a piece of egg pancake, poured me a cup of tea. Then she sat down across from me to watch me eat.

"You have to wear a mask. The playing card people saw you last night. They'll be coming now. You have to put a mask on so they won't recognize you."

"Why wouldn't they recognize me? I recognize you."

"You think you do," she said, her long-lashed eyes vivid and humorous. "Playing card people wouldn't know you behind a mask. It's their Achilles heel. They take everything at face value. They're very one-dimensional thinkers."

"Ha ha," I said. "When's the appraiser coming?"

"Sometime. Later. I don't really know. I'm not sure there even is an appraiser. I might've made that up."

"I've only been awake twenty minutes and I'm already bored. Couldn't you guys have found a babysitter for me and come up here for your weird mask-wearing, baby-making weekend by yourselves?" As soon as I said it, I felt myself starting to blush, but I was pleased that I had it in me to needle her about their masks and her black underwear and the burlesque game they had going that they thought I was too young to understand.

She said, "I'd rather have you along. Now you won't be getting into trouble with that girl."

The heat in my cheeks deepened, the way coals will when someone sighs over them. "What girl?"

"I'm not sure which girl. It's either Jane Redhill or her friend. Probably her friend. The person you always go over to Luke's house hoping to see."

Luke was the one who liked her friend, Melinda; I liked Jane. Still, my mother had guessed close enough to unsettle me. Her smile broadened at my stricken silence.

"She is a pert little cutie, isn't she? Jane's friend? I guess they both are. The friend, though, seems more your type. What's her name? Melinda? The way she goes around in her baggy farmer overalls. I bet she spends her afternoons reading in a treehouse she built with her father. I bet she baits her own worms and plays football with the boys."

"Luke is hot for her."

"So it's Jane."

"Who said it has to be either of them?"

"There must be some reason you hang around with Luke. Besides Luke."
Then she said, "Jane came by selling magazine subscriptions to benefit her
church a few days ago. She seems like a very wholesome young thing. Very
community minded. I wish I thought she had a sense of humor. When you're a
little older, you should cold cock Luke Redhill and drop him in the old quarry.
That Melinda will fall right into your arms. The two of you can mourn for him
together. Grief can be very romantic." She took my empty plate and got up.
"Find a mask. Play along."

She put my plate in the sink and went out. I finished a glass of juice and
meandered into the great room after her. I glanced at the master bedroom,
just as she was pushing the door shut behind her. The man who I took for my
father still wore his disfiguring mask of ice, and had pulled on a pair of jeans.
For a moment our eyes met, his gaze dispassionate and unfamiliar. He put a
possessive hand on my mother's hip. The door closed and they were gone.

In the other bedroom, I sat on the edge of my bed and stuck my feet into
my sneakers. The wind whined under the eaves. I felt glum and out of sorts,
wanted to be home, had no idea what to do with myself. As I stood, I happened
to glance at the green mask made of sewn silk leaves, turned once again to face
the room. I pulled it down, rubbed it between thumb and forefinger, trying out
the slippery smoothness of it. Almost as an afterthought, I put it on.

My mother was in the living room, fresh from the shower.

"It's you," she said. "Very Dionysian. Very Pan. We should get a towel. You
could walk around in a little toga."

"That would be fun. Until hypothermia set in."

"It is drafty in here, isn't it? We need a fire. One of us has to go into the
forest and collect an armful of dead wood."

"Boy, I wonder who that's going to be."

"Wait. We'll make it into a game. It'll be exciting."

"I'm sure. Nothing livens up a morning like tramping around in the cold
foraging for sticks."

"Listen. Don't wander from the forest path. Out there in the woods, nothing
is real except for the path. Children who drift away from it never find their way
back. Also — this is the most important thing — don't let anyone see you,
unless they come masked. Anyone in a mask is hiding out from the playing
card people, just like us."

"If the woods are so dangerous for children, maybe I ought to stay here and you or Dad can go play pick up sticks. Is he ever coming out of the bedroom?"

But she was shaking her head. "Grown-ups can't go into the forest at all. Not even the trail is safe for someone my age. I can't even see the trail. Once you get as old as me it disappears from sight. I only know about it because your father and I used to take walks on it, when we came up here as teenagers. Only the young can find their way through all the wonders and illusions in the deep dark woods."

Outside was drab and cold beneath the pigeon-colored sky. I went around the back of the house, to see if there was a woodpile. On my way past the master bedroom, my father thumped on the glass. I went to the window to see what he wanted, and was surprised by my own reflection, superimposed over his face. I was still wearing the mask of silk leaves, had for a moment forgotten about it.

He pulled the top half of the window down and leaned out, his own face squashed by its shell of clear plastic, his wintry blue eyes a little blank. "Where are you going?"

"I'm going to check out the woods, I guess. Mom wants me to collect sticks for a fire."

He hung his arms over the top of the window and stared across the yard. He watched some rust colored leaves trip end-over-end across the grass. "I wish I was going."

"Then come."

He glanced up at me, and smiled, for the first time all day. "No. Not right now. Tell you what. You go on, and maybe I'll meet you out there in a while."

"Okay."

"It's funny. As soon as you leave this place, you forget how — pure it is. What the air smells like." He stared at the grass and the lake for another moment, then turned his head, caught my eye. "You forget other things too. Jack, listen, I don't want you to forget about —"

The door opened behind him, on the far side of the room. My father fell silent. My mother stood in the doorway. She was in her jeans and sweater, playing with the wide buckle of her belt.

"Boys," she said. "What are we talking about?"

My father didn't glance back at her, but went on staring at me, and beneath his new face of melted crystal, I thought I saw a look of chagrin, as if he'd been caught doing something faintly embarrassing; cheating at solitaire maybe. I remembered, then, her drawing her fingers across his lips, closing an imaginary zipper, the night before. My head went queer and light. I had the sudden idea I was seeing another part of some unwholesome game playing out between them, the less of which I knew, the happier I'd be.

"Nothing," I said. "I was just telling Dad I was going for a walk. And now I'm going. For my walk." Backing away from the window as I spoke.

My mother coughed. My father slowly pushed the top half of the window shut, his gaze still level with mine. He turned the lock — then pressed his palm to the glass, in a gesture of goodbye. When he lowered his hand, a steamy imprint of it remained, a ghost hand that shrank in on itself and vanished. My father drew down the shade.

I forgot about gathering sticks almost as soon as I set out. I had by then decided that my parents only wanted me out of the house so they could have the place to themselves, a thought that made me peevish. At the head of the trail I pulled off my mask of silk leaves and hung it on a branch.

I walked with my head down and my hands shoved into the pockets of my coat. For a while the path ran parallel to the lake, visible beyond the hemlocks in slivers of frigid-looking blue. I was too busy thinking that if they wanted to be perverted and un-parent-like, they should've figured a way to come up to Big Cat Lake without me, to notice the path turning and leading away from the water. I didn't look up until I heard the sound coming toward me along the trail: a steely whirring, the creak of a metal frame under stress. Directly ahead the path divided to go around a boulder, the size and rough shape of a half-buried coffin stood on end. Beyond the boulder, the path came back together and wound away into the pines.

I was alarmed, I don't know why. It was something about the way the wind rose just then, so the trees flailed at the sky. It was the frantic way the leaves scurried about my ankles, as if in a sudden hurry to get off the trail. Without thinking, I sat down behind the boulder, back to the stone, hugging my knees to my chest.

A moment later the boy on the antique bike — the boy I thought I had dreamed — rode past on my left, without so much as a glance my way. He was dressed in the nightgown he had been wearing the night before. A harness of white straps held a pair of modest white-feathered wings to his back. Maybe he had had them on the first time I saw him and I hadn't noticed them in the dark. As he rattled past, I had a brief look at his dimpled cheeks and blond bangs, features set in an expression of serene confidence. His gaze was cool, distant. Seeking. I watched him expertly guide his Charlie-Chaplin-cycle between stones and roots, around a curve, and out of sight.

If I hadn't seen him in the night, I might have thought he was a boy on his way to a costume party, although it was too cold to be out gallivanting in a nightgown. I wanted to be back at the cabin, out of the wind, safe with my parents. I was in dread of the trees, waving and shushing around me.

But when I moved, it was to continue in the direction I had been heading, glancing often over my shoulder to make sure the bicyclist wasn't coming up behind me. I didn't have the nerve to walk back along the trail, knowing that the boy on the antique bike was somewhere out there, between myself and the cabin.

I hurried along, hoping to find a road, or one of the other summer houses along the lake, eager to be anywhere but in the woods. Anywhere turned out to be less than ten minutes walk from the coffin-shaped rock. It was clearly marked — a weathered plank, with the words "ANY-WHERE" painted on it, was nailed to the trunk of a pine — a bare patch in the woods where people had once camped. A few charred sticks sat in the bottom of a blackened firepit. Someone, children maybe, had built a lean-to between a pair of boulders. The boulders were about the same height, tilting in toward one another, and a sheet of plywood had been set across the top of them. A log had been pulled across the opening that faced the clearing, providing both a place for people to sit by a fire, and a barrier that had to be climbed over to enter the shelter.

I stood at the ruin of the ancient campfire, trying to get my bearings. Two trails on the far side of the camp led away. There was little difference between them, both narrow ruts gouged out in the brush, and no clue as to where either of them might lead.

"Where are you trying to go?" said a girl on my left, her voice pitched to a good-humored hush.

I leaped, took a half-step away, looked around. She was leaning out of the shelter, hands on the log. I hadn't seen her in the shadows of the lean-to. She was black-haired, a little older than myself — sixteen maybe — and I had a sense she was pretty. It was hard to be sure. She wore a black sequined mask, with a fan of ostrich feathers standing up from one side. Just behind her, further back in the dark, was a boy, the upper half of his face hidden behind a smooth plastic mask the color of milk.

"I'm looking for my way back," I said.

"Back where?" asked the girl.

The boy kneeling behind her took a measured look at her outthrust bottom in her faded jeans. She was, consciously or not, wiggling her hips a little from side-to-side.

"My family has a summer place near here. I was wondering if one of those two trails would take me there."

"You could go back the way you came," she said, but mischievously, as if she already knew I was afraid to double back.

"I'd rather not," I said.

"What brought you all the way out here?" asked the boy.

"My mother sent me to collect wood for the fire."

He snorted. "Sounds like the beginning of a fairy tale." The girl cast a disapproving look back at him, which he ignored. "One of the bad ones. Your parents can't feed you anymore, so they send you off to get lost in the woods. Eventually someone gets eaten by a witch for dinner. Baked into a pie. Be careful it's not you."

"Do you want to play cards with us?" the girl asked, and held up a deck.

"I just want to get home. I don't want my parents worried."

"Sit and play with us," she said. "We'll play a hand for answers. The winner gets to ask each of the losers a question, and no matter what, they have to tell the truth. So if you beat me, you could ask me how to get home without seeing the boy on the old bicycle, and I'd have to tell you."

Which meant she had seen him and somehow guessed the rest. She looked pleased with herself, enjoyed letting me know I was easy to figure out. I considered for a moment, then nodded.

"What are you playing?" I asked.

"It's a kind of poker. It's called Cold Hands, because it's the only card game you can play when it's this cold."

The boy shook his head. "This is one of these games where she makes up the rules as she goes along." His voice, which had an adolescent crack in it, was nevertheless familiar to me.

I crossed to the log and she retreated on her knees, sliding back into the dark space under the plywood roof to make room for me. She was talking all the time, shuffling her worn deck of cards.

"It isn't hard. I deal five cards to each player, face-up. When I'm done, whoever has the best poker hand wins. That probably sounds too simple, but then there are a lot of funny little house rules. If you smile during the game, the player sitting to your left can swap one of his cards for one of yours. If you can build a house with the first three cards you get dealt, and if the other players can't blow it down in one breath, you get to look through the deck and pick out whatever you want for your fourth card. If you draw a black forfeit, the other players throw stones at you until you're dead. If you have any questions, keep them to yourself. Only the winner gets to ask questions. Anyone who asks a question while the game is in play loses instantly. Okay? Let's start."

My first card was a Lazy Jack. I knew because it said so across the bottom, and because it showed a picture of a golden-haired jack lounging on silk pillows, while a harem girl filed his toenails. It wasn't until the girl handed me my second card — the three of rings — that I mentally registered the thing she had said about the black forfeit.

"Excuse me," I started. "But what's a —"

She raised her eyebrows, looked at me seriously.

"Nevermind," I said.

The boy made a little sound in his throat. The girl cried out, "He smiled! Now you can trade one of your cards for one of his!"

"I did not!"

"You did," she said. "I saw it. Take his queen and give him your jack."

I gave him the Lazy Jack and took the Queen of Sheets away from him. It showed a nude girl asleep on a carved four-poster, amid the tangle of her bedclothes. She had straight brown hair, and strong, handsome features, and bore a resemblance to Jane's friend, Melinda. After that I was dealt the King of Pennyfarthings, a red-bearded fellow, carrying a sack of coins that was splitting and beginning to spill. I was pretty sure the girl in the black mask had dealt him to me from the bottom of the deck. She saw I saw and shot me a cool, challenging look.

When we each had three cards, we took a break and tried to build houses the others couldn't blow down, but none of them would stand. Afterward I was dealt the Queen of Chains and a card with the rules of Cribbage printed on it. I almost asked if it was in the deck by accident, then thought better of it. No one drew a black forfeit. I don't even know what one is.

"Jack wins!" shouted the girl, which unnerved me a little, since I had never introduced myself. "Jack is the winner!" She flung herself against me and hugged me fiercely. When she straightened up, she was pushing my winning cards into the pocket of my jacket. "Here, you should keep your winning hand. To remember the fun we had. It doesn't matter. This old deck is missing a bunch of cards anyway. I just knew you'd win!"

"Sure she did," said the boy. "First she makes up a game with rules only she can understand, then she cheats so it comes out how she likes."

She laughed, unpolished, convulsive laughter, and I felt cold on the nape of my neck. But really, I think I already knew by then, even before she laughed, who I was playing cards with.

"The secret to avoiding unhappy losses is to only play games you make up yourself," she said. "Now. Go ahead, Jack. Ask anything you like. It's your right."

"How do I get home without going back the way I came?"

"That's easy. Take the path closest to the 'any-where' sign, which will take you anywhere you want to go. That's why it says anywhere. Just be sure the cabin is really where you want to go, or you might not get there."

"Right. Thank you. It was a good game. I didn't understand it, but I had fun playing." And I scrambled out over the log.

I hadn't gone far, before she called out to me. When I looked back, she and the boy were side-by-side, leaning over the log and staring out at me.

"Don't forget," she said. "You get to ask him a question too."

"Do I know you?" I said, making a gesture to include both of them.

"No," he said. "You don't really know either of us."

There was a Jag parked in the driveway behind my parents' car. The interior was polished cherry, and the seats looked as if they had never been sat on. It might have just rolled off the dealership floor. By then it was late in the day, the light slanting in from the west, cutting through the tops of the trees. It didn't seem like it could be so late.

I thumped up the stairs, but before I could reach the door to go in, it opened, and my mother stepped out, still wearing the black sex-kitten mask.

"Your mask," she said. "What'd you do with it?"

"Ditched it," I said. I didn't tell her I hung it on a tree branch because I was embarrassed to be seen in it. I wished I had it now, although I couldn't have said why.

She threw an anxious look back at the door, then crouched in front of me.

"I knew. I was watching for you. Put this on." She offered me my father's mask of clear plastic.

I stared at it a moment, remembering the way I recoiled from it when I first saw it, and how it had squashed my father's features into something cold and menacing. But when I slipped it on my face, it fit well enough. It carried a faint fragrance of my father, coffee and the sea-spray odor of his aftershave. I found it reassuring to have him so close to me.

My mother said, "We're getting out of here in a few minutes. Going home. Just as soon as the appraiser is done looking around. Come on. Come in. It's almost over."

I followed her inside, then stopped just through the door. My father sat on the couch, shirtless and barefoot. His body looked as if it had been marked up by a surgeon for an operation. Dotted lines and arrows showed the location of liver, spleen and bowels. His eyes were pointed toward the floor, his face blank.

"Dad?" I asked.

His gaze rose, flitted from my mother to me and back. His expression remained bland and unrevealing.

"Sh," my mother said. "Daddy's busy."

I heard heels cracking across the bare planks to my right, and glanced across the room, as the appraiser came out of the master bedroom. I had assumed the appraiser would be a man, but it was a middle-aged woman in a tweed jacket, with some white showing in her wavy yellow hair. She had austere, imperial features, the high cheekbones and expressive, arching eyebrows of English nobility.

"See anything you like?" my mother asked.

"You have some wonderful pieces," the appraiser said. Her gaze drifted to my father's bare shoulders.

"Well," my mother said. "Don't mind me." She gave the back of my arm a soft pinch, and slipped around me, whispered out of the side of her mouth, "Hold the fort, kiddo. I'll be right back."

My mother showed the appraiser a small, strictly polite smile, before easing into the master bedroom and out of sight, leaving the three of us alone.

"I was sorry when I heard Upton died," the appraiser said. "Do you miss him?"

The question was so unexpected and direct it startled me; or maybe it was her tone, which was not sympathetic, but sounded to my ears too-curious, eager for a little grief.

"I guess. We weren't so close," I said. "I think he had a pretty good life, though."

"Of course he did," she said.

"I'd be happy if things worked out half as well for me."

"Of course they will," she said, and put a hand on the back of my father's neck and began rubbing it fondly.

It was such a casually, obscenely intimate gesture, I felt a sick intestinal pang at the sight. I let my gaze drift away — had to look away — and happened to glance at the mirror on the back of the dresser. The curtains were parted slightly, and in the reflection I saw a playing card woman standing behind my father, the queen of spades, her eyes of ink haughty and distant, her black robes painted onto her body. I wrenched my gaze from the looking-glass in alarm, and glanced back at the couch. My father was smiling in a dreamy kind of way, leaning back into the hands now massaging his shoulders. The appraiser regarded me from beneath half-lowered eyelids.

"That isn't your face," she said to me. "No one has a face like that. A face made out of ice. What are you hiding?"

My father stiffened, and his smile faded. He sat up and forward, slipping his shoulders out of her grip.

"You've seen everything," my father said to the woman behind him. "Do you know what you want?"

"I'd start with everything in this room," she said, putting her hand gently on his shoulder again. She toyed with a curl of his hair for a moment. "I can have everything, can't I?"

My mother came out of the bedroom, lugging a pair of suitcases, one in each hand. She glanced at the appraiser with her hand on my father's neck, and huffed a bemused little laugh — a laugh that went *huh* and which seemed to mean more or less just that — and picked up the suitcases again, marched with them toward the door.

"It's all up for grabs," my father said. "We're ready to deal."

"Who isn't?" said the appraiser.

My mother set one of the suitcases in front of me, and nodded that I should take it. I followed her onto the porch, and then looked back. The appraiser was leaning over the back of the couch, and my father's head was tipped back, and her mouth was on his. My mother reached past me and closed the door.

We walked through the gathering twilight to the car. The boy in the white gown sat on the lawn, his bicycle on the grass beside him. He was skinning a dead rabbit with a piece of horn, its stomach open and steaming. He glanced at us as we went by and grinned, showing teeth pink with blood. My mother put a motherly arm around my shoulders.

After she was in the car, she took off her mask and threw it on the backseat. I left mine on. When I inhaled deeply I could smell my father.

"What are we doing?" I asked. "Isn't he coming?"

"No," she said, and started the car. "He's staying here."

"How will he get home?"

She turned a sideways look upon me, and smiled sympathetically. Outside, the sky was a blue-almost-black, and the clouds were a scalding shade of crimson, but in the car it was already night. I turned in my seat, sat up on my knees, to watch the cottage disappear through the trees.

"Let's play a game," my mother said. "Let's pretend you never really knew your father. He went away before you were born. We can make up fun little stories about him. He has a *Semper Fi* tattoo from his days in the marines, and another one, a blue anchor, that's from —" her voice faltered, as she came up suddenly short on inspiration.

"From when he worked on a deep-sea oil rig."

She laughed. "Right. And we'll pretend the road is magic. The Amnesia Highway. By the time we're home, we'll both believe the story is true, that he really did leave before you were born. Everything else will seem like a dream, those dreams as real as memories. The made-up story will probably be better than the real thing anyway. I mean, he loved your bones, and he wanted everything for you, but can you remember one interesting thing he ever did?"

I had to admit I couldn't.

"Can you even remember what he did for a living?"

I had to admit I didn't. Insurance?

"Isn't this a good game?" she asked. "Speaking of games. Do you still have your deal?"

"My deal?" I asked, then remembered, and touched the pocket of my jacket.

"You want to hold onto it. That's some winning hand. King of Pennyfarthings. Queen of Sheets. You got it all, boy. I'm telling you, when we get home, you give that Melinda a call." She laughed again, and then affectionately patted her tummy. "Good days ahead, kid. For both of us."

I shrugged.

"You can take the mask off, you know," my mother said. "Unless you like wearing it. Do you like wearing it?"

I reached up for the sun visor, turned it down, and opened the mirror. The lights around the mirror switched on. I studied my new face of ice, and the face beneath, a malformed, human blank.

"Sure," I said. "It's me."